THE EX ASSIGNMENT

VICTORIA PAIGE

Edited by: edit LLC
Content Editor: Edit Sober
Proofreader: A Book Nerd Edits
Photography by: Wander Aguiar

1

LOS ANGELES

THE TIP CAME at fifteen hundred.

Gabrielle Woodward had just come home from her father's funeral. You would think it was a Hollywood premiere with the who's who in attendance. The reporters were ready with their cameras, waiting for when the stars, dressed in Armani, and Stella McCartney would make their way past them.

No one paid attention to Gabby. She wore no labels, just a simple, ill-fitting black dress. No one questioned why she was at the back of the funeral crowd rather than in front with Peter Woodward's ex-wife and son. She'd shunned the spotlight such a lifetime ago that people had forgotten the famous Hollywood mogul had a daughter.

Crossing the threshold of her apartment, she pulled the dress over her head and walked to the utility room, tossing it into the hamper, probably never to be needed again. Her LAPD blues, perfectly pressed and laundered, hung ready in her closet for when she would attend the next funeral of a victim or a fallen officer.

As a detective with the LA Gang and Homicide Division (GHD), death was her constant companion, and she'd witnessed its brutal ripple effect on the loved ones left behind. And yet today her emotions laid dormant inside her. Granted, she and her father had not spoken for years, but she should feel something, right? A wave of grief? Gabby was still waiting for the first one to hit.

Heading into her bedroom and straight for her closet, she kicked off her equally uncomfortable pumps and dragged her black tactical clothes from behind columns of gray suits and white button-down shirts. With the hours she put into her job, this self-imposed uniform made it easier as if she had her shit together.

Her phone buzzed with a message from her partner and adrenaline breathed new life into the numbness of her muscles and limbs.

There was a high probability that the crime lord of LA was meeting his minions in the house on Zamora Street. Since the fentanyl aerosol attack in a downtown shopping center eight months ago, Raul Ortega had become public enemy number one. Going after him had wrung every bit of blood, sweat, and tears from her team. Endless stakeouts, monitoring money drops and exchanges, and going undercover as drug addicts took a toll on everyone. The price of getting Ortega couldn't have been higher after one of their own was killed a few months ago.

She thought about her LAPD blues again.

Wash.

Repeat.

GABBY SQUATTED beside the puddle of blood. A low current of rage zipped through her veins as her brain struggled to comprehend how the operation had gotten fucked up beyond recognition.

A mother was dead and a child had been traumatized.

Ortega was nowhere on the property. Their sting operation failed.

Off to the side, a CSI tech documented the carnage.

"You okay?" asked Brock Kelso, her partner of five years.

"No." Her lips pressed into a straight line. A child had witnessed her mother's death. The girl would have nightmares for years if not her entire life. The higher ups would have to answer to the press, but bad publicity was the furthest from Gabby's mind. "They better not pull us from this case."

"I don't think they will, but it's not looking good for us."

"It should've been our call. We've been on Ortega's case since the beginning. Captain wouldn't have okayed the op with the patchy intel we received."

GHD was in charge of the case, but the order for the raid involving different units of the LAPD—SWAT, Narcotics, and GHD—came from the top. The mayor needed a win for his reelection and pressure cascaded down the chain of command.

"Tell me something I don't know."

"They should've let us do our job!" Gabby exploded. "We've only alerted Ortega."

Eighteen months of work derailed by damned politics.

"Kelso! Woodward!" Captain Frank Mitchell strode into the room with his distinctive gait, as if his ramrod-straight back was held up by a plank. Tall and lean with a shaved head that gleamed, the whites of his eyes were a stark contrast to the deep mahogany of his skin. "Why are you still here?"

"This"—Gabby pointed at the pool of blood—"This shouldn't have happened."

"Agreed," the captain replied. "But it did. And it will be

investigated. So, go home, both of you. Nothing else to be done here."

"How's Lucia?" Gabby asked.

The lines around the captain's mouth softened. "She's with a patrol officer. She's shaken but you did a good job calming her."

Gabby gave a somber nod. In all her years on the force it was a constant balance to stay emotionally detached on the scene while at the same time showing compassion when called for. The latter was easy when a child was involved. When the girl rushed toward her, Gabby's instinct was to shield the child and not let her see the horrific state of her mother's body. "Is she going to be okay?"

"Social services is taking over. It's out of our hands," Mitchell said. "Go home. It's Friday. I don't want to see your faces until Monday morning."

"The reading of the will is tomorrow, right?" Kelso asked.

Her mouth flattened and she gave a brief nod.

"Not looking forward to it, huh?"

Gabby shrugged. "Just want to get it over and done."

Long and short of it was, she didn't care.

"And your brother?"

"Half-brother," Gabby corrected, getting slightly irritated that her partner would bring up such a matter now. "He's got money of his own. I'd be surprised if he didn't apply for emancipation."

"If you need more time to get your personal affairs in order, take some vacation," Mitchell said.

"I'll take that under advisement." Gabby jerked her head to the CSI techs who seemed to be interested in their conversation. The last thing she needed was to have one of them talk to the tabloids.

"It's okay to slow down, Woodward." Mitchell exhaled an effusive breath and studied the carnage in the room. "Hope we don't start from square one. Ortega is a slippery bastard."

"That's what happens when you go in half-cocked."

Kelso coughed.

Mitchell raised a brow.

"Which is why you need all hands on deck at Division, sir," she quickly added.

Mitchell's shoulders sagged and it pained Gabby to see him this way. He'd been her mentor for fourteen years, taking the wide-eyed rookie under his wing, but their bond went back much further than that. The captain was a hard ass, a legend in the LAPD who gave up rank and position so he could remain on the streets where his experience was needed the most.

He put a hand on her shoulder and gave it a brief squeeze before striding to the door. He paused under its frame and turned back to her. "The dead are important to us, but so are the living. In this case, I think your brother needs you more."

NORTHERN VIRGINIA

STARING at ceilings was nothing new for Declan Roarke. Getting thrown into jail wasn't new either, but he'd never been incarcerated on U.S. soil before. As a former mercenary, he was no stranger to dungeons and prisons in foreign countries. What he did was not always legal.

After the Judge Advocate General (JAG) disbanded their private military company, banning them from any form of international work, Declan thought personal protection was the way to go. Turned out, the void left by his former life couldn't be filled with new businesses, more money, or the first world comfort of booze and functional indoor plumbing.

The cot was comfy for short-term confinement in

Loudoun County, but he hadn't been comfortable in his own skin for a while.

He shifted his gaze to the cracked cement wall he shared with a drunk who was brought in at the same time he was. The eardrum-shattering snore of his jail-mate assured him he wasn't getting any kind of sleep tonight, and Declan wondered if the man's off-key singing earlier would have made a better companion. He winced in remembrance. Probably not.

The door to the drunk tank opened, and a shadow danced on the arrow of light before a lanky man in khakis appeared at his barred door.

"You're free to go."

Declan swung his long legs off the cot, got up, and approached the deputy. "I made bail?" He'd been in here for twenty-four hours.

"Charges dropped," the deputy said shortly and slid the cell door to the left. "You're lucky the Congressman didn't press assault charges."

It took all of Declan's self-restraint not to say that Congressman Tomlin deserved it. He merely nodded at the officer and stepped out to his freedom.

DECLAN GLANCED over to his business partner, driving their company vehicle. Kade Spear opened Elite Shield Security— ESS—a year ago and asked him if he wanted to join in. Declan thought it was a good idea at that time. Now he wasn't sure if personal protection was the right fit for him. Bodyguard duties were an intrinsic part of private military work, but there was usually a level of imminent threat. Protecting someone whose politics he didn't agree with had never been a problem either. But being here in the Capital, he'd witnessed how vicious politicians could get in pushing their agendas. Constituents only saw the packaged message, not the behind-the-scenes ugliness and machinations it took to get there. And when a clear abuse of power went against the wrong side of his mercenary heart, he couldn't turn away.

"Do I have Yara to thank for Congressman Douche not pressing charges?"

Kade huffed in slight exasperation. "No. But she would have intervened."

Yara was Kade's fiancée and their last client as PMCs. The CIA had hooked them up with the Saudis to do a targeted assassination of the humanitarian aid's hosts, but the op ran into a snag.

Kade fell in love.

It all turned out for the best, and Declan was one hundred percent behind his friend's decision to break the contract with the Saudis. Getting trapped in a foreign country as hostile as Yemen was no picnic. Declan and a few other contractors loyal to Kade got thrown into a Yemeni jail controlled by the rebels. And yet he'd been more in his element in that dank prison than he'd been in the Loudon County one.

The traffic on the DC beltway was stop and go, amplifying the silence in the SUV.

"I wish you had come to me instead of taking matters into your own hands," Kade said finally.

"The man is a pedophile. He was making a fifteen-year-old student squirm—"

"And you decided breaking his nose was the answer?"

Snapshots of the other afternoon came back to mind. The congressman was meeting with the student council from a high school. One of the students was a pretty cheerleader. Congressman Douche had no business putting his hand on the curve of her ass regardless whether she was wearing a short skirt.

The first time. Declan took notice and gritted his teeth, telling himself it was an accident.

The second time. He was clenching his fists.

When it happened yet again, the girl flushed and flinched away from the politician. The damned congressman grabbed her arm and was speaking to the girl in a sickening skeevy voice.

Declan saw red and before he knew it, Tomlin was on the floor with blood all over his face.

"Didn't mean to put the company in a bad light." He stared out the window.

"Fuck the company," Kade growled with such vehemence, it pulled Declan's gaze back to his friend. "I told you to get help. You're having trouble transitioning into civilian life and I get that. Fuck. Do I get that."

"The congressman wasn't an ideal client."

Kade smirked. "No, he wasn't. No immediate threats against him to feed the adrenaline junkies in us. He doesn't really need a bodyguard, but it makes him look important. We wouldn't have taken the job if it wasn't a favor to Yara's dad."

The traffic began to move and Kade changed lanes as their exit came up.

"Let's stop playing the politics game, shall we?"

His friend cleared his throat but didn't respond. It was a gesture Kade was doing more lately when he didn't know how to broach a subject. Transitioning into civilian life wasn't easy on him either, but he had Yara to keep him centered.

As for Declan, he didn't need a woman. He'd figure this shit out eventually. Or maybe the JAG would lift the restrictions on them and let them take jobs where they were needed.

Kade made the turn into the exit leading to Declan's condo. "How about the Hollywood game?"

"What?"

"I know you used to live there, Roarke."

"And I left for a goddamned reason."

"Whoa there, buddy." Kade laughed but threw him a shrewd look. "I know you changed your name from O'Connor to Roarke before you got accepted to Ranger school. At the time I checked, your records were sealed by the military."

"And yet you never pried, so why bring it up now?"

"It's relevant."

"I'm not going back there."

"Hear me out."

"No."

But his friend wasn't easily dissuaded. This was confirmed when Kade parked the SUV instead of dropping him off at his condo. Declan lived in a maintenance-free high-rise building in Reston. The two-bedroom unit was enough for his needs given a job could send him across the country at a moment's notice.

Since it was late in the evening, the front-desk concierge had left, so Declan punched in his code to open the glass doors of the vestibule that led inside the building.

"You like the area?" Kade asked as they stepped into the elevator.

"Yeah."

"How much is it costing you?"

Declan told him how much then asked, "You and Yara plan to stay in Manhattan?"

"Both her office and ours are there so it makes sense, but we're thinking of getting a place in Brooklyn."

The elevator doors opened on the tenth floor. Declan had the unit farthest on the right near the stairwell. When they entered his residence, he didn't apologize for the state of his place.

Stacks of unpacked boxes, some opened and some still sealed, laid in a row.

He had one couch, a leather recliner, and a coffee table. Strewn on its glass top were tactical magazines and stacks of books.

"Still don't watch television?"

Declan shrugged. "No need. I'd just use it for the news, but I can get that on the tablet or my laptop. Want a beer?"

"Sure." Kade surveyed his surroundings. "What do you do for entertainment?"

He walked to the kitchen. "Ever heard of reading, Spear?"

His friend chuckled. "When your fiancée is a staunch supporter of the performing arts, you can't just not have a television."

Snagging two beers from the fridge, he popped the cap off each and handed one to Kade. He leaned against the counter and took a long pull from the bottle. "You haven't told me why Congressman Tomlin didn't press charges."

"He decided to forget the incident. Can't you leave it at that?"

Kade was messing with him judging from the twinkle in his eyes and the twitch at the corners of his mouth. The grumpy soldier was a memory. Now his friend was quick to smile and was rarely in a bad mood. It was sickeningly sappy.

But he was thrilled for Kade and Yara. They deserved all the happiness after what they went through.

"Nope. Start talking, man."

Kade contemplated his beer. "Let's just say we found other shit on the congressman. Nothing to do with his predilection to underage teens, but we have damaging information that would turn off a majority of his conservative base."

"Who's we?"

"Garrison."

"What the fuck? Is he dragging us into his shit again?"

"Well, not me," Kade said. "But you definitely."

"Let me guess. You volunteered me?"

"No. He said you were who he needed, and it was for your own good."

"Motherfucking spook," Declan snorted. "Let me get this straight. He expects me to do his shit, no questions asked."

"Pretty much. Says he saved your ass, he's collecting a favor."

Declan crossed his arms. "Tell me exactly what he wants and maybe ... I'm gonna do it."

"You know we have a gig with the net streaming giant, right?"

"Primeflix? Teaching their actors survival skills. Isn't it for some kind of sci-fi supernatural series?"

"You really need to watch TV or start streaming shows at least."

"No thanks."

His friend scratched his jaw. "Yara said you had movie-star good looks. Were you an actor? Wasn't in your file."

"You were talking about Primeflix."

"Their main producer is Revenant Films."

Lead weighed down his chest, making it difficult to breathe. "Go on."

Kade eyed him closely. "You knew Peter Woodward and his daughter."

"Why the fuck is Garrison digging into my old files?"

"It seems that it was buried in the Army's special section recruitment databases."

Declan took another pull from the bottle. "Not doing this. Not stepping back in fuckin' LA."

He looked anywhere but at Kade as uncomfortable emotions rattled around the chambers of his heart. Seconds passed and his friend stayed silent but the burn on his face from Kade's intense stare forced him to meet his eyes. "If there's something you want to say, say it."

Kade cleared his throat. "Gabrielle Woodward—you were married to her."

Hearing her name was like the proverbial gunshot to center mass.

"I'm not sure if that's a question or a statement." Declan couldn't help the sarcasm that crept into his tone. "I'm assuming it's the latter. So, let's cut this introductory bullshit and get to the point."

His friend exhaled heavily, a somber expression darkened over his face and suddenly, a sensation akin to panic seized Declan's chest. "Is ... is Gabby all right?"

"Peter Woodward was found dead in his Beverly Hills mansion a week ago."

"And Gabby?" he pressed fiercely. "How ... how is she?"

"As far as I know, she's fine."

His mouth turned dry and he swallowed with difficulty. Declan drank his beer, trying to buy himself time as he absorbed this news while wrestling with the memories that came roaring back, trying desperately to keep them in a compartment he could control. "Was he murdered?"

"Still under investigation. Detectives working the case are trying to see if it's more than robbery and homicide. Garrison thinks it's related to what he's investigating."

His eyes narrowed. "What is he investigating?"

"He wouldn't say."

Declan snorted a derisive laugh. "And he expects me to pack up my things and do his bidding?" He hated himself for wanting to jump on that plane to make sure his ex-wife was all right. Not that he knew where she was at the moment, but with Revenant Films as a client, Kade had a file on her for sure. "Is Gabby in danger?"

"How much of her life did you keep up with?"

Declan clenched his jaw and averted his gaze, not wanting his friend to see the pain in his eyes he was sure he couldn't hide. LA took two people who meant the world to him—his sister Claire, and then Gabby.

Draining his beer, he turned back to his friend. "Pretty much none of it after I left LA."

"That bad, huh?"

Bad was an understatement. Gabby married someone else three months after the dissolution of their marriage. It showed

how little he knew her, what she thought of him, how dispos-
able and forgettable he was. From that moment on, and for his
own sanity, he avoided news of her, refusing to look her up.
Whatever part of his heart that was capable of love was
crushed in that place, and he'd gladly exchanged it with one
encased in ice.

And now it was laughable how thin that ice was because
given the suspicious nature of Peter's death, there was no
doubt Declan would never be at peace until he saw for himself
that Gabby was all right.

Call him a sucker.

He'd been better off in ignorant bliss, which explained his
avoidance of the television. But he was ignorant no more,
wasn't he?

Damn Kade.

And damn Garrison.

Circumstances had left him with one reluctant choice.

"Nothing I can't handle," he clipped with more conviction
than he was feeling. "When do I leave?"

2

LOS ANGELES

THE GOODMAN LAW Office was rarely open on Saturdays, but Peter Woodward was a prominent client. Mr. Goodman had always dealt with the legal matters pertaining to Revenant Films—her father's production company—and was now handling his estate.

Aside from the attorney, Gabby was the first to arrive. This wasn't a surprise since her ex-stepmother loved to make a grand entrance. As for her half-brother Theo, well, he was like any other entitled teen who thought the world revolved around their time.

She sat in the waiting room, drinking the coffee she'd made from the fancy brew station in the corner. Gabby sat facing the door—a habit she'd acquired as a detective. So she fully observed the glass doors sliding open as her brother swaggered in.

Theo Woodard, more popularly known as Theo Cole, was the seventeen-year-old star of the hit streaming series *Hodgetown*, a show about teenagers in a small town battling monsters from another dimension. Its fandom exploded in the second season and, from what Gabby had gathered, Theo was making as much as three million dollars for the entire third season. This didn't include all the endorsements for cereals, drinks, or even the sneakers he wore on the show. His net worth was north of ten million.

But all this was insignificant compared to Peter Woodward's fortune.

"Hey, sis."

Gabby ground her molars. Theo's hazel eyes twinkled with mischief and his face bore the beginnings of a smirk. He was aware of her aversion to him and—Theo being Theo—wanted to push her buttons. He had no idea that it hurt to look at him, especially in these last three years as his baby fat melted away and he grew more and more in the likeness of … no … she wasn't thinking of him today. She vowed Claudette's mindfuck of the past would never affect her again.

Trailing behind her brother was a big, muscular man with bronzed skin and golden-flecked brown eyes. She recognized Levi James— the series weapons and fight consultant. *What is he doing here?*

Her brother must have read her mind. "Levi's here for my security."

Gabby felt like she'd been caught flat-footed. "Have the detectives on Peter's case mentioned you were in danger?"

"They said something," Theo shrugged. "Didn't think you were interested."

She resisted the urge to look at the ceiling for divine intervention, leveling her gaze at her brother. "And that something?" she asked. "Is someone after you, too?"

"Playing the concerned sister card now?"

"You know as a relative I can't be involved in the investigation."

Her brother's reply was cut short when the doors slid open again and Theo's mother walked in.

Now they could be one big happy family.

Yeah, right.

Gabby never knew why her father divorced Claudette or how he got full custody of Theo. The divorce happened quickly although the tabloids were full of speculations, like Claudette being caught in bed with a lover.

Nothing new there. A bitter smile formed on her lips.

"Gabby, darling."

Don't darling *me, you bitch.* She successfully avoided her stepmother's air-kisses—something else she hated that Claudette did all the time—and took a step toward Levi.

"We haven't met." Gabby extended her arm in greeting.

Her brother's bodyguard shook her hand. There was a slight squeeze that sent 'I know all about you, too' meaning loud and clear. "Detective Woodward."

Gabby felt immediate confidence in the man, although she'd previously done a background check on Levi James which came up with no red flags. His Irish-Hawaiian blood was evident in his sturdy build, but she was unsure from which ancestry the thick wavy hair came.

"The detectives said they wanted to talk to you," Levi said, volunteering information that Theo refused.

Gabby frowned. "Okay."

The investigation of Peter's suspicious death was the domain of the Robbery and Homicide Division (RHD). Her boss specifically ordered her to stay out of the case. She had mixed feelings about sticking her nose in it, but if Peter's death was not an isolated incident and her brother was in danger, a familial obligation compelled her to get involved.

"After the reading of the will, fill me in on what you know without compromising the investigation."

"YOUR FATHER REQUESTED that the initial reading be done with only the three of you."

Levi was asked to stay outside, and the only ones permitted in the office were Gabby, Theo, and Claudette.

A ghost of a smile touched Gabby's lips. Peter liked his multi-layered existence, seeing how he excised her from his life when she defied him and shunned the Hollywood life. Though she wasn't surprised that he left her something in his will. What surprised her was Claudette. After what Peter put her through in the divorce, Gabby would think his ex-wife would spit on his grave.

"Why is she here?" Her half-brother nodded to Claudette.

Apparently, Theo didn't think highly of his mother either.

Claudette hardly winced at her son's jab, although it could be all that surgical enhancement had frozen her face. She had her own skin care line that she marketed only to the top Hollywood spas and plastic surgeons. Her beauty was timeless, only showing the merest signs of aging through the years. Claudette flicked a curtain of platinum blond hair to the back of her shoulder at the same time she regarded her son with a brittle smile. "Theo, *mon cher*, what did I say about manners?"

Theo responded in French, saying something that annoyed his mother more.

Mr. Goodman looked imploringly at Gabby.

She sighed. "Okay. Both of you. Can you do this family drama somewhere else, so we can get this damned will reading over with?"

Anger flashed through Claudette's eyes, but the only indication of her temper was in the pursing of her lips.

"Please proceed." Gabby gave the go ahead to the lawyer. She spied her brother slouched in his seat with his long legs stretched in front of him in a position that reminded her again of the man she'd buried in the back of her mind.

Shaking her head to clear the cobweb of memories, she concentrated on the lawyer's words.

· · ·

"I, Peter Woodward, a resident of Beverly Hills, California, and the United States and being of sound mind and memory..."

THE LAWYER DRONED on with the legalese about revoking and nulling past wills and testaments. Then he mentioned his children, Gabrielle and Theo.

"I SPECIFICALLY, and intentionally, and with full knowledge included Claudette Dumont in this will even though we've been divorced for three years and she was fully compensated and has no claim on my estate. The reasons will be stated later."

MR. GOODMAN WENT on about the debt agreements and fees and taxes arising from the execution of the will.

"MY SPECIFIC BEQUESTS will be the following:
One, to my son, Theo Woodward,
My car collection except the red Mustang which will be given to my long-time friend and managing partner, Nicholas Carter.
My house in Malibu, Bel Air, Montouk ..."

GABBY ROLLED her eyes as her father basically signed all properties over to Theo.

"IF MY SON doesn't survive me, all bequests will be given to Gabrielle.
Two, to my daughter Gabby, I bequeath the house in Beverly Hills though she doesn't give a shit about it. She will not be allowed to sell it. If she does, the money will be distributed to the charities listed in the following."

. . .

GABBY WONDERED what was her father's motive. Did Peter think she would care if the money went to charity? It was probably the best option anyway. The lawyer went on about specific items like the charity distribution, art collection, libraries, and other assets.

"REVENANT FILMS WILL CONTINUE to be run by the board and all shares and monies due to me will be split equally between Theo and Gabrielle."

"Is THERE anything in there for me at all or did I waste a transatlantic flight from Paris?" Claudette flared.

"Classy, Mother," Theo drawled.

"Why you—"

"I'm getting to that section," the lawyer interrupted in a louder voice than normal. The lines on his forehead more pronounced as he stared at the document before him.

"IF BOTH MY children survive me, I have a special request before bequeathing them the sum of twenty-five million dollars each. They will live together for a period of three months and spend time together as siblings. It is my deepest regret that I've never mended the rift within my family. It is my wish that Gabrielle will remain Theo's guardian until he reaches eighteen. If he files for emancipation immediately after my death, the money bequeathed to him will be distributed evenly to the charities mentioned prior to this section.

"Now, to Claudette Dumont, I bequeath the sum of eight million dollars and my apartment in Paris, France as long as she stays out of my children's lives. She shall not interfere or try to gain custody of Theo while he has not reached legal age."

. . .

MR. GOODMAN's throat bobbed and he stole a glance at her father's ex. "This is a direct quote to you Ms. Dumont.

"STAY the fuck away from my children, Claudette. Even in my death I have ways to hunt you down if you hurt them in any way. Let them get to know each other with none of your vile manipulations. Keep your people away. I mean it."

YOUR PEOPLE?
"Did Peter amend his will recently?" Gabby asked.
"A month ago." Mr. Goodman's eyes darted toward Claudette.
Before Gabby could say anything, Theo sprung to his feet and stalked toward his mother. "Was it you? Did you have him murdered?"
"I was in France!" Claudette exclaimed. "I have my money and my boyfriend is rich enough to buy out Peter ten times over. Eight million dollars is nice, but I don't need it." She sniffed. "I've agreed to talk to the detectives. Peter always thought someone was after him. You should talk to Nick. Your father's been on a cocktail of medication for his heart condition and a bad back, and they've made him depressed and paranoid. He always had trouble distinguishing between his movies and reality."
Gabby's mind was swirling at this turn of events. Live with her brother? What was their father thinking? And what was that cryptic threat against Claudette? Did Peter know he was in danger? She would request a copy of the prior will and the current one to compare the differences. Maybe robbery wasn't the intention and just a front. She debated whether she should

inform Captain Mitchell of these developments and get clearance to get involved in the case.

"Is there anything else in the will?"

"Yes. This one is a direct quote to both of you."

"GABRIELLE, I've watched you struggle with what happened all those years ago. You needed your family and I've been selfish, thinking of my own happiness and didn't consider your own. I tried to contact you, but you never returned my emails, calls, or texts. I hope you view Theo in a different light than me and Claudette. He's a good kid—if not spoiled, but I hope spending time with you will teach him about the real world. Because of that, I would like for Theo to move in with you for the duration specified in this will."

"WHAT?" Theo growled. "No way. You live in a dump."

Gabby was amused if not a tad terrified. "A dump? Have you seen my place?"

"No. But I'm sure it's not Beverly Hills."

"You're right. But maybe that's Peter's best idea yet. You need a lesson in humility."

"Pleaaase." He rolled his eyes. "Do you have room for Levi?"

"Three bedrooms." Gabby paused. "Shit. Am I agreeing to this?"

"Do you have parking for my Ferrari?" Theo demanded.

"I suggest you downgrade your ride if you don't want it stripped, or worse—stolen." She lived in a gated apartment complex, but her brother didn't need to know that.

For the first time since Gabby had to deal with this teen version of her brother, he was the one who was speechless. Was it petty that she derived immense satisfaction in seeing his face pale and his lazy nonchalance evaporate?

Theo glanced at Goodman. "Is there a way to contest this?"

"Over sleeping arrangements?" Gabby laughed.

"I'm not finished," Goodman interrupted.

"By all means, please continue," her brother muttered.

"THEO, son, I'm proud of the success of Hodgetown, *but I'm afraid you might become a child-star cliché without proper guidance. You need a lesson in humility."*

GABBY SNORTED a laugh and Theo shot her a death stare.

"IT IS my hope you do not give your sister a difficult time. In the end of all this, you will find how much the two of you are alike. If you success-fully live together for three months, besides the money, you will be given the key to a safe deposit box. I am certain you will discover you share the same blood more than you know, and the contents of the box will put all doubts and questions to rest."

GOODMAN CLEARED his throat again and peered at them. "Any questions?"

Claudette stood. She'd been unusually quiet during the reading of the will. "This was a waste of my time. I wouldn't even try to gain guardianship of Theo anyway. See how much my son hates me?"

"You know why, Mother."

"All right." Gabby stood and extended her arm to the attorney. "Thank you for your time. I presume you have a copy of the old will?"

Goodman nodded. "I was afraid you might ask that."

"I'll talk to my captain, see if these wills need to be pursued in the investigation of my father's death."

"I'm leaving," Claudette announced as she strutted to the door and yanked it open.

"Don't leave town, Claudette."

The blonde flipped her off before her stilettos clacked away on the marble floor.

"So, roomie." Theo walked up to her. "Are you sure you don't want to live the high life in Beverly Hills?"

"So slum it for a while."

He raised a brow, took in her white blouse, gray slacks, before wincing at her brown loafers. "Maybe we can work on your wardrobe game."

Gabby scowled at him before addressing the attorney. "I'll keep in touch. I'm not the detective on the case, but I'll make sure they're aware of this turn of events."

"This office will cooperate," Goodman assured her. "Both of you are the main beneficiaries and as executor of this will, it is my duty to be on your side."

"That'd be appreciated." Gabby turned to her brother. "Should I go with you to pack your things?"

"Whoa. Stop right there," her brother growled. "You may be my guardian but I'm almost eighteen."

"Your point?"

"I don't need a babysitter." He stalked out of the office. Gabby sighed and trailed behind him.

Levi was waiting for them, leaning against the wall beside the door.

"Then what do you call this dude?" She thumbed at the big guy.

Her brother's bodyguard was instantly alert, his dark brows cinched in a frown. "What's going on?"

Gabby continued to walk ahead. "Theo is coming home with me."

"That's not happening."

She stopped and faced Goliath. In her estimate, Levi stood six-four and his broad shoulders easily dwarfed Gabby twice over.

Not that she was insignificant. At five-six, she wasn't tiny, and she kept in shape with weights and martial arts, but she had a feeling Levi wasn't a lumbering idiot, and she'd have to think long-term. She'd have to lure him to her side with sugar and not vinegar if she'd have hopes of managing Theo.

She was his guardian. Somehow that still didn't compute in her brain.

"Look, it's in my father's will. Theo stays with me."

Levi considered this. "I'll have to clear it with ESS. It's our reputation on the line if anything happens to Theo."

"Understood. What do you need from me?"

"Address and what levels of security you have."

Oh, they're going to love my address. "You got it. Anything else?"

The big guy exhaled a breath. "Several things, but it's better if we discuss this somewhere else."

"Hate to interrupt you all." Theo moved between them. "But I'm the one with a busy schedule and ..." he checked his watch. "We can work on this sibling bonding time after the awards show tonight ... unless you want to go as my date?"

"Ugh ... People's Choice is tonight, isn't it?"

"Hey, there's hope for you after all."

She was more amused than annoyed as she sighed in Levi's direction. "There was nothing stated in the will that this arrangement has to take effect immediately. We'll reconvene on Monday? I need the weekend to digest this."

"You make it sound like I'm some bad seafood being forced down your throat," Theo grumbled.

Gabby walked up to her brother. Even at seventeen, he was already over six feet. "Listen, pal. You and I will have to make the most of our situation. Peter's death is suspicious and something in the will has triggered some red flags."

"What red flags?" Levi asked.

"Let's put it this way … Revenant Films was right in hiring you as Theo's security." Turning her attention back to her brother, she continued. "I've lived without Peter's money for a long time and it may sound trite, but I don't care about the money. I do care that you may be in danger."

"Wow, I'm touched."

"Don't be an asshole."

Theo grinned, but for the first time that day, Gabby noticed it didn't reach his eyes and a twinge of guilt settled on her chest. He was doing his utmost best to hide his grief, a grief she had yet to feel.

And like the detective she was, she filed away that information for further processing and handed Levi her card. "I'll be in touch this weekend."

She was already at the sliding glass doors when Theo hollered. "No group hugs?"

Despite the belated sympathy she'd felt for him, she flipped her brother a middle finger salute and left without another word.

3

HOLLYWOOD.

A city where dreams come true or your heart gets ripped to pieces. For Declan, the moment he found his wife in bed with another man killed all his dreams of having a family. Scavenging whatever was left of his heart, he forged a new path in the Army, forming a band of brothers. It was a different kind of belonging, but he never again experienced that level of unbridled happiness he'd shared with his ex-wife.

He dragged his gaze from the famous sign and turned his attention back to the taxi that took him from LAX to this address on Stone Canyon Road. The vehicle rolled to a stop in front of a massive ranch house sprawled behind ornate black iron bars. After paying the driver, Declan exited the cab and slung his large duffel over one shoulder, heading up to the gate.

Embossed in small print on a brass plate: Revenant Films.

He tightened his grip on the duffel strap, as he prepared himself for the past to clash with the present. It was only a matter of time before he ran into his ex-wife. He'd come a long way from the impulsive idealistic nineteen-year old he'd been. He was in a better place, wasn't he? He gave a brief snort. He just broke the nose of a congressman—"better place"—was relative.

Peter Woodward had wanted him nowhere near his precious daughter, much less have him as a son-in-law. Back in the day, the producer and director made big waves with his post-apocalyptic movies, managing to inject realism into his films that touched at the core of people's fears. Presently, his outfit dominated a niche market of the net-streaming business. The man had the Midas touch, but apparently, that didn't save him from his own mortality.

So far, the investigation indicated an armed robbery at his Beverly Hills mansion.

He punched the button for the outside call box. A voice on the box told him to hold up his driver's license. After a few beeps, the gate slid open and he was informed where to find Levi James.

Peace of mind, Declan repeated to himself. It was all he was here for, but mentoring teen actors seemed like a steep price to pay. He winced at the thought.

It wasn't hard to figure out where everyone was. The driveway wrapped around the house and stopped at a clearing with a drop off to the canyon. A row of expensive cars lined the grassy area and a group of people surrounded what resembled an outdoor fitness camp.

Declan was about fifteen minutes early and sauntered under the shade of a tree. He leaned against its massive trunk and lowered his bag to observe the activities. He didn't want to interrupt the session which appeared to be wrapping up anyway.

Just like Declan, his partner on this gig, Levi, had worked for Kade's defunct private military company. Declan had never worked with the former SEAL, but he'd heard nothing but praise. Apparently, his home life was a mess and he was separated from his wife. It seemed everyone was having a hard time adjusting to this civilian life except Kade, but he had Yara to keep him in line.

The huddle broke up and Levi turned to wave at him before talking to a couple of girls who giggled at what he said. Declan wondered which one was Peter Woodward's son. The dossier had a blurry picture of a bottle-blond boy with dark eyes. Declan couldn't identify anyone with that shade of hair among the gaggle of teenagers who dispersed and headed his way. A dark-haired boy walked alongside Levi making gestures as if asking for tips on his fighting stance.

A couple of teen girls got excited when they spotted Declan.

Fuck, they probably thought he was that *Captain America* actor with the beard.

"I'm not him," he called out when one of them batted their lashes. He proceeded to ignore them, until they finally gave up trying to gain his attention and got into their cars and drove off.

Jesus. That never changed.

As Levi and the boy got closer, instincts honed by his years as an Army Ranger throttled his senses into high alert. No threats of a roadside bomb or lurking terrorists were imminent, so this feeling of getting ambushed threw him off. Lightheadedness gripped him and quick bursts of breath sawed through his lungs. A panic attack? He hadn't had one of those in a long fucking time.

Five feet away, he saw that the boy was clean shaven as opposed to his trim beard. He took in Theo's face—its angles, his jawline, his nose, even the shape of his eyes. Declan finally realized why seeing the teenager gave him a strange feeling of déjà vu, why he kept comparing the boy to himself.

It was like staring at a mirror into the past.

In fact, Theo Cole could have been him at seventeen, and the only difference was the color of their irises. Hazel to his green.

What the fuck is going on?

"You must be Roarke," Levi called out as ground-eating strides diminished the last few feet between them. Declan straightened from his slouch against the tree and held out his arm.

"Yeah."

"Levi James—Levi."

He barely acknowledged his colleague, his eyes riveted on the teenager. "You must be Theo?"

The boy gave him a chin lift.

Forcing his eyes to Levi's, he said, "He wasn't what I was expecting. The image on the file is different."

"Dude! Ever heard of the internet?" Theo smirked.

"Wasn't me who arranged the dos— the file," Levi said.

Did Kade mislead him? Although, Declan suspected Garrison had a hand in it.

"So you're Peter Woodward's grandson?" Declan asked. He shoved his hands into his front pockets to refrain from grabbing the boy and demanding answers.

Levi and Theo frowned.

"Roarke, you—" his partner started.

"Didn't you read the file?" Theo glanced at the other man. "Your back-up is messed up, Levi."

"You're seventeen?"

"What's with all these stupid questions?" the teenager snapped. "Read the file. I'm not doing your job for you."

Peter Woodward is your father as much as he was the Pope.

"You okay, man?" Levi asked, a sharpness entering his tone. He realized he wasn't making a good first impression, but Declan was past giving a fuck.

But creeping out the teenager with his staring wasn't going to get him any answers.

"Give me a minute." He raised a finger and spun away from the duo.

"I'm gonna go get cleaned up at the house," Theo muttered to Levi. "Fix this mix-up. Because this guy …?"

As a tornado of possibilities tumbled in his head, Declan imagined Theo miming the crazy circle gesture with his fingers.

At that moment, Declan wasn't sure whether he was trapped in a dream, a nightmare, or a hallucination.

But regaining control of his equilibrium evaporated when a sedan rolled down the driveway and, before he could stop himself, he went stalking toward it to confront the driver.

"Roarke, man, what the fuck?" Levi shouted from behind him.

He reached the vehicle and yanked open the door, about to snarl his questions, but he wasn't prepared for the full blast of magnificent brown eyes that still had the power to captivate him and render him speechless.

Gabby.

They stared at each other for an eternity.

He gritted out a brusque. "Get. Out." His own voice sounding foreign to him.

"Dec?" His name a whisper. Disbelief etched on her pale face… disbelief and something else.

"What the fuck is going on?" Levi growled, coming up beside them.

"Stay out of this, James."

Gabby slowly stepped out of the vehicle as if any sudden movement of hers would incense a wild animal.

She shot Levi a dazed look. "I got this."

"Not sure you do," Levi replied which pissed off Declan more.

"Call Spear," Declan snapped. "Tell him no thanks for this clusterfuck he sprang on me."

"Roarke …"

"Now!" he growled.

Levi crossed his arms. "Not until you fucking calm down and I know you're not gonna do stupid shit."

His lungs refused to expand with much needed oxygen, so he waited one beat, two beats, fully aware that the woman who'd haunted him for seventeen years was standing right in front of him. Seeing Theo also blindsided him, and words he had carefully rehearsed was lost in the chaos of his mind.

When he'd regained a semblance of composure, he spoke in a controlled voice. "I'm good. Ms. Woodward and I need to talk."

"I'll be fine," Gabby assured the other man. "He gets out of line, I know kung-fu."

Levi chuckled at the attempted levity and backed away. "I'll call Spear."

Declan shot the man a glare. "Do that and give him a 'fuck you' from me."

"Still charming, aren't you?" Gabby said, pulling his attention back to her, his gaze critical as he studied the woman before him like he would an adversary. She was not the Gabby from his past. Her face was thinner, making those blasted eyes that seemed to see into him more arresting. Missing was the sparkle he remembered. It was replaced by world-weary flatness. Not that he cared.

"Theo Cole is not your father's son."

Her face lost all color and her body swayed and for a second, Declan thought he might have to catch her from falling. Then her face hardened, a chill taking over her eyes. "Not here." She walked ahead of him.

"What? Afraid the world will know the truth?"

When they reached the tree line, she wheeled around and had the gall to look hurt and angry. "The truth?"

He had never felt such an urge to do violence to a woman as much as he wanted to throttle her at that singular moment. All thoughts of comforting her on Peter's death fled from his mind, overcome by a rage from the unforgivable.

"He's mine," he choked.

"You're right," she said without inflection. "He's yours."

"Why?" he said hoarsely. "Why did you lie?"

Her brows drew together, head rearing back. "What?"

"Why did you keep him from me?"

"What the hell are you talking about?"

Feeling like a caged tiger with no outlet for his rage, he paced. "That scene at the hospital. Was that staged? Guilt me enough to get out of your life?"

Her eyes turned from icy fury to fire.

"You bastard," she whispered. "That scene? Was a woman who'd just lost her baby. That scene? Was a woman whose husband handed her divorce papers three days after she'd lost that baby." The devastation on her face was awakening long-forgotten emotions in his heart. He squashed them viciously, because he couldn't feel this and understand what she was telling him.

He stopped his pacing. "You're not making sense."

"That day I lost everything," she said dully.

Confused, he stated, "He's our son."

"No, Declan, only yours." Her shoulders drooped as if the weight of the world was on them. "I thought he was my brother all these years. But this ..." she pointed to him. "Claudette wasn't just messing with my mind." Her mouth twisted in disgust. "That bitch," she whispered as if lost in her own world. "She was telling the truth."

"What are you talking about?" He moved to put his hands on her shoulders, but her arms came up in a defensive gesture, eyes slitting in warning.

"I'm done with this shit. Done with you." Her voice was determined. "I'm glad you know. You deserve to get to know him as his father. I don't have the answers you need," she said in rapid speech before exhaling deeply. "Take it up with Claudette."

"Claudette?"

"Yes. Are you forgetting my ex-stepmother? That day I came to you to beg you to reconsider the divorce because I found out I was pregnant and who did I find?"

Declan's head was spinning as the memories he'd tried to block came rushing back.

No. No. No.

"My stepmother with a towel wrapped around her body," she said slowly through clenched teeth—"answered your door."

"That was fucked up," he groaned.

"Yes, it was."

"Gabby ..." The situation still wasn't making a lick of sense. He grabbed her arm.

And just like that, she had it twisted behind his back, his chest pushed up against a tree trunk, drawing all his awareness to the body pressing against his.

He didn't fight her. He knew she was a cop, but, fuck, he was impressed. The gears in his brain spun in place trying to reconcile the Gabby he knew to this version of his ex-wife.

"Fucking touch me again and I'm throwing your ass into jail so fast, you'll be wishing you'd never stepped foot back into my city."

"Your city, huh?" he couldn't help the teasing that crept into his words. Years melted away, and in between anger, bitterness, and pain, the natural way they clicked was still there.

She must have felt it too because she quickly released him. He turned to look at her, catching her wiping her fingers at the back of her gray pants.

The way she dressed was new. Her whole demeanor was so alien to him, he had to recalibrate every way he would deal with this version of his ex-wife. But his top priority was getting to the bottom of the mystery with Theo.

And judging from her reaction, she didn't have the answers either.

"If you're backup for my brother's security, there's something you should know." She switched to all business and he let it go for now. He needed to regain his bearings after seeing Theo and coming face-to-face with her, so he forced himself to focus as Gabby told him the gist of her father's will.

Before he could comment on it though, Theo's voice rang out through the clearing. "Hey, sis, what are you doing over there? That man is crazy."

They both looked in Theo's direction as the teen approached them. He had a swagger Declan never had at his age.

"He's got a mouth on him," he observed.

"Tell me about it," she grumbled as she started toward Theo and he walked alongside her.

"From his reaction, I gather he still thinks Peter Woodward is his father?"

"Yes. It's up to you how you want to break it to him. I want no part of it."

Declan stopped walking. Surprised how those words cut into him and his shields slammed up. He needed to be an observer first. He watched Gabby greet her brother, sensing no warmth coming from her, and Theo had the rascal attitude going. What the hell was going on?

THE PAIN of a thousand daggers pierced through the center of her chest as she turned away from Declan and turned to face her brother—who she knew now, without a doubt, had never been her brother. He was the lovechild of her ex-husband and Claudette.

"What did he say to you?" Theo demanded. "Was he a dick to you?"

A choked laugh escaped her lips. "Nothing I can't handle."

Declan's son, but never hers. Oh, god.

"You look like you're about to throw up or spit nails," he observed. "And why can't you look at me unless you're lying…"

Because it hurts to look at you.

For a second, his words receded in a vacuum. All these years since Theo hit puberty, Gabby thought she'd imagined seeing a replica of her ex. She avoided dwelling on it because she refused to let the past haunt her anymore. The years had blurred Declan's features in her mind and it was easy to make up her own reality. Her relationship with Theo depended on it, but now with Declan's return, the ugly truth just smacked her in the face.

"Still not looking at me," her brother growled. "Should I kick him in the ass?"

Her brother. She needed to think of Theo as her brother. This was the only way she could survive this farcical drama.

She raised her gaze to meet his. "If there's any ass-kicking to do, that'll be my job."

"Huh." Theo shifted in his stance and puffed out his chest. "I'm almost a foot taller than you."

"You exaggerate. And I can kick your ass as well."

The teenager's eyes broke away from her and narrowed over her shoulder. Feeling Declan's scrutiny burning down her back, she gathered the pieces of herself that lay scattered at her feet and turned to him, proud of the woman she'd become in his absence.

"Theo's riding with me," Gabby informed them. "I know you're his security, but I figured you guys want to touch base privately?"

Declan shrugged, but Levi nodded.

"We'll follow your car," his partner answered.

Gabby's attention returned to Theo, and her breath hitched. The teen was slightly pale beneath his tan and with his gaze boring into Declan, she had a feeling a big secret was about to be blown wide open.

"Theo? You ready?"

The younger man's gaze wavered, jaw tightening as he gave a brief nod, before he walked ahead of them toward her car.

Her sedan was rolling down Stone Canyon Road, Levi's Escalade following behind her, and had just passed the Hotel Bel-Air when Theo spoke his first words since leaving Revenant Ranch.

"What's up with the new guy?"

His question snapped her out of her rough trip down memory lane. A trip she wasn't prepared to take. And she fumed at the nostalgia her thoughts evoked. Because wasn't nostalgia a person's unwillingness to let go of the past? How dare Declan show up here in Los Angeles and send her world in a tailspin.

Switching to the logic of her cop's brain, she evaluated the events that led up to her ex-husband showing up. The timing wasn't a coincidence. It was as if chess pieces were being moved into place. Peter's suspicious death. Claudette was in town. Now Declan showing up? Not to mention the odd warning in the will.

"I knew him from way back."

"He's ... not ugly. Was he from your acting days?"

"You can say that."

"What? Was he bad at it?"

"Oh, he's good." So good that he fooled her into believing love conquered all.

"Then what?"

"Why don't you ask him?"

"I'm asking you."

Though Gabby hadn't spent enough time with Theo to know his every quirk, it didn't take long to figure out that he could be persistently annoying.

"He realized he preferred to serve his country."

Theo fell silent. Gabby glanced at him and realized his face was contorting from the effort to maintain a straight face.

He exploded laughing. "That's so cheesy."

"What's cheesy about wanting to serve your country?"

"It's the way you made it sound. Can't you just say he wanted to join the Army? He's Army, right? Levi said so."

"There's nothing wrong with the way I said it."

"Be all you can be, huh?"

Gabby bit her tongue. It wasn't her place to teach patriotism to this kid. Declan would do it soon enough, if he chose to be a dad.

A dad. At least one of them got their dream, even if it was seventeen years late. They'd talked about having a family right before they eloped to Vegas. Yes, they'd been that cliché. They'd been so in love. She'd just turned eighteen, ready to defy her dad and commit career suicide. Declan was barely a man, a boy of nineteen, and yet he carried a responsibility no one his age should have borne. The odds were stacked against them and they'd been too arrogant to think that they had enough love between them to survive.

But life turned on a dime, didn't it? And when it turned, there was a fifty percent chance you'd lose.

And Gabby lost it all.

She tried to shake off the shiver that went through her, annoyed how the past easily returned to haunt her. She lost the baby because of a brutal mugging.

Did Declan think she staged the mugging, too?

It was one of the darkest days of her existence, and yet the only thing she could remember was the agony of a life being ripped away from her.

Somehow the reminder of that crime prickled her consciousness and she checked the rearview mirror just in time to see a motorcycle run parallel with Levi's Escalade before overtaking it. Alertness pushed the past out of her mind, and defensive instincts kicked into high gear. She glanced over at Theo to make sure he was buckled in.

"What?" her brother quirked a brow.

A screeching sound screamed behind them, just as a blur of black shot past her.

"Watch out!" Theo screamed.

Gunfire sprayed their vehicle and their tires blew.

"Hang on!" Gabby yelled.

Her car fishtailed and swerved as she tried to regain control. Wheels grated against concrete, and she gritted her teeth. She almost had it under control when a van barreled out of nowhere and rammed the front of their vehicle. Her world spun and flashed into frames of muddled color.

They smashed into something unyielding. Excruciating pain slammed into her and a line of fire burned across her shoulder and chest before her breath was stolen.

Gabby struggled to stay conscious. "Theo, are you all right?" A groan sounded beside her, but her attention refocused on the masked men who got out of the van.

Her fingers frantically searched for her Glock, closing over its grip, but her vision dimmed.

Before the darkness swallowed her, she heard fireworks.

4

"GET that needle away from me, Bristow."

He watched the ginger-haired nurse attend to Gabby who was turning out to be a grumpy patient. As for Declan, he was only now recovering from the adrenaline high and terror that seized him when he witnessed the attack on her and Theo.

Thank fucking Christ, Levi managed some *Fast and Furious* maneuvers to get around the garbage truck that tried to stop them from following Gabby's car. This enabled them to head off the masked assailants who attacked her vehicle. Declan flexed his jaw, but kept his arms folded across his chest to keep from touching his ex-wife and checking for himself that she was indeed all right.

"Tsk. Tsk. Always trying to be tough, our Detective Hottie." Bristow didn't look like he belonged to the Bellevue emergency room. But with sleeve tattoos and longish red hair held back by a leather tie, he reminded him more of a cage fighter than a nurse.

"I take it she's a regular visitor," Declan asked.

"Oh, we reserve emergency room five for her every Friday," Bristow continued, still holding up a needle. "We were worried we'd have to look for her in the morgue—"

"Jesus," Declan muttered. Not something he needed to hear.

"You have to get used to their morbid humor." Gabby glared at the nurse. "I'm serious, Bristow. No shots. I hate how they make me feel after. Throw some pills at me."

Bristow lowered the needle. "Fine. I'll get the doc to write you a script. No running around chasing bad guys, lady. The only thing you're gonna be doing is finding out if that dagger is gonna kill the Qadonac monster and stop the virus from spreading."

"What the hell are you talking about?" Gabby demanded.

What she said, Declan thought.

The nurse rolled his eyes. "Don't you watch your brother's show?"

"Do I look like I have the time?"

The other man grinned at Declan. "Well, Detective Hottie, looks like you'll have plenty of time now."

"Bite me."

"Is she always this testy?" Declan asked.

"Yup. Always. With her weekly visits, I'm used to her orneriness. I'm the only nurse who can tolerate her."

"Guys. I'm right here," Gabby huffed indignantly. "And just for the record. I'm not here every week and the nurses love me."

Bristow grinned and slid back on the stool and stood. "Hang tight, Detective. I'll get the doc."

"I'm outta here," Gabby grumbled after the nurse closed the door. She swung her legs off the bed, but Declan blocked her.

"Don't think so."

"Get out of the way, Dec."

For the first time since they'd seen each other again, it was just the two of them in an enclosed area. Awareness thickened the air between them. Dragging oxygen into his lungs seemed to be his issue today. Maybe he needed a doctor to look at him too.

Gabby was finding the floor interesting, so he was staring at the top of her head. He braced both his hands on either side of her hips and—he'd probably call himself all kinds of stupid later—pinned her body to the bed. Her frame stiffened against him and when she tipped up her chin to look at him, he found himself sucked into the depths of her thick-lashed brown eyes. The oddest compulsion to kiss her seized him.

"What are you doing?" she whispered.

"Fuck if I know," he muttered. "You need to be cleared by the doctor."

He lost her eyes when she stared at his shoulder, her throat bobbing. "Any news on Theo?"

"He's fine."

"Why aren't you with him?"

His jaw clenched. "Because, I don't know how, Gabby. He's better off with who he's familiar with right now ... who he trusts, and that person is Levi."

He shouldn't feel a stab of pain in his chest. He barely knew the kid and he didn't quite know what to do with Gabby, and yet his instincts were screaming at him to keep her safe. Fuck if that didn't make him an idiot, but the attack had shaken him. And he wasn't easily shaken. The only way to restore his balance would be to take control of the situation.

"This is what's gonna happen," he told her. "You're—"

"Oh, hell no!" She shoved him with the palm of her hands, but he didn't budge. Her face flinched in pain.

He stepped back and caught her biceps. "What the hell are you doing?"

"Getting away from you," she snarled.

"What's going on here?" A voice spoke from the doorway.

They both turned to the newcomers.

One was an older man in a cop's uniform. The other man was wearing a suit.

He released Gabby and introduced himself. "Declan Roarke. I work with Levi James, Theo Cole's security."

"Frank Mitchell," the black guy said, shaking Declan's outstretched hand. "I'm Gabby's boss." He nodded to the dark-haired man beside him. "Kelso here is Gabby's partner. We have you and Mr. James to thank for chasing off their attackers. Doesn't explain why you have your hands on my detective," Mitchell said in a no-nonsense tone. "I can book you right now for assaulting a police officer."

"Are you all right, Gabby?" Kelso shot him a glare before moving to her side. "Heard from Bristow you've rattled your noggin' real good."

"I've got a hard head."

"That you do." Kelso grinned faintly. "You look like shit."

"Thanks. Always so flattering there, pal."

"That's why you love me." Gabby's partner shot Declan a look, one that was staking a claim. A familiar possessiveness locked Declan's muscles, and he had to remind himself that things were different between him and Gabby now. He had no right to feel jealous.

But fuck that, was she dating her partner?

"Knock it off you two," Mitchell said, eyeballing Declan. "Well?"

"She wanted to leave and I stopped her. Nurse told her to wait."

"There are one too many people in this room," a new voice joined the conversation.

When Mitchell moved from the doorway, a man in a white coat and with a stethoscope around his neck strode into the room. By the way he greeted them, the doctor clearly knew Mitchell, Kelso, and Gabby

After introducing himself to Declan, the doctor said, "I'll have to ask one of you to leave and it'll have to be you."

Declan clenched his fists. He could stand here and argue,

but the sooner Gabby got examined by a doctor, the better. "I'll wait outside."

"Can you check on Theo?" Gabby asked after him.

That he could do. He nodded and left the room.

Declan headed to emergency room two to see Theo but paused when he saw Levi talking to a man he recognized as Nick Carter, Peter's right-hand man, and from the dossier—Theo's manager. He was also the man who played a huge role in breaking up his marriage. Now all they needed was Claudette to show up to complete this fucking circus. Anger boiled close to the surface and an image of Congressman Tomlin with a bloody nose flashed through his head, but instead of Tomlin, it was Carter on that floor bleeding.

He couldn't afford to lose his shit now when he had so many questions. And getting locked up in jail wouldn't get him any answers.

Like how the fuck did Theo become Peter and Claudette's son ... unless.

No. It was impossible. Peter wouldn't be that cruel and Gabby wouldn't have been complicit. There was no trace of a mother's love in her eyes when she regarded Theo. Their interactions hinted more like he was a thorn in her side, and for some reason that made Declan want to lock them all up in a room and have it out.

A sound of a closing door clicked down the hallway and he locked eyes with the doctor who had told him to leave. Declan waited for the man to reach him.

"She's been ordered to take it easy for a week."

"I'll make sure she does."

"You think you'll succeed where Captain Mitchell didn't?"

Declan's mouth thinned.

"I know a spec ops guy when I see one," the other man said. "I was an army medic with the Joint Special operations ... oh, a decade ago."

At this, his brow raised.

"I don't know what's going on, but that girl has been through a lot. She needs someone to look after her, even stand up to her and tell her not to kill herself doing this job." His eyes peered into his. "There's more story between you two. Tension was thick." He huffed a laugh. "Give it a week, okay?"

"A week?"

"Before you have sex."

"Jesus. You always this crass with your patients, Doc?"

"I'm a physician. Sex is a clinical act to me." He paused. "When talking to my patients."

"Noted," he muttered.

"One more thing. I told the captain and Kelso, but someone needs to stay with her tonight."

"Wake her up every hour?"

The doctor nodded.

"She's got me."

"That's what I thought." The doctor gave him a brief smile before walking away.

Gabby's door opened again. This time it was Gabby's partner who emerged. He and Declan exchanged a look across the hallway. He didn't care who she fucked now but he winced at the thought. He tried another track in his brain … that his concern for her was related to Theo. That was all there was to it.

But his gut called him a liar and he'd gone and gotten pissed at himself all over again.

"Kelso sees he's got competition." Bristow appeared by his side, and both of them started for Gabby's room.

"They've been partners a long time?"

"I think five years, but they're just friends though."

Declan shot a disbelieving look at the nurse. "Then I don't see—"

"Cops and their partners, man." The nurse grinned at him. "Almost as good as married, right?"

When they got to the door and Kelso, Bristow asked, "She ready for me?"

"Give her two minutes," the detective said.

Declan's phone beeped with a message. It was from Levi.

Levi: "Theo's about to be discharged. Ms. Woodward?"

Me: "She's almost ready."

Levi: Change of plans. Spear got us a residence on Brentwood. More security."

Me: "You think Gabby will agree to this?"

Levi: "Use your charm, Roarke."

Me: "Doubt that's gonna work."

LEVI DIDN'T REPLY, but Declan imagined he was laughing his head off.

5

"YOU'RE BACK, HUH?"

Declan didn't look at Nick. He managed to tamp down the bitterness and rage and kept his eyes staring ahead as he watched Bristow and another nurse reunite Gabby with Theo.

Peter's right-hand man, who happened to be Gabby's ex-husband number two, registered shock when he saw Declan, but quickly recovered and even had the audacity to stand beside him.

"Yes."

"Theo doesn't need any upheavals in his life so soon after Peter's death."

This time he turned cold eyes toward Nick. "Upheavals. That's a favorite term of yours, isn't it?"

"You're bad news, O'Connor. Always have been, always will be."

"Name's Roarke now. O'Connor's long dead."

"Then you shouldn't have come back," Nick whispered harshly. "You destroyed Gabby's career. Look at her now."

Declan raised a brow. "Such concern for her. Didn't even see you peek in her room to see if she was okay."

"Theo needed me more."

"You mean, Theo, your cash cow?"

Gabby took that moment to look at them, a frown creasing her brow. "Everything all right?" Must be awkward for her seeing her ex-husbands side by side. Resentment overwhelmed him. At least she finally wised up and didn't go for husband number three.

Theo glanced at them. "You two know each other?" The boy wasn't stupid. He already figured something was up, judging by how nonchalant he was asking the question.

"Nothing to worry about, kid." Nick walked up to the boy and put his arm around his shoulder. Declan wanted to haul him back and flatten him. He didn't want that man anywhere near Theo. But he was held impotent by what little he understood of the situation. At this point, Gabby's captain and Kelso exchanged strange looks. Because Declan didn't want anyone else to speculate when they saw him beside Theo, he made the decision to hang way back from his son.

The captain was able to request provisional police protection for Theo Cole and a detail would patrol their temporary residence. Gabby didn't consider herself under police protection. She'd been stubborn as shit arguing with her superior. Said it was part of her job and if that Ortega guy came after her—to use her as bait.

Declan gritted his teeth at that.

Before they headed to the secure residence in Brentwood that Spear arranged for them, Gabby needed to pick up items from her apartment. He was accompanying her, with Kelso dropping them off. They would be using Gabby's private vehicle since her cruiser was a total wreck.

When they walked out to the waiting room, it was crowded with patients and fans. There were hospital security present to make sure nothing got out of hand. Declan almost felt sorry for the teenager, except Theo seemed to be in his element, smiling and waving even as Levi body-checked someone who tried to slip past him. His partner's size alone was intimidating. Declan huddled protectively around Gabby.

One reporter tried to shove a mic at her, but he knocked the device away.

"Boy, you're useful," Bristow told him.

"Detective Woodward." The reporter was persistent. "Is this related to your father's death? There are reports calling it a gang hit."

Another one asked, "Is this a gimmick for the show's ratings? Last season it was the strange virus that hit the set."

"Captain Mitchell! Captain Mitchell!" The reporter rushed off when he spotted Gabby's boss.

The outside of the emergency room was infinitely worse. It was a zoo. News vans were everywhere. Guess the show was really popular. Declan might even consider watching it.

Questions, camera flashes, and the crowd's frenzy grew in decibels. Cold fingers clutched his hand and he glanced down to see Gabby's face etched in pain with a thumb and fore-finger pinching her forehead.

Shit, her concussion. This was too much for her.

"I'm double parked here," Kelso said grimly, also noting his partner's distress. "Let's go."

WHEN THEY REACHED Gabby's apartment, Kelso had started to rub Declan the wrong way, especially after Nick had already pushed him to his limit. Her partner was going to be a problem if he didn't quit that protective bullshit with Gabby. The tidal wave of revelations that hit him one after another was stripping him raw, pouring salt on a wound that never healed right. He was powerless to stop the confusing emotions tearing at him, and he had no desire to run away from them either.

"You sure you don't want me to wait for you?" Gabby's partner asked.

"No. Thanks. I have my Pilot."

Declan helped Gabby down from the Explorer. Both men's eyes clashed in an unwavering challenge.

"Knock it off with the alpha male posturing, you two," Gabby groaned. "Dec, can you fish my key from my messenger bag?"

Grabbing her purse and his duffel from the back seat, Declan pushed the SUV door closed as Kelso grunted his "Later."

Gabby lived in a gated apartment complex in Hawthorne. There was no guard at the gates, but the equipment seemed to be the latest in multi-home security.

"Beverly Hills's not your thing?"

"No." She winced.

"Want me to carry you?"

"Hell no."

Declan bit back a retort. This was not his sweet Gabrielle. That girl was gone, and a part of him ached at that loss. They continued their slow walk to the wide steps that led to her second level unit. Gabby limped up the steps, putting her weight on the hand holding the banister. She had bruised ribs and hips, and when she nearly face-planted in the middle of the staircase, Declan had witnessed enough and took over. He secured his duffel on his back and swept her up in his arms.

"Put me down!"

"Shut it, Gabby."

"How dare you!" She had the sense not to struggle and risk sending them tumbling down the steps.

"Which unit is yours?"

"I can walk."

"Which one, goddammit!"

"Two-twelve."

"Thank you."

When they got to her apartment, he lowered her to her

feet and opened the door. Gabby quickly turned off the alarm and moved into the kitchen.

"There are drinks in the refrigerator. I may take a while to gather my things."

Declan ignored her plan to blow him off. They needed to get a few things straight. He looked around. Gabby Woodward was a minimalist. Her furniture had simple lines, all wood frames with olive green canvas cushions, almost like seventies type furniture. There were no plants in the house, no clutter on the coffee table. A gray area rug beneath it. Magazines were in their racks. No photographs.

What happened to the woman who couldn't wait to frame their Vegas wedding pictures and display them on the mantel? He passed her kitchen. At least there were dirty dishes in the sink and she still cooked. His Gabby liked to cook.

His Gabby?

Shit.

He followed her where she disappeared down the hallway. Three bedrooms. Yeah. This wouldn't work for all of them. He could imagine Theo's horror if he was forced to live here. Though it would do the kid some good to experience simplicity.

As a private military contractor, Declan lived without fear, without a care for his own life, and in search of the next adrenaline rush, but at this moment, there was a rattling anxiety at facing a seventeen-year-old boy.

He heard a curse and a thump from the last bedroom on the right. As he made the turn, he saw Gabby with a suitcase on the bed.

"Let me help—"

"I can manage!"

"I know, but you should have waited for me," he replied calmly.

"What? So you can gloat how the mighty has fallen? It's

my choice you know," she said bitterly. "Oh, don't look at me like that."

"Like what?"

"Like you pity me."

Anger flared inside him. "Pity? Pity is the last thing I'm feeling. Try guilt."

"Don't," she bit out, her face crumpling. "I don't want to hear about you and Claudette."

Throwing Claudette in his face had gone on long enough. He had to come clean.

"See," Declan exhaled deeply. "I didn't sleep with Claudette."

Her eyes widened and then scathing doubt crept into them and she chuckled darkly. "Don't try to change your story because that'll be a lie. You're trying to ease your guilt."

"And how about yours, huh? You broke our vows. Slept with another man!" His voice rose as the image of Nick on top of her flashed through his head.

"I told you I didn't."

"I. Was. There," he gritted, his breath ragged. "I nearly killed the man. I dragged your almost naked body ..." His voice broke off as he squeezed his eyes shut as pieces of that night came back like shards of glass piercing his chest.

All he saw was red.

That was the night Declan understood the phrase *blinded with rage.*

"Nothing happened, I ..." She gripped her head in a sob. "I tried to tell you over and over."

"You fucking married him before the ink was even dry on our divorce papers!"

"It's my fault, okay? Everything! Happy now? Just please ... I don't want to talk about this anymore. We're only hurting each other. And my head hurts, dammit."

Gabby sank to the bed and sucked in a strangled sob.

Declan clenched his fists. He wanted to hug her and

throttle her at the same time. He ended up doing nothing, just staring at her bowed head. He was frustrated he couldn't get the truth out of her and was worried he was not helping her concussion by bringing on emotional stress. If the physical pain in his chest was a prelude to what this unfinished business between them was going to bring, he could only imagine what she was feeling in her concussed state.

He didn't want that for her.

Even after all the hurt they'd caused each other, he still hurt when she did.

"I'll help you pack, okay?" he said quietly. "Just tell me what clothes you want to bring. And don't fucking move."

"Were you always this bossy?" she grumbled, toeing off her shoes as she scooted back to the headboard, leaning against it. Her eyes drooped.

"Do you need to take any meds?"

"I'm good until morning. That damned Bristow shot me up with something," her voice slurred.

"I was there. He didn't. It's the concussion." He glanced at the columns of clothes in the closet. "Where are your lounge clothes?"

"Drawers on the left."

"Underwear?"

"Same. Don't forget to pack pants and shirts. Hanging right in front of you."

"You're taking it easy remember?"

Gabby yawned. "Bristow exaggerates. I'm fine."

"Uh-huh. You know, you are kind of loopy right now, right?"

"So tired." She closed her eyes.

"Gabby."

No response.

"Gabby!"

Her eyes shot open and she sat forward. "What?"

"I need to wake you up every hour."

She huffed. "Okay."

"It's probably better to head out tomorrow morning. I'll lock up."

"You're not sleeping with me."

Declan didn't respond. She was out of it and she fell sideways smack into her pillow, burrowing her face into it. He slipped out his phone and shot a text off to Levi, informing him of the change of plans. He pulled the suitcase off the bed. He could pack tomorrow.

He stood there staring at his ex-wife, looking so peaceful with a hand tucked under her cheek. His lungs felt raw and his ticker was doing double time with the nameless emotions coursing through him. The ache in his chest felt new yet vaguely familiar.

"What happened to us?" Declan whispered. When Gabby shifted and a groan escaped her lips, he forced himself to move so he could get her more comfortable. He picked the least revealing pajamas, but she still seemed to favor her sleeping shorts.

He glanced back at her sleeping form. Maybe, she was fine the way she was?

What are you afraid of, Roarke? Can't handle your ex-wife naked?

Dropping the sleepwear on the mattress, he tried to be as clinical as possible as he repositioned her on the bed. However, the second his fingers undid the first button of her top, feelings from the past reverberated in the present. Of how he felt when he cared for her when she was so tired from a week of filming.

Fuck.

His fingers shook as he unbuttoned her shirt and pulled it out from her damned gray pants. He sucked in his breath at the swell of her breasts. They were fuller than he remembered.

He quickly slipped her tee over her bare skin and dragged

her pants over her hips more slowly so as not to wake her. Gabby was dead to the world, and here he was, sweat beading his forehead with the simple task of undressing her.

Her body had changed, and it was obvious she took care of it by lifting weights. And it seemed she went heavy, judging from her shapely, toned thighs, and firm ass. And she mustn't have been kidding when she told Levi that she knew kung-fu, even when it sounded tongue-in-cheek.

His ex-wife was hot as fuck underneath her starched clothes. But more than the physical chemistry that was still apparent between them, he didn't know what to do with these complicated emotions—scratch that—conflicting emotions that warred inside him.

Declan should despise her, but admiration was winning out, for Gabby forging her own path after they divorced, for taking on a male-dominated profession. And yet he was saddened at the colorless life outside her job if the contents of her house and her closet were his yardstick.

But was her life so different from his own?

She mumbled a protest when he moved her under the covers. Heading out to the living room to pick up his duffle, he made sure everything was locked up for the night. Levi responded that Captain Mitchell ordered extra patrols in her neighborhood anyway, and whoever attacked them would be thinking twice about striking again so soon.

Declan took a quick shower, put on athletic shorts, and threw on a tee which he'd normally forgo at night. But he was sleeping beside Gabby, on top of the covers of course, so she wouldn't feel so outraged if she woke up in the middle of the night.

To be sure she didn't shoot him—accidentally or on purpose—because fuck knows how she felt about him at the moment, he unchambered the round in the Glock that was in her nightstand. He found other guns hidden under the kitchen counter, the hallway bathroom, and the laundry room.

Another trait he was having trouble reconciling from the wife he left behind.

Seventeen years was a long time, and people did change.

He set his phone to alert him every hour so he could wake her up.

Then he crawled into bed and slept beside his ex-wife.

6

GABBY STARED at the rumpled bed covers. A sign that she, indeed, had slept beside her ex-husband last night. She recalled getting annoyed hearing the alarm that roused her every hour, the tapping on her shoulder, if not the shaking. A voice, sometimes cajoling, sometimes stern, and sometimes sexy, forced her to respond.

Speaking of sexy, her cheeks flamed at the idea that Declan undressed her. He left her bra and panties on her though. Her skin still smelled of hospital antiseptic. Not to mention her mouth was dry and she could imagine what it smelled like—sewer on a humid summer day. Horrified at the thought, she bolted out of bed. Her concussion reminded her why that was a bad idea.

The room tilted and her sore ribs crashed against the dresser, the pain so sharp, she couldn't even utter a sound. Her hands gripped its edges, thankful she didn't hit her head again, and she bit her lip to keep from crying out. Gabby's gaze dropped to the glass, keys, and medicine bottles scattered on the carpet. Did she knock them off? Geez, she was more disoriented than she first thought.

"What are you doing?" A calm voice asked from the doorway.

There stood a version of her ex-husband she couldn't connect to the nineteen-year-old boy she'd known. He was leaning against the doorframe, one foot crossed over an ankle, arms folded over his chest, biceps bulging, observing her struggle to straighten up, but doing nothing to help her. His eyes were guarded, his mouth tight. Declan of seventeen years ago had packed on maybe twenty pounds of muscle. No trace of the young man she used to know remained. He was broader, seemed taller, and there was nothing safe about him. At least that was what her cop's instincts were yelling at her.

"Trying to get to the bathroom."

His eyes flashed with frustration and he stalked into the room.

Gabby took an unsteady step back, and when he reached out to her, she put a hand up.

"Don't—"

"Christ, Gabby, I'm not gonna hurt you."

"Didn't think you would."

"I was just going to help you. Don't want you to fall and hit your head again," he growled. "Like you almost did."

"I'm fine!"

He moved closer.

"Don't—"

He took a step back, scrubbing his face and then sighing. "Don't want me to touch you? Fine, but let me stay close to you—"

"I stink," she mumbled, covering her mouth.

His head reared back. "What?"

"I. Stink."

Realization dawned on his features, and a corner of his mouth hitched up. "I promise I won't hold your physical hygiene against you today."

Trust her ex-husband to bring out the prissy Gabby of

long ago. If it were Kelso in front of her, she wouldn't have cared. She'd done overnight stakeouts, navigated through sewer tunnels—which was the foulest smell on earth—and belly-crawled through disgusting tight spaces of dilapidated homes. But deep down she was just like any woman who had come face-to-face with an ex who dumped her. Clearly, appearing her best for that encounter wasn't in the stars. In fact, the universe was conspiring against her.

"I'm just being polite."

A dark brow raised, and his green irises grew closer. "Polite? Are you forgetting, Angel, that I've seen you naked?"

She sucked in a breath at his words, not to mention the endearment she thought she'd never hear from his lips again.

"I've been inside you, know how you sound when you come." His voice lowered perceptibly. "Knowing all that, you think we can just act *polite*?"

"It's been seventeen years, Declan. We're nothing more than strangers now."

His jaw worked reflexively as his eyes hardened into emerald ice. "If that's how you wanna play it." He paused. "You're still not using the bathroom alone."

"What are you suggesting?"

"You want a shower? I'm getting in there with you."

"Oh, I don't think so."

Amusement played at the corners of his lips. "Then no shower for you."

"That's hardly your decision!"

"Two of us in this house and you've been given into my care. I'm following doctor's orders."

Gabby had enough of this conversation and the rancid taste in her mouth. She edged her way past the looming presence in front of her (was he really this tall before?) and scooted into the bathroom. He followed her closely but kept a respectable distance. After freshening up with a toothbrush and mouthwash, she stared at his reflection in the mirror. His face was impassive.

"You can sit there." She nodded to the toilet. "And wait until I finish. Is that acceptable?"

She took his shrug as agreement. She grabbed the edge of her shirt and pulled it over her head, tossing it to the hamper in the linen closet. Her bra followed and she walked to the shower to turn it on. As she let the water steam up the glass enclosure, she inhaled deeply. Her whole body was tingling.

She turned to face him. Declan's chest rose and fell as if he was having difficulty breathing. His face was still expressionless, but there was an all too familiar heat in his eyes.

"You changed your tune fairly quickly." His voice was rough.

This time it was Gabby who shrugged as she removed her sleeping shorts and panties. She had to get within a foot of him to throw the rest of her clothes into the hamper. She also grabbed a towel, but she didn't wrap it around her even when she felt her nipples hardening.

"I work with men. We're a special division down on seventy-seventh. Only one locker room. Can't suffer modesty now, can I?" There was actually a sectioned-off area in the locker room for women.

"You're saying you're treating me like one of the guys. Is that it?"

"That's exactly what I'm saying."

His eyes glittered ominously as he stepped closer. She held her ground, chin tilted up in challenge and forced herself not to shiver at his proximity. Their gazes locked in challenge. His hand came up and it took all her willpower not to flinch. A finger tucked a stray curl behind her ear before it made its way down the line of her chin, her neck, flirting on the skin above the swell of her breasts.

"Do the guys do this, too?"

"Stop with your games, Dec. I don't know what you're trying to prove."

She spun away from him. As dizziness hit her, his hands caught her under her armpits, brushing against her breasts.

"Stop being so reckless," he hissed in her ear. "Or I'll think you're doing this on purpose just to feel my hands on you."

"In your dreams," she snapped. "Let go."

"You got it?" he asked tightly.

"Yes."

"I'll be right here." He sat on the closed toilet lid as she stepped into the glass enclosure.

"Try not to slip, okay?" he added sarcastically.

She had the oddest urge to stick out her tongue, but she didn't. The hot water spray instantly soothed her poor banged up body.

"This feels so good …" she groaned as she began to lather her hair, and then reached for the soap to get rid of the last traces of the hospital smell. She loved her peaches and vanilla shampoo, some of the last luxuries from her old life she couldn't give up. She mentally regrouped, reminding herself that it took real strength to become a detective in LAPD's toughest division, and hell would freeze over before she let her ex-husband rattle her. For three years she was that broken woman, marrying Nick on the rebound, thinking another baby would fill the hole inside her. But she lost that one, too and that last miscarriage took with it her desire to become a mother. She had to find a new purpose.

"You all right in there?"

"Yes! Almost done."

"Don't shrivel up into a prune, okay?"

"Ugh, stop rushing me. The water just feels so good."

"Yeah, I heard you."

When she washed up the last of the soapy residue and wrung out her hair, she stepped out of the shower and a towel was immediately wrapped around her.

"You're gonna get your shirt wet," she warned.

"Don't care." He dried her brusquely, yet carefully.

"Seriously, Dec, I'm not helpless."

"Fine!" he muttered and let go.

"I don't know why you're"—her eyes dropped to the bulge behind his shorts—"Oh, my."

"Ignore it."

"It's hard to ignore because it's staring right at me." She laughed.

His eyes narrowed. "Haven't you learned that it's insulting to laugh at a man's erection?"

Was she pleased that she could still turn him on? Not that she was going to do anything about it, but it soothed her pride somewhat, especially after feeling like a sewer rat this morning.

Wrapping the towel snuggly around her, she smiled impishly. "You're on your own with that." She fled into the bedroom. She was probably playing with fire, but payback's a bitch, right? Especially after his sexual taunts this morning.

She tossed her towel on the bed and paraded past him to the closet.

"You're playing with fire, Angel."

"Am I, really?" She shot back and couldn't help digging into the past. "Because last I remembered, you shut me out for four months. No amount of sexy underwear would interest you."

"I was mourning my sister!" he exploded, startling her, his face a thundercloud. "And you couldn't even give me that!"

"Four months, Dec? We took vows. For better or worse, remember? And when worse happened, you shut me out. Her voice caught on emotions that wanted to break free and, in a garbled voice she soldiered on, unable to hold back the hurt she'd held so deep in the heart of her. "And then two weeks before we separated, you fucked me as if you hated me, and after that you blamed me for your sister's death."

His face twisted in a sneer. "I should never have married you."

Declan pivoted away from her and left the room. Gabby stood motionless, his words slamming into her with the force of a forty-five caliber pistol.

Boom!

Staring at the empty space he'd vacated, his barb ricocheted around her like an echo. And in that echo, there was one statement he hadn't uttered in the present.

"I should have never married you and maybe, just maybe, my sister would still be alive."

That had been their biggest fight. Somehow Gabby knew their marriage was over then, his words ripping out her young insecure heart and unleashing a vindictive vixen. She almost slept with another man. Declan thought she did, declared them over, and changed the locks of their apartment. She tried to explain, stalked him until he put a restraining order on her and, ultimately, he served her divorce papers on grounds of adultery.

She would have accepted that their marriage was over and wallowed in self-destruction had she not found out she was pregnant. For a time she hoped a child would fix their marriage, so she made one last ditch effort.

But that final effort shattered her further when Claudette answered their apartment door wrapped in a towel. Gabby pulled another t-shirt over her head and chuckled bitterly. How naive she'd been. The child wouldn't have fixed their marriage. They would have only brought an innocent baby into a union that was already broken.

Did Declan still blame her for his sister's death?

Maybe it was time for closure.

––––––––––––––

You're a fucking moron.

Declan imagined Claire O'Connor reaching out from the grave just so she could smack him upside of the head.

He found some gluten free waffles in the freezer and popped those in the toaster oven. There was weird green juice in her refrigerator, and he wasn't sure if it was going bad or it was meant to look that way. At least there were eggs. He reached for the carton and began cracking a few into a bowl to scramble.

Simply put, Declan was at a loss in handling this new Gabby. So different from the girl who captivated him from across the room at a Hollywood party, and yet the way she could twist him inside out had not changed. And that pissed him off. *Why? Why only with her?* He prided himself on his self-control when it came to women but watching Gabby shower through the glass was hot as fuck and he couldn't look away if his life depended on it. Add to that her moans of pleasure and he was instantly hard.

So, he lashed out.

Old hurts.

Buried resentments.

The scars from their shared previous life blistered, opening forgotten wounds that never healed right, and words from that past made a dissonant refrain. There was one difference. They didn't fester, and the second he left the room, he regretted his outburst.

Footsteps shuffled behind him. The barstool scraped back. "You didn't have to cook."

"I'm hungry," he replied without turning around. "You can eat that green shit in the fridge, but I want real food."

"Kale juice is real food."

"Whatever you say, babe."

Silence reigned for the duration of his cooking. The toaster popped up the waffles and Gabby stepped up beside him and dished them on a plate. They worked side by side, each lost in their own thoughts.

He poured coffee into a mug and brought out the milk without asking if she still liked milk with it.

She poured it into her mug. Guess she still did.

Declan crisped the scrambled eggs at the corners the way she liked it. Whether he did that consciously or not, he didn't know.

There was tension in what was familiar.

Existing beside each other was weird as fuck right now.

Declan grabbed the other stool and sat facing her.

"Guess no green shit for you today, huh?"

"Stop calling it green shit."

"Where's the girl who liked her medium rare burger?"

"That girl still likes her burger medium rare. She just reserves it for cheat days."

"That's health nut mumbo-jumbo."

She rolled her eyes and took a sip of her coffee.

"I still like my food, but I *am* getting older. I eat all the junk food when I'm around Kelso or at Division, so I call it balance." Gabby primly cut at her waffle and forked it into her mouth.

"Junk food like donuts?"

"Yep."

"That's so cliché, Gab."

"It's the stress."

Declan shoveled the scrambled eggs in his mouth. "You close to your partner?"

Her brows furrowed. "What kind of question is that?"

"It's a simple one. He married?"

"He's single, and if you're fishing to see if I've fucked him, the answer is no. Not that it concerns you."

"Just wondering."

"Kelso is family. We have a close-knit team. Even the wives. Captain Mitchell's wife is like our mother hen. They're the family I've always wanted," she whispered that last statement wistfully.

Something twisted in his chest. An unexpected pain. He and Gabby *were* supposed to be family. Guess she didn't want what they had. His fingers tightened on his fork as he forced himself to finish his breakfast, which tasted as bitter as his thoughts.

Her gaze dropped to the corner of the countertop, her finger circling the rim of her mug as if in contemplation, then her eyes lifted. "I need to ask you something."

His body froze, but he nodded.

"We made a big mess of our marriage and it took me a while to get my life on track and I really don't want to re-hash things about the divorce. You're clearly in a better place and so am I."

If she only knew he came straight from jail to California. And was she delusional to think that this lifeless apartment she lived in was a better place? But who was he to judge? Declan thought of his own condo. Was he in a better place? Were they in a better place?

He called bullshit.

"I need to know," she whispered. "Do you still blame me for Claire's death?"

His eyes slid shut. "No, Gabby."

"Really?"

Opening his eyes, he gazed at her steadily. "Claire was sick. She'd always been on borrowed time with the Cystic Fibrosis." Seventeen years ago, the drug that would have given his sister a real chance at life wasn't available yet. "She wanted us together."

"But I made you stop working—"

"You didn't make me do anything. The only way we could be together was if I stopped working as a male escort." He had other jobs, but the high cost of Claire's medical treatments made him resort to desperate measures. Competition was steep in LA for modeling and acting jobs, and he also worked construction, but the compensation was abysmal. His sister's life mattered more than his self-respect.

"I told you I had money, but …" Her voice trailed off.

Declan clenched his jaw. A typical Hollywood story, they met at a party and hooked up. Their relationship became tabloid fodder, but they didn't care. They were in love. Six months to the day they met, they eloped to Vegas and tied the knot. Then reality and bills hit them. His pride took a beating when he couldn't be the main breadwinner, but the desire to be with Gabby trumped all that. Or so he thought. Cracks in their marriage started to show, became harder to ignore. Gabby's father thought he was a gold-digger, so the bastard cut off his daughter's finances, even withheld her paycheck from acting. "You underestimated how much your dad hated me, that's all."

"We could've gotten better treatments for Claire!"

"We managed as much as we could."

Gabby's smile was sad. "But that time … You really blamed me, didn't you?"

"I did," he said shortly. "Claire's death was sudden. She was doing so well and I thought …" He shook his head and pondered how he could have fucked up everyone's life by putting his heart first. "I thought I deserved to be happy … with you. When she died …the guilt was crippling. I should have spent more time with her. I thought I had more time with her."

"Instead you spent most of it with me."

"It took me years to get over the guilt." He held her eyes. "Claire wouldn't have wanted me to put my life on hold for her. She wanted me to be happy, but for the longest time I wondered if I'd been on top of her situation, if I could have prevented that lung infection." He blew out a breath. "After I joined the Army, after seeing my brothers blown up by IEDs despite being so careful, I realized just how little control we have over death."

"Believe me, I know," she mumbled.

He stared at her, still not able to wrap his mind around the woman she was now. "What made the young star of *Dead Futures* give that all up and become a homicide detective?"

"That's a long story." She smiled and glanced at the clock. "And we need to get moving."

"Yeah." He stood and gathered the dishes. There were many things left to be said, but those would have to wait. At least he could give her this. Closure for the harsh words he said to her that started the death spiral of their marriage. A marriage that only lasted seven months and left a tragic, mangled history. One part of his past was at peace, but there was more to the wreckage that followed.

"Claudette is in town," she said suddenly as if reading his mind. "I'm sure I can get the lawyer to—"

Throwing that woman at him was getting old. "I don't need to talk to Claudette."

"But Dec, you need to discuss Theo. You missed—"

"Listen to me," he growled. "I want to get to the bottom of this. Theo is a smart kid and he'll soon realize I'm his father, but I'll be damned if I let him think I slept with Claudette."

"You did … at least before me, you did."

Declan scowled at her. "That's a low blow. Before we decided to see each other exclusively, I told you everything I did as a male escort and we agreed never to talk about it again." The first thing he admitted was sleeping with her former stepmother. Gabby was able to get over it because it was at a time before Claudette married Peter. It did take Gabby a week to digest this information, and when she decided to take a chance on Declan, she also had to tell Peter. "Are you gonna throw that in my face now?"

She lowered her head and rubbed her brow. "I'm sorry. You're right."

"All I want is what's good for Theo and to figure out what security is needed around him."

"Understood."

"Is your head hurting?"

"Not too bad."

His phone buzzed with a text message.

"It's about damned time," he muttered when he recognized the sender.

"Who is it?" Gabby asked.

"Business."

Her eyes narrowed. "Regarding Theo?"

"Could be. Listen, I may need Levi as well. Can you call Captain Mitchell and see if he can spare a uniform to watch over Theo?"

"No need. The Cap and Kelso are coming over to the Brentwood house."

Declan frowned. "Do they have additional information on who the target was yesterday?"

"That's what I'm about to find out."

7

"WE NEVER FINISHED OUR CONVERSATION YESTERDAY," Levi spoke beside him.

Declan was driving the Escalade through the steep and winding road that was Blue Heights Drive. The rendezvous point with Garrison was at the summit of Hollywood Hills.

"It's obvious you and Gabby are not strangers," his partner continued in a cautious tone. "And personally, it's none of my business, but to do this job properly, you need to give me a heads up of what's going on."

"It's complicated."

"Figured." A pause. "Noticed you and Nick Carter had some tension going on there as well. But seeing you and Theo side-by-side tells me there's a story there."

"Gabby and I married and divorced young."

"No shit?" Levi appeared to digest this information and Declan stiffened as he felt the other man's eyes take him in. "Theo takes after you. Clearly, he isn't Woodward's son."

For a moment, Declan thought he was referring to Gabby. "How about you, Levi? What's your story?" He decided to redirect the subject, unwilling to discuss his ex-wife since he was seeking answers himself.

"Nothing as complicated as yours," Levi exhaled in resignation. "Kelly got tired of my shit and asked for a separation."

"You have kids, right?" Declan cut a glance to his partner and caught his sad smile.

"Yeah. Two girls. Six and four."

"Must be hard on them."

Levi emitted a derisive laugh. "Actually, nothing is different. The life we had as PMCs? Wasn't fair to Kelly or the kids. I was hardly home." His partner turned to look out the window. "I'm a better father now than I ever was compared to when we all stayed under the same roof."

At his questioning look, Levi added. "We take turns staying with our girls at the same house instead of shuttling them back and forth between homes. Why I asked that I do this gig two weeks at a time."

That was something Declan had never heard before, but it made sense, especially for the welfare of the children.

He could hear the regret in his partner's voice and Declan thought of his own shortcomings as a husband. He always wondered if he got his shit together sooner after Claire died, would his marriage have survived?

Their turn came up the road and he guided the Escalade down a lane that was narrower than the main one with sections unpaved.

"Anyway." Levi grabbed the handlebar as the vehicle rocked from side to side before getting back on a wider, smoother plane. "Not giving up on Kelly. Just need to do whatever it takes for her to take me back. I sure as fuck hope she doesn't serve me divorce papers before I've convinced her."

"Sorry, man," was all Declan could say, and a twinge of guilt hit him as he remembered that it was he who'd served Gabby with divorce papers.

Levi suddenly chuckled. "Have you been taking lessons

from Garrison? I asked you the question and I'm the one spilling my guts."

He grinned. "Better you than me."

"Fucker," Levi said under his breath. "But thanks. Better you than a bunch of teenagers I guess."

"Anytime, bro." Declan raised his hand in a fist and Levi bumped it with his own.

A cluster of houses of different architectures loomed before them, lining the street on both sides. Each of them partially hidden with solid metal gates. Assassin's Hill was no longer a myth. It really existed as Declan was now finding out. It was a group of properties carefully vetted by the CIA—real estate for their operatives who chose to lay low or retire. The choice to live in houses built at the edge of the cliff had its advantages as security efforts were focused on attacks from the street.

Levi pointed to a rust colored gate and after entering codes into an app the CIA had provided, the gate swung open and Declan drove thru and parked. John Garrison emerged from the house and leaned against an Escalade that was a twin of theirs except with blacked out windows and bulletproof tires. He liked to live dangerously and probably made enemies everywhere. Behind John was a boxy, multilevel home with sweeping windows typical of the structures in the area that took advantage of the view. Declan would bet all his money that those windows were also retrofitted, bulletproof glass.

"How's the reunion?" John asked, a smirk on his face.

"A little heads-up would've been nice," Declan called out as he stepped down from the vehicle.

He and Levi walked toward the other man.

"Didn't have time to hold your hand," John Garrison replied.

"Asshole," Declan muttered.

He hadn't seen John since the Yemen mission, but he knew he kept in contact with Kade.

He and Levi stopped their approach when another man came out of the house.

"It's clear," the guy said. His gaze landed on the newcomers, expression neutral.

"Let's talk inside." John motioned to his colleague. "Migs Walker. Declan Roarke. Levi James."

The men exchanged chin lifts and entered the house. Walker had thick dark hair, eyes almost black, maybe of Hispanic or Italian heritage. His dark faded denims, white tee, and keychain hanging around his hips, reminded Declan of a biker in a motorcycle club. Scuffed boots and full sleeves of ink on each arm completed the image. It wouldn't be a stretch if the man was working undercover if he was with Garrison.

"Have a seat." John motioned to the chairs around a ten-person dining table.

"Is this gonna take long?" Declan asked, pulling out a chair and planting his ass in it. Levi took the one beside him. Walker remained standing behind John. "I wanna get back to Gabby and Theo."

"I'll get to the point then," John said. "Contrary to what you might think, Roarke, this has little to do with your newfound fatherhood. That was just a bonus of our investigation."

"Of course." He didn't think he was so important as to get special treatment from the CIA.

"The agency is concerned with Ortega's LA criminal network."

Declan's gaze flicked briefly to Walker before returning to John's. "So, this is about Gabby? You want me to spy on her?"

"That and other things."

A protective instinct reared inside him. "You don't think she's dirty, do you?"

"We have no reason to believe she is."

That didn't give him any relief.

"Local LEOs are hunting down Ortega for his role in the

fentanyl attack. That's no reason for us to get involved, but it's concerning. It's even more concerning that he may have acquired a biological weapon."

"What? In LA? How and why?"

John glanced at Walker. "Care to elaborate? Migs has been undercover in the Ortega organization."

"If he's undercover why doesn't he know where Ortega is?"

"Let me rephrase that," John replied, a hint of irritation crossing his face. "He's newly undercover. Ortega is extremely paranoid and divides his network into cells that have no idea what the others are doing. It's how he maintains control," John said. "We're lucky Migs has been assigned to Ariana— Ortega's sister."

"If you have an in via Ortega's sister, why do we need to be involved?" Levi asked.

"Because we're not sure when Ariana will see her brother again," Migs replied. "There's recent intel that Ortega has cancer and is trying alternative medicine as well as chemo. His sister runs one of those vitamin therapy spas in Beverly Hills, but we doubt that's where Ortega will go."

Declan gave John a look. "Vitamin. Therapy. Spas?"

"Don't ask," he muttered.

"It's a thing," Levi grinned. "They stick an IV in you and pump you full of the good stuff."

Declan wasn't sure if he was more perturbed by the idea of a vitamin therapy spa or the fact that his partner knew what it was.

"How do you know that?" he asked the question anyway.

"My wife mentioned it." Levi scratched the scruff on his chin sheepishly. "I'm trying to turn over a new leaf. Listen to her more. Pay attention to the things she talks about related to her job."

Declan fought back a smile. "You never mentioned what she does for a living."

"Make-up and special effects," he said, then added proudly. "With the rise of net streaming, she's in demand and has to travel sometimes."

"Sounds interesting," John cut in. "Maybe we could find some work for her."

Levi scowled and his mouth zipped shut.

Rescuing his friend, and in case John wasn't kidding, Declan asked, "Is Ortega's sister involved in his brother's criminal enterprise?"

"Not that I could determine," Walker said. "All her clients seem legit. She does charity work at a clinic in the Valley. I haven't gone along on any of those yet."

"Well, I'll be damned," Declan chuckled, but more out of an incredulous epiphany than humor. "Of course. IV injections in a spa? Makes a great front for drugs."

"Bingo," Levi agreed.

"I haven't found anything that incriminates Ariana yet," Walker growled with more ferocity than Declan expected from an undercover agent talking about his target. "So let's not jump to fucking conclusions."

"Are we having trouble staying objective, Walker?" John asked, frowning.

"Not sure what you're asking."

"No danger of falling in love with Ms. Ortega, right? 'Cause I don't care for a repeat of the Yemen fiasco." At this last statement, Garrison stared pointedly at Declan, who smirked. Things would have ended so differently in Yemen if Kade hadn't gone rogue.

"Don't know what went down in Yemen, but I assure you that's not happening," Walker snapped. "Anyway, we're getting off track. Two of Ortega's trusted inner circle were killed in the Friday sting by GHD. He's pissed and the whole criminal underworld is bracing for him to declare war on the city. The fentanyl attacks are only the beginning."

"I'm still not seeing how Levi and I come in? We're merely

bodyguards at this point, and I doubt we'll be privy to Gabby's briefing with her boss, especially if she's on leave." Declan's eyes narrowed. "Was it Ortega who called the hit on Gabby and Theo? Payback for LAPD's Friday op?"

"Probably," Walker said. "Like I said, Ortega is on a rampage."

"So, let's cut the crap. What exactly do you need from Levi and me?"

"You in particular," John said. "How well are you acquainted with Claudette?"

He managed to keep his seat. "What about her?"

"What do you know about her and Ortega?"

"What?" Declan whispered. This time he leaned forward. "What does Claudette have to do with that fucker?"

Garrison pushed a file toward him. "She appeared on our radar only recently. But the DEA has a file on her that goes back twenty years. More so in the last three since the popular party drug XZite exploded on the Hollywood scene. She and Ortega were lovers. She was his connection to the Hollywood elite. They'd met up over the years, but it was DEA's belief that Ortega was just stringing her along, using her position as Peter's wife as a Hollywood insider." The CIA officer leveled him a stare. "What do you remember of your relationship with her?"

"Never had a relationship with her. I slept with her once before I married Gabby," Declan gritted out. "I'm surprised that isn't in the fucking file like everything else."

"And the time Gabby found her in your apartment?"

Declan's chair scraped back and he surged to his feet. "Where the fuck are you getting this?" He slammed his palm on the table.

"Calm down, Roarke," John said. "We're just establishing how well you know her."

"How about you tell me something? How the hell did Theo end up being Peter and Claudette's?" Declan growled.

"You tell me how the hospital fucked up that badly and maybe …" his voice shook with fury. "Maybe, I'd consider prostituting myself to her again."

Everyone flinched, including Garrison. Declan left the table and stalked to the windows, staring at the city he loathed. Did he ever regret his time as a male escort? No. Because it gave his sister almost two years to live comfortably. Claudette was a reminder of what he hated of that life. One of the few clients he'd slept with at a time when he was backed into a corner, when the insurmountable debts made him feel like he was drowning. So fucking Claudette for information? He'd kill her first for stealing Theo.

"We can only go by the hospital records," John replied evenly. "And we're talking seventeen years ago. It seems the quickest way to find your answers is to go straight to the source."

"Was Peter complicit in the switch?"

"We wouldn't know, but then again, the answers are right here in LA. Gabby should have access to his files, right?"

"Yeah."

His stomach turned as it was looking more and more likely that he needed to play Claudette. "How does she figure into this Ortega mess now?"

"Claudette Dumont runs her own skin care line," Garrison said. "She's never been destitute, but she's ambitious. She gives off the bored Hollywood wife vibe, but she's cunning and a survivor. After Peter Woodward divorced her, she moved on to Antonio Andrade."

"The same Antonio Andrade of Andrade Industries?" Levi interjected. "He owns several pharmaceutical subsidiaries, doesn't he?"

"Yes. He's the manufacturer of XZite. Claudette hooked up with Andrade right around the time the drug appeared on the Hollywood circuit. Again, the party drug is not our concern," John answered. "But I've tapped into a reliable source that one of Andrade's labs has developed a bioweapon. He has numerous facilities, all legit on paper, and we're not certain which lab is our target."

"So, she has a habit of latching on to men in power and switching babies," Declan muttered in disgust. "But why Theo?"

For a long time, the CIA officer didn't say anything. Frowning, Declan turned away from the windows and faced the men at the table. "What are you not telling me, John?"

"There was a rumor," John stated carefully. "And this was merely speculation in a DEA report that Claudette's baby was not Peter's but Ortega's."

Declan's brows shot to his hairline. "Well, that's bullshit."

"We know," Walker piped in after having been on the sidelines in the discussion. "Ortega's been erratic these past few months. Some say it's the cancer, but my two cents? It was because he found out that Theo wasn't his son and why he had Peter killed."

"I'm surprised Claudette is even in LA," John said. "Which is why we think she's agreed to become a go-between for Andrade and Ortega."

"So Ortega wouldn't call a hit on her?" Declan asked.

All the men assented.

Claudette did hold all the answers. "I don't know if I can even look her in the face. I'd kill that bitch."

"Roarke. We're talking about a bioweapon."

Declan knew he had to do it. Didn't mean he had to act like he was gung-ho about it.

"We can't alert Ortega," John added at his continued silence. "We also have rough intel that Ortega is in a power struggle with the Mexican cartels. We can't rock that boat right now in case they're after the bioweapon as well. This has to look like a lover's reunion."

Just that thought caused bile to rise up his throat. "The fuck? I thought you said she's in love with Ortega."

"She was attracted to you once. Charm her. You can make her talk."

"Weren't you an actor?" Levi asked.

"A shit actor," Declan muttered.

"You said he could get to Claudette," Walker scoffed at John. "Looks like he doesn't have the balls to do it."

Garrison leaned back in his chair, eyeing Declan. "Are you hoping to get back with Gabby?"

"That ship has sailed," he said shortly.

"Then what's the problem?"

"The problem is Theo will hate him," Levi interjected. "Jesus, you two are a bunch of morons. You need to go and have kids to figure this out. If Theo is led to believe that Roarke cheated with Claudette, it's a double betrayal. On Peter Woodward who he has only known as his father and Gabby. The kid hates his mother, and the way I see it, he does like Gabby who prefers not to give him the time of day right now. So, if Roarke goes ahead with this ..."

John smiled. "This should be interesting."

"Fuck you, Garrison," Declan growled.

8

"You shouldn't be reading."

Gabby glanced up from the documents on the table and looked at Kelso. He and the captain were already in the Brentwood home when she arrived this morning with Declan. They were sitting under the shaded patio beside the pool, escaping the activity in the living room. Theo had largely ignored her.

Before Levi left with Declan to do whatever they needed to do, she asked the bodyguard what was up, but Levi didn't know either. Then the parade of teen actors marched through the Brentwood house. They were supposed to be practicing their scripts, but instead they were watching *Dead Futures* DVDs and Gabby's young fifteen-year-old face appeared on the screen in a show about the zombie apocalypse.

Kill her now.

"I'm fine," she assured her partner. Her head was beginning to throb again even after taking a couple of painkillers, but she was sure it was from obnoxious reactions of the teenagers to the series that had been a big part of her adolescent years. Concentrating on Peter's previous will would help her ignore their boisterous comments about the special effects that weren't as advanced back then. "My father changed his will a month ago. From what I can see, all that was added was a clause regarding Claudette and the adjustments in the amounts as Mr. Goodman pointed out. Why did he suddenly include her?"

The captain looked thoughtful. "Maybe he knew she would contest it."

"But why? Their divorce was three years ago."

"Peter Woodward's net worth is better than six hundred and thirty million. Claudette only got twenty million in the divorce settlement," Mitchell said. "The detectives on the case gave me the numbers. She was a suspect."

She picked up another stash of papers. "These phone records between the two don't show anything unusual. Obviously, even after their divorce they communicated regularly."

"And you're not surprised about that?"

"Not really," she responded. "They moved in the same circle which is why if you cross-reference their phone records, you can see they also call the same numbers. Have the detectives run them through a crosscheck?"

"They have. That's what they're doing right now. Calling them one by one."

Gabby emitted a puff of laughter. "That's a part of detective work I hate the most."

"I looked into your ex-husband," Kelso said. At her glare, he added, "I was concerned, all right? After you told me how he and Ms. Dumont fucked you over, and seeing you with him yesterday, you have to admit that something smells fishy."

"You're wasting your time looking in his direction. He's clean." The hammering in her head intensified.

"You're not even a tad suspicious?" Kelso pressed.

Gabby glanced at Mitchell. "Did you put him up to this?"

Her captain shrugged. "Maybe."

"Okay, I'll play," she gritted. "Declan wasn't in LA when Peter was killed, so it couldn't be him. Let's say being a PMC, he'd have plenty of contacts, right? Easy enough to hire one without scruples and kill Peter. But Peter changed his will and according to the lawyer, it's airtight. Claudette has no way of milking the estate for more. So why is Declan still here?"

"You have to admit, after seventeen years of absence, his timing is impeccable," Kelso said.

A sinking feeling settled in her belly. How well did she know Declan now? He'd been a mercenary. He was capable of killing in cold blood.

"He was mighty concerned about you yesterday," Kelso made air quotes over the word 'concerned.' "And you two seemed to be hitting it off this morning."

"If you're implying I'm falling for him again, I assure you, he was anything but charming. And even though we made a mess of our marriage, I would like to believe that we've matured enough to act like civilized adults."

"No need to get sarcastic there, partner," Kelso said quietly.

Rousing laughter erupted from the direction of the living room, while on the widescreen TV, her young face covered in black zombie blood was on full display.

Red hazed her vision.

Among Theo's co-stars, she recognized Emma Haller who was as popular as Theo with her all-American girl-next-door looks. The sixteen-year-old was also rumored to be Theo's girlfriend. Because of the sheer star power of the two and the rest of the *Hodgetown* cast, the reporters and paparazzi were camped at the gates.

"Aren't you glad this shindig isn't at your apartment?" Captain asked.

"I would have murdered them by now," Gabby said.

"I've watched the entire five seasons you know," Kelso said. "Sad when you weren't in the fifth one. Can't believe you let down your fans."

"Bite me." She flashed her teeth in her best zombie snarl. She was feeling pretty stabby. Now would be a good time for a zombie to show up so she could drive a hunting knife through its skull.

When a louder raucous jeer reached her ear, she surged from her seat. "That's it."

She stomped over to the eight teenagers scattered all over the living room.

"Party's over, kids," she announced.

There were grumbles and groans as everyone's eyes turned to her brother.

Theo was sitting in the middle of the couch with Emma beside him. He was stroking her hair absentmindedly, but had this broody thing going on like a tragic King Arthur.

"But we just got here," a brown-haired, lanky teen with freckles protested.

"Rex Smith, right?"

"Sure am." He grinned. On the *Hodgetown* series he wore braces, but in real life? His teeth were straight and gleamed white like a toothpaste commercial. Gabby also knew he did Theo's dirty work and was like his mouth of Sauron.

"Listen, Theo has a concussion. And the doctor limited his screen time. So, TV?" Gabby lowered her voice as if conspiratorially, but it came out full of snark. "Bad idea."

Seven pairs of eyes swung back to Theo. "No one's leaving," he declared, face tilting up in challenge. "Revenant Films is paying for this house, so technically, I'm paying for this roof over your head. My money. My rules. And I say they stay."

Emma pushed away from Theo, glaring at him. "Your sister's right. You need your rest." She moved to get up, but her brother yanked her back to him. "Sit your ass down."

"Are you serious right now?" Gabby fumed at the way her brother talked to Emma.

"Ooh, sibling fight," Rex crowed.

"Don't I look serious?" Theo raised a dark brow.

Gabby narrowed her eyes. "Fine."

She stalked away from the teenagers, her anger escalating

as more laughter and cheers followed her every step. She'd be damned before she let Theo Cole step all over her. Gabby didn't know what crawled up his ass that changed his playful banter from yesterday to this pain-in-the-ass kid right now, but he just drew a line in the sand. She marched past the captain and Kelso who both rose to their feet, looking worried.

The thing with these entitled teens, they weren't afraid of anything because they had the money to get them out of shit. She knew this because she used to be one. She doubted they'd be stupid enough to carry drugs in their cars. So, she would do the next best thing. Her brother hadn't witnessed her wrath yet.

She marched outside to her Honda where it was parked in the motor court and bleeped the locks to open the vehicle. She grabbed the baseball bat she'd always kept behind the driver's seat and strode past Mitchell who was gaping at her in alarm.

"Jesus, Gabby, what are you going to do, beat them up?" Mitchell asked.

"No. Something better."

"Ms. Woodward! Ms. Woodward!" The press called from behind the gates. She waved and smiled brightly at them despite the sun killing her eyes. Her head was throbbing by the time she entered the house again.

"Dude! Your sis is gonna paddle your ass now."

Theo continued to sit unconcerned with a smirk on his face.

She passed him and the living room, shooting him a smile full of malice and made a beeline for the kitchen, then out to the garage, right where his precious red Ferrari was parked.

Without hesitating, she smashed the side view mirror on the driver's side.

Shouts came from inside the house and she grinned. Despite her blinding headache, she felt catharsis. It was as if the Ferrari represented everything that was wrong in her life.

Gabby rounded the sports car and swung her bat at the taillight.

"Are you fucking insane?" Theo stood at the door staring at her in disbelief.

"You better get that fixed." She pointed to the left taillight with the bat. "Or I'll make sure you get a ticket the next time you take your precious baby for a ride." She smashed the other one. "Oh, look. Two taillights out."

Her brother flew down the steps and prowled toward her, intimidating her with his size as he tried to grab the bat from her. She pulled him forward, twisting his arm behind his back and slammed his body on the trunk of the car.

"Did you just assault a police officer?" she asked sweetly, then glanced up seeing Kelso grinning wide. "Did you just see this jerk assault me?"

"Sure did, Detective Woodward."

"Fuck you!"

Theo tried to rear up, but Gabby had the bat wedged between his thighs and close to his balls. "You should pay closer attention to your fight lessons."

"You're fucking insane!"

"What the fuck is going on?"

Gabby released her brother and straightened to see a bewildered looking Declan and Levi standing inside the garage.

"Some kind of bodyguards you are!" Theo yelled. "Both of you are fired. I'm calling Nick right now." The teenager stalked back into the house.

"Gabby, what happened?" Declan asked.

"Putting a teenager in his place," Gabby twirled the bat like a marching band girl, passing by Kelso who gave her a high five.

"By destroying his car?"

"There's no XBox to take away."

"Jesus, you're a cop."

"Nope. In this case I'm his older sister laying down the law."

She left him standing there and went back inside the house, but not before she overheard Declan snipe at Kelso about letting things get out of hand, to which her partner responded it wasn't his place to interfere.

"What exactly was the problem?" Declan caught up with her in the hallway where she spotted the captain holding off the other teens. Smart. No other witnesses.

"The problem"—she glared at him—"is letting people do your job."

"You said you were okay with watching him for a while."

Gabby started seeing double. "Shit." She gripped Declan's arm.

"You okay?"

"Just need to sit down."

He led her to the nearest chair and sank into it, but she was still feeling the high of releasing her pent-up annoyance from that morning. "That felt good."

"Thrashing a million-dollar car?"

"He deserved it."

"The car didn't—"

"You do find this kinda funny, right?"

Instead of answering her, he studied her face. "Gabby, does your head hurt?"

"A little." A lot.

"You need your pain meds."

"This is not brain-chemistry induced. It's called want-to-kill-a-teenager rage."

Declan was shaking his head, but there was an amused slant to his mouth.

"You better go talk to him," she sighed. "The last thing I want is for your company to lose the contract. You and Levi asked permission to meet up with your boss, and the LAPD was covering, so none of this was your fault."

"I got her." Kelso appeared beside them. "Go talk to the kid, Roarke. Captain is sending the rest home."

"Thank God," Gabby said.

Declan hesitated. A slew of emotions flashing across his face.

"Go," she prodded again.

He gave a tight nod and went looking for the teenager.

DECLAN FOUND his son arguing with Levi in a bedroom.

"I got this, Levi." Somehow, he had a feeling this whole thing had something to do with Gabby and him spending the night together. He noted the teen's sour mood the moment they entered the house this morning.

His colleague nodded and left the room. Declan closed the door.

"Mind telling me why you were giving your sister a hard time?"

"Me giving her a hard time? Are you blind? Didn't you see her wreck my car?"

"Gabby wouldn't be pushed to that extreme if you didn't do or say something."

"Gabby, huh? You think you know her so well, right? And as it turns out she's not my sister, is she?"

He knows.

The sneer, the narrowed eyes, so much like his when he was pissed.

He knows.

"You're him. Gabby's first husband."

This was the confrontation he dreaded the most and the sheer relief he felt was welcome. One hurdle over. A thousand more to go.

"Yes."

"It wasn't hard to find out, you know? What with the

internet and all. I talked to Nick this morning after I found stuff about you two and he confirmed."

"And did he add that I ruined her career?"

"Are you denying it?" He started pacing. "A former escort lands Hollywood's hottest teen star. Must have been a coup for you."

"You should know better than to believe the tabloids."

"Are you denying you used to be a male escort?" Theo jeered.

"I'm not going to defend what I needed to do to take care of my sister." Declan kept his voice even. "You don't get to judge me when you've lived this entitled existence all your life."

Theo looked away as if chastised, but his eyes returned to Declan with fury in them. "You know the worst thing about all this? What I couldn't wrap my mind around." His voice broke. "How you could cheat on her with my mother."

"There's a lot you don't know."

"Oh, please tell me," he taunted. "Nick said you're gonna say Gabby cheated first."

Declan didn't say anything. This was his burden. He wasn't going to taint her in Theo's eyes. "She didn't."

"But you left her. After she lost your kid. You simply left her."

"I had to." His throat caught. "I failed her, Theo."

"Yes. You did. It's probably for the best. At least it gave Nick a chance."

"How did that work out for him?" he shot back.

"He said you'd broken Gabby too much for him to be able to help."

"Bull-fucking-shit," he growled. "He couldn't wait to get Gabby back to acting."

"And would that be so bad? Look at where she is now? Her life is always at risk. She lives in that dump. She refuses to acknowledge we're family." He gave a bitter laugh. "It's because we're not. Not by blood at least. I always wondered why she acted as if she couldn't tolerate me and I understand now." He glared at him. "It's because I reminded her of the man who broke her fucking heart."

"Theo—" His arm reached out.

"Don't," he warned. "I have only one dad and that's Peter Woodward. You're a sperm donor. Plain and simple."

Sperm donor. Those words. They fucking hurt.

"Don't expect us to be one big happy family. Don't expect me to call you dad. I'm not gonna fire you yet. I'd rather keep an eye on you until I figure out what you're up to. You came back to California when Dad died because of the inheritance, didn't you?"

"That's not why I'm here. You were as much a surprise to me as I was to you."

"Please," Theo scoffed. "You were a mercenary, right?"

Private military contractor, you little shit.

"Stay away from my sister."

Declan crossed his arms and braced on his feet. Wiping all emotions from his face, turning it cold, calculating. The kid noticed and took a small step back.

"You done?" He asked softly.

Theo nodded.

"Here's the thing. I'm not after anyone's money. I've got money. Mercenary, remember? And my clients were rich as sin. They don't have to act or entertain anyone for a living.

"I'm doing this gig as a favor. Turned out, my friend thought he was doing me a favor." Declan scrubbed his face. "I'm fucking glad that you're almost eighteen. I'm actually glad Peter got you away from Claudette. I'm not going to force a relationship with you, but if you need me, I'll be right here." Declan strode to the door. "One more thing. You can't tell me to stay away from anyone. I'm not after Gabby, but I have to work with her to make sure you're safe. Got it?"

Theo stared at him with a contempt that gutted him.

"Yeah." Then the kid turned his back to him, head bowed. "Just leave."

Declan wanted to go to him, wanted to put his hand on his shoulder and say they'd figure this out. But he didn't; he couldn't.

He left the room and gently closed the door.

9

"Please pass the salt."

Gabby reached for the salt shaker and passed it to Kelso, who handed it to Theo who sat at the end of the eight-seat dining table. The rest of them were collected on one end with Declan at the head.

After the fiery confrontation in the garage, the house descended into chilling politeness—at least between the teen star and the adults. The captain didn't stay long. He said his wife Vanessa was expecting him for dinner and like the mother hen she was to her husband's team, she prepared three casseroles in nine-by-eleven aluminum baking trays.

Levi reheated two of them—a baked spaghetti and lasagna.

Gabby stared at her plate, contemplating how many of the calories she needed to burn. Her metabolism wasn't what it used to be in her twenties. If she didn't work hard enough at it, given her love for carbs, she'd be sporting a healthy muffin-top by the time she hit forty. She convinced herself it wasn't vanity, but a desire to remain healthy. Maybe she was lying to herself.

"Not enough protein for you, Woodward?" Kelso teased.

"I'm already feeling this pasta settle on each hip."

Her partner feigned looking at her bottom. "You could use a little padding."

"Easy for you to say, Mr. I-can-bench-three-fifty."

"You don't do too bad yourself." Kelso leaned and nudged her on the shoulder.

At that moment, Gabby felt twin blasts of displeasure from opposing ends. She glanced at Theo first who was glaring at Kelso, and then she casually turned her head to look at Declan, who'd dropped his gaze to his plate and started attacking his pasta.

That was weird.

Levi kept the conversation easy, talking about his girls.

"I'm sorry your plans changed," Gabby said.

"Yeah. They were bummed they can't see me this week-end, but they understand daddy's job is unpredictable." Gabby felt sympathy for the man as his disappointment was etched on his face, although there was also pragmatism. She knew he and his wife were separated and wondered if it was his job that caused the rift in their marriage.

Her thoughts returned to Theo, and as much as she wanted to leave her brother to sulk, a muscle tugged at the center of her chest. "How about you, Theo?" She turned to the sullen teen. "When are you going back to work? You can probably do the indoor shoots, right?"

At first, Gabby thought the teenager was going to ignore her, but the man-child's face actually brightened up at being included in the conversation. "Yeah, no action for a while. We just finished the big mid-season finale anyway." His lips tilted up. "You can help me with my lines."

She snorted. "No fucking way."

"Come on, sis. It could be fun. Besides, you owe me a Ferrari."

"They were just lights."

"And a side mirror," he deadpanned. "Maybe you can do a cameo. Maybe I should tell the writers—"

"Theo Woodward," Gabby warned. "Do not even think about it."

"We're going to be living together anyway. Consider it bonding?"

The other guys at the table snickered.

She split a glare between Levi and Declan and kicked Kelso under the table.

"Yow," Kelso mumbled. "What was that for? I think it'd be cool. Think what it will do for the ratings."

"Ha … you're beginning to sound like Nick and everyone at PrimeFlix and Revenant Films."

"Helping him read his lines might be a good idea," Declan commented.

"Do you like wearing your spaghetti, Roarke?"

Her ex-husband's eyes gleamed with a challenge.

"And you," she asked Theo. "Do you want to find your Ferrari in the junkyard?"

He shot her a comical look like he wasn't sure whether she was serious or not. "Damn, sis. Remind me not to piss you off again." He stabbed his spaghetti and shoveled it into his mouth, but the corner of his lips threatened to pull into a smile.

The mood in the house lifted a bit, but there was an underlying tension that ran from one end of the table to the other. It wasn't her problem though. Father and son could duke it out.

Kelso left after dinner. His bachelor life meant no one was waiting for him at home, but he was a gym rat and getting up at the crack of dawn to do his workout was his religion. Gabby caught the gym bug from him. She was getting antsy that she couldn't do anything physical, so she decided to go over the murder book of her dad's homicide that the captain had brought in earlier.

Theo made an excuse to go to his room, and Gabby hoped he wasn't playing his video games, but there was only so much she could do. That boy was seventeen going on thirty. He should know what was good for him.

Declan and Levi were in the library, probably discussing Theo's schedule. The captain agreed to extend their police protection since the attack on their vehicle seemed to be targeting Gabby. A meeting would convene tomorrow with the mayor and the police chief to discuss the failed sting operation last Friday.

A text message pinged on her phone. It was Kelso, letting her know he was home and secure. Threats like this were common and she'd learned to live on the edge. The difference now was that she had Theo to worry about.

Danger by association. Ortega definitely didn't like their move last Friday and was quick to retaliate.

"Shouldn't you be resting?"

Her heart skipped when Declan sat beside her on the couch.

"How did you manage to sneak up on me?"

An eyebrow rose. "Ranger here. We're stealthy and shit."

"Ha. Ha."

"Bruised your detective's ego?"

"Not really. Maybe it's the concussion."

"Maybe." He frowned at the binder in front of her. "What's that?"

"Dad's murder book."

"I thought it wasn't your jurisdiction."

"Captain pulled some strings, got the RHD detectives on the case to make me a copy." She patted the box beside her. "These are Peter's files—papers. Or what's left of them that was in his home office."

"What's left? What do you mean—thieves took them?"

"His laptop, back-up drives, discs. They made sure to take the television and sound system, but the detectives are puzzled."

"How so?"

Gabby showed him the crime scene photographs. "They didn't touch any of the artwork. Fair enough—maybe they didn't know its value. But they didn't touch his bedroom either, where he had his watch collection and that's worth a mint. But they ransacked Theo's room and targeted very personal stuff."

Declan stiffened. "How personal?"

"His bedsheets, sneakers, his toothbrush?" She turned to the page that showed the toppled tumblers, a stripped mattress, and an empty trashcan. "One theory is that it's a deranged fan or stalker. A very deranged fan. Nothing new in this part of California, but it still gives me the creeps just thinking about it."

"Nothing on surveillance?"

Gabby puffed a derisive laugh. "None. Those CSI shows are making it more difficult for us to do our jobs."

"I can imagine," Declan smiled briefly before turning serious. "They briefed us that a stalker was a possibility, but they didn't share specifics. Levi was going to meet with the detectives tomorrow. I guess this was what they were going to show us?"

"Yes," she sighed and averted her eyes.

"There's something else," he pressed, and her gaze returned to his face. His brows were drawn together. "Out with it."

She shook her head. "I can't really say."

"You can't really say," he repeated. "But I suspect this has something to do with Claudette. And by extension—me—because I supposedly fathered a child with her."

"Why are you still denying it?" She lowered her voice into

a whisper. "Theo looks like you. The color of his eyes is almost a carbon copy of Claudette's." And that was the one damning feature that Gabby couldn't deny and it tore her heart every time she thought about it, which was why for her sanity she tried not to dwell on it. It was an open-and-shut case.

"I knew you'd say that, so I did a bit of research. Hazel eyes, Gabby? Given the color of our eyes, hazel is difficult to predict."

"Mine are plain brown——"

"Yours are a gorgeous brown—the color of warm whiskey," he rasped.

"I can't even begin to comprehend what you're trying to imply. That there was a conspiracy to swap my baby with Claudette's? But why?"

"Hasn't that ever occurred to you?"

"What, Declan? That I wished it was her baby who died and mine survived? Is that a better reality for you?"

"There's only one way to resolve this."

"Oh, great, let's ask Theo for a buccal swab and say, *oh, by the way, I think your sister who isn't your sister might actually be your mom!*"

He stared at her for a long time, frustration swimming in his emerald irises. "You're not in the right frame of mind to talk about this," he muttered.

"Oh, that's rich coming from you," she scoffed. "Short of rehashing our past ad nauseam, I wasn't the one with communication problems. Besides, what would be Claudette's objective? She didn't even want a baby. Peter was crazy enough for her. Crazy enough that he moved her to another country just to get away from me. She said I was too caught up in my grief, that I might hurt her child."

"Jesus, she did quite a mindfuck on you, didn't she?"

"Come to think of it, she was right to be scared. I was crazy."

"You weren't crazy," Declan said quietly. "You were grieving, Gab."

She took her time to respond, momentarily lost in that
dark time. "I was," she admitted.

That time was her rock bottom, a time in her life when
everyone abandoned her except Nick. So she latched on to
him, and it only got worse before it got better. Gabby Woodward burned to ashes, only to be reborn into the person she
was now.

"You asked how I became a detective?" She closed the
murder book and leaned back against the opposite end of the
couch, her chin inching up, a flare of defiance sparking
inside her.

There was surprise in his eyes, but also blatant interest in
what she had to say, and that melted the frost in her heart to a
degree—that he wanted to hear about the watershed moment
that corrected the course of her life.

"You were right. I was grieving. The months following the
mugging were hard. I was an emotional mess. Not being able
to protect my baby, losing you—I'm telling you this not to
make you feel guilty but to let you know where my headspace
was."

"I get it. It was my own guilt that sent me away, too,"
Declan's voice was gruff.

"The long and short of it was I tried to fill the void. I felt
so empty. So I married Nick. He was there for me—don't
interrupt—I think I know how you feel about him. That he
was interested only for the *Dead Future* series."

"Wasn't he?"

"I wanted another baby. I was foolish enough to think that
I could easily replace the one I lost. It took us a year for me to
conceive. I was obsessed with getting pregnant—" she stopped
when she saw the murderous look on Declan's face. "Yes, we
had plenty of sex, Dec, get over it."

He jumped to his feet and began to pace. "Go on." His tone was harsh.

"I miscarried after eleven weeks. I was devastated and I was done. I withdrew into my shell and filed for divorce. I was twice divorced by my twenty-second birthday." She laughed briefly, bitterly. "I was on my way to becoming a Hollywood cliché, a has-been because *Dead Futures* had been cancelled too after the one season I wasn't in it." Her face hardened. "One day, I decided to overcome my fears, go back to the place where I was mugged. On my way home. I stopped by a super-market there. It was late and I saw a pregnant woman being harassed by two men. It brought back memories of that night. And I just felt this uncontrollable rage. Since that attack, I've always kept a baseball bat behind my driver's seat." At Declan's curse, she added. "Don't worry, I made sure I knew how to use it.

"I went in swinging. The pregnant woman—I think I scared her too—later told me I let out the most horrific keening wail ..." Gabby inhaled a raspy breath.

"Don't keep me in suspense ... what happened to them?"

"Cracked the skull of one and shattered the cheekbone of the other including other parts. They threatened me with a knife, so I was within my rights to defend myself. That's when I met Captain Mitchell. He was a detective then, and it turned out he was also the same investigator who worked my mugging case all those years before. He remembered me. Who wouldn't at that time? The star of *Dead Futures* taking an indef-inite leave was the biggest news that year."

"He offered you a job?"

"No," Gabby smiled. "He gave me back my life."

Declan appraised her with a face full of wonder and her skin prickled with a sensation low in her belly. Then his brows drew together as if jolted from a trance and Gabby wondered if he remembered he wasn't supposed to like her.

He leaned forward and fished out his phone from his back pocket and frowned. It continued to vibrate in his hand.

"Not answering that?"

"Thinking …"

"That's mother." Theo walked in, barging into their conversation. "Figured she should know you're here."

Gabby clutched her throat instinctively as she realized exactly why the tension was thick between these two. Not that she doubted Theo's powers of deduction. The boy was nothing but observant.

The phone stopped buzzing. Declan's eyes were glued to it.

"Call her back." Theo's voice dripped with mockery.

The phone vibrated again and Gabby saw the shutters fall on her ex's face as he got up and excused himself, turning his back on them as he answered the call.

"Cat's out of the bag, huh," Gabby said.

Theo, who was staring daggers into Declan's retreating back, turned to her. "Yup."

He took the spot on the couch that his father vacated. "As far as I'm concerned, he's only a sperm donor."

"Ouch."

"Peter Woodward will always be my father," he declared.

"Theo, you have to understand he was young then."

"Doesn't excuse him cheating on you."

"Says the guy who juggles girlfriends."

"I'm not married to them. They're not even my girl-friends," he defended.

He had a point. "So, you and Emma?"

"We hang out."

"I like her," Gabby said.

"You've only met her once."

"Any girl who stands up to your rudeness has my auto-matic like."

"She's mad at me." His shoulders sagged. "Girls."

"Is that why you were sulking at dinner?"

"No. Maybe." Annoyance marred his features. "I think I'm more pissed at Declan—Roarke. I think I'll call him Roarke." His mouth curved.

"Not liking that smile, Theo."

"He and mother deserve each other."

A part of Gabby wanted to agree, but she couldn't find it in her heart to simply give Declan to that woman. And yet, she didn't have the right. She was an ex.

"You should give him a chance. Get to know the man he is now." Gabby found herself saying.

"No thanks." He narrowed his eyes at her. "You're not pawning me off on him, are you?"

"What?"

"You are," he smirked. "You don't like me. And I get it." He leaned in conspiratorially. "Honestly, I think I was a pain in the ass when you got home because I was jealous."

"Jealous?"

"Yeah, don't let it go to your head." He leaned away and grinned at her cockily. "Get that I'm a star, and we may no longer be related by blood, but I'll always consider you my big sister. Of course, I look up to you."

"I'm …" she pressed her lips together so she wouldn't burst out laughing. "Really touched."

She must not have hid her humor well, and that seemed to bother Theo. His face lost his initial arrogance and he stared at the floor, worrying his lips between his teeth. "I'm sorry about earlier."

"I was the one who thrashed your car."

"Yeah, but I was a dick for inciting the guys to make fun of your series. That was not cool, especially when you're the one who inspired me to go into acting."

Gabby's eyes slitted, studying her brother to see if he was pulling her leg, but he said those words guilelessly and— with

her cop's instinct that could spot a bullshitter a mile away
—sincerely.

"You watched my series?"

He glanced up and smiled, almost sheepishly. "Yeah. Got
my hands on them when I was ten." Then as if remembering
he was the great Theo Cole, he added. "As I said, don't let it
go to your head."

Rascal.

It was kind of ... endearing.

Declan stalked back into the living room, his face dark and
angry.

He pointed his phone at Theo. "You invited Claudette
here tomorrow?"

"Don't you want us to be one big happy family?"

Declan's eyes switched to Gabby and she sucked in her
breath at the raw yearning reflected in them. Theo stiffened
beside her.

"That's not possible," he rasped.

"Damn straight, that's not possible." Theo stood and
stepped into his space. "Because you can't keep it in your
pants and you had to cheat on my sister. "

"Theo!" Gabby exclaimed. Declan had no defense. He
figured out he couldn't lie about it now that her former stepmother was back in the picture.

"You're gonna defend him again?" Theo yelled at her. "I
just ... can't deal with you all right now."

He stalked off.

"I'm sorry."

"Why are you sorry?" Declan's voice was cold.

"I don't know how to tell him"

"That you cheated first?"

A lump formed in Gabby's throat as his statement registered. "Why can't you just admit that you slept with
Claudette?"

"I have no defense. She's gonna say that we fucked."

Gabby flinched at the coarseness of the way he said it.

"And the only other possibility is that you would be his mother," he added. "Which according to you would sound crazy, right?"

The sneer on his face almost broke her. Why was he being so cruel?

And why the hell was she trying to be the better person. "He's hurting, Dec. He just lost Peter."

"Don't need you to tell me that. I get where some of this teenage rage is coming from. At least I had the sense not to go wreck his car."

Her cheeks burned as her momentary lack of control came back to bite her, but Theo wasn't the only one hurting and she tried to make it right again. "Dec, do you want me to talk to Theo?"

He glared at her. "No Gabby. I don't need your help with my son."

It was like a slap to the face but, more than that, it tripped something inside her. A tremor of the past reverberating in the present.

The disgust on Declan's face when he found out she was pregnant didn't do as much damage as the words he'd said.

"Pregnant? I'm not the sucker I once was, Gabby. Trying to pawn off another man's child? When you deliver that kid? I'll be demanding a paternity test."

He slammed the door on her open-mouthed face. It was the final jolt she needed to accept that she'd lost her husband.

10

THE FIRST THING Gabby wanted to do when she opened the door to her perfectly coiffed former stepmother was slam it shut again. She contemplated answering the door with a towel wrapped around her body, but she'd like to believe she wasn't that vindictive person anymore. Besides, the effect would be severely diminished with two other people in the house.

Instead, her lips did their best effort to smile. "Claudette."

"Gabby, darling." This time no air kisses. Claudette anxiously looked past her shoulder. "Dec?"

"He had to help Levi with something." She kept her face from reacting when the other woman used her nickname for Declan. "I'll let him know you're here."

The *Hodgetown* cast was coming in for a table-read and furniture needed to be moved around. Since Theo was giving his concussion as an excuse not to help, he was being deliberately difficult with furniture placement. Gabby wouldn't be surprised if a chair flew out the window. Theo with it.

Her brother hadn't realized yet that these men were dangerous. These men had faced death, and had no problem killing if killing needed to be done.

"Are you not inviting me in?"

Gabby looked at the other woman in confusion. "I'm holding the door open and you're not a vampire."

Claudette held her nose high and strutted through. "We used to be such good friends."

"Was that before or after you slept with my husband?"

Her head whipped to Gabby, face indignant. "I beg your pardon. You cheated on Declan first, remember?"

A throat cleared, and both women jerked their heads toward the sound.

There stood Declan, Theo, and Levi as witnesses to Claudette's last statement and maybe more.

Gabby's cheeks flamed especially with Theo's eyes boring into hers. *Now he knows too.*

What a fine mess they were in. They were the classic Hollywood cliché. Musical partners, musical beds.

But she couldn't stand the expression on Claudette's face as her gaze landed on Declan. Clearly she prepared for this meeting. Her Brigitte Bardot emulation, with the elaborate bouffant hair style to showcase her platinum blond hair, was completed with the sex-kittenish baby doll dress that hit mid-thigh. And God help Gabby before she stuck out her foot and tripped the other woman—Claudette slow-walked to Declan as if she were in a trance and then went on tiptoes to kiss him like a damned Hollywood heroine seeing her lover after a long period of separation.

Bile rose in her throat.

Body-language wise, Declan was stiff, but he didn't avoid the other woman's lips either. He allowed the kiss, but only briefly, before he grabbed her biceps and pulled her away.

"Where have you been?" Claudette asked him huskily. "You just disappeared."

"I had to go away."

Claudette turned to Theo. "I'm glad you know."

"What? That you're a slut?"

Quick clacking of heels and a slap resounded in the foyer.

"That's enough," Declan growled, holding back Claudette who lost all her poise and wanted to go after her son with her claws. "Let's go. We can talk someplace else."

He dragged her out the still-open door while she was still cursing her son in French. Levi walked calmly to the entrance and let the door swing shut.

Gabby couldn't look at Theo.

"I'm really, really confused," the teenager announced before disappearing down the hallway.

Gabby wanted the ground to swallow her up and she could tell Levi was uncomfortable with the dead silence in the foyer.

"When will the kids arrive?" Gabby asked, finally glancing up at him.

He checked his watch. "Within the hour."

"I can't stay here."

His brow arched. "You can't go anywhere. You shouldn't be driving."

"Don't worry. I'm not. I can ask Kelso to pick me up."

The man sighed. "Can't stop you. You're not my charge."

"No, I'm not."

"Roarke won't like it."

She bristled. "Well, it's a good thing I don't give a damn what he likes."

She escaped to her bedroom to call her partner, but her lungs were choking her. It was pain—unbearable pain in the center of her chest—that ripped straight to her gut. Her cheeks were wet before she even knew she was bawling. Piteous wracking sobs interfered with her ability to suck in oxygen. She tried to rein it in, but her legs were like rubber and she sank to her knees, arms wrapping protectively around her belly. She wasn't prepared to see Declan and Claudette together, wasn't prepared to see their lips touch and walk out the door together.

It killed her.

It excavated the brutal memories from that night she lost everything … the night Claudette called her to tell her that she was frightened. What if Peter found out that the baby she was carrying was not his.

"What if it's Declan's?" she wailed. "What if the baby has green eyes?"

"Then you'll have to tell Declan," she snapped. "Goodbye, Claudette."

"Wait! Please, Gabby, don't hang up."

Her grip tightened on her phone. She didn't owe this woman anything. It wasn't Gabby's place to tell her father either, although she really wanted to, so he could kick that backstabbing woman out of their lives. But Claudette knew Gabby wasn't going to say anything. Peter suffered a mild stroke six months before and another shock could kill him.

"What. Do. You. Want?"

"Maybe I should disappear until the baby is born."

"Are you crazy? Where are you going to go?"

"A friend of mine is going to Cancun and knows of a good birthing clinic there."

"You're out of your freaking mind."

"That's what I'll do."

"Claudette! Don't you dare hang up."

"My friend is leaving tonight."

"Where are you?"

"I'm in the Valley."

"You come back right this instant."

"I'm scared, Gabby."

"You shouldn't have slept with Declan!" she screamed. "You're such a fucking bitch!"

"I know," Claudette started crying. "I'm sorry, all right?"

Gabby started crying too. "I'll come get you."

She didn't know she'd signed the death warrant for her baby when she got into that car to retrieve her stepmother. She wouldn't be easily recognized in Van Nuys, but she still took precautions and tucked her hair under a hat and wore a trench coat with a turned-up collar, using the belt to hold the coat around her almost nine-month belly. Claudette said she was waiting inside the La Familia bodega. The Our Lady of Lourdes Clinic was a landmark beside it, Claudette said.

Gabby remembered parking the car, noting with trepidation how the area was dimly lit. There were very few pedestrians. She stepped out of the vehicle and went into the convenience store and saw Claudette. Her stepmother appeared very relieved to see her.

She remembered leaving the convenience store with Claudette. Remembered her head exploding in pain and she wished she had drifted into blessed numbness, but instead, excruciating agony eviscerated her insides. It was her baby being born, her baby never getting a chance to cry. Gabby almost bled out and died.

Then the voices came as she floated in and out of consciousness.

"She lost a lot of blood."

"Get out of here!"

"I'm staying, Peter ... I'm her husband."

"You abandoned a pregnant wife and she nearly died, you son of a bitch—"

"Things were complicated between us. You wouldn't begin to understand."

"Do the right thing. I beg you, Declan. Give her back the life she deserves."

After three days, she woke up and the first person she saw was Declan, sitting in a chair, his head buried in his hands.

She didn't say anything, just stared at the top of his head. Her hands drifted to her belly and it felt so empty. A sob rose in her throat.

His head jerked up and he walked briskly to her side and pushed the button for the nurse. His face had aged, eyes were bloodshot, and his usually clean-shaven face was darkened by several days' worth of stubble. He briefly closed his eyes and his mouth moved as if saying a prayer, but he didn't touch her.

"You're awake," he said gruffly. His eyes were suspiciously bright with emotion, but not a single tear fell.

"My baby?" she whispered.

Devastation was written all over Declan's face, and he started shaking his head.

"You didn't want him," she accused.

"Gabby ..."

"You didn't believe he was yours."

"I'm sorry—"

"Get out! Get the hell out!"

The nurses rushed in and then the doctor. Declan stayed behind them, his fingers digging into his hair as she continued to curse him and blame him for their baby's death. The medical staff tried to calm her down but there were no words to drive out the excruciating pain that was tearing her up from the inside. She fought everyone who tried to give her comfort until finally they sedated her.

The next time she woke up, the only person she saw was Nick. He was the one who broke the news that her father had taken Claudette and their new baby to France.

By her bedside was a thick folded document.

Divorce papers.

She stared at them dispassionately. Her world already imploded the day her baby died.

GABBY REALIZED she'd stopped crying. And, instead, a ball of anger formed at the base of her throat. Anger was good. It was better than despair. With anger came adrenaline and what followed adrenaline?

Clarity.

Our Lady of Lourdes Clinic.

She scrambled to her feet and grabbed the phone off the charger and called Kelso.

He answered on the second ring. "Hey, partner, was about to call you."

"Do you have a lead on Ortega?"

"Uh, no?" His voice sounded very baffled.

"Well, I do, and don't give me bullshit about taking it easy because I have a damned concussion."

There was silence and then, "You all right, Woodward?"

"I will be if you tell me there's an Our Lady of Lourdes clinic in our case file on Ortega."

"That sounds familiar, but I'll have to take a look."

"That'll take too long. Just come and get me."

She ended the call without waiting for his response, and jumped into the shower with a renewed purpose.

"WHAT'S YOUR GAME, CLAUDETTE?" Declan navigated the Porsche SUV out of the Brentwood district. He figured they could drive around. He still didn't know how to handle her, how to pump her for information without showing his disgust. The urge to shove her away when she kissed him was so strong, it was a wonder he stood as still as he did.

He glanced at the rearview mirror. Her bodyguards were following them in a black Explorer. It figured if her boyfriend was a billionaire.

"I missed you, Dec."

His skin crawled. He hated that name since he was a kid and forbade anyone to call him that except Gabby. Somehow it felt right for her to use it.

"Don't call me that."

"Gabs does."

"She was my wife."

"Exactly. Was. So why does it matter if I call you the same?"

Claudette could be dense. She didn't get it.

"Why don't you tell me how Theo came to be your son?"

"He was better off with me and Peter." Out of the corner of his eye, he noted Claudette squirming in her seat.

"Don't feed me that bullshit."

"She was only keeping the baby to hang on to you. It was for the best!"

"So your answer was to steal our kid?"

"I did you a favor. I set you free. If you found out you had a son, would you have gone on with your dream to join the Army? You hated her. You were going to divorce her. But you had second thoughts, didn't you? You had the restraining order on her, but you were the one stalking her."

Declan glanced sharply at Claudette. "How did you know?" It took months before he was able to think about Gabby and the baby. Deep down he knew it was his, but he couldn't erase the image of her in bed with another man, letting his rage keep him physically away. Watching over her from a distance was all he could do. But that one night he got hung up on a modeling job, she got attacked. Guilt crushed his heart and he let her go.

"How, Claudette?"

"I had you followed," she said slowly. "I got involved with a very dangerous man."

"Raul Ortega?"

"How …" There was surprise on her face, but also satisfaction. "Of course. This is why I contacted you. You have connections that I need."

"Tell me how Ortega is connected to this baby switch."

"I wish you wouldn't call it that. Theo will always be my son."

He was fast losing his patience. "Talk, Claudette. Why did you do it? Did yours really die?"

"How dare you! Are you suggesting I killed my own baby?" she gasped. "I cried for days when I found out my baby was dead in my womb."

He stilled.

"Are you saying," he had to space out his words, fury curdling the blood inside him. His knuckles turned white on the steering wheel. "The switch was premeditated?" He had to continue driving. If he pulled onto the shoulder, he might murder her and damn the consequences.

"You don't understand!" she sobbed. "Ortega would have killed me if I had no baby to show for it."

"He was the father." His voice was dead quiet.

"Yes!"

Declan took a couple of deep breaths to process this confirmation. He waited until they reached the next traffic light before he spoke again. "Let's back up a bit. How serious was your affair with Ortega?"

Claudette started talking. Telling him that Ortega was obsessed with her and prized her connections into Hollywood via her marriage to Peter Woodward. A jealous lover yet selfish when it came to what she did to his bottom line. She admitted her infatuation with the crime lord and the danger he represented. She loved the thrill it gave her and then she got pregnant.

"He deliberately planted his baby inside me," she whispered. "When Raul found out I was pregnant, he was scarily ecstatic. He threatened me. Said he would kill me if I had an abortion. For all his criminal activities, he is a very religious man. Fanatically so."

"Why didn't he just ask you to divorce Peter and live happily fucking after?" Declan snarled. That would have spared everyone a lot of grief as it looked like Ortega and Claudette deserved each other.

"He said I could never be his queen because the cartels can't be trusted. A wife and a son would be his weakness. That

I had to be patient. But my baby died a month before I was to deliver. I panicked."

His jaw clenched. "So you lured Gabby to Van Nuys that night. Took our baby instead. Who did you bribe, Claudette?"

She didn't answer and looked out the window.

"Answer me!"

"I'm not telling you anymore until I know you'll help me," she said.

Declan lapsed into silence as he concentrated hard not to floor the gas. They reached the intersection of Sunset Boulevard and he made the turn to head to the Valley.

"Where are you going?" Claudette asked.

"What did you think was gonna happen?" he asked. "That we're gonna have a cozy breakfast on Rodeo Drive?"

She gave a nervous laugh. "I wouldn't dare be seen there."

"What's the matter, Claudette? Ortega found out you were a lying bitch and put a hit on you?" Declan cast a glance at her. She was staring at her linked fingers on her lap, twisting them in a sure sign of anxiety.

"He did, didn't he?"

Her chin trembled. "It's quite the opposite. Raul used me and now Andrade thinks I've connived with him, and I think he has the cartel looking for me."

"Andrade?"

"Yes," she whispered. Her mask of perfection cracked and revealed a very frightened woman. Declan almost felt sorry for her. Almost.

"But it was all Raul, I swear," she continued. "I thought the shipment I brought in was XZite pills." At his snort, a defiant look crossed her face.

"You're a drug mule."

"That's harsh. The XZite pills are a perfectly acceptable party drug in Europe." She crossed her arms and hugged her biceps, giving a sniff. "I don't do cocaine or the heavy stuff. Oh, I still gave Raul targets, but I stayed far away from trafficking or using. I was a good mother to Theo. Peter didn't see that and had to ruin everything. He had suspicions about Theo being his son, especially when the boy started losing the baby fat. And then in one of our fights, I threw Raul at his face." She laughed bitterly. "Peter couldn't divorce me fast enough. Packed up and moved back to Los Angeles. Left me in Paris, scared that Ortega would come after me."

"Did he order the hit on Peter?"

"It's very possible," she whispered almost too softly that Declan wasn't sure those were her words. "The reason Raul wanted Theo to grow up with Peter was to shield him from his enemies. Before the fentanyl attacks, Raul used to be more visible in public. He and Peter were acquaintances. Peter confided in me that Raul had been inordinately fixated on Theo in the common gatherings they attended. Only Peter already knew that Gabby was Theo's mother because he'd run a DNA analysis after our divorce three years ago."

"When was the last time you talked to Peter?"

"Three months before his death. He was pissed. Told me to tell Raul to fuck off or he would."

"Ortega was harassing Peter? He was in hiding by that time, right?"

"Yes. He's a crime lord, Declan. He has people."

"They threatened Peter?"

She shrugged. "I told him to leave well enough alone. Let Raul continue to believe that Theo was his. That's all I really know."

"Not everything. I want to know about you, Andrade, and Ortega."

She looked out her window. "I found out from my bodyguard that I've actually handed a dangerous prototype to Ortega."

"What prototype?" His voice was low and controlled.

"Some kind of biological weapon."

"Jesus Christ!" Even when he expected her to say this

because Garrison had already given him a heads up, it was still too much to be having this conversation and driving around. He scanned the road up ahead and looked for an exit. He pulled into a Denny's parking lot, put the Porsche in park but kept the engine running. He twisted in his seat and faced her. "Why the hell would you do that?"

"I told you I thought it was the XZite pills. Even Andrade found out too late it was a biological weapon."

Declan was confused. "Wait a minute. Back up. It wasn't Andrade who sent the bioweapon?"

Claudette laughed bitterly. "I don't know what to believe anymore. I'm in deep shit. I think I'm being set up." Her eyes stared at him beseechingly. "You have to help me."

"Always thinking of saving your ass," he snarled. "Never even thinking about the people who might die or get hurt as long as you get your way."

"I didn't know."

Declan laughed derisively. "Ignorance isn't an excuse. You need to be in jail for the baby switch alone and all the lives you've ruined by putting people in Ortega's path."

"Well?" Her mouth flattened and her face had a closed-off look that said she wouldn't budge if he didn't help her. Or tried to at least.

"Look, I may have contacts, but nothing short of giving me information on where to find Ortega or this bioweapon is going to buy you safe passage out of the States."

"I can do that." A look of relief came over her face. Did she think she was going to get away with it?

"I want immunity first," she said.

Well, fuck me. Maybe she's not as dumb as she lets on.

"I don't have that power."

"Yes, you do. You work for the CIA," she smiled. "Never underestimate me, Declan."

"I may have worked for them once."

"I'm not talking unless I get immunity. Also, I want to get out of this country as soon as possible."

"You can't make demands unless you give me something, so start talking."

She told him everything. What happened that night, how the baby switch happened and a possible, current location of Ortega.

"This is what's gonna happen," Declan managed to say, even when the promise of the ultimate answers was looming. He looked back to where her bodyguards were idling in their SUV. "I'm gonna take your Explorer and go to the clinic you mentioned, the one in Van Nuys. You better make that call. If homeboy doesn't give me any actionable intel, I can't go to bat for your immunity."

"What should I do then?"

"Go back to our house in Brentwood. I'll give Levi a heads up."

"Why should I go there? Can't I just go ahead and find a safe place to hide out and then call you?"

"Because I don't trust you. And it's not because I can't find you, because like you suspected I know people who can. But I don't want to get pissed off at you any further by wasting my time looking for you."

They got out of the Porsche which prompted her bodyguards to get out as well. Declan took a good look at them. South African mercenaries if he were to guess. Blond, built, Dolph Lungdren wanna-bes down to the buzz cut and spiked hair. Claudette informed the one driving to give up the keys. As she and the two guys walked back to the Porsche, Declan called out, "Oh, and Claudette, please don't piss Gabby off."

"I never …"

"Just. Don't."

Claudette gave an offended huff, and with chin held high, climbed into the luxury vehicle.

Declan got into the Explorer. He had some calls to make.

11

THE GANGS and Homicide Division was located in an old square building on 77th street near the 101. A task force was formed in response to problems in information sharing when crimes crossed lines from gangs into narcotics, vice into homicide, and all other possible combinations. Because of its proven efficacy, the task force was converted into a division. Not everyone was happy with this move because other individual tables were territorial about GHD encroaching on their turf.

GHD was comprised of two teams—Bravo and Charlie. Gabby belonged to Charlie team which was made up of six detectives. An administrative staff included an adjutant, watch officer, crime analyst, clerk and a liaison officer who supported all the teams. Captain Mitchell oversaw the entire division.

When Gabby and Kelso arrived in the squad room, the area was buzzing with activity.

She spotted Lt. Chen who was the officer-in-charge after Mitchell, who was currently talking to his partner Detective Delgado. The other detective pair was off the watch.

"What's going on?" Kelso asked. "Is the captain in?"

"He's on his way back from his meeting with the mayor,"

Chen looked at Gabby. "Aren't you supposed to be on leave, Woodward?"

"I was getting cabin fever," she quipped.

"You sure wouldn't want to miss this fun, white girl," Delgado piped in. "Your hunch on Our Lady of Lourdes Clinic hit pay dirt. Nadia is out and about in the Valley doing another surveil for the suits on Bravo team and hopped over a couple of blocks to Van Nuys. And guess who joined us?"

Gabby's heart was thumping. "Well don't keep me in suspense, homie."

"Ariana Ortega," Delgado chortled. "She's doing some of her charity work in the OLL clinic."

Her heart sank. It wasn't that Ariana wasn't important, but she was easily accessible at her Beverly Hills vitamin juice spa. "You think she's scheduled to give ole bro his vitamin boost?"

"Possible," Kelso said. "It's around the time he should be getting his next chemo round. We fucked up the last time when we thought it was down in South Central, but recent intel is pointing to the Valley. Maybe in one of the clinics."

"Problem is Guzman from Bravo went undercover in that clinic the last time Ariana was there six weeks ago and nothing was out of the ordinary," Delgado said.

"He did? Why weren't we informed?" she demanded.

"Beats me. It was on the shared division database when I pulled up what we had on the clinic," the Hispanic detective replied.

Just then, their captain walked in. "Tell me good news, people. Nadia just informed me that Ortega's sister is at the clinic. Do we have enough intel to investigate?"

Nadia Powell was their crime and forensic analyst. She wore several hats. After the fentanyl attacks, she'd been reassigned from the Criminalistics Laboratory to work for the GHD full-time. Her state-of-the-art lab was located in the adjacent room, a bit out of place in the old building, but it had the necessary equipment such as a glove box to isolate a toxin. She also had the technical skills for analyzing trigger devices. The ones used in the shopping mall attack was pressure activated similar to stepping on a landmine.

"Might be a good idea to walk in, look around," Gabby said. "I could go in with Delgado. Less suspicious. If we see any of Ortega's associates hanging around, he should be close by. We hear he never goes months without seeing his sister and our intel is telling us, he is due."

"You should be resting, Gabby," Kelso said.

"I'm already here and I don't care if this sounds personal. I'm sure he was the one who attacked us last Monday."

Delgado grinned at her partner and Chen. "You know you can't stop Woodward. Concussion or not." Then he turned his eyes on Gabby. "You sure you're up for this, white girl?"

"Just try and stop me," she replied.

THE DRIVE to the Valley was uneventful, but it was laced with trepidation. She'd made this drive regularly and had no idea why this time was different. The San Fernando Valley had seen a surge of gang-on-gang violence in recent years. Studies showed it was mainly turf wars due to the rise in the drug trade, prostitution, and sale of illegal weapons. For Gabby it was so much more. It was the place where her young dreams died, and the place where she rose up from their ashes.

This was her city and she would continue to fight for it and, try, as much as possible, to make it safe for the citizens of Los Angeles. That was her oath when she graduated from the academy.

She looked at Kelso, who was driving their department-issued Suburban. He was unusually quiet, his jawline tense, lost in his own thoughts. Rather than engage him in conversation, she let her eyes take in the diverse skyline of Los Angeles as their SUV traversed the 101.

The City of Angels.

A city of ten million souls.

And they were its guardians.

Buildings rose high and low. The smog the city was known for was surprisingly missing today and yet the traffic was the usual. Cars crawled at a snail's pace— impatient drivers, blaring horns, and road rage—just another day in LA. Neighborhoods so different from one zip code to the next. From the luxuries of Beverly Hills to the graffitied walls of Van Nuys.

A sigh escaped Kelso when he took the exit for the Valley. Under the overpass, the marks of the gangs were painted on full display. There were four hundred gangs just in Los Angeles. Major groups splintered into smaller ones and spread, but someone held them all in the palm of his hand.

Ortega.

His connections to the cartels and arms dealers were making this possible but allegiances shifted all the time. The power struggles, and his rumored cancer, sent the crime boss into hiding. There was another rumor that he'd arranged for Ariana to marry a cartel boss, cementing their alliance, but she was resistant to the plans and was under heavy guard.

They turned from Haynes Street onto Van Nuys, passing commercial streets with more short-term and long-term storage companies and warehouses per mile of road than any other area in LA. The scenery turned into single-story homes like bungalows. Barred windows and gates to yards held warnings saying the "property was protected by Smith and Wesson."

Yep, they were in the Valley.

A couple of nondescript vehicles were parked up the side of the road, but Gabby recognized their surveillance van.

"Let's see what Nadia has for us," she said as Kelso pulled behind the commercial vehicle. She turned the visor down to check her make-up. She'd gone with pale goth, dark circles under her eyes. Her hair was teased to death, reminiscent of

Madonna's *Material Girl* days. She had on jeans and wore a thin bulletproof vest behind a tee beneath a bomber jacket.

"Sure you're up for this?" Kelso asked worriedly. "No headache?"

"A bit. Less than a hangover." She put on her aviators. "Besides, shades help and go with the look." She hopped out of the vehicle and immediately regretted it. The jolt gave her a spike of pain in her skull.

Kelso gave two raps to the back of the van, paused, and another double rap before Nadia opened the door, smiling at them

"Come on in, detectives. How's the head?"

"Hard as ever," Gabby quipped as she and Kelso climbed in. By that time, the captain and Delgado joined in.

"Chen's scouting the perimeter, but good job with the drone, Nadia," the captain said.

Nadia nodded, but her attention was riveted on Gabby, giving her a head-to-toe appraisal. "Love the disguise. Now we're sisters." She held out her fist and they exchanged a fist bump. Their crime analyst was dressed all in black, her right arm was inked with tattoos. Black square-rimmed glasses and slicked back blond hair gave her a scholarly yet edgy look. "Now all you need are bangles and bangs."

Gabby laughed. "No bangles. If I have to follow a suspect on the sly, I don't want to be jingling all over the place." Everyone laughed, though the air in the van felt fraught with tension or maybe it was just too crowded, making it difficult to breathe.

"I'll be watching you all on the Wasp."

"The Wasp?"

"The Wasp ten-k." The analyst gestured toward a row of silver colored bugs that looked more like beetles than wasps.

"They're shiny. Don't they attract attention?" Gabby asked as everyone picked up a set of earpieces and put them on.

"Nope. What they do is camouflage. Once activated, little

mirrors reflect the surroundings and they're nearly transparent. Can't tell they're even there."

"At least this comm stuff looks like ear buds and …" Gabby checked her Tac-watch. "And it's linked."

They did a couple of tests with their communication equipment and finally Delgado turned to Gabby.

"Ready to rock?"

A COUPLE of people stood in front of the clinic. A Hispanic woman with two children waited right by the door; a woman with coppery hair sat against the wall. She was so emaciated, her eyes were sunken. She didn't even bother to hide the track marks on her arm.

"Be advised there are women and children around the perimeter," Gabby muttered to her comms as she and Delgado entered the clinic.

There were varying affirmative responses. It was just a formality for the sake of recording the op.

The first thing Gabby noticed when she entered the facility was that it was clean, but it was crowded and noisy. Benches lined the walls and people of all ages and races sat against them, and children were scattered on the floor.

An announcement stood to one side. "Ariana Ortega Wellness drive today." There was a translation in Spanish, and a red bar across the sign indicated appointments were fully booked.

"Oh well," Delgado murmured by her ear. "I guess no vitamin infusion for you today."

A large oval counter was flanked by the two hallways that led to the rooms in the clinic. Nurses ushered patients to and from the reception area. The disparity in personnel was obvious. Ariana brought her own staff to these events. The nurse in a polished and vibrant uniform clashed with the one wearing drab, faded scrubs, but they seemed to be getting along and exchanging good-natured ribbing.

She approached the front desk which was manned by three people, one of whom was a harried looking nurse, busy shuffling paperwork around. "We're full," she announced without looking at Gabby. "But you can take a bottle of vitamins from the box at the end of the counter."

"Thanks," she said. Delgado signaled with his eyes that he was going around the other end to peek down the corridor.

Her earpiece crackled.

"We have two vehicles circling the clinic," Nadia said.

"Suspicious?" Chen asked.

"Four men. Silver Toyota, old model. Driver looks Latino, thirties, ink on left arm."

"Do you recognize the tats?" This from the Captain.

"Checking now."

"How about the other vehicle?" Delgado asked while pretending interest in a mural on the wall.

"Caucasian male, facial hair, thirties, black Explorer with rental tags. He just moved out of drone range."

"Might be a tourist lost in the Valley," Chen joked.

"Do you want a packet of vitamins?" A voice pulled Gabby's attention to the woman behind the counter asking the question. She was one of the polished ones.

"Oh, I'm actually a reporter," she said.

The woman froze up, eyes turning into slits. "Ms. Ortega is not giving any interviews."

Gabby pointed to the reception area. "But this would go a long way to show the good she is doing for the community. You know, after what her brother did?"

"I'm going to have to ask you to leave."

A distraction over the comm channels drew Gabby's ear.

"Fuck, get out of there now," Nadia said urgently. "These men are cartel."

"Are they heading toward the clinic?" Gabby asked.

"They just parked."

"Both of you heard Nadia," Cap ordered. "Abort."

A door slammed further down the hallway and Gabby heard arguing and she leaned back to see Ariana and a man she didn't recognize.

"I'm not leaving like a coward," Ariana said vehemently.

"If I have to remove you bodily, I will," the man threatened.

"I'm not running. They're after Raul, not me!"

Gabby signaled to Delgado who was already holding the door to the clinic open and he was scowling at her delay.

"Ma'am, I told you to leave," the woman offering the vitamins repeated, but her eyes were getting shifty.

"Damn you, let me go!" Ariana shouted.

Turning her attention back to the fighting couple, she saw the man did as promised and was physically hauling Ortega's sister out the back exit. Gabby dashed down the hallway just as her comms broke into chatter and—gunfire?

What the hell?

Chaos and screaming erupted from the front of the clinic.

She hesitated and glanced back, not seeing Delgado, and decided to follow Ariana and the man who Gabby tagged as a biker thug.

Pushing the exit bar, the door opened to a small parking lot that led to a narrow street lined with houses surrounded with steel fencing.

"Gabby, where the fuck are you?" Kelso yelled in her ear.

"In foot pursuit of Ariana Ortega."

She spotted the pair in front of the first house facing the clinic.

"My brother needs me!" Ariana shouted, twisting her arm away from Biker Man and ran to the house, but he caught up with her and kept a firmer hold on her.

Gabby drew her weapon, pointed it down, and crouched behind one of the parked cars.

"And my job is to protect you!" The man looked angry enough to toss Ariana over his shoulder.

Her bodyguard? He didn't exactly fit the bill of Ortega's soldiers. More like an independent bruiser for hire.

"Ortega could be in the house behind the clinic," Gabby spoke into her comms. "Nadia, do you copy?"

"Roger that. Repositioning drone."

"I'm on it," Kelso said. "Chen, cover me. First house you said?"

All the while there were sporadic gunshots echoing around them.

"On the corner." She paused. "I have an idea ..."

"Gabby ... what the fuck?" Kelso rasped.

"You've gone off script enough!" the Cap cut in.

She ignored the mix of protests and assents that crackled in her earpiece, but she had to follow her instincts. She broke her concealment behind the car and Biker Man spotted her instantly.

He was a quick draw—surprising her—reaching for his pistol and pointing it at her as he shoved Ortega's sister behind him.

Gabby had raised her gun at the same time he did. "Police! Let her go. Drop your weapon."

"Don't come any closer," he snarled as he backed away with Ariana.

"Ariana," Gabby said. "We just want to ask you questions. Tell your pit bull to stand down."

"You want to arrest my brother."

"You know what he did was wrong."

"He's very sick."

"We know. And we'll make sure he gets his treatments, but he must be taken off the streets."

She was shaking her head. "He's not going to die in prison. I can't let that happen."

"Ariana, the cartel is out there, my unit is holding them back."

The blare of the sirens echoed in the distance. "Hear that? You're safe." She inched closer. Slowly. She had instincts about the jumpiness of a person with a gun and Biker Man was as cool as ice.

She swallowed. He could shoot her and not blink an eye.

As for Ariana, she seemed to be relenting. This was a woman who went against her brother's criminal lifestyle, but blood was blood. She thought she could save him.

Gabby took another step forward. "I won't repeat myself. Drop your weapon. We can work this out."

The biker's eyes darkened, and his expression took on a look Gabby couldn't decipher. When he stared past her shoulders and smirked, her blood ran cold.

"Gabby!"

Two shots rang out. She instinctively dropped to a knee, finger still on the trigger, gun pointed down. She must have blinked because Ariana and Biker Man disappeared and Declan was pulling her into his arms, his fingers securely clasping her wrist—the hand that held her weapon.

"What the fuck are you doing here?" she yelled.

He flinched. She must have screamed but she didn't care. She surged to her feet, shoving away from him. Her head pounded with a thousand jackhammers. "I could have shot you!"

"But you didn't." His face was calm, which infuriated her more.

She gestured furiously to where Ariana and the biker had stood. "You let them get away."

"Gabby, where the fuck are you?" Kelso's voice crackled through comms. "We're about to go in."

At that moment, Delgado jogged up to them. "Let's go, Woodward." He looked at Declan. "Thanks, detective."

Detective? *What. The. Fuck.*

Declan shot her a warning look, and it was then that she spotted the badge clipped to his belt. "Come on, your squad needs back-up."

The three of them converged with Kelso, Mitchell, and Chen at the corner of a Mediterranean-style villa surrounded by galvanized steel fencing. Black mold stained the exterior walls and the overgrowth of shrubs and leggy flower bushes indicated the landscaping hadn't seen maintenance in a while. Crab grass had overtaken the front lawn. Some suits from Bravo unit showed up while two Valley PD cruisers blocked the street, and their patrol officers started securing the area. Judging from Kelso's scowl, there was a new development.

"What's going on?" Gabby asked.

"SWAT's taking over," Mitchell announced. He narrowed his eyes briefly at Declan before addressing the rest of Charlie and Bravo team. "They'll be in charge of initial assault. We'll do clean up. Make sure to tag every item, disk, or document we could use as evidence to nail his ass."

"Is our warrant solid?" Gabby asked the Cap.

Mitchell nodded. "Standing arrest warrant from a month ago holds. I'm going to direct the patrol officers and set up a command post." His gaze landed on Kelso. "This is not reflective on our division. We follow protocol so the sixth floor won't have our asses when the op goes pear-shaped. Got it?"

ORTEGA'S MEN didn't put up much of a fight when SWAT swooped in. There was a brief exchange of automatic weapons, but the whole takedown was over in ten minutes.

One would say it was anticlimactic, but the shock was seeing the elusive crime lord in a fragile state. Ortega wasn't a tall man, probably five-ten. Gabby could picture the man he once was. Expensive silk pajamas hung loosely on a body ravaged by cancer. As the officers helped him up and cuffed him, he maintained an arrogant posture and exchanged a defiant look with Mitchell—his mouth firmly pressed in a straight line. State of the art medical equipment surrounded a hospital bed and a stash of vials and syringes lay on a hospital caddy.

"Gabby," Nadia called her over to a room. She walked into a space full of boxes, but her eyes landed on a familiar laptop. It was scuffed, but she recognized the stickers on it from the different Revenant productions of the past two years including *Hodgetown*.

"That could be Peter's," she whispered. "Why is it here?"

"I'm going to dust it for latents," Nadia said. "Then I'm gonna take it back to the lab and try to get into it." She heard the other woman vaguely, but she was already looking around. There was a box that contained a bunch of memory sticks and backup drives.

"Oh my God," she choked, her mind trying to absorb this new information, misfiring like faulty wiring that couldn't quite make the connection. It gave her an almighty pounding headache.

"Gabby!" Nadia gasped.

She had sagged into a column of boxes and would have fallen if the analyst hadn't held her up.

"Told you to go home," Kelso growled, stalking into the room. "We got this, Woodward."

She pointed weakly to the laptop, unable to speak.

Kelso stared blankly at the computer, then his brows shot to his hairline, eyes bugging out. "Oh, fuck."

12

DECLAN GLANCED WORRIEDLY AT GABBY. Her head was tilted against the headrest of the Explorer. He was back on the 405, heading home to Brentwood. After the SWAT team raid, and with Ortega in custody, GHD was able to take a breather to reassess, and all eyes landed on Declan who stuck out like a sore thumb. Mitchell ordered him back to the command post. At least he wasn't kept at the outermost circle with the other spectators. Declan figured the captain didn't want him disappearing just yet. As if he could, with his stubborn, concussed ex-wife knee deep, sorting through the evidence in Ortega's latest safe house located behind the clinic.

Seeing Gabby leaning on her partner like a crutch when they left Ortega's hideaway was a kick in the gut. He hated seeing her hurt and protectiveness won out over the fury. Worry had coursed through him when he found out from Levi that she had left the house with her partner.

And if that wasn't enough, finding her in an alley in a standoff that challenged his loyalties pissed him the fuck off even more. He did what he had to do.

"Is your head still hurting?" he asked. The paramedics at

the scene gave her a painkiller shot that would give her relief quickly.

"Not for the reasons you think."

He sighed. "I'm the reason."

"Why would you think you're the reason?" Gabby retorted, opening her eyes and shooting him a glare. "Oh, let me guess," she added sarcastically. "Was it because you impersonated a police officer?"

"Your guys were outgunned, and if I didn't step in there would have been casualties."

"You're a smug sumbitch," she slurred, closing her eyes and rubbing her temples. "What the hell was that scene in the alley? You're lucky we got Ortega or I'd have Mitchell tear you a new one for letting Ariana get away. Maybe a night in lockup would do you good, seeing that you stuck your nose in a police operation."

She turned her head to look out the window and gave an effusive sigh. There was something else on her mind. And he was still trying to wrap his head around the fact that his ex-wife was a cop. It was her job and danger was a part of it, but he couldn't help that old feeling of protectiveness that he'd always felt toward her. Even when they first separated, it was only his hurt and anger that kept him away, but without that between them now... Hell. As if the attack on her car and subsequent concussion wasn't bad enough. Now, seeing her in a hostile situation, seeing her going after a suspect with a gun, had pushed him into unknown territory. He was thankful the SWAT team did the assault, otherwise he wouldn't know what he would've done. He sure as fuck wouldn't be standing by the sidelines. He wasn't confident enough in the men around her to have her back.

He wasn't prepared to address that problem.

"There's going to be an investigation," she said finally. "When field investigators review the case, and with the op probably uploaded to YouTube by now with your mug all over it, shit's going to hit the fan."

"I'll think of something," he muttered. Garrison would shit a brick that he used his fake badge for the unintended purpose, but what did he expect when he put Declan in close proximity to Gabby. His ex-wife who never lost the power to twist him up inside, and he would damn the consequences to keep her safe.

"Oh, you'll think of something," she groused.

He should be irritated, but he was amused. Gabby had turned into quite a spitfire. He liked it and, oddly, his dick did too.

Down boy.

"What the hell are you finding so funny?"

"You've got quite a mouth on you." He looked up the 405 and was thankful the traffic was moving. He couldn't wait to get Gabby home and have it out with her. Then he remembered Claudette. He shifted in his seat and he fished out his phone, and thumbed Levi's number.

"That's illegal," Gabby grumbled.

"It's an emergency," he deadpanned.

He imagined her rolling her eyes at him.

On the third ring, Levi answered.

"Claudette get there?"

"Nope."

Figured. "Dammit." She probably skipped town. "Did you get a hold of G?"

"No answer," Levi replied. "You have an update for him?"

"Yeah. Need to run something by him."

"Did you fuck up, Roarke?"

What? Did this guy have ESP? "Gabby and I will be there in …" He checked the stream of traffic again. "Half an hour."

He tossed the phone into the console between them and glanced over to Gabby, noting the disapproval on her face.

"What?" A grin threatened the corners of his mouth. "Still annoyed I used my phone while driving?"

"Who's G?"

"A contact."

"What did you fuck up?"

"I didn't." If he had to do it all over again, he would do the same thing—use his fake badge to get to her.

At the moment, he was confused by what he was feeling. Was it concern for someone who used to be the most important person in his life, or did it go deeper? Did he still love her? Declan couldn't allow himself to be that vulnerable again. He wasn't even that same person, one who loved with everything he had.

After he maneuvered the SUV to the center lane to coast back to Brentwood, he noted that Gabby didn't respond, that she was watching the LA scenery pass her by.

"Why didn't you ever leave?" he asked.

"What?"

Declan fell silent, surprising himself that he asked the question. What was the point? "Forget it."

He could feel her gaze burn the side of his face. Scowling at the traffic, he bit out, "What?"

"Were you asking me why I never left LA?"

"Yes."

"Is this small talk? Or are you really interested to know why."

"What's the difference? We've got thirty minutes to kill anyway."

"Or we could spend thirty minutes in blessed silence," she said. "If there's any talking to be done, we need to figure out how to explain your presence at the scene. I just don't have it in me right now."

He glanced at her with concern. "Are you feeling all right? Head hurt?"

"It's a dull throb. It's really better, but with the adrenaline crash …" Her hand reached for the tuner on the dashboard. "You mind if I find something on the radio?"

"Go ahead."

The strains of Coldplay came over the speakers and Declan swallowed a groan. Maybe silence was indeed better. He gave his attention to the 405 on the way back to the house. It wasn't rush hour yet and traffic was moving at a steady pace, not the regular four miles per hour. The next time he looked at Gabby, her eyes were closed, her hands laying loosely on her lap.

He had a strong urge to reach over the console and take her hand in his. Like they used to when they'd been married, back in happier times. Declan would drive with his left hand on the steering wheel, their linked fingers settling on her lap or on his chest as he kissed the back of her fingers.

They'd been young.

They'd been in love.

And now?

They were different people, with different paths in life. He snorted a self-deprecating chuckle. He was rudderless. Sure he had money. Enough to keep him comfortable for the rest of his life, but he needed the rush of a high-risk mission to feel alive.

Until now.

The whole situation with Gabby and Theo was fucked up at best, but he didn't feel the need to be elsewhere. The thrumming energy that made him want to crawl out of his skin was a memory. LA wasn't his home anymore. He took a deep breath, and for the umpteenth time on the drive, glanced over at the woman beside him. So why did it feel like he'd come home?

GABBY KEPT HER EYES CLOSED, pretending to still be asleep when Declan gently nudged her to let her know they were almost to Brentwood. It wasn't her intention to fall asleep. Was her mouth open? Did she drool? Had she snored?

"Better wake up, Angel, unless you want me to carry you."

One eye popped open. "Not happening."

His chuckle was at the same time annoying as it was endearing. That brief amusement letting her know that he was on to her tricks of avoidance.

"You haven't changed, have you?" His voice was light.

"Not sure what you mean."

"You know."

She caught him shooting her a quick glance from the corner of her eye. There was a sharp twist in her heart, a tweak of a memory, and she couldn't help the smile that tugged at the corners of her mouth.

"For all your acting skills, you still can't fake being asleep." His voice lowered. "At least not with me."

A sensation pulled low in her belly. A feeling she hadn't felt in a long time. The last time she felt it was when she first laid eyes on Declan. It had nothing to do with lust or love, but more of anticipation, a yearning for something just within her reach.

Sleep had addled her brain.

"You sound very confident." She straightened in her seat and faked a yawn.

"Gabby, Gabby," he chided. "We may have spent seventeen years apart, but you can't deny that it's still there."

What the hell did he mean? Her heart quickened its pace, and she forced a smile. "Care to enlighten me?"

"Chemistry."

Unbidden disappointment settled like a barrel on her chest. The last thing she expected was for Declan to declare undying love, but something deep inside her wondered if he still cared. That she thought about the idea infuriated her. "We're not young and stupid any longer, Dec. Chemistry can only get us so far, right?"

He didn't respond.

The silence that fell between them was thick with not quite anger, not quite annoyance, but it was uncomfortable enough for her to want to escape from the SUV. The moment he pulled the Explorer in front of the house, she flung the door open before he switched off the engine and ignored her name growled out in irritation.

Several cars were parked in the motor court. Among them was a silver Mercedes SL500 she'd recognize anywhere.

Nick was here.

The man in question strode out of the residence's double-doors. Theo followed him with Levi a step behind.

"Were you there?" Nick's usually slicked back blond hair was mussed as though he'd raked his fingers repeatedly through it. "That raid. Christ almighty. Ortega was your case, wasn't it?"

"SWAT did the heavy lifting," she said.

When Nick reached her, he pulled her immediately into a hug. "I was so worried," he muttered near her ear. His body stiffened right before they pulled apart. She glanced up to see Nick looking over her shoulder, his mouth flattening.

Having her two ex-husbands within striking distance of each other wasn't how she envisioned ending her day. Nick kept his left arm around her waist as she turned to Theo who stopped short of any physical contact.

Her brother's relaxed posture with his thumbs hooked in his belt loops belied the intense concern in his eyes. "You okay, sis?"

"What possessed you to go into work today?" Nick burst out before she could answer her brother. "You're concussed. I thought you were on leave."

"Hey, back off," Theo told ex-husband number two. "Give her a break, would you, man?"

Gabby pulled away from Nick, crossing her arms over her chest, keeping her temper in check, and just stared at him.

Nick hung his head. "Sorry. Out of line."

"Glad we have that clear. You're forgetting I'm not your wife anymore and I'm just doing my damned job."

She pushed past them to get into the house. Levi and Declan had gone off to the other side of the motor court to discuss something private.

Gabby's blood boiled. Declan was hiding something. She didn't want to open the can of worms regarding why he was at the clinic the same time her team was. So she avoided the topic. As drained as she was right now, she didn't have the mental, physical, or emotional capacity to get into a discussion with him about it. It had something to do with Claudette. The clinic was a common ground for the two women. They both had their babies born there; the difference was Gabby's didn't survive. Was Declan still insisting there was a baby swap and went to investigate?

She forced herself to wave at the teenagers huddled in the living room. They watched her walk by as if she was a performer in a high-wire act. The raid in Van Nuys was playing on the television flashing a picture of Ortega. He was rarely seen in public this past year. Their profiler said it was his way of perpetuating his myth, especially after the fentanyl attack.

When she got to her bedroom, she unbuckled her holster and deposited her gun in the nightstand drawer, then she checked messages from Division.

Nada. They were leaving her alone, but that wouldn't last. Declan's involvement was going to raise a lot of questions and she was already trying to formulate a cover up in her head if Internal Affairs got involved.

But first, she needed a shower.

She grabbed her robe and a change of underwear and headed to the bathroom. There, she let the hot spray wash away the grit of the day. As she mulled over the many questions she had for ex-husband number one, she found herself getting more and more pissed at him. Why couldn't he leave well enough alone? Why dig up the past and subject them to this emotional torture? Hadn't they gone through enough?

Why did he walk back into her life when she needed to concentrate on the biggest case of her career?

At least they got Ortega and it was looking more like he put the hit on Peter as well. It was too soon to jump to conclusions, though. She'd rarely stepped inside Peter's Beverly Hills mansion so it might be difficult to positively ID any of the items in the crime lord's possession. She'd hate to bring Theo into this, so she'd let Nadia do her magic first. And if that laptop was confirmed to be Peter's? She closed her eyes as the synapses in her brain fired wildly. She was off the case and she had plenty on her plate to manage. First of all, sleep. The shower relaxed her muscles and she could almost fall asleep on her feet.

After toweling herself dry and donning a robe, she wrapped a towel around her head and exited the bathroom.

And stopped in her tracks.

Declan was sitting on her bed, back against the headboard. His hair was wet and he was wearing a tee and athletic shorts. How long had she been in the shower?

"Glad to see you didn't drown."

"Ha ha," Gabby said with more candor than she intended. She glanced at her door. "Did you just break into my room?"

He nodded at the set of keys by the nightstand. "Not a break in if I have those."

"Having the keys doesn't give you the right to go through a locked door without permission." She instinctively tightened the belt of her robe, drawing Declan's intent gaze to the action. "What do you want?"

"Thought you wanted to talk. Explain my presence at the raid."

"You bring all kinds of trouble, don't you, Declan Roarke?"

He swung his legs to the floor, surged up and stalked toward her, erasing any smidgen of personal space. "And you take too many risks."

"You make it sound as if I was reckless. I wasn't. I was simply investigating the clinic. I had backup."

"And the cartel guys just happened to drive up?"

Despite her resolve not to mention his suspicious appearance at the clinic, she blurted out. "How about you? How do you explain your presence there?"

"I was in the neighborhood."

This pissed her off. "Damn you, Roarke. You get to know my business, but you get to keep all yours?"

"Don't turn this back on me." His voice became deceptively low, a sign that he was about to lose his temper, but Gabby had already gone through several cycles of that emotion on her own and she was beyond caring.

"It has everything to do with you!" she fumed. "You interfered in a police operation. The captain could have you arrested."

"After I helped you guys beat back the cartel soldiers?" Declan's head reared back incredulously.

"That's not the point!"

"Well, kindly explain the point."

"If you got hurt, can you imagine what hell Division would answer for?"

"Fucking hell, Gab, glad to know that your division's welfare is more important than my damned life," he derided.

"That's not fair. Stop twisting my words!" God! He was

infuriating, and she had the strongest compulsion to stomp her foot. "Clearly this is not the time to discuss this."

"This is the perfect time to discuss this." His face darkened to the color of rosewood, the vein in his neck apparent.

"I don't think so." Gabby pivoted away, indicating the end of this discussion. "Kindly leave and lock the door behind you," she threw over her shoulder.

She didn't manage one step toward the bathroom when fingers gripped her bicep and swung her back. Somehow, she expected this and something inside her snapped.

Yes, she was prepared as she gripped the wrist of the hand that was holding her, but she'd underestimated her ex-husband. Declan quickly had both her wrists manacled behind her back, and her breasts were slammed into a wall of muscle.

"I'm not some damned patrol officer you can order about," he said, eyes glittering ominously.

"Let me go," she gritted out.

"Or what, Detective?" he taunted. "You gonna arrest me?"

She struggled. But when it came to brute force, Declan was superior in strength, and he was holding her in a way that limited her movements and that angered her even more. They wrestled against each other, tightly entwined. Gabby thought she heard him groan as she strained against his body, her robe coming loose, one flap falling off her shoulder. The towel fell off her head, hair spilling out in wet curls around her face.

Suddenly he let go, stepping back, taking her in. The fury in his eyes morphed into that familiar heated lust and the area between her legs pulsed wet heat.

"Fuck this," he muttered, moving forward and grabbing both sides of her face, his mouth crashed down on hers, sparking every nerve ending in her body.

She gasped. His tongue took advantage and dipped in. Every hard part of his body molded to her softness, and she was spun, backed against the bed, and they fell on the mattress. Declan continued to kiss her feverishly. His hands roaming the contours of her body with desperation, fingers seeking the heat between her thighs and he stroked her wet folds, eliciting a moan from her.

A choked sound came from the back of his throat as he continued his exploration, one hand coming up, cupping a breast, squeezing, thumb flicking a nipple, and her whole body ignited.

He broke the kiss only to continue down her chin, her neck, and then lower. Wetness circled a nipple and Gabby couldn't help arching up for more. Meanwhile a finger entered her, sliding in and out.

"You're begging for me right here," Declan murmured as he continued to pump his fingers into her sex as his mouth moved down to her belly.

Her fingers dug into the sheets, legs thrashing in anticipation. His tongue hit her core and jolted her spine. She grabbed his head to stop him.

"Dec, we shouldn't." Her voice came out breathless.

His answer was to lick her harder and faster. His tongue speared her entrance, causing her thighs to squeeze his head. Another moan escaped her mouth as heat built in her pelvis and she was squirming for that release … and then.

Pounding on the door.

The delicious lashing of his tongue stopped, and Dec's head came up as he glanced in the direction of the interruption.

"Roarke in there?"

Theo.

"I'm going to kill that kid," Declan growled softly.

A sheen of sweat bloomed over her skin as mortification hit her. Gabby scrambled to a sitting position, glaring at Declan between her spread thighs, their position a testament to how far the situation had gotten.

"Now what?" she whispered in panic, eyes wide.

"What do you want, kid?" Dec called out.

"Have to talk to you about tomorrow's plans."

"Tell Levi. I'm not your security anymore."

"What?"

"Go ask Levi."

Gabby already gathered her robe and was getting off the bed when Declan stopped her.

"Where do you think you're going?" he asked.

"What are you doing in there with my sister?" Theo continued talking through the door.

"Declan will be out in a minute!" Gabby called.

"What are you guys doing in there?" the teenager insisted.

"That kid isn't fucking serious," Declan muttered. "Come here." He pulled Gabby toward him and gave her a quick kiss. "We're not finished."

"Oh, yes, we are," Gabby returned. "We can't do this."

"Roarke? Are you coming out?" Theo wasn't going anywhere.

"Fucking kid." Declan got off the bed and stalked toward the door, ignoring Gabby's *What do you think you're doing?*

He opened it a crack to speak to her brother. "Be with you in a minute. Go wait in the living room or be prepared to hear things you'd rather not."

Theo made a gagging sound, but Gabby heard his footsteps filter away and made a dash for the bathroom, but Dec caught her around the waist.

"Dec!"

"Where do you think you're going?"

Gabby tipped her head toward the rumpled sheets. "That shouldn't have happened."

"That's what you think? 'Coz I seem to remember you moaning and pushing that pussy against my mouth."

Her cheeks were on fire. "Don't be crass."

"Crass? You liked my dirty mouth, remember?" He

surveyed her up and down. "I don't think LA has turned you into a nun."

"Don't be hateful."

The mocking in his eyes died and his gaze dropped to the floor. "We still haven't talked about how to address my presence at the raid."

"Consultant."

His gaze snapped back to hers and a dark brow rose. "Of what?"

"I'll figure something out or you can think of something."

"I'll run it by Levi and Kade."

"Not Mr. G?"

A slow smile broke through his face. "Can't get anything by you, can I, Angel?"

"I'd like to see you try." She took a step toward the bathroom and nodded to the door. "Better see what Theo wants before he comes back ... Dad."

At his pained face, Gabby laughed. "I'm glad I have you to pawn him off to."

"He doesn't like me much," he said it with a self-deprecating twist to his mouth, but there was a flash of frustration on his face.

Gabby didn't know why she did it, but she couldn't help bumping his shoulder gently with a fist. "He'll come around."

Declan sighed. "Not sure about that." He smiled at her. "He likes you though."

Gabby didn't deny it, remembering Theo's concern when she came home. "Does it bother you?"

His brows furrowed. "Not at all. In fact ..." his words trailed off.

She cocked her head, waiting for him to elaborate.

He shook his head as if changing his mind. "You're right. He'll come around." There was something in his eyes that communicated 'later' and there was a reluctance in his gait as he headed to her door. He exited the room without looking back.

"And that's that," Gabby said to the wall, but an uneasiness coiled in her gut. Declan wanted to tell her something but changed his mind. All signs pointed that it was about Theo and she was either too tired to press him, or she was just plain chicken shit to talk about it.

13

GABBY SLEPT like the dead for twelve hours. She woke up more refreshed than she'd ever been. This wasn't new. She'd have days where she'd operate with a buzz followed by days she'd walk around like a zombie and that was when she knew a recharge was needed. Which was why she blocked everything from her mind except the need for sleep. If she didn't, she'd be useless to everyone.

Her stomach grumbled, reminding her she hadn't eaten before bed. Exiting her bedroom, she headed to the kitchen and noticed light flickering in the darkness, most likely from the television. She had an idea who it was. She'd been a teenager once.

Theo sat in the middle of a sectional sofa with earphones on, eyes focused on the screen with his hands on a gaming controller. She wondered if she should just return to her bedroom, but she was really hungry, and she'd be damned if she'd tiptoe around her brother for three months. Might as well establish a comfortable coexistence—"comfortable" being a relative term.

His eyes flicked briefly in her direction.

"Feeling better?" he asked, still riveted on the screen.

"Like a champ." She shrugged. "Concussion feels like a memory." Turning her attention to the TV, she asked, "Whatcha playing?"

"Call of Duty." He paused the game and gave her his full attention, yanking off his headphones. "You know how to play?"

Gabby shook her head. "Not really. That's Kelso's territory." She pointed to the kitchen. "Going to grab something to eat. Want anything?"

In the dim light of the living room, Theo's face was shadowed, his eyes dark, but they were studying her. "If I say I do, are you going to eat with me or retreat to the bedroom?"

"I was planning to eat with you. Bring something here. So we could kick back and chat." Gabby frowned. "Got a problem with that?"

"Nah … figured you would." Theo cocked his head. "I believe there's some of that mac and cheese left. Your Captain … Mitchell?"

"Yes?"

"His wife dropped by with some fried chicken." His teeth flashed briefly. "Sorry. We ate it all."

Gabby chuckled as she made her way to the kitchen. "Guess that's expected with teenagers in the house."

From her peripheral vision, she saw her brother rise from the couch and follow her to the kitchen. The under-cabinet lights were on, so she didn't have to fumble her way toward it. She flicked on the main switch and flooded the area with light. She took out the lone aluminum pan in the fridge and set it on the counter, and took a peek at the mac and cheese. "You guys did put a dent in this. There's probably two cups of mac and cheese left in here." She wondered why no one transferred it into a smaller container instead of squeezing the aluminum pan in the refrigerator. "You want this?"

Theo shrugged. "What will you eat?"

She glanced back into the depths of the fridge and saw

some Chinese takeout containers. Her empty stomach roiled. Nope. Not at four in the morning. She spotted a few apples in the produce drawer and her mouth watered, hoping the rest of the ingredients were handy.

Grabbing the fruit, she walked over to the pantry.

"That's not gonna hold you." The teenager informed her.

"No shit," she said. Her eyes fell on the whole-grain bread and peanut butter. "Hallelujah." She turned to Theo, a triumphant smile on her face. "I'm good with this."

Her brother looked at her doubtfully. "That'll be enough?"

"Carbs, protein, and fat," she declared. "Perfect balance."

Theo rubbed the stubble on his jaw, still not looking too impressed. "Mind if I try it with you?"

Gabby hitched her shoulders, indicating she didn't mind, while Theo put the mac and cheese back in the fridge.

A few minutes later, she had arranged several pieces of bread smeared with the organic peanut butter from the farmer's market. Then she topped them off with slices of apple. She ordered Theo to make some coffee—a no brainer — since one corner of the kitchen was a barista's dream coffee station with a setting that made a carafe of coffee at the touch of the button.

The click-clack of the coffee maker graduated to the loud grinding of coffee beans. Gabby wondered if they would wake up Declan or Levi, but maybe the cinder block walls were a good insulation against the noise. She barely heard anything from the outside when she was in her bedroom, which was good and bad, considering the situation.

"I don't think I saw Emma today," Gabby remarked as she walked over to the living room holding her platter of peanut-butter apple sandwiches.

"She didn't have any lines to rehearse," Theo mumbled, setting the coffee and a carton of milk on the coffee table. "Crap. Mugs."

Gabby switched on a lampshade and sat, eyeing her

creation. Not waiting for Theo, she took a slice and started munching. Funny how something as simple as a peanut butter toast was imminently satisfying when you hadn't eaten for eighteen hours. Her brother returned and poured the brew into a mug and handed her the milk. When she was done, he poured his own then he sat down beside her and grabbed a piece of bread, eyeing it suspiciously before taking a bite, then another.

"Well?" Gabby asked when he polished off his first slice.

He went for another one and shrugged. "It's okay."

When Gabby didn't say anything, he smirked. "What? It's nothing special. It's peanut butter and bread."

"Such appreciation," she mocked and helped herself to another one.

"Kidding," he chuckled. "It's good. Okay?"

They ate together in silence. After Gabby satisfied her gnawing hunger pangs and got more energized by the dose of caffeine, she asked, "Aren't you supposed to be laying off those video games?"

"I'm fine, *Mom.*" As soon as the words came out of his mouth, a stricken look came over his face. "Sorry. You must hate Claudette. If it's any consolation, I call her Claudette or Mother." He looked away. "I kinda get your dislike for me. You're not even really my sister and Peter kept forcing me on you to make a relationship.

"I know you and Dad had issues," he continued. "Claudette made it sound like you were a bad influence on me, which by the way is one of the reasons why she and I don't get along. At first, I believed her, but then the few times Dad talked about you, there was regret in his voice."

"He talked about me?"

Theo gave a sad smile. It pained him still to talk about Peter no matter how much he tried to hide behind a mask of teenage arrogance. "He did. He was very proud of *Dead Futures*. We watched it together, you know. When I was ten."

"You did?" she whispered, emotions for her father she thought she'd never feel again formed a lump in her throat. She released a deep breath as the first wave of grief she was waiting for swelled. She pinched the corners of her eyes.

"There it is," Theo muttered.

She shot him a questioning glance.

"I never saw you cry for Peter. You were just there at the funeral. Stoic."

Gabby was disconcerted at being called out on this. There was a lapse of silence as she considered it. "I guess that was my way of coping when it came to Peter," she said slowly. "There was resentment, you know, hurts buried deep from his abandonment. That Beverly Hills mansion was like a crypt. Money and luxury were not what I needed at that time."

"So, you married Nick."

She gave a small nod. Gabby wasn't proud of how she'd reacted. She knew Nick loved her in his own way, but he wasn't Declan. Besides, filmmaking would always be Nick's priority.

"I felt like I was tossed at sea and Nick was my lifeline. I didn't know how to cope. Losing the baby, Peter bailing. The divorce." She didn't know how to handle grief. Her own mother died in a car accident when she was three. She had no memories of her at all. Some of her father's girlfriends tried to nurture her, while others treated her like a nuisance until *Dead Futures* made her a star. She'd been pampered all her life. Claudette was Peter's fourth and last wife and was closer to Gabby's age than Peter's. Their relationship was like siblings —best friends one day, mortal enemies the next. "Peter tried to get in touch with me in the past three years. Cutting him off permanently is my one regret that I'm realizing now."

"Thought you simply didn't want anything to do with me." He gave a lopsided smile. "It's why I deliberately misbehaved at school when Peter was out of the country so you'd be forced to see me."

Gabby shook her head and gave a wry smile. "You were a pain in the ass, you know that?"

"Sorry, not sorry."

"Why am I not surprised?"

They shared a brief chuckle before she turned serious again. "I've always thought of you as my brother regardless of blood. It was just hard to look at you, you know."

"That too," he said, lifting his eyes and searching hers. "I'm surprised you didn't kick Roarke in the nuts when you saw him again."

Gabby set down her mug. "Let's get something straight. The breakdown of my marriage to your dad—"

"Sperm donor," Theo growled.

"No," she reiterated. "Claudette was right. I was the first one who stepped out on our marriage." She closed her eyes. "With Nick."

Silence.

She opened her eyes. Theo was staring at her, mouth open.

"Dec and I were having problems and it was really bad." Gabby pursed her lips, remembering. "Really bad." Her brother was still staring at her and she realized she hadn't clarified the situation. "Nothing happened between Nick and me that night. I came to my senses before it went further, but Dec's timing was the worst. Let's just say the damage was done. Irreparable." She shook her head in regret. "Declan and I ... we were young. I was barely nineteen and he wasn't even twenty. We weren't prepared for how volatile our emotions were, and we didn't know how to handle it without hurting each other."

Theo gave a brief nod.

"Anyway, I'm telling you this, because I don't want you to miss out on having a relationship with Dec." She grinned wryly. "You should give him a chance." It was on the tip of her tongue to say he was a good man. She felt he was. A cop's instinct and all, but she couldn't equivocally say that because she knew Dec had been a mercenary.

"Are you reconciling?"

"God, no," she responded instantly.

"Then why was he in your room last night?"

"We had something to discuss regarding what happened yesterday." She did her best to hold his stare.

Theo angled his head and a corner of his mouth kicked up. "Riiiight."

Gabby made a tsk sound at his teasing, batted him on his arm with the back of her hand and then leaned forward to pick up another piece of toast. "Are you going back to the studio tomorrow?"

"Maybe. Need to get clearance first from the doc. Nick's orders."

One thing she couldn't fault about ex-husband number two was he liked to play by the rules. He took care of his actors.

"Dec going with you or Levi? I might need your dad … what?" she asked when she saw the teenager grimace.

"Referring to Roarke as my dad doesn't sound right. I called our father Dad, you know. My dad has just been buried. As far as I'm concerned, it's not about blood, but the person who really cared for you."

"I agree," Gabby enunciated. "But—"

Theo cut her off by raising his palm. "Stop. Taking it slow, okay?"

"Fair enough." She'd stuck her nose in it too much already.

"And yeah, Dec said you might need him for some shit he started."

"That'd be right."

"What did he do?"

"Can't really tell you." Gabby leaned back against the sofa

and put her foot up on the table. "Maybe you should go to bed."

Theo looked at her. "That's how it's gonna be?"

"What do you mean?"

"I ask you something personal and you try to deflect or send me to my room?"

Her brow quirked up. "You're not a child. Just pointing out what the doctor ordered."

Theo jumped to his feet and stretched, a yawn overcoming him. "Guess I am tired. See ya around, sis."

14

DECLAN TURNED AWAY from the mouth of the hallway and moved down the corridor. He stopped, leaned against the wall, his knees threatening to buckle beneath him. Hearing Gabby's side of the story about Nick was a sucker punch to the solar plexus and his mind tried to wrap around the enormity of what it meant, what he needed to face.

To top it off, hearing how logical she was, how she'd taken his side, he couldn't help comparing her to the spoiled young actress she was seventeen years ago.

Somehow, he made it back to the bedroom, the tightness in the center of his chest making it difficult to breathe. The rumpled sheets on his bed recalled the sleepless night he'd had. Even reading a book couldn't take his mind off how Gabby felt in his arms, how she tasted on his tongue. But all that took a back seat to the memory of that night years ago when she broke his heart.

It was the night of the Serpentine Film Awards, only three months after Claire died. He'd been at the bar, using a fake ID to get alcohol because he wasn't old enough to drink, drowning his pain in whiskey when he should have been at home donning a tux to accompany his wife to the ceremony. Gabby had been nominated for best actress.

The awards ceremony was on the screen and he tried to ignore it. But he heard her voice.

"Where's the husband, Gabby?" the red carpet reporter asked her.

"He thinks he's coming down with the flu." For all her accolades as one of the greatest teen actresses of her generation, Gabby couldn't disguise the sarcasm in her voice. Declan tensed as she leaned into Nick, who tucked her arm into his. "Thank God Nick agreed to be my escort."

The reporter gave a fake laugh and asked them about *Dead Futures*.

They both smiled and answered questions and then posed against a wall to have their requisite pictures taken. With each flash of the camera, anger mounted inside him, his own sorrows momentarily forgotten.

Declan clenched his jaw. He should have been there with her, not that motherfucker. He signaled the bartender for another drink.

"I'm gonna have to cut you off. This is the last one."

"Whatever," Declan growled. "Just pour it."

But one more drink hadn't been enough. He left the bar and went home where he could drink in peace. He sat in front of the TV, the awards show on. He ate cold pizza, washed it down with beer and, as the night wore on, discontent festered deep in his heart.

Gabby didn't win.

At first Declan thought he was too drunk, and he'd heard the emcee call it out wrong, but as another actress took to the stage and the camera split-screened to the nominees who didn't win, his eyes were riveted on Gabby.

She was smiling big and she was clapping. But he knew her fake smile and it broke his heart to recognize the disappointment on her face even through the filter of television.

Through the alcohol haze, Declan had the strong urge to comfort her, and his anger took a back seat to the guilt that he let her down. Making up his mind to go to the after party, he checked the details on the invitation that was pinned on the kitchen cork board where they kept their schedules in sync. He quickly took a shower and put on slacks and a polo. He squirted eye drops to alleviate the redness of his eyes.

He jumped into his pickup and raced to the Bel Air villa owned by Revenant Films. Declan didn't have a problem going through as the guards recognized him. The parking valet was a different matter, his face etched in disdain as he took in the battered pickup truck. Declan had a better ride. The Maserati was a gift from Gabby right after Claire died and after Gabby had a row with Peter about withholding her earnings from the series. Money started flowing in again but as far as Declan was concerned, it was too little too late. No amount of money would bring back his sister.

The party was in full swing, he barely acknowledged Peter who was entertaining some bigwigs in the movie business. He was taller than most of the people there and scanned the crowd for his wife, knowing her hair was up in an elegant twist and that she was wearing a white off-the-shoulder dress. But what if she changed after the awards show? Frustration gnawed inside him as he ignored the eyes that followed him, the whispered conversations behind his back. The press was going to have a field day again. In the beginning of their marriage, the tabloid headlines calling him a gold digger didn't bother them. But when cash got tight and Gabby had to borrow money from a friend for Claire's funeral, the headlines were scathing. Needless to say, that friend was no longer a friend, but it only deepened the rift between him and Gabby.

But that ended now. Yes, he let his wife down, but he was here to make it right.

Gabby—his Gabby must be disappointed. She was excited to be nominated. Another stab of guilt cut to his heart. Still reeling from Claire's death, he hadn't been excited with her. Why couldn't he have pretended to feel something when she showed him the gold-embossed nomination notice?

Regret was always an afterthought. So was guilt.

"I thought you had the flu." Claudette stepped into his path, running a finger down his arm. The hair on the back of his neck stood on end—she was the last person he wanted to see.

"Have you seen Gabby?" His tone was curt.

"Oh, lover's quarrel?" She tilted her head and batted her eyes.

"If you haven't then—"

"She's busy."

"Do you or do you not know where she is?"

Claudette sighed. "I don't think she wants to be disturbed."

Something in her tone, in the way she studied her blood-red fingernails, raveled a knot of anxiety in his gut.

"Don't have time for this shit." He made to move past her.

"Last bedroom on the second floor," she said. There was almost pity in her eyes.

His chest went tight and he had to force himself to inhale and exhale as he took the steps two at a time.

The second floor was mostly empty of revelers and he walked briskly to the last bedroom. There were two facing rooms, but the door to the one on the right was slightly ajar.

He approached, heart pounding, and he pushed it open.

The light of the hallway illuminated two bodies writhing on the bed. So involved in fucking they didn't even know someone had entered the room.

"Oh, Gabby, waited so long, baby."

"Nick ...st—"

"Let me. I'll—"

"Declan?" Gabby gasped when her eyes fell on him. She couldn't see his face, but she recognized him, nonetheless.

What followed was a blur. He remembered yanking Nick off Gabby and breaking his nose, relishing the crunch of cartilage. Rage. So much rage. He spun around to deal with his cheating wife as she hastily put her dress back to rights. He gripped her shoulders and she yelped. He wanted to crush her, strangle her.

"Why?" He roared into her face before throwing her on the bed. "You fucking slut." Then he glared at Nick. "You two deserve each other."

Anger vibrated through him as he made himself walk to the door, bile rising to his throat as fury mixed with the horror that he'd been so close to hitting Gabby.

"Dec ..." her voice croaked.

He stopped at the door and turned slightly, not looking at her. He couldn't stomach the evidence of her betrayal.

"We're done," he told her in a flat voice. "I'll pack your clothes and send them to the studio. Don't you fucking come to the apartment if you know what's good for you because ...." He hissed in a ragged breath. "I might just kill you."

Steeling himself against the thought that he was leaving his wife with another man, he walked out the door, out the house full of people who never thought he was good enough, and out of Gabby's life.

HAD he judged Gabby harshly that night? Declan wondered as he realized he'd been staring sightlessly at his bed, taking a much-needed peek into the past. He walked further into the room and sank into the mattress.

"Nick ...st—"

Did Gabby try to stop Nick? Had second thoughts? Declan never got the full story from her. But did it matter now? Pride destroyed their relationship. They both were at fault with what happened to their marriage. He realized that over the years when the Army made a man out of the boy, far away from the glitz and glamour of Hollywood.

Sleeping around for revenge wasn't in the cards for him because he didn't trust women even for a one-night stand. Even when Gabby married Nick, he didn't go on the rebound. Instead, he gave his best to the Army and was fast-tracked for Ranger school.

The rest was fucking history.

There'd been women eventually. Some were faceless one-night-stands and others were short-term girlfriends. Certainly no one became close enough for him to want commitment.

Bitterness had slowly faded away and he thought he'd put the past behind him. But seeing Gabby again turned his world upside down. This infuriated him, as well as gave him relief that he hadn't become too jaded. That he hadn't turned into someone like Garrison who'd throw his own mother under a bus if it was for the fucking greater good.

So what should he do now?

The dawn light filtered through the slats of the blinds. Sunrise was a few minutes away. There were so many things he wanted to tell Gabby. Many times since yesterday morning, he almost blurted out that Theo was their son. He didn't want to keep it from her, yet he was at a loss on how to break it to her. Instinct was telling him now was the time before she got embroiled in finding the evidence to keep Ortega off the streets.

They needed to talk away from this house.

He knew just the place.

Griffith Park was a Los Angeles landmark located right smack in the middle of the city. It's known for the Observatory and it's one of the best places to see the famed Hollywood sign. A little less famous was the vintage carousel built in the 1920s that inspired Walt Disney to create Disneyland.

For Declan, it was the place he and Gabby went on hikes and picnics. Their relationship thrived when they shunned the places the Hollywood elite were known to haunt. He and Gabby had been happy preparing their meals at home and taking them some place to eat. She was naturally empathetic to what he needed. She let him be the man when he pursued her and didn't throw her wealth and popularity at him.

"So I think I know where you're taking me," Gabby cautiously said beside him. Declan glanced at her, giving her his mysterious smile which she pretended to hate. It still had that effect on her and she laughed nervously, and he imagined, gave him an eye roll.

They took her Honda and left Levi to watch over Theo even though the threat levels were reduced since Ortega had been taken into custody.

The SUV made a turn on Crystal Springs Drive and Gabby sucked in a deep breath. "What are you doing, Declan?" There was a sadness in her tone that made him want to hit the gas so they could get to their destination sooner and have their talk.

"Making things right."

"I don't want to dig into our past again."

"But you already did. I heard your talk with Theo."

She didn't respond for several seconds, and then, "You were eavesdropping?"

"Yes."

"Unbelievable," she huffed. "What were you doing awake anyway?"

"Couldn't sleep."

That shut her up, probably because to ask why was useless. That had always been Gabby. She didn't ask useless questions, but he could hear her thinking. The sun was already rising on the horizon as he guided the vehicle to the parking for the merry-go-rounds. He knew it didn't open until ten that day.

They both got out of the vehicle and unlike the last time

they'd been here, they simply walked side by side instead of wrapped up in each other's arms.

Gabby stopped walking and he turned to look at her.

Tears welled in her eyes; her lips trembled. "Why bring me here, Dec?"

"Because this was the place I asked you for forever," he stated softly.

"Forever was a lie," she whispered.

"Only because my pride got in the way." He closed what little distance was between them and put his hands on her shoulders. "Forgive me, Angel. I don't know if you can. I fucked up our marriage."

"Why are you taking all the blame?"

Dec glanced at the merry-go-round. The sun's rays hit its roof and illuminated the antique gold. Without saying another word, he urged her forward, an arm keeping her close to his side.

She leaned into him, much to his relief.

When they reached the ancient ride, he boosted her up on a marble pony as he leaned against it. There was something magical about a structure that had withstood the test of time. That was why he proposed here.

She wrapped her hands around the pole and rested her head there. "What if you never heard me talk to Theo? Would we be having this conversation?"

"I'll admit knowing you stopped Nick facilitated our talk, but I've been meaning to have it out with you anyway."

At her doubtful look, he said, "You're a detective, Gabby. Figure out why I injected myself into a police operation if it wasn't because I care for you. And last night? You think I'd simply lose control like that?"

"Sex was never our problem."

"I pushed you away physically and emotionally when Claire died."

"That hurt me more than you know. I was supposed to be the person you turned to. For better or worse, remember?"

He nodded tightly, thinking about what his grown-up self would say to his younger version. Probably smack him upside the head. "I'm partly to blame. Driving you to seek comfort in another man's arms." The image flashed through his mind again and he scrubbed his hand over his face. Tumultuous emotions reared inside him, jealousy that another man had touched his wife, and anger at himself for making it easy for Nick to move in.

Was that why he wanted to rip Nick's head off yesterday, and why he almost had sex with Gabby? Re-stake his claim?

"Have you really forgotten and forgiven?" Gabby asked.

Declan turned away to stare at the tree line surrounding the park. Joggers, walkers, and dog owners started their morning activities.

"I have. I have no anger left against you, if that's what you mean." He stretched an arm up against a pole and gave it his weight. "The moment I laid eyes on you again, I knew I've never gotten over you."

A suppressed sob sounded beside him. It was as hard for her to hear as it was for him to get the words out. He needed to regroup a bit before he dropped to his knees and begged her to take him back. Somehow he knew he had to go slow, so he went with humor and a side of cocky.

When he turned back to face her, his mouth was turned into a slight smirk. "Can you honestly say you've moved on from me?"

The melancholy left her eyes and outrage flashed in them.

Good. He didn't want sad Gabby. He wanted her vibrant, but not defiant. Damn, it was like navigating a tightrope.

Tread carefully, Roarke.

"I didn't do too bad, did I?" she defended. She straightened from her seat and glared at him. "I happen to be a good detective. Check my closure rate."

He leaned against a horse and crossed his arms and ankles. "Is that right? I've seen your apartment. You call that moving on?" Declan felt like a hypocrite knowing his own condo didn't fare any better, but she didn't know that.

"I just happen to like the minimalist lifestyle. What's wrong with that?" She got down from her figurative and literal high horse to step into his face. "I've found gratification in the job I do. I speak for the dead who needs justice. It's more than I can say for the work you do."

"Hey, no harping on my job."

"If the shoe fits."

"I can show you what else can fit."

Her luscious lips tilted into a smile. Even without lipstick they had an appealing rosy color. And the generous lips begged to be wrapped around his erection.

His dick stirred to life.

Down boy.

It didn't help that Gabby's eyes lowered to his crotch.

"My eyes are up here, Angel."

This time it was her turn to smirk. "Oh, don't pretend you didn't do that on purpose."

He uncrossed his arms to grab her, but she bounced out of his reach.

"No. Stop." She raised a hand between them. "Spell it out for me exactly what you want. I know you think just because I'm a detective, I'm an expert in reading between the lines, but nothing beats going on record."

Declan chuckled. "Jesus, you drive a hard bargain."

"What?" Her brow raised. "You can't draw me into your sexy web and then throw a restraining order at me." Her eyes were full of accusation.

His amusement fled. "That was the second biggest mistake of my life."

Her throat bobbed. "And the first?"

Damn, she really did want him to spell it out. "The divorce. Leaving you."

She turned away from him. Her arms wrapped around herself as she rubbed her biceps. "It wasn't a mistake."

He tensed. "What?"

"We were too young, Declan. For the love we had. We both needed to experience the world. Grow up. You needed to get out of LA and be the man you were meant to be. I had to find my own way without my dad's influence."

He took a step toward her, resting his hands on her shoulders and eased her around to face him. "And now? Are we ready for each other now?"

"I'm scared, Dec," she whispered, eyes clouding. "Afraid to feel so much again. Losing the baby and losing you. I almost never came back from that."

"But you did," he growled. "You came back stronger. I wasn't good enough for you then," he said. "I can be that man for you now."

"How do you explain Claudette—" her statement cut off, and her eyes went past his shoulder. Declan felt it too, someone's eyes on them and he turned.

"That's Nurse Bristow, but who's with him?"

Two men approached from the parking lot.

"Garrison," he growled.

15

WHAT THE HELL was going on, and why was Bristow with the spook? The two formed an incongruous duo that didn't compute in Declan's brain. Was something wrong with Gabby that was held back?

"Who's Garrison?" Gabby asked in a matter-of-fact voice.

"He sent me here."

"Sent you here to spy on me?"

"If that was the case, I didn't know."

They had this conversation without looking at each other. He was frustrated that Garrison's timing just derailed his progress in breaking down Gabby's walls. He could already feel her withdrawing from him.

As the newcomers came closer, Bristow called out, "Hey, Detective. Roarke."

"You don't work for ESS, do you?" Gabby eyed the man beside the nurse.

"No. John Garrison, ma'am," he held out his hand. "I work with, rather than for, Roarke's company."

After handshakes were exchanged, Garrison turned to Declan. "Have you told her anything?"

"Anything could be anything," Declan replied. "But, no."

He could feel Gabby's glare on the side of his face, so he glanced at her. "Time and place, detective."

Declan ground his molars at the way he addressed her. It was a force of habit. Turning things impersonal when he didn't know what the hell was going on, especially around someone like Garrison who could exploit a weakness.

But the man didn't get to the top of the CIA game without being astute. "Having a lover's tryst?"

"We were discussing something personal, yes," Declan informed him. "So, none of your business."

"As personal as when you injected yourself into a police operation?" Garrison shot back, eyes glittering. "When you misused the ID I gave you for *personal* use."

"Mr. Garrison, need I remind you that you are in the presence of a police officer and you are referring to a fake ID Declan used to impersonate a cop. The FBI wouldn't do that without informing us," Gabby said. "The CIA, though and I'm assuming that's who you work for"—her chin inched up in challenge—"cannot operate in the homeland except through a federal or local partnership. Get in line and get off Declan's back. If we're going to work together here, you need to fill us in on what you know."

At that moment, Declan was on Gabby's side, proud of her for standing up to John and unfazed by the man's position in the CIA, showing she had the balls and grit to hack it in a profession dominated by men.

"You tell them, detective," Bristow added his two cents, his eyes quietly laughing.

"Well," Garrison cleared his throat and looked around. "I doubt there are any bugs around here. It's as good a place to tell you what we know."

"First, I want to know what he's doing here?" Declan asked, tipping his chin at Bristow. He wanted any health crises concerning Gabby out of the way.

"Was there anything wrong with my x-ray?" Gabby asked

the nurse. "Did you suddenly find out I have superpowers and that's why you brought in the CIA to haul me in?"

Garrison smiled tightly.

"Oh god," Gabby whispered, her hand automatically reaching for Declan's arm, and he steadied her. "Tell me."

"Fuck, sorry about that," Garrison muttered. "Nothing to do with your health, detective." He paused, "At least not with your concussion."

"You're not making sense, Mr. Garrison," Gabby said.

"Ortega was in possession of a biological weapon that we believe was part of the cache your team confiscated in the raid yesterday."

"You mean chemical," she corrected. "Our case is about the fentanyl aerosol."

"We know that," Garrison reiterated. "But Z-91 is a derivative of the Ebola virus and we believe it's been weaponized."

Gabby's face paled. "What?" She checked her phone. "There's nothing from Division except to show up for a field investigator interview at eleven."

"Homeland Security plans to make an announcement today. Everyone who's been in contact with Ortega is required to take the vaccine," Bristow said. "That's why I'm here."

Gabby looked at the nurse strangely, probably wondering as much as Declan how long Bristow had been working for Garrison.

"How contagious is it?" Declan asked. "Claudette wasn't sure because she said she heard it secondhand from her bodyguard."

"Claudette?" Gabby screeched. "What has Claudette got to do with this?" Her calm reception of Garrison seemingly dissipated at the involvement of her former stepmother.

"Ms. Dumont was either a complicit or an unwitting accomplice to an arms deal," Garrison informed her.

Gabby turned on Declan. "You knew about this?"

"Not until yesterday."

"And you didn't tell me?"

"I wasn't sure until I got it out of her."

"Oh my god, Declan. You should have said something."

"That was why I was trying to contact Garrison."

Gabby backed away from them, eyes furious. "You put everyone who was there in danger."

"Homeland Security was informed of this threat," Garrison said. "It was up to them to disseminate the information. Not our place to tell local law enforcement directly."

"But Claudette told you." Her eyes shifted to Declan.

"It was secondhand information. I had no proof," he gritted out.

"Still not his place to inform you," Garrison said. "Depending on how you received it and where you'd gone with the information, you could cause a panic."

"Do I look like someone who'd go cause a mass panic?" Gabby snarled.

"Gabby, calm down," Declan said. "Things were just moving too fast."

"You can say that again," Bristow mumbled.

Something in the way Garrison and the other man exchanged glances sent a riff of unease up Declan's spine.

"What exactly is going on?" he asked.

Garrison's jaw hardened. "It's our belief that Ortega had ingested the virus."

"What?" Gabby and Declan exclaimed at the same time.

"He's infected with Ebola."

DECLAN WAS SPEEDING down the 101 to get to GHD. They all piled into Gabby's vehicle so everyone could get updated on all fronts. Garrison sat beside him, but he kept his ears peeled to the conversation Gabby was having with her partner on the phone.

"Yes, everyone," she told Kelso. "Everyone who has ever had contact with Ortega since the raid."

Bristow was in the backseat with Gabby. They marched … or rather sprinted after her when she raced to her Honda, wanting to get to Division quickly. Declan drove while she made all the calls she needed to make. He found it curious that she let Garrison ride shotgun. She was directly behind Declan's seat so maybe it made sense. She could talk to the guard at the gate when they got to her building.

"I have no time to explain. I don't have a lot of information myself. Yes! Thanks." She hung up and scooted between the console. "Kelso is organizing everyone together and activating the bioterrorism protocol. The SWAT will take care of their own for quarantine. Screw Homeland Security. They can take my badge later. I'm not sitting on this information now that the virus could be out there.

"I'm putting my neck on the line scaring the shit out of everyone at Division, and maybe half of the LAPD leadership," Gabby said. "I get why this information needed to be handled delicately, but if someone doesn't explain how Claudette is involved, then you guys better be scrambling for bail money."

"Ms. Dumont carried the virus into the country," Garrison said.

"What?" she gasped.

"She had a long clandestine relationship with Ortega behind your father's back," he said. "One could say it was a physical and emotional affair, and a business partnership. I don't have confirmation of any of that." Garrison glanced at Declan. He didn't give the CIA officer the details of what Claudette told him, so John had jack shit to tell Gabby. "All we know is that the Z-91 biological weapon was destined for an arms dealer operating in South America. But Ortega reneged on the deal and decided to screw with everyone who's trying to overthrow him or bring him down."

"That's a lot of risk for revenge."

"He's a megalomaniac. He wants to do things big and leave an impression." Disgust colored Garrison's voice. "Hence, the shopping mall fentanyl attack."

"Captain Mitchell …" she whispered.

"Yes. I believed their enmity has spanned almost two decades."

"His son's friend was a snitch. Ortega found out and killed the captain's son and friend in a drive by."

"And since Mitchell couldn't get to Ortega, he went for his associates and made it difficult for them." Garrison turned in his seat to look at Gabby. "Mitchell took you in and used your own tragedy to fuel his own vendetta against the crime lord."

"The Cap may have a personal stake in seeing Ortega off the streets," Gabby said. "But he's a fair man. He's pushed the line sometimes, but Frank sacrificed any promotion due him so he could stay connected to the streets and not sit in a pretty office on the sixth floor, embroiled in politics. He could have been chief of police ten years ago, if he wanted that."

"Sounds more like a crusade to me—"

"You don't know him—"

"G, just shut it, okay?" Declan growled. He was also trying to work out how to tell Gabby that her ex-stepmother was in a way responsible for her father's death, but that would involve divulging the truth about Theo's parentage. He needed to grab some coffee somewhere, but it looked like the Division's brew was gonna be it. Knowing now about Mitchell's son, he realized how many lives the crime kingpin of LA had destroyed. Garrison might have a point regarding Ortega taking the fight to the cops.

"Still doesn't make sense that he'd risk his life," Declan said.

"Ortega?" Garrison asked.

"Yes."

"His cancer is terminal," the CIA officer told him. "This is his FU to the LAPD. He's taking as many down with him as he can."

Gabby was quiet.

Their eyes met in the rearview mirror. She looked like she was about to throw up.

"Headache, Angel?"

"I'm fine." She edged to the window so he couldn't see anything but the top of her head.

"We're almost there," Declan said. "We'll get everyone immunized and it'll be okay, right, Bristow?" He tried to keep the doubt from his voice, knew it wasn't that simple, but someone needed to inject some positive to the gloom and doom saturating the air in the vehicle.

When Bristow didn't answer, he cut his gaze to the rearview mirror again and met the nurse's stare. "Right?"

"Theoretically."

Declan's fingers tightened on the steering wheel as he changed lanes seeing their exit ahead. "What do you mean?"

"The vaccine has an eighty-five percent efficacy and has only been tested on the Congolese and Liberians," he paused. "Honestly? I'm putting it at fifty-fifty."

"Those aren't very good odds," Gabby said. "How about people we've come in contact with?" She thought of Theo and Levi.

"If you came in contact with Ortega yesterday, you're still within the forty-eight hour safe zone," Bristow said. "We'll do a blood kit to be sure. Our bioterrorism trailer is on its way to Seventy-seventh street. I've texted the driver where to go. How soon will we arrive?"

"We'll be at Division in under ten," Declan replied. And that was ten minutes too long.

16

An eighteen-wheeler was parked beside the gates housing GHD. The bioterrorism trailer contained equipment that could rapidly check for contagions.

Kelso was standing by the guard house and met them before they hit the gates.

Gabby rolled down the window. "Everyone here?"

"Just about."

"Ortega?"

"They're bringing him in a specialized ambulance," Kelso said. "Waiting for you guys to arrive. Would have appreciated a heads-up with this trailer showing up."

Gabby's partner moved to his window. "Roarke," Kelso greeted, but his eyes were on Garrison, so he made the introductions.

"Sorry about springing the eighteen-wheeler on you," Garrison said in a no-way apologetic tone. "But we need to move this party along." The CIA officer nodded pointedly to the pedestrians taking an interest in the semi-trailer truck.

"You'll have to sign here," the guard told Kelso who signed the clipboard while Gabby initialed beside his signature.

"We're doing this at GHD?" Gabby asked.

"Yup. Cleared other departments to the other building as a precaution."

As their vehicle passed the gates, Declan took a survey of the compound that housed the GHD. He remembered Gabby saying that they shared their building with an LAPD forensics lab. The other building was being used by the special Vice task force. She directed them to the one-story building that was typical of the construction in the seventies with red brick and concrete blocks.

The medical trailer pulled into the far end of the parking lot.

"Bristow has respirator masks," Garrison said. "Use them before entering the building."

Everyone complied.

When they entered the building, Mitchell was talking to Chen who scowled at the newcomers. The detective's partner, who Declan remembered as Delgado, was standing beside him. He smiled at Gabby, but speared Declan and Garrison with the same chilly look that Chen awarded them. Delgado's initial appreciation of his help yesterday had dissipated with the knowledge that he had used a fake badge.

"What we got?" Gabby asked as she joined the huddle.

"Let's head to the war room," Mitchell said, his eyes landing on Garrison. "You the spook?"

"John Garrison," the man beside him replied. "And I wasn't here."

Mitchell nodded briefly. "Someone needs to liaise with our department. The feds are busy briefing the governor."

"They're probably scared to show up here," Delgado piped in.

Everyone chuckled, but there was no humor in their tone.

"Well?" Mitchell prompted, his eyes landing on Declan.

What the fuck?

"Guess it's you, Roarke," Garrison muttered.

Gabby, who was talking to Chen, glanced over. "That'll work, especially since you stuck your nose in our op anyway."

"Dammit," Garrison mumbled. "Guess you're really up. Nice job, Roarke."

If this was the only repercussion he had to face from his actions yesterday, then he was more than willing to step up.

Declan dipped his chin in an affirmative.

Satisfied, Mitchell turned back to his team and the group moved into a big room with a row of two open bullpens, each desk separated by low partitions on three sides, with its opening against the aisles. It allowed the cops to stand up and confer over the partition or slide around in a chair to talk to a person further down the row.

Gabby picked up a folder from her desk and as Declan passed it, he noticed a map of Los Angeles with red pins stuck to some areas, as well as post-it notes with phone numbers. A tall coffee mug and a stress ball sat on her desk. No photographs just like her house.

Garrison nudged him lightly as he passed him. "Keep the puppy-eyed look for later."

Declan glared at his friend. "Fuck you."

They entered a room with a wide conference table surrounded by wall-to-wall white boards. Link charts of different cases were scrawled on the surface as well as images held up by magnets. Mitchell walked to one featuring a picture of Ortega, and mugs of his known associates. Several dates and events were listed beneath it and one encircled in red was the fentanyl aerosol attack.

Mitchell added a line below it. "Possible Ebola."

"I've received a high-level briefing from the feds," Mitchell started, momentarily distracted by other officers and detectives entering the room, bringing their number to twenty. "The San Fernando Valley Police Department is holding their own briefings. Their patrol officers were involved in the raid yesterday but didn't have direct physical contact with our suspect. Chen and I interviewed Ortega in an interrogation room. He didn't look healthy at all, but we found chemotherapy drugs at the raid yesterday and we've known he has cancer which we thought would account for his physical condition when we arrested him." He paused, his jaw tightening. "Last night, before the Lieutenant and I stood to leave, he slumped over and was running a low-grade fever."

Declan was braced against a wall behind Gabby who was seated at the table. She straightened in her seat and leaned forward, alert.

"Ortega was immediately admitted to a hospital. We thought he was battling an infection due to reduced immunity from the chemo drugs, but we were informed early this morning via an emergency call from Homeland Security that he is in possession of a bioweapon. This has been confirmed by Detective Woodward. Thankfully, Ortega had been kept in an isolation room at the jail so he had little to no contact with the other inmates." Mitchell tilted his chin toward Roarke and Garrison. "Declan Roarke is our contact with the feds."

"Is it really Ebola?" one of the detectives asked.

"Nadia is analyzing the glass pearls contained in a pelican case we recovered from yesterday's raid," Mitchell said. "They're the size of golf balls. Our first thought was that this was another medium for weaponized fentanyl, so we delayed its analysis, making sure we have our I's dotted and T's crossed, so we can use it as evidence in court. SWAT and GHD were able to perform the raid yesterday with Ortega's outstanding arrest warrant, but the search warrant for the raid was retroactively approved this morning and Nadia immediately got to work with the knowledge that this could be Ebola."

As if on cue, the door to the war room opened again and a woman Declan recognized from yesterday's raid stepped in. She wasn't a woman easy to forget with her sleeve tattoo on one arm, Goth makeup, and pale skin. She talked with Gabby briefly after the raid, and her contrast against Gabby's natural olive skin was distinctive.

"Nadia, you have something for us?" Mitchell asked.

"I've conferred with my contact at the CDC," Nadia said. "The genetic code of the liquid in the pearl I tested matched several benchmarks of the Ebola virus, but we both agree, it was modified. To what extent, I am still testing."

"How contagious is it?" Delgado asked. "Have we infected our family?"

"Your family is fine. Ebola has an r naught of 1.5 to 2 which is unimpressive," Nadia said. "That's because it's not airborne and transmission is only through bodily fluids only when a person exhibits symptoms."

"Where are the rest of the pearls?" Garrison asked.

"Excuse me," Nadia's brow arched. "Who are you?"

The CIA officer didn't say anything and merely treated the CSI tech to a penetrating stare.

"Garrison is with the feds."

"The pelican case and its contents need to be turned over to us," Declan said.

"Now wait a minute," Chen spoke up. "We worked our asses off to get Ortega. Those pearls? That's evidence to nail his ass on local terrorism charges which will carry a heavier penalty than the original RICO shit the feds wanted us to pin on him."

"I doubt Homeland Security will leave something like this in your hands for long," Declan replied. "Where is it exactly, Ms. Powell?"

Nadia's eyes widened when Declan said her last name. They weren't introduced, but he'd spied her nameplate when she walked in. She probably realized this after the fact when her face relaxed. "I have it in my lab's containment unit." She turned to Mitchell. "What do you want me to do, Captain?"

"Expect we'd be receiving a direct request from the CDC to transfer this into their custody," Mitchell blew out a breath.

"I agree with Roarke. A bioweapon of this magnitude is beyond our ability to handle." Mitchell's gaze turned to Declan and Garrison. "I expect you guys have more information?"

He turned to Garrison who shook his head. "We can't share that intel with the whole room—"

There were varying degrees of protests and agreements.

"That's bullshit," Delgado growled. "You should have shared that information sooner. You put people's lives at stake by withholding it."

"Time and place, Delgado," Kelso spoke up.

"Then what the hell is the purpose of this meeting?"

"We're waiting—" Mitchell started when Bristow stepped in.

"Most of you are familiar with Hank Bristow," Mitchell said. "Our favorite nurse seemed to be holding out on us and works with the feds. As a precaution, and for everyone's peace of mind, he and his team will be taking blood samples from each of us to check for the virus with a new test that could detect it before the onset of symptoms. Should take a few hours, I believe?"

Bristow nodded.

"In the meantime, we request that no one leaves. Food and refreshments will be brought in throughout the day. We won't be confiscating your phones. I trust you all know the panic that would ensue if news of this leaks out prematurely. If you break that trust, I'll confiscate your badge instead—permanently," Mitchell said. "Woodward, Kelso, please step into my office. You too, Nadia, and bring the laptop." The captain walked up to Declan and Garrison. "Now is a good time to tell me everything you know."

"Cap," Chen started. "You can't leave me out of it."

"Yes, I can," Mitchell said. "I've been instructed by Homeland Security to keep this case as tight as possible but will let you know once I can share."

"Why them?" the lieutenant snarled.

"Know your place, L-T," Mitchell responded quietly. "That's an order."

———

GABBY DIDN'T KNOW what Mitchell had to say that the other detectives couldn't hear. She sat down in front of the captain's desk, while Declan took the position behind her, his hands on her shoulders, giving them a squeeze. That only served to make her more anxious. This had something to do with Claudette, and with Nadia holding Peter's laptop—the laptop from the raid—she was sure that her ex-stepmother was involved in her father's death. Did she pay Ortega and put a hit on him? Why? Because Theo was becoming very popular and she wanted control of his fortune?

When Mitchell's eyes locked with hers in an expression of sympathy, she could feel emotion push up against her throat, a tightening that felt like she was choking.

"Gabby," the captain said and nodded to the computer in Nadia's hands. "That laptop did belong to Peter."

A sob that she was holding in escaped her lips briefly, but Declan squeezed her shoulders again and this time it gave her support.

"Because of that, we were able to establish that Ortega did order a hit on Peter. He ordered the attack on you and Theo. We can even establish probable cause, but we're missing some pieces." Mitchell looked at Declan. "We're hoping you have the answers."

"I do."

Gabby craned her neck and glared at him. "You knew all along?"

"I've been trying to tell you, but the timing was never right."

The blood drained from her face, and she turned back to Mitchell. "Please go on."

"We've tried to piece the documents in chronological order," Mitchell said. "Right after your father divorced Claudette, he ordered a DNA test for him and Theo. According to Nadia, the results proved that Theo Woodward received only 22% of his genetic makeup from your father."

"That means—" Gabby broke off, trying to understand what the captain was telling her.

"Theo is his grandson," Mitchell confirmed. "We also found a copy of a DNA report that simply says Raul Ortega doesn't match the DNA of a subject. We're assuming it was also on Theo. This was more recent. The date of the report was a few days before the attack on your vehicle."

"The personal items," she whispered. "That's what they took from the house. They also killed Peter. But why did Ortega think that Theo was his son?"

Her captain glanced up at Declan. "Roarke, care to fill in the rest?"

"Claudette was having an affair with Ortega. From what I understand, the man was obsessed with her and got her pregnant. Threatened to kill her if she had an abortion," Declan said the words rapidly, as if he'd been holding on to them for a while.

"You were right? She swapped our babies?" Gabby's eyes filled with tears. "Did her baby die?"

Declan nodded. "Her baby died in her womb two days before she called you to Van Nuys. She already had an arrangement with the doctor at the Our Lady of Lourdes clinic. Apparently, he was also Ortega's doctor at that time and was the one providing Claudette's prenatal checkups and reporting her progress to the crime lord. The doctor was terrified himself and was the one who suggested the switch to Claudette since she was also panicking. The mugging was the perfect excuse to explain her going into labor at the same time as you did."

"I want to apologize, Gabby," Mitchell said quietly. "I was the detective on your case and we focused on the attack on two pregnant women. We were so outraged by it that we didn't even consider that another crime was committed at the clinic."

Her eyes locked with Declan's and lowered when he crouched in front of her. There was a cautious look on his face, yet it was tender. He picked up her hands that were clenched into fists and loosened her fingers, intertwining them with his.

"Angel," he said gently. "Theo is our son."

She saw the truth in his eyes and now she had the evidence. *Oh, god. Theo was her son, the baby she thought she lost.*

The choking feeling worsened, her lungs constricted, and she needed to escape.

"I ... I can't ..." she choked. She wrenched her fingers from his grasp and sprang toward the door, yanking it open and sprinting out. There were people in the hallway— colleagues—and they looked at her curiously and then behind her from where she'd fled.

She ran past Chen.

"Where are you going?" he called. "You can't leave!"

She bumped into Bristow.

"Detective Hottie, ready for your blood test?"

"Not now, Bristow." She went around the nurse, stumbling, needing air. She couldn't breathe. The damned respirator was killing her. Pushing the exit bar open, she yanked down her mask and sucked in oxygen. She fell back against the wall, bent forward, and rested her hands on her knees.

The exit door opened again, and she knew it was Declan, but she couldn't look at him. She was drawn back into the vortex of feelings of that day everyone abandoned her. An event that also alienated her from her father.

Was that why Peter tried to reach out to her after his divorce from Claudette?

"He tried to contact me," she whispered. "I didn't give him a chance. Why wasn't he more insistent?" Her voice rose angrily. "Why didn't he just force me to listen to him?"

Declan leaned against the wall beside her, not touching her. "Maybe he wasn't quite willing to let Theo go as his son."

"And me?" she said angrily. "I was his daughter. He didn't have any problem leaving me, did he? The idea that I tanked *Dead Futures* outweighed the fact that he left me. Did he even care what he put me through? Was that what the will was all about? Absolution for his abandonment? Well, fuck him!"

"Gabby ..."

"How did he expect me to simply forgive that? He started a new family somewhere else!"

"I don't think he expected you to forgive him, Gabby, but he didn't want you to go on blaming Theo for his shortcomings."

"I never blamed Theo." Her eyes slid shut. "He was just hard to be around because he reminded me of you." Then an unbidden smile touched her lips. "But the kid found ways to ingratiate himself in my life."

She opened her eyes to see a smile curve the corner of Declan's mouth, then he turned serious. "From Claudette's conversations with your dad, she wasn't sure if Peter had straight out told Ortega that Theo wasn't his son. But things were tense between the two."

Another thought about her former stepmother nagged at her mind. "You didn't sleep with Claudette again, did you?"

Unlike Declan's reaction the last time when she insisted he must have slept with Claudette, an almost relieved expression crossed his face. "I was telling the truth. She knew you were coming to see me, and I was desperate enough to fake sleeping with her to get you out of my life."

The stab of pain in her heart must have shown in her eyes

for he quickly added, "It hurt to look at you then, Gabby," he said. "I felt like a failure. First as Claire's brother, and then as your husband. I thought I've hit rock bottom when I've alienated you after Claire died, but finding you in bed with Nick sent me straight to hell."

"What are you saying? That you and Claudette staged the scene at the apartment?"

"Yes." Declan averted his eyes, a muscle ticked at his jaw. "Not proud of what I did. How I let that woman manipulate me." He glanced back at her. "I regret hurting you like that."

Gabby blew out a breath and with it another weight was lifted off her chest. She couldn't believe how twisted their marriage had become. No wonder it didn't survive. This reaffirmed what she told Declan that morning at the carousel. They'd been too young to deserve the love they had in the past and that left a question. Were they ready now?

Unable to process that question on top of all the revelations battering her that day, she changed the subject. "I just ran out of there." Gabby jerked her head toward the door. "Maybe Nadia had more she could tell us. Breadcrumbs of their pissing contest at least. What else would cause Ortega to throw caution to the wind and have a prominent Hollywood player killed?"

"That's the million-dollar question, isn't it?"

Another thought occurred to her and anxiety rippled through her as she stared at Declan. "Shit. What do I do? Do we tell Theo that I'm his mother?"

"Of course we do!" Declan's eyes flashed in irritation. "Why would you ask that?"

"I don't know, all right?" Her voice rose. "I'm scared. What if he hates me? I mean … I can't just feel like a mom."

"Welcome to the club," Declan muttered.

Gabby laughed, albeit, not entirely in humor, but with a little bit of terror. She hugged her arms. "I don't know, Dec.

I'm glad I don't actually hate him, you know. Just tried not to feel anything for him."

"Oh, I don't know. I think you guys were bonding this morning."

"I don't know if I can—"

Hands gripped her shoulders, turning her toward him and his head dipped, emerald eyes blazing deeply into hers. "We're in this together, Angel. Theo doesn't need a mother. He needs you and he needs you to acknowledge that you're family."

"We," Gabby said. "No matter what happens between us, I'll never make it difficult for you to know your son."

"Our son," he said, giving her a reminder shake.

Gabby shook her head, unable to speak through the giant size boulder lodged in her throat.

"We have a son," she whispered. The tears she'd been holding back finally streamed down her cheeks.

"Heaven help us," Declan chuckled.

She punched him lightly on the chest before resting her face on it. He held her through her shifting emotions of joy, sadness, bittersweet fury, and back to joy.

The exit door opened again, and she heard Declan murmur to someone. Gabby didn't care who saw her crying on her ex-husband's chest.

The shell around her heart cracked open and tentative tendrils of hope sneaked through. And hope was what everyone needed right now.

17

KILLING someone in cold blood had never crossed her mind until today.

Watching Raul Ortega struggle to breathe while lying on a cot in his cell didn't even come close to giving her the satisfaction she needed. Floor-to-ceiling safety glass took the place of prison bars. The holding cell was big enough to accommodate a portable patient monitor.

The captain allowed her to see Ortega after she and Declan gave their blood samples. She'd been watching the crime lord for over ten minutes, not saying a word, letting her hatred of him drive her thoughts to a morbid turn.

Maybe she had a fever.

Some of the guys in the war room looked flushed, their temperatures were elevated and they'd been separated from the rest of the group. Bristow was cautiously optimistic that their response was simply mass hysteria, which wouldn't be unusual under the circumstances.

Ortega shifted on his cot; his skin was almost purple and glistened with sweat. He turned his head and opened his eyes. A ghost of a smile touched his mouth.

"Detective Woodward," he said. "This is an honor." He

heaved himself to a sitting position. Swiping under his nose, his hand came away with blood. He sighed as he reached for a tissue on the makeshift nightstand beside him. "If I'd known this was going to be messy, I wouldn't have exposed myself to the virus."

Gabby didn't say anything.

That seemed to irritate Ortega. "I despise the silent treatment. Talk to me. Tell me how much you admire my cunning for running circles around the LAPD all these years."

"Not so untouchable now, are you?" she asked.

"I blame the chemo," he returned. "Fried some of my brain cells."

"I know what you did," Gabby pushed the words out with difficulty. This bastard would not see how much he'd hurt her.

Ortega's eyes grew shifty. "The shopping mall incident. Bah, I was making a statement to your mayor. Thinks I'll give up LA." He gave a brief snort which ended in a coughing fit. More blood. "I'll tell you this. Better me than the cartel. I have no proof, but I know someone in the cartel has his ear."

Gabby had heard that rumor but pushed it away so she could state her purpose. "I know you killed my father. I know about your affair with Claudette."

The man's shoulders stiffened, and he glowered at her, his mouth curling, baring teeth. "*La puta.* She sang like a canary, didn't she?"

Gabby pushed back from the wall and approached the enclosure, pulling down her mask. "Your big dick was little after all, wasn't it?"

"You dare talk to me this way?" he snarled.

She laughed, a grating mocking sound, and judging by how Ortega's eyes flashed in fury, she succeeded in hitting a nerve. "Tsk. Tsk. The once mighty Raul Ortega, reduced to shitting in a pot in the corner." The man before her vibrated with so much rage, he sputtered but didn't manage to say anything—anything that she understood at least.

"I'm going after your cronies." A smile touched her lips when Ortega grew wary. "And your sister, Ariana? I'm going after her too."

The once powerful crime lord tried to rise from the bed but fell back weakly.

"Leave her alone," he gritted. "No one threatens Ariana. Haven't you learned from what happened to your father?"

Ortega's face grimaced. Gabby wasn't sure if it was from the virus ravaging his body or because of an unintended slip. "Did my father threaten Ariana? Is that why you had him killed?"

Silence.

"Everything's falling apart," she continued to taunt him. "The cartel you double-crossed? They probably already got to her."

"You have to protect her." He said finally and dropped his gaze to the cold jail floor, his whole demeanor was extremely troubled. Then he lifted his eyes and held her stare. "Your mayor will let the cartel take over South Central and the Valley. I'm the only one standing in their way."

The door to the cell block opened and a nurse came in flanked by two guards. All three were wearing biohazard suits.

"We're going to open his cell," the nurse told her. "He's exhibiting advanced symptoms."

Gabby glanced up at the surveillance camera at the corner ceiling. She was being monitored after all. Her eyes fell back on Ortega and they exchanged an unspoken challenge.

"You need to leave," the nurse added.

"I'm done here anyway," Gabby said and walked to the exit.

She left the block of cells and left the man who'd murdered her father. Because of his sordid affair with Claudette, she had lost years with Theo and the feelings she should have enjoyed as a mother. She and Declan might still be divorced, but she'd never gotten so much closure in one day.

Yet her instincts were telling her this was far from over.

AMONG ALL THE dozens of blood samples, only Captain Mitchell and Chen's revealed traces of the Z-91 virus and both were admitted immediately to the quarantine wing of Downtown Medical Center in accordance with bioterrorism protocols. With Mitchell and Chen out of commission, Kelso and Gabby were put in charge of GHD by the mayor and the LA Chief of Police.

The pelican case containing the Z-91 virus pearls was handed to Garrison who shepherded them to the Los Angeles quarantine station of the CDC, along with Raul Ortega who was for all accounts patient zero for this particular derivative of Ebola. Further tests needed to be conducted on him while he was still alive.

As Gabby packed case binders into a box, she muttered. "Why are we doing this again?"

"Bioterrorism protocol 101," Kelso said one desk over. "GHD is on mandatory leave for at least three days after both of us were put in charge. How's that for a vote of confidence?"

"Not me," Delgado piped in. "Apparently I get guard duty."

"Hey, you volunteered," one of the patrol officers attached to their division muttered. "Someone couldn't stand to spend three days babysitting his kids."

"Fuck you, asshole." Delgado threw a stress ball at the speaker.

"How about you, Nadia?" Gabby asked.

"You think I'm gonna leave my lab unsupervised?" their crime analyst said and turned slitted eyes at Declan. "After your friend commandeered my evidence?"

He chuckled as he grabbed another box for Gabby to fill. "He's not my friend."

"Of course, I'm just a small shrimp in the ocean," Nadia said. "I'm not the CDC." She gestured air quotes around the acronym.

Gabby inwardly smiled as Nadia continued to rant. The exchange between Nadia and Garrison had been hilarious. She was very territorial about items that crossed the threshold of her lab.

"Kelso, I'm just about done. Can you handle these two boxes?" Gabby said. "It's our shared case files."

But her partner knew why Gabby was anxious to get home. No one except the people in the captain's office knew about Theo.

"Go ahead, Gab," Kelso's eyes softened. "Go see him."

18

"WE CAN'T TELL HIM YET," Gabby said, staring at the house, frozen in the passenger seat, unable to make her limbs move to get out of the car.

"I agree." Declan tapped his fingers on the steering wheel. It was nine in the evening and they'd been gone since dawn. He'd turned off the engine a few minutes ago, but it seemed he was giving her time to get her wits about her. "Come on, Angel. He's just a seventeen-year-old kid."

She angled her eyes at him, noting the flash of his grin in the darkness. "You and I know Theo is not an ordinary teenager."

"Didn't think you'd let his star status intimidate you."

"I'm not intimidated."

"Could've fooled me."

"You can quit being annoying," she grouched and pushed open her door, slamming it with more force than she intended, and stalked toward the house.

She heard footsteps behind her as Declan pulled back her arm. "Hey ... are we fighting already?"

His question rubbed her the wrong way, so she got into his

face and snarled, "Let's get one thing straight, Roarke. We're not in a relationship. In no way have I agreed to one. The boy in there"—she pointed toward the house—"is our priority. Not our feelings. Not our guilt over how we fucked things up between us. Clear?"

Declan stepped back and crossed his arms. "What's up your ass?"

"Argh!" Gabby wanted to smack the befuddled look off his face. "I would think seventeen years would have taught you more about women. You're still clueless. God!"

She stomped away from him, and this time, he did not try to catch up with her, but she saw his reflection in the sidelights of the door, following her a few paces behind.

Levi opened the door, brow raised questioningly.

"We're fine," Gabby muttered, pushing past Theo's mammoth bodyguard. "Where's my brother?"

"He's getting ready."

"For what?"

"Some shindig down at Revenant Ranch," Levi said.

"How did his check-up go?"

"Cleared and permitted to party," Theo called from the hallway, striding up to them. He was freshly showered, and he was wearing some rock band's tee, tight-fitting black jeans, and a pair of his special edition Converse sneakers. Gabby had seen his ad on a Sunset Boulevard billboard. Theo larger than life.

A feeling of inadequacy filled her. Did Theo even need to know she was his mother? From where she was standing, he was doing fine all on his own. "That doesn't mean you can go ahead and stay out all night. You're still on meds, right?"

"I stopped after the first day," Theo replied, eyes looking over her shoulder and hardening at the sight of Declan. The teenager muttered an unintelligible curse, cutting his gaze to the side before blasting her with the full potency of his hazel-eyed glare. "You know what? I'm not even gonna pretend that

I'm okay with this." He pointed his finger between her and Declan. "We were supposed to be spending time as a family—bonding time. Remember?"

"We were called downtown, I should've—"

"And you!" Theo inched his chin up at Declan. "Father and son, huh? You're full of shit. What's happening here? You just want to screw my sister over—"

"Dec!" Gabby shouted when, quick as a flash, her ex-husband had gripped their son by the collar and backed him against the wall—thankfully, without slamming him.

"Apologize to Gabby," Declan snarled.

"Fuck you!" Theo snarled back, spittle flying, both his hands gripping the unyielding arm that had him pinned.

Gabby forcibly inserted herself between the two, breaking them up. "That's enough." She faced the angry teen. "We were summoned to Division. I know we left early this morning. Unfortunately, Dec had to take me because I haven't been cleared to drive yet and Mitchell wanted to talk to him because of his role yesterday."

"Whatever," Theo said, shifting to the side and heading for the kitchen toward the garage.

"We won't get along if you don't respect my job!" Gabby called after his back, becoming more frustrated by the second.

"It seems nothing has changed." Theo threw a glance over his shoulder and shrugged. "I don't know why I'm forcing this. I don't need Dad's money. You have the house to yourselves. Have at it."

Levi glanced at them, tight-lipped, as he followed Theo.

"Keep an eye on him, man," Declan said.

"Will do," his partner said. "I'll make sure he doesn't do anything stupid." A half-smile curved the other man's lips. "And you kids behave."

Gabby felt her cheeks flame as Levi disappeared into the garage.

"I believe we were given permission to fuck," Declan
drawled beside her.

Tingles skated over her skin, her nipples tightened. What
the hell? She was exhausted, and yet there was a need to
release all this pent-up frustration.

She shot Declan a nasty look before spinning away to
escape to her room. She needed a long cold shower.

GABBY FROZE her ass off under the cold spray before flipping the
dial to hot—which was how she liked it. The bathroom was
steaming when she emerged from the glass enclosure. She put on
her sleep shorts and a tank before she headed out to the bedroom,
half expecting Declan to be on her bed again, but he wasn't.

"Good. He's learning," she muttered, even as a slight
disappointment rooted in her chest. She berated herself for
her mixed feelings. And as she sat on the vanity and dried her
hair, she wondered if she was giving those same mixed signals
to Declan. She played back all their conversations from that
morning—whatever she could recall at least—and determined
that no, she didn't lead him on.

Gabby stared at her reflection. Her usually pale olive
complexion turned bronze in the California summer and the
heat of the shower gave it a pinkish glow. Although she didn't
have patience on most days for makeup, her routine included
a concealer, a peach-colored lipstick and a color-correcting
powder that was all the rage. She tried as much as possible to
take care of her skin. She was overworked, not dead. Her skin
was one of the few vanities leftover from her previous life as a
Hollywood star, and she protected it fiercely.

She grabbed the two-in-one serum and moisturizer that
was worth a chunk of her salary and was about to scoop a
measured amount with the tiny spoon it came with when a
knock rapped on her door.

Her heart skittered, and she let herself exhale slowly before saying, "What do you want?"

"Open the door, Gabby." Declan's muffled voice held a hint of irritation.

Good, maybe he'd learn to stay out of her way if she gave him enough ulcers.

"Go away. I'm tired."

"I made us dinner."

"Not hungry." Her stomach growled, making her a liar, but he didn't know that.

"You need to eat."

"Go. Away. What's so hard to understand about that?"

"Don't be a child. You're trying ..." the words got muffled as if he moved away, but then he returned and the knock became a pound.

Fed up, Gabby jumped to her feet and marched toward the door. "This is ridiculous. I've had enough of immature men who need things to be their way or the highway. I've just showered. I'm sleepy. Leave me in peace."

"You showered?" His voice lowered.

"Of all the—I'm going to sleep. We can talk tomorr-"

The knob started to rattle as if a key was being inserted.

"Don't you dare use your keys, Roarke!"

There was an exasperated, "Fine," followed by, "Then step back if you're behind the door."

Something in those calm words sent her heart racing.

A loud thump shook the door.

He was kicking it!

"Are you insane?" she shrilled.

"... warning. Stand back, Gabby."

She stumbled back a couple of steps as another crash hit the door, and it exploded inward.

Declan stood between the frames like a pillager about to ransack the village of its prized virgins and she stood frozen with her mouth open even as shameless arousal pulsed between her legs.

"You … you … " Words failed her.

He strolled in casually, critically assessing the door before closing it. "Could have taken it down in one, but having it hit your face would defeat my purpose."

When he faced her, his jaw was set tight, and his stormy gaze scorched her from head to toe, with said toes curled in thrilling anticipation.

He wanted her. He wanted to eat her alive. A visual of his head between her thighs when he was avidly tongue-fucking her came to mind and her prickling awareness morphed into a raging inferno in her veins.

"Perfect." He bit his lower lip and she saw a flash of his tongue. "Having trouble breathing, Angel?"

Gabby realized she was panting in short breaths, and she wasn't sure if the damp heat at her sex was from the shower or from his stare.

"This caveman attitude doesn't work on me." Her voice held no conviction. "Leave."

An arrogant brow lifted. "Make me."

"I don't want you." Her voice caught, making her words barely discernible. Why was she saying the opposite of what her whole body was screaming? Good god, she wanted Declan to throw her on the bed and just fuck her. And judging by the way he continued to look at her, he knew she was lying.

And he wasn't playing fair. Perfectly cut shoulders on a man was one of her weaknesses, and Declan wearing a tee with its sleeves cut off exposed obscenely defined muscles that made her want to explore those ridges beneath well-worn cotton.

He approached like a jungle cat, invading her space, overwhelming her with his heat, his breath sending a quiver she felt straight through her core.

"Your nipples say otherwise," he said. "And I bet if I sink my fingers into your pussy, you're wet and ready for me. So tell me. Why are we wasting time?"

A tightness lodged in her throat. She couldn't lie. She needed him inside her, to fill her. A low moan escaped her as his lips brushed the edges of her mouth and sought the pulse at her neck. His tongue briefly touched it and her knees nearly buckled.

He held her up, chuckling. "Still the magic place, huh? Give in, Angel."

The bastard! He was pulling out all the big guns in this seduction game.

"I will," she replied with a bored tone she was far from feeling. "But this will only be a fuck."

He flinched, but recovered quickly. The heat in his eyes disappeared and turned chilling, as if he'd taken a step back from his own body. "Fuck each other out of our systems you mean?"

She gave a tight nod.

Without another word he lowered his head and captured her lips, slowly at first and then devouring. Her hands were trapped between them and she fisted his shirt as they kissed. Their tongues tentatively touched, stroking and seeking what was familiar. His hands burned a trail down her body and gripped her ass, lifted her and walked her to the nearest wall.

Pinning her against the hard surface, her legs were lowered, her feet finding purchase on the floor as he continued to explore every inch of her skin as if learning her curves all over again. Her fingers tangled in his hair as he teased the pulse at her throat and then lowered to the swell of her breast. When he sucked her nipple through cotton, she gave a small cry of pleasure, eyes closing.

"Fuck," he muttered, and his mouth was back on hers, nipping at her. Her eyes flew open.

He slipped his finger behind her sleep shorts and his lids shut briefly. "Fuuuuck." When his eyes opened, she reeled at the determination etched in them. "I feel you gripping me," his breathing was ragged. "Sopping wet." He fitted another finger and she gasped as he curled them. He knew her sweet spot.

"Oh my god," she breathed.

"Feel that," he snarled softly. "Just to be clear, this is not like the last time we had angry sex. This is not me fucking you as if I hate you. You're not fucking me out of your system, Angel, because I'm fucking myself into you so deep, there isn't a chance in hell you can get me out."

His mouth descended and there was no finesse in the way he kissed her, it was pure savagery. He jerked his head away with a growl and dropped to his knees, yanking her sleep shorts on the way down, fumbling with them as he lifted one leg over his shoulder and put his mouth on her.

His tongue speared her, lapping her slickness as if he'd been starved for her taste. The flat of his tongue pressed on that sensitive trove. Sucking on her clit, he sent her spiraling into a chasm of pulsing pleasure. Her back arched back and she cried out.

"Stop, I can't …" She couldn't breathe. She couldn't come down and suck in air because he continued to torture her with the beauty of multiple orgasms.

Stars. She was seeing stars.

"Declan! Let me breathe!" She pulled at his hair and he eased back the pressure of his mouth, transferring his attention to the juncture between her leg and pussy. It was one of his favorite spots to nibble just before …

Assault number two.

Less intense, but equally torturous pleasure. He worked her sensitized flesh, moving that skilled tongue from her clit to the pulsing liquid heat at her core.

As she came down from another high, Declan rose,

framed her face with both hands and captured her lips in another long, searing kiss. Tastes mingled, tongues dueled, and their breathing fractured into desperate exhalations.

"You taste so good," Declan rasped. "I need inside you." He went in for a quick kiss before lowering his hand between them. His hard cock pressed briefly against her before she was boosted up against the wall and without another word, he surged inside her.

Filled her. Stretched her.

He gave her a chance to adjust, tugging her hair with his left hand as he went in for more bruising kisses. His right arm held her leg hooked around his hip. Then he started pumping, upthrusts that were slow and deliberate before quickening into a rhythmic pace.

Declan pulled back and they watched each other, his face etched in some kind of pain that regret could only bring.

Gabby's hand cupped his jaw, the bristly texture of his beard was unfamiliar, yet it symbolized the years that had passed and the time they'd spent away from each other. She gave a watery smile.

"Angel." Her name on his lips was tortured and ragged. He thrust harder, more brutal and she broke again under the ferocity of his possession. He inhaled sharply before releasing a soft grunt. His eyes squeezed shut and warmth filled her womb.

He shuddered against her and she continued to ride her own wave, allowing herself to indulge in this moment that she thought she'd never experience again.

Declan relaxed against her, his face buried in her neck as he let go of her leg. Slight tremors rippled through his muscular frame. Finally, he backed away an inch, his mouth feathering hers as if tasting her in small doses and wonder. Then he laced their fingers together and pulled her away from the wall and led her to the bed.

She resisted. "We can't."

His brows drew together, nostrils flaring. "Don't want to hear can't, Gabby." He jerked his head in the direction of the wall. "We definitely can. We—"

"Door is broken, you neanderthal. Theo could come home any minute."

"He hasn't been gone an hour."

"He probably went to the Revenant party because he's sulking. No telling when he'll decide to come back."

He tugged her hand and, unbalanced, she fell into him. Her eyes narrowed. He hadn't even taken off his shirt and she was naked from the waist down.

"He's a grown kid. He doesn't need his parents breathing down his neck. Hell, he seems to have his shit together more than we do."

She tried to pull away, but he held on tight. "You don't get it," she said. "Not every teenager is you. You matured quickly because you had to care for your sister. Theo—he's at that vulnerable age, you know? Veer a little to the side of drugs and bad decisions, we'll have a big problem on our hands."

"Gabby—"

"I work gangs and homicide, Dec. I've seen enough teenagers fucked up by heroin and oxy to know that we need to keep an eye on Theo—"

His face softened in understanding and the back of his hand caressed her face. "Sometimes …" he shook his head, mouth twitching wryly. "Sometimes I forget that you're not the girl you used to be."

"Is that good or bad?" Her tone lightened from earlier.

"Oh, definitely good." He sighed. "You're right." He edged his face closer. "Mom."

Gabby laughed. It was too soon to get used to the word.

"My room then?"

She tried to break free from his arms but he'd cleaved her to him in a bear hug. "Dec … I just said…"

"Uh-uh, Angel. I'm not letting you go until we're clear about what this is."

She looked down at her half-naked state. "I'm feeling at a disadvantage."

He chuckled. "Totally on purpose."

"You sneak."

Declan kissed her nose. "I get your concerns about Theo. We can switch rooms if you feel more comfortable with a lock. I'd rather you move into my room, but I understand the need to ease Theo into the idea of us."

"I can stay here." She puffed a short laugh. "And Dec, you're moving too fast. Now let me go so I can put on my shorts."

He stared at her a beat and then let his arms drop to his side. Gabby could feel his eyes on her.

And before long, he pulled her back into his arms and was kissing her again.

When they broke apart, he murmured. "Come into my room later."

"No."

"Hang out with me then? We can stream something."

She smiled up at him. "That I can do."

THEY SETTLED in front of the widescreen, but Gabby didn't last very long and fell asleep on Declan's shoulder. He shifted to the end of the couch, taking her with him.

"What? Is the episode over?"

"No, sleepyhead, we barely got to the middle."

"Oh." She snuggled closer. "So comfortable."

Somehow, he managed to get her feet up on the couch. Gabby was on her side, her hands cradling the side of her face on his lap. Declan couldn't see if she was watching TV.

"You awake?"

"Hmm."

"Hmm yes, or hmm no."

A brief burst of laughter came from her and she tilted her head up and down as if to scratch the side of her face, but fuck any movement from her was torture to his self-control. If she didn't stop her fidgeting, she'd have his erection for a pillow.

"We didn't use a condom," she mumbled.

Now that came out of nowhere.

"No. I trusted you to stop me if it wasn't okay."

"I trusted you not to put me at risk," she said.

"I'm safe. I've always suited up, and my last check-up was three months ago."

"You're saying you haven't had sex since then?"

"That's exactly what I'm saying."

She didn't say anything else. Well, hell, was he expecting her to share? Did he actually want to know of the men in her past? He suppressed the growl that threatened to rise.

He leaned forward and saw her thick lashes blinking. She was awake and watching TV.

"That's the bad guy," Gabby said. "I'm sure of it."

They were watching a detective show, one where Declan had read the books and Gabby idolized the main character for his tenacity and sense of justice even if he was fictional.

"If you say so, detective."

She turned her face toward him. "Wanna bet?"

"I'll only bet if it's for more sex."

"You're one-track-minded, aren't you?"

"I haven't even begun to get my fill of you." He let his fingers comb through her hair and let them stroke down her neck. He smiled when her body shuddered.

"Stop with the seduction routine and watch."

"I'm watching," he replied. "I'm a multitasker."

"You're so cocky. Now, stop distracting me."

"Yes, ma'am."

They watched the show quietly for the next twenty minutes until the villain was revealed and Gabby was right.

As the series credits rolled by, Declan asked, "How about you? Dated a lot?"

Gabby shifted on her back and stared up at him. "You wanna know when I last had sex."

His jaw hardened. "Not really."

A delicate brow arched.

"Okay, yes. I've always been possessive, Gab. You know that."

"Four months ago."

When she wasn't forthcoming with more, he prodded. "Go on. Who was he?"

"Promise not to hunt him down."

"Scout's honor." He'd never been one and Gabby knew this.

She rolled her eyes. "A lawyer. He was the assistant DA."

Declan's mouth flattened, the itch to look up the guy online was overwhelming.

Gabby's brow went higher. "I don't like that look in your eyes."

"What look?"

"Like you're about to commit murder," she grinned. "You don't have to worry about competition. He moved to the east coast. I wouldn't even call it a relationship. I think his term was serial monogamy." He gave a tight nod, wondering how he would have handled the situation if Gabby was actually seeing someone. Probably not well. Yup, not well at all.

"Does it bother you that I work with men?"

"As long as no one hits on you and … I hate it," he gritted. "That you share a locker with guys. That they see you naked." Declan swore his eyes actually bled red.

Seeing his reaction, a corner of her lip tipped up.

"I'm not finding this funny," he growled.

She burst out laughing and sat up. "I was just pulling your

leg. The women's area is sectioned off. Guys don't see us naked."

His chest whooshed with relief, but the predator in him was poked.

"Why you—" He dragged her back to the couch and started tickling.

"Dec, stop! I'm sorry." But she started laughing that tinkling laughter that warmed his heart and held a direct line to his dick.

He was about to kiss her when they both heard a sound. Declan grabbed his phone and checked the surveillance app. It was the garage, and the volume on the television had muffled its sound.

"Theo and Levi are back."

"They're early." Apprehension suffused her face.

"It'll be fine."

"Remember what we talked about."

Declan didn't say anything.

"Dec," she censured.

"We're not gonna hide what's happening between us," he said. "But I'm not gonna grab your ass in front of him."

She rolled her eyes.

The next episode started playing. "It's started."

Gabby's attention was drawn to the garage.

He nudged her. "It's best if we act as if nothing happened. That our son didn't throw a tantrum. At least, I think that's what we're supposed to do." It was like the blind leading the blind. "Got me?"

She blew out a breath and sat back on the couch, six inches away from him.

A few minutes later, Theo walked in.

Both Declan and Gabby turned and said "hey" and turned back to the TV.

He could feel anxiety rolling off her and didn't think she was even breathing normally. His hand moved towards hers and touched his pinky to hers. A slow smile started on her face.

"The party was boring, so I came home," Theo shared as he walked up to them.

"Watching *Bosch*?" Levi asked as he joined them in the living room.

"Shh ..." Gabby said.

"Aren't you tired of watching cop shows when you're a cop?" Theo asked.

Gabby grabbed the remote and paused the episode. "And don't you know it's rude to interrupt someone when they're binge watching a series?"

Theo's mouth twitched. "Mea culpa, sis."

Somehow, to Declan's ears, it was an apology for more than interrupting the show.

"You guys wanna hang out with us? We can pick a movie to watch instead," Declan said.

The teenager shrugged. "Sure." He eyed the empty bowls on the table. "What did you guys eat?"

"Made enchiladas," Declan said, then looked at Levi. "There's plenty."

"Thanks. They served rabbit food over there." His partner laughed.

"I can—" Gabby made to get up, but Declan tugged her down. "Levi and Theo can help themselves. Right, guys?"

"Of course." His son shrugged again and accompanied Levi to the kitchen.

He yanked Gabby to his side. "Relax." He murmured into her ear. "See, I told you it'll be fine."

"I just don't know how to do this mommy shit," Gabby hissed.

They both gave a puff of laughter. Declan pulled up the selections of the net streaming providers and brought up a list of new releases.

When Theo and Levi returned from the kitchen, they

didn't only bring back their dinners but some chips, dips, and beer.

They argued about what to watch, but the guys let Gabby win.

The midnight hour was about to strike, and the tumultuous day ended on a high note.

19

"I NEED A TUXEDO."

Gabby looked up from her laptop and took off her reading glasses. Theo was standing in front of her with his arms crossed. His stance was so similar to his dad's when he was telling her something important that she knew she had to give him her full attention before any other information was forthcoming. Being his father's son definitely had its advantages when it came to deciphering body language.

"What's so funny?" the teenager demanded.

"Nothing. Tuxedo—don't you have like ten of them?"

He rolled his eyes and before he could respond, Emma came up behind him and wrapped her arms around his torso. The puzzle of the boy's difficult behavior two nights prior before he left for the Revenant party was solved. It wasn't about Gabby and Declan getting together, it was because he was having girl problems. Levi hinted that her boy made up with Emma at the party which explained his good mood when he came home. Though Theo made an effort to spend movie night with them, he spent half the film texting someone with that mysterious smile Gabby knew so well.

She'd been in love and a teenager once.

"He has six," Emma piped in. "Still one too many if you ask me."

"But I'm a presenter," Theo protested. "And I've outgrown half of them." He puffed up his chest and this time it was Emma who rolled her eyes.

"Don't you have a new gown for every awards show," Theo added.

"It's different for the ladies," Emma said, grinning at Gabby. "Tell him, Ms. Woodward."

Gabby dropped her gaze to the screen and coughed uncomfortably. "Well—"

"Actually." Theo snapped his fingers like he had an epiphany. Gabby's eyes pulled back to him at the sound and he pointed at her. "You, sis, need a new wardrobe."

Oh, hell to the fucking no.

Emma clasped her hands together. "Oh, that's exciting." The teenage girl gave Gabby a once-over, at least what she could see from her sitting on the couch. Gabby was wearing gray sweatpants and a well-worn LAPD sweatshirt.

"Why do I get the feeling," Gabby said slowly, "that I'm being set-up? And if you need a tuxedo, I'm sure you have a personal shopper. Or could have them deliver it."

"I haven't had my measurements taken in a few months." He flexed his arms and shrugged his shoulders the way she'd seen Kelso do when he was showing off his traps.

"Okay, suppose I bite. Where exactly are we going?"

"Where else?" Theo chortled. "Rodeo Drive."

Gabby felt the blood drain from her face. Good thing Levi and Declan walked in from the pool area while she digested that info.

"Been looking for you two," Levi said.

"I told you to leave your sister alone," Declan said, but there was amusement on his face.

Gabby narrowed her eyes. Were they in on this too? After finding out Theo was her son, somehow she'd reverted to being his sister and hadn't overanalyzed how to treat him. Her situation was different from Declan's. He had no prior relationship with Theo. Having to work from home while Division underwent a deep clean was a blessing in a way. She could figure things out in her personal life now that the Ortega case would be drawing to a close. He was probably already dead, but there was no news from the LAPD or the CDC. Gabby was sure they needed a formal death certificate to close the case. Meanwhile, Chen had been released from the hospital to home quarantine after the virus had shown inactive levels, but the captain had developed a fever. Gabby had been convincing herself that he was going to be okay, that he'd received the antiviral in time.

There was still the question of the missing Claudette. The clinic doctor who'd helped her was found dead and buried in a shallow grave in a Nevada desert. At first, the Vegas PD thought it was a mob hit, but when Gabby followed up with the doctor's last known address, they'd linked their cases together and had been sharing information on their investigation. Gabby had just shot off an email to the Vegas detective-in-charge, thanking them for their cooperation when she was interrupted by the teenager.

"Theo informed me he needs to go shopping," she told Levi. "Rodeo Drive."

"Yeah, I was making necessary arrangements." Levi grinned. "We're going on a field trip."

"We?" Gabby repeated, and then glanced at Declan who raised both his hands like he had nothing to do with it.

"Weren't you guys supposed to be practicing field stripping an M9 blindfolded?"

The script of *Hodgetown* was quickly rewritten to give Theo a break from the action scenes. His character was stricken with temporary blindness, so the teen suggested that Levi teach him to disassemble and assemble a gun while blindfolded. They'd been rehearsing this for the past two days, even went to Revenant Ranch to practice shooting blind. It had been hilarious watching the guys time each other. Declan could field strip an M9 and put it back together in twenty seconds without looking at what he was doing.

"I got it done in forty seconds this morning," Theo said.

"That's really good," Gabby said.

"It's still twice Roarke's time." The teen shrugged in disappointment.

"You'll get there," Declan said.

"It'll look badass on film, baby," Emma said, kissing his cheek.

Theo slung his arm around her and pulled her closer. "What kind of kiss is that?" he chided before planting a big, sloppy one on her lips.

"Ew, that's disgusting," the girl protested and pushed away from Theo who proceeded to tickle her. It ended up with Emma running away giggling and Theo chasing her.

Gabby burst out laughing, but stopped short when her eyes landed on Declan. He was watching her with an intensity that made her squirm. They had not had sex since that night, but he'd been dragging her into corners for quick kisses or make-out sessions.

They'd been behaving like a couple of teenagers themselves.

A cough sounded beside them. "Annnnd, I know when I'm the fifth wheel," Levi chuckled. "You think you can leave within the hour?"

"Wait a minute, guys." Gabby pointed at her screen. "I'm not exactly on vacation here."

"Call Kelso and tell him you need to spend some time with Theo," Declan told her.

"Are you managing me, Mr. Roarke?" She arched a brow.

He sat beside her on the couch, reached for her laptop, and shut the lid.

"Your bossiness is getting out of hand," she informed him.

"Don't see you protesting too much."

"I'm saving all my energy for when you all drag me kicking and screaming onto Rodeo Drive." Her mouth turned wry. "Besides, most of the SAs there probably know me."

"Oh, you worked Beverly Hills before?"

"Patrol officer," Gabby said and then she thought of the polished Claudette. "I guess I should just get it over with." She looked around them before lowering her voice. "When the truth comes out that I'm Theo's mom, I guess I need to at least try and look the part."

A pissed off look crossed Declan's face. "If you think you have to change the way you dress to be accepted as Theo's parent, then let's not do this. Be who you are. I've known you and I like the person you are now, but I feel like you're holding back that core of the girl you used to be." His green eyes searched hers. "Let go, Angel. Set her free. That's who Theo needs."

It was unnerving how Declan could see into the heart of her.

That part of her chained to the remnants of buried pain.

But between him and Theo, she had a feeling she was about to break free from those shackles.

⸻

AT LEAST THEO didn't lie about needing to be measured for a suit, but it took less than half an hour for him to get his stuff done. Gabby thought she could still get out of it, but apparently, they'd lassoed Emma to pull her into different designer shops.

For most of the hour she indulged Theo's girlfriend as she showed her the trouser suits of Chanel, Valentino, Armani, and other big-name designers. When she was about to pull her into another boutique, she put her foot down.

"Honey," Gabby said gently. "You know what I do, right?"

Emma shot her a confused look. "Of course."

"Being a detective is not what you see on television. We don't walk around a crime scene or simply sit behind a desk or meet the big cheeses in the war room and discuss a case that's on a whiteboard."

"Hey, what's going on?" Theo put a protective arm around Emma.

"I told you it's not what she likes," his girlfriend said. "She'd look good in something sportier though."

"We need to do something about your gray suits."

God save her from teenagers who wanted to give her a makeover.

"All right, then can we go someplace where the price tag is not ten grand a suit?" she sighed.

"I'll pay for it," Theo said. "My credit is good in every store." He slyly rubbed his forefinger beneath his chin as if saying his face was his credit card.

"Well, good for you," Gabby said, resisting the urge to snort. "But, I'm paying for these or we go home right now."

She wasn't offended. She had her money too that came from her share of Revenant Films as the owner's daughter. It wasn't anywhere near Theo's slice of the pie, but it was more than enough for emergency funds for a wardrobe change.

"Consider it a gift," Theo said darkly. "I want to do something for you."

People were starting to recognize the stars of *Hodgetown* despite Theo's baseball cap. Both he and Emma were wearing sunglasses, but seeing them as a couple identified them easily. Maybe that was why Theo hung back with Declan when they first got to the shopping mecca in the Golden Triangle.

"And you're not going to feel bad if I take that ten-k Chanel suit and go crawling into a tunnel or into a sewer?"

Theo and Emma's faces both blanched with horror.

Declan's chuckle sounded behind her and she spun around and poked him in the chest. "Some help you are—" she stopped short when she spied the approaching paparazzi. "Let's keep walking. Theo, stay with Levi. Declan and I have Emma."

The crowd of paparazzi seemed to grow exponentially.

"Are you and Emma back together?"

"Does Mr. Haller approve?"

Emma's father was a popular criminal defense attorney, and a few of Gabby's colleagues had squared up against the man in the courtroom—and hated him. Gabby had no issue with who Emma's father was, but she found out from Theo that Mr. Haller was the main reason for their previous break up.

"Is that your sister?" Another reporter asked.

"Ms. Woodward, where is Ortega?"

"Do you approve of Emma?"

Fortunately, another big-name star was walking down the street and the herd of independent photographers moved toward him. Some remained and continued to snap pictures. When they entered the Michael Kors boutique, Emma tugged her to the row of suits. "I think you'll like it here."

Gabby had a feeling she would too. It wasn't as pricey as the other designer brands, but it was modern and sophisticated in its simplicity.

Declan and Levi waited on the couches at the entrance, flipping through their phones, maybe catching up on emails. She quickly checked hers but there were no messages from Kelso.

Theo and Emma were conferring on one of the suits and Gabby was secretly amused. She looked back at Declan who was watching them, and he gave her a two-thumbs up.

Gabby shook her head and mimed strangling her neck. Declan smiled and she returned her attention to the teenagers before they got carried away trying to dress her up.

It wasn't all that bad, and if Gabby were honest, she liked each suit the sales associate brought to her to try as selected by her brother … son … shit, her brain did the double stutter, and she decided to refer to him as her brother for now so she wouldn't slip before she was ready. This idea that Theo was making an effort to take care of her? She liked that and she got it.

The price tags were as she expected as she went inside a fitting room. She found herself not minding dipping into her emergency fund to cover the purchase which would probably amount to twenty thousand by the time she was done. Still, she wasn't wearing these suits to chase a suspect or when she knew she was doing field work. And it wasn't because it would get dirty or ruined. She didn't want people intimidated by what she wore when she had to interview a vic or a witness. She'd known a couple of homeless people who used to live in Beverly Hills. Drugs and gambling were a fast track to the soup kitchen. And, homeless or not, they'd never forget pawning off a prized Chanel bag to pay off an addiction.

After several changes of suits and doing a mock fashion show for Theo and Emma, Gabby was relieved that the two were satisfied with her selections. Three trouser suits, four button-down shirts, and why wasn't she surprised to see shoe boxes waiting for her to fit?

"I'm not wearing heels," she said before anyone could say anything.

"Do these look like heels to you?" Theo smirked.

Gabby peered into the box he was holding. Nestled inside was a pair of dark loafers. Her fingers couldn't resist touching them.

Lambskin.

Soft.

Her feet were begging to try them on. Not that she didn't have sensible shoes.

"You gotta have new shoes to go with your clothes."

Since they were black, they'd still work well with her gray

suits, not the clashing color of her brown loafers, but she bought those because they were damned comfortable.

"Oh, all right. But if I can't run in these, I'm not buying them."

Theo burst out laughing.

"What?"

"Roarke was the one who brought these three pairs over. Said to get them all and don't worry, you'll be able to chase your suspects in them."

Gabby couldn't name the emotion that came over her heart, but it made her smile. And to keep her face from pulling into a silly grin, she bit her bottom lip, and sat on the dressing room settee as the others encouraged the would-be-fitter to max out her credit card.

She slipped on the first pair, a black one, and gave it a walk through. She didn't want to take them off.

The same thing happened with the other two, a chocolate pair, and another black that was shinier than the first, and a different style.

"I don't need three pairs," she told the SA. "I'll take the black one and the other black shiny one." She could use them when she visited City Hall or had to go to court.

"Are you sure, ma'am?" their shopping assistant asked. "We don't have these often as they're specially made in Italy."

Impeccably soled detectives were not unheard of, especially in LA, but Gabby noted she'd be giving Delgado a run for his money. He was the most snazzily dressed cop, not only in their Division but most of Hollywood.

"I'm sure." She glanced at Theo, daring him to object, but he simply shrugged as he slung an arm around Emma who was busy scrolling through her phone.

Thank god their make-over project was over. She quickly checked the fitting room to make sure she didn't forget anything. Then she and the kids exited the lounge area of the dressing room.

Declan rose immediately when they emerged. A panty-melting grin she hadn't seen in a long time broke through his face. His beard was the sole barrier from making it an exact replica of that memory, but it was as if the years peeled away, and she was seeing the boy she once loved.

A pang of longing stabbed her chest and she couldn't help returning the smile.

"Shoes good?" he asked.

"Perfect. I can't believe you remembered my size."

Declan didn't respond, but the thoughtful look on his face made her heart pound extra hard. She moved past him and walked up to the check-out counter where the lady assisting her was busy putting the purchases in shopping bags.

"I don't recall the last time I shopped this much. If one suit fits, I'd order five of the same color and size," Gabby laughed, looking over her shoulder at Theo and her ex-husband.

"Yeah, gray's not a good color for you," her brother said.

"Okay, sport," Declan chuckled. "Ease up on the tough love before she returns everything."

Shaking her head, she pulled out her credit card and handed it to the cashier.

The lady smiled and looked over her shoulder. "Mr. Roarke has settled your purchases."

"What?" She turned on him accusingly. This time Declan's eyes held a wary glint, while her brother and Emma hugged each other, looking mighty pleased.

"It's a gift," Declan said.

"You just can't give me a twenty-thousand-dollar gift," she sputtered. It was much more with the shoes. "That's insane."

"I just did," he muttered and stepped up to the counter to sign the receipt.

"Wait a minute." She looked at the cashier. "Refund his money."

The cashier winked at her. "Don't fight it. Let him spoil you."

"I'm not—" Gabby protested but fingers gripped her upper arm and Declan ushered her away.

"Come on, Angel." He lowered his head and murmured by her ear. "Like the lady said. Don't fight it." He turned to Theo. "Grab the bags and load 'em up in the car."

The teenager gave a mock-salute as Gabby was led, still bewildered, out of the store.

"Declan," she sighed, but the man's purposeful strides told her he wasn't backing down. "It's not the same. You're asking too much before I'm ready."

When they were outside by the entrance, he tugged her to the corner so they wouldn't get mowed down by pedestrians. He put both hands on her shoulders. "I'm beginning to understand the new Gabby."

She narrowed her eyes. "Oh, really? This I've got to hear."

"Not here," he grinned. "But long and short of it? We're not getting anywhere if I don't knock down that wall you've erected around you with a sledgehammer."

"That's a mighty expensive sledgehammer."

"I have money now," he stated simply, but there was a hard set in his eyes and Gabby regretted sending him back to the past when he straddled a thin line with his pride.

"I didn't mean it that way."

"Hey." His head lowered. "That insecure boy you knew doesn't exist anymore. Doesn't matter if you're an heiress to a mansion in Beverly Hills. Money doesn't faze me, Angel. It can be made. But our relationship needs all the help it can get, and I don't mind a proper courtship."

"Well." Gabby nodded to the bags that Levi and Theo were holding. "If that's the way you want to put it."

"It is."

They were about to take a step to rejoin the others when

she added, "Well, darn I should have gotten the third pair of shoes then since you're being so generous——"

Declan's eyes twinkled. "You did."

"You didn't——"

He grinned that heartbreaking grin. "Just say 'thank you, Declan.'"

"Thank you, Declan," she repeated.

And then he kissed her—slow and deliberate.

Gagging noises from the peanut gallery.

"Seriously, dude," Theo hollered. "That's my sister."

Gabby blushed to the roots of her hair and immediately sprung back but he kept her close.

A familiar black SUV pulled up to the curb and the lightness of the day sifted away, and her anxiety from this morning came rolling in.

Declan stiffened beside her when the window lowered to reveal Kelso at the wheel with Delgado beside him.

"What happened?" she twisted away from Declan and rushed to their side.

"It's the Cap," Delgado said grimly. "Took a turn for the worse two hours ago."

"We need to head there now," Kelso said.

"I'm coming with you," Declan said. He turned to Levi. "You got them?"

His partner nodded, but Gabby was already pulling open the door to the SUV. She paused and turned back to Theo.

"I have to go," she said. "I know we planned——"

"It's okay," Theo said with the most understanding look she'd seen on his face and her heart clenched.

Her son.

She reached out and squeezed his shoulder and then hurried into the vehicle, Declan following in closely behind her.

Kelso snapped the police lights on, pulled into traffic, and sped away.

20

Downtown Medical Center was swarmed in blue. The news that Captain Mitchell had gone critical struck the LAPD at its core. At fifty-seven, the captain had been on the force for more than thirty-five years. He had made enemies, but he was well respected among his peers, not to mention by lawyers, politicians, and case victims like Gabby.

Because Gabby, Kelso, and Delgado were directly under his command, they were allowed into the Center for Infectious Disease wing of the hospital. The hallway was wider than the regular ones they'd passed in the hospital. A clean room divided the corridor in the middle and that was as far as they were allowed to go. Chairs and benches were arranged along the wall. Gabby spotted the police chief and his wife who were comforting Vanessa—the captain's wife of thirty-two years.

Seeing her, Vanessa's face crumpled as Gabby approached. The two women hugged. "Oh, Gabby, I'm so scared."

"What did the doctor say?"

They broke apart and Mitchell's wife swiped the tears from her eyes. "The antiviral seemed to have little effect."

"But it worked on Chen."

"The doctor said it might be because of his age and health … the stress." Vanessa put a hand over her mouth as her voice grew garbled from the effort not to sob. "A weakened immune system."

"I've called Steven and Eric," she continued. "They're flying in tonight. I should have called them sooner …"

Gabby hugged the woman again. At least their sons were all grown up and were successful in their careers. Steven was a lawyer. Eric followed in his father's footsteps in law enforcement and was now an FBI agent.

She, Kelso, and Delgado continued to comfort Vanessa. They eventually migrated to an area with a couch. After a while, Gabby excused herself to look for Declan who seemed to have disappeared. So much for keeping her company. On her way to the vending machine, she spotted him coming in from a stairwell.

He didn't look pleased and, when he saw her, the look of regret in his eyes made her more anxious than she already was.

"Where did you go?" she demanded.

"Garrison."

"He's here?"

"Not anymore."

Getting information out of Declan regarding the spook could be a knuckle-dragging affair. "What did he say?"

"Gabby."

"What. Did. He. Tell. You?" she enunciated. "If it has anything to do with the Z-91 virus, I need to know."

Declan blew out a breath. "Can't tell anyone. It's gonna cause a panic."

"Do I look like I earned my stripes yesterday? I know how to handle information, Dec," she snapped.

He regarded her carefully and then reached out his arm. "Come here."

"Don't." Her eyes warmed with tears.

She tried to ward him off, but he caught her arm and pulled her close. "I know you're scared for Mitchell."

"It doesn't look good," she choked.

Declan didn't say anything, but continued to soothe her, rubbing her back. Gabby leaned away and peered up into his face. "You know something."

He gave a tight nod. "The strain that infected Ortega and Chen was different from what Mitchell has."

"How is that possible? It couldn't have mutated so easily."

"Some DNA of the virus has been altered. The virologist with the CDC believes how easy it attaches to a host will determine its pathology."

"English, Declan."

His jaw worked reflexively. "It's a virus that has the ingenuity of a parasite. Parasites know which hosts it can feed on to grow stronger. The strain that has developed in Mitchell is aggressive. I don't think they'll allow anyone past the clean room who's not suited up properly."

"They won't allow Vanessa to see him?"

Declan's eyes softened. "They will. They're coming up with a new protocol to handle entry into the area."

"Does he have a chance, Dec?"

"I don't know, Angel."

He held her eyes, but she couldn't see any hope in them. She inhaled a ragged breath and buried her face on his chest again. She was just coming to terms with Peter's death, but with Mitchell the sorrow was instant. Her heart was feeling all the agony of an impending loss. She couldn't count how many times she'd gone to Mitchell's home for Sunday dinner, and she remembered Vanessa dropping by her place bringing chicken soup the couple of times she'd been sick.

She blinked and tears rolled down her cheeks and soaked Declan's shirt. His arms tightened around her. Uniforms walked by, probably people she worked with, witnessing her break down, but she didn't care. She knew that they understood. The LAPD could be wrought in politics, division conflict, and sometimes even racism plagued their ranks, but when the life of one of their own was on the line, everyone bled blue.

RADIO STATIC ... 14242 ... *static* 14242 ... final call for badge 14242.

Captain Frank Mitchell of the LAPD answered his final call on September 28, 2019. He served the department with outstanding leadership and an integrity admired by his peers.

Badge 14242, you are cleared for end of watch.

Captain Frank Mitchell has gone home for the final time.

SEVERAL MEMBERS of the LAPD gathered at the GHD for the dispatcher's end-of-watch transmission for Captain Mitchell. It was emotional and full of sadness. For Gabby, it held an undercurrent of helpless fury. Captain Mitchell was cremated, and his remains wouldn't even be turned over to Vanessa. The funeral the next day would be an empty casket. Gabby understood the concerns for public safety and the captain's widow did too, but that didn't lessen the unbridled anger rioting inside Gabby, seeking to find its target.

After the last call was announced, everyone turned to each other for comfort. There was hardly a dry eye in the office. Nadia was quietly sobbing in the corner, sitting on a bench against the wall. Gabby walked over to her and sat beside her, taking her hand as they leaned against each other without saying a word.

Kelso soon joined their duo.

Delgado's desk was in front of them, and when the detective came up to them, he opened the bottom drawer and reached for the Maker's Mark bourbon—the captain's drink of choice.

"I know I'm not cliquey with you all, but my man Chen is still under home confinement, and I'm feeling lonely," the well-dressed Hispanic man said. "And I know Captain would frown at all them long faces, no? He'd prefer it if we gave him a toast. How about it?"

Gabby and Kelso looked at each other and shrugged almost in unison.

"Sounds like a plan."

"I'm game."

"Tomorrow's the funeral," Nadia said. "Early. Don't want to miss that."

"Did I say we were getting drunk?" Delgado shot back. "Hey, guys," he called to the other huddle of officers who had remained after the call. "We're heading over to Tripp's to toast the captain, what do you all say?"

"I'll be there."

"Cool!"

"Guess I need to go, too," Nadia said.

"It'll do us good." Gabby got up from the bench. She hadn't gone drinking with the guys in a while. Maybe a tumbler or two of bourbon was what she needed. She also needed to keep an eye on Nadia who she knew had a low tolerance for alcohol.

As they filed out of the room, Gabby told Kelso, "I wonder why I didn't think of this."

Her partner gave her a wry smile. "You've been in your head too much these past few days. You and the captain were closest to the Ortega case."

Gabby gave a shake of her head. "You should have shaken some sense into me."

"I would have. Except I think someone else has that job right now."

She looked away. Gabby had been a bit distant to the men

in her life in the two days following the captain's passing. Levi, Declan, and even Theo had steered clear of her as she roamed the house like a lost soul, although she was aware of their eyes on her.

Time to remedy that and join the land of the living. After the captain's funeral tomorrow, they needed to get back to their cases. Gabby wasn't giving up on finding Claudette.

Her former stepmother had a lot to answer for.

DECLAN CHECKED the time on his watch. It was almost one in the morning. He couldn't count the many times he'd gotten up and paced the living room with the urge to call Gabby.

Levi was playing video games with Theo, but he was sure they'd noticed his unease.

Gabby had withdrawn from everyone since Captain Mitchell died. She and Kelso were closest to the Mitchell family, and they'd been allowed into the room after the area around the bed had been contained with a plastic bio-sealant. Vanessa couldn't even hold her husband's hand as he took his final breath.

Even as a hardened mercenary, Declan couldn't comprehend the depth of this tragedy. His interaction with Vanessa had been limited, but it was clear that she and the captain had a good marriage. Thank god their sons arrived in time to support their mother. When they left the room, Vanessa and Gabby were like ghosts, the men—tight-lipped, faces etched in unfathomable grief.

Gabby shut down, her answers monotone, so Declan gave her space. When they arrived at the house, Theo asked how Mitchell was and all she answered was …

He didn't make it.

Then she announced she was tired and disappeared into her room. The door closed and locked. At that time Declan regretted fixing the door the day after he broke it. Not that it would have made a difference. She deserved her moment to grieve for the man who'd been like a father to her.

He glanced at the text she sent at nine that evening. *Having a drink with the guys. Don't know when I'll be home.*

The funeral was tomorrow. Declan knew she had to be with her department and he understood that. As a soldier, nothing hit harder than the loss of a brother. The shared grief with the surviving team, shooting the shit and remembering the good times were a way of moving on, getting unstuck from the cycle of grief.

This end-of-watch ritual would be hard on everyone.

Declan convinced himself that seeing Gabby through this difficult time would strengthen their relationship. Still, he couldn't help the angst that took hold when she wasn't within his sight. An issue he was trying to ignore.

"Dammit!" Theo yelled. "I'm dead. You win."

His partner's chuckle followed another disgruntled groan from the teen. Declan wasn't much of a gamer; he was damned glad that Levi was.

"It's past one, you should go to bed," Levi told the teenager. "The call sheet says you're due on the set at nine."

"Yeah, yeah, I need my beauty rest," Theo said as he stood and stretched, but headed in Declan's direction instead of toward his room.

Levi announced he was turning in and disappeared to his side of the house.

"Worried about Gabby?" Theo asked.

"Not necessarily a worry, more like a concern."

"It's tough being a cop. Tougher being related to one."

Declan glanced sharply at his son.

Theo hitched his shoulders. "They say it all the time on TV. It's harder on the loved ones wondering if their cop is safe."

It was uncanny how Theo had zeroed in on the thing that was bothering him.

"You're tougher than most men I know," the teen continued. "Certainly more than Nick and I love that guy." The teen's eyes widened as if realizing the insensitivity of his words, but his mouth turned up in a half grin. "No offense, but he's been like my second dad."

"Sometimes." Declan exhaled through his nose because what Theo said hit the bullseye—straight through his fucking heart and then some. "You need a helluva filter on that mouth. I will never, in any goddamned dimension of this universe, be like Nick."

"Yeah, just calling it as it is."

"Kid, you're too young to call it as it is," he said. "Stop trying to act older than you are. There are a lot of things you don't know—"

"I know this," Theo cut him off. "I know you may be the best man for Gabby after all."

He stilled. "I'm sorry. I don't think I heard you right."

Theo laughed. "All I'm saying is it takes a strong-minded man to handle my sister. I can see why you got together in the first place ... sparks and all. But can you handle her being a cop? The risks? She'll always be my sister no matter what, and I'll worry about her for an eternity, but you? You can walk away now."

"Now, not later?" Declan asked, curious with his phrasing.

"Before it goes any further. Before one of you gets hurt."

"I'm not going to hurt Gabby. Not this time."

"I'm also thinking about you, Roarke," Theo said. "What if she was the one infected and not the captain?"

"Jesus." He scraped his face with a hand. The thought did occur to him. He'd had nightmares about it the other night. Gabby with tubes going through her, keeping her alive, blood pouring from her eyes and nose. "I get the risks, bud. I've lived the risks before, worked side-by-side with men and women who had loved ones back home."

Theo nodded, seemingly satisfied. "You waiting up for her?"

"Yeah. Go to bed. You need your beauty sleep."

His son snorted and clamped a hand on his shoulder and squeezed.

He'd just received comfort and a heart-to-heart from a teenager. Theo had probably experienced more meaningful relationships than he had, judging from how smitten he was with Emma, although his son tried to act all cool and shit. He chuckled at the thought.

Declan only had Gabby. Had fallen in deep and wanted to marry her despite their vastly different social statuses.

A sound of a vehicle came rumbling down the driveway. The tension in his muscles loosened as he walked to the window to take a peek, recognizing the sound of Gabby's vehicle pulling in, wondering if someone else had driven her home. He knew she wouldn't be idiotic enough to get behind the wheel under the influence. The engine cut off and she exited the Pilot and gingerly closed the SUV's door as if mindful it was early in the morning.

Gabby approached under the glow of the porch lights, her steps dragging, but in no way straddling the drunk line.

She had her key in hand but, before she could notch it into the keyhole, Declan opened the door.

Her face registered surprise, but there was gladness in it too, and that settled him a bit. "You didn't have to wait up for me."

Declan stepped aside to let her in and closed the door.

"How did it go?" He followed her into the kitchen where she retrieved a glass and filled it with water.

"Hard." She leaned against the countertop and took a sip of water as if contemplating the question further "But it was good." She nodded effusively, her mouth set in determination.

"We talked about the good times, our favorite Frank Mitchell moments."

"What was yours?" Declan asked while he took his place beside her.

"Oh, several," she said. "The time he called me an idiot when I was a patrol officer and messed up his crime scene. I wanted to slink away then and quit."

"You were a rookie?"

"Rookie or not, you learn fast enough under Mitchell."

"Tough love?"

"Oh yeah, but he was fair and he had your back no matter what."

Declan waited for her to elaborate. She took another sip and continued, "Officer-involved shootings. Those are always tough, often scrutinized by the rat department."

"As in Internal Affairs?"

"Yes. In my fifteen years as a cop, there've always been bad apples in that division. Don't get me wrong, majority of them are just doing their job—checks and balances and all. But sometimes there are those who are out for revenge."

"Gotcha."

"IA is always hated. I'd rather quit than have to join them." She glanced at him. "Your involvement in the raid might still be investigated, you know."

"I wouldn't worry about it," Declan assured her.

"Garrison handled it?"

"He did."

"Good." Gabby pushed away from the countertop and lowered her glass. "Guess I'll turn in." She started to walk away.

"Gabby …" He clasped her arm, stopping her.

She didn't look at him, keeping her head bowed, but he could feel the need rolling off her. She needed something from him. In what capacity, he wasn't sure, but what he was sure about was he couldn't leave her alone. Not tonight.

"Gabby," he repeated.

She raised her eyes and the raw agony in them tore at his heart.

"I'm here, Angel."

"I can't stop thinking." Her voice cracked. "I keep running things through my head if we could have done things differently. If I didn't bring up the clinic—"

"Angel, I don't think—"

"Not my fault?" she said fiercely. "I was the one who put us there. If someone had to die, it should have been me, not him."

"Don't," Declan said harshly. "Don't say that. You said Mitchell was all for it and you got Ortega off the streets."

"Yes! And Mitchell is dead and Vanessa didn't even get to hold his hand when he died!" she cried. Wrenching herself out of his hold, she fled from the kitchen. Declan didn't hesitate. He followed her to her room.

She didn't bother closing the door, tossing her messenger bag on a chair, and spun around to face him.

Fury and grief couldn't have mixed more acutely on her face.

"What do you need, Angel? Tell me," he asked quietly, shutting the door behind him.

Without saying another word, she stepped up to him, grabbed his jaw and kissed him hard. His arms instinctively wrapped around her, keeping her flush. She bit his bottom lip and he made a sound in the back of his throat as he fervently returned her kisses.

She pulled back a breadth and whispered, "Make the pain go away."

Declan scooped her up in his arms and carried her to bed.

"I need you now," she growled. "I want you to fuck this pain away."

He dropped her on the bed. "That's not how it's gonna work."

She glared up at him.

"Trust me, okay?" Declan said, pulling his shirt over his head and tossing it on the floor. Next, he lowered his sweatpants over his ass and stepped out of them. Putting a knee on the bed, he reached for the button of her trousers and yanked them off her as she kicked off her shoes.

Gabby looked like a sex kitten on the bed, just wearing her button-down shirt, bare legs and still wearing socks. He held one ankle, hauled her under him and switched their positions, having her straddle him.

"Take it out on me," he commanded.

Her eyes flared.

Declan was usually the dominant one when it came to sex, but if he read Gabby right, what she needed was control after the events of the past few days left her with so little.

"Take it from me, Gab," he repeated. "Take—"

She slammed her mouth on his, her tongue jabbing inside his mouth, aggressively tasting him. He dueled with her stroke for stroke. She shimmied her ass lower and he levered himself up, unwilling to lose her mouth as she rubbed her pussy over his erection.

Fuck, that felt good.

She yanked her shirt apart and buttons flew in every direction. Her full tits jutted at him at eye level. "Suck me," she ordered.

Words barely left her mouth when his own wrapped around a breast. He avidly speared his tongue around her nipple and her moaning was all he needed to know she was on fire. She was burning as hot as he was. He could tell how wet she was just in the way she was dry fucking herself with panties and boxer briefs as their sole barrier.

"Oh, my god, oh my god. I need you inside me."

He lost her tit, as she wiggled one way and then the other to remove her undies, then she freed his cock and before Declan could take another breath, she sank onto him.

"Jesus, fuck!" he hissed as the exquisite grip of her inner muscles wrapped around him like a tight wet glove. Both her hands gripped his shoulders and as she rose, the suction on his dick made his eyes roll back.

She started rocking slowly at first, up then down, hips gyrating, torturing his poor dick that wanted to come in her so bad, but he bit back a snarl as Gabby fucked him with abandon. He felt her clench around him with the most exquisite torturous pleasure. Declan gritted his teeth and refused to come until he'd tasted all of her.

"Declan," she gasped as she continued bouncing on top of him. "You come, too."

"Not until I fuck you with my mouth," he said.

He flipped them over and without giving her another chance to protest, shoved her legs apart and buried his head between her thighs.

Her scent in his nose, her taste on his tongue—all these he hungered for endlessly. As her legs thrashed on his back, he gorged on the addictive sweetness of her that turned him into a mindless rutting beast. Every drop that slicked her pussy was every drop his tongue licked with abandon. Her clit was swollen with her arousal and he drew it between his lips and sucked, and somehow her muffled scream came to him. Her body shook, her fingers dug into his scalp as her orgasm ripped through her and he didn't relent until he'd wrung every tremor from her. He bolted up her body and slid back inside. He laced their fingers together and braced their hands on either side of her head.

"Look at me, Angel."

Her glazed eyes tried to focus on him. "Declan ..."

"You have me." He sped up his thrusts. He couldn't hold back any longer. His cock was rock hard and ready to explode.

"You'll always have me." A couple of hard thrusts and with one final push, he planted deep.

He grunted, shuddering as he jetted into her. He rolled on

his back before he could crush her, taking her with him, letting her sprawl on his chest. They were both breathing hard and a sheen of dampness glistened on her brow as he reached up to gently brush it.

Gabby glanced up and rested her chin on the rise and fall of his chest. "Thank you," she murmured.

His mouth pulled into a grin. "You did all the work."

"I needed that."

"I know."

She traced her finger on his skin, in the area where his heart was still thumping from the force of his climax. She lowered her face and feathered her lips there.

"Gabby?"

A sigh escaped her. "It unsettles me how you can still read me after all these years. And I'm not talking about the way Kelso reads me as his partner." Her eyes returned to his which were getting heavy after the relief of having her home, not to mention the mind-blowing sex that followed. "Hey." She shook him. "I'm about to have a profound conversation with you and you're dozing off."

"All ears, Angel." His grin widened, but his lids were like lead. He was too relaxed.

A biting pinch dug at his ribs. "Yow." His eyes popped open. "What was that for?"

"Thank you," she said simply and touched her lips to his before pushing back to get off the bed.

"Where are you going?"

"Showering off the smell of the bar."

He folded his arms under his head. "Thought we were having a life-altering conversation."

She rolled her eyes at him before showing him her delectable ass as she headed into the bathroom.

"Hurry back," he mumbled, looking down at his semi-erect cock before his vision blurred.

Later, the heavenly scent of lemon and vanilla mixed with

eau-de-Gabby assailed his nostrils and a warm body slipped into bed beside him.

"Took you long enough." He breathed in her hair and she snuggled into him.

"You staying here?" she asked.

His arms tightened around her. "You betcha."

She was silent and he squeezed her shoulder. "Don't worry about Theo. He gave us his blessing."

"Dec ..."

"Sleep, babe."

"Okay."

THE NEXT MORNING, Gabby woke up bright and early and put on her uniform. After the memorial service at the church where the mayor and other city officials gave speeches honoring the life of the captain, a procession of LAPD blue marched through the streets of downtown LA. Flanked by her sons, Vanessa stood strong even as the bagpipes played the haunting tune of "Going Home."

Gabby stood with her brothers and sisters in blue.

The honor guard rendered the 21-gun salute and Captain Frank Mitchell was laid to rest.

21

Two weeks later

"Cut!"

That ended "Take Three Fight with the Moon Beast."

Theo's character, Billy Mayhem, had broken out of a stranglehold that the Moon Beast had on him. In this case, it was a six-five stunt man who would later be CGI-ed onto the scene.

Applause erupted from the ecstatic film crew. It was supposed to be one of the most complex scenes on the penultimate episode that would set up the finale. Theo refused a stunt double and Declan couldn't be prouder.

His son practiced hard with him and Levi in perfecting the scene of a blind teen faced with the most dangerous life form he'd encountered since the series began.

And yes, references to the Karate Kid were mentioned given they blindfolded Theo to teach him how to use his senses to give credibility to his character.

Was it perfect?

No, but with careful choreography with the Moon Beast

stuntman, Declan knew by the third take that Theo was going to ace it.

"Our boy did good," Levi declared beside him.

Declan flashed him a proud grin. "More than good. Spectacular."

"Reckon Gabby's gonna quit reaming our ass?" Levi's mouth pulled into a self-deprecating smile.

He gave a shake of his head. "Hope so."

The blindfolded fight didn't go over well with Gabby—she all but fumed and growled at them when she found out. But after being outnumbered three-to-one, she acquiesced.

The first time it was mentioned to her, she dragged Declan into their bedroom and they had their first parenting fight.

"I thought he was going with the blind gun fight," she growled.

"Theo wasn't feeling it."

"Whose idea was it for hand-to-hand?"

"Theo's."

Gabby's brow lifted.

Declan coughed. "I might have said it was doable."

"He's coming off a concussion."

"So are you and yet you went chasing after a perp the other day." Declan was holding his tongue then, not wanting her to know that the risks she took with her job rattled him, but he couldn't stop blurting it out now.

"We're not talking about me."

"Right. You think our son is gonna fly with that double standard?"

"It's not the same. I've had years of training." She threw up her hands in exasperation. "Why are you not seeing this?"

That irritated him. "Are you saying I'd knowingly put our son in danger?"

"Stop twisting my words!"

His jaw clenched. "Not at all. It's either that, or you think

I'm a clueless backwoods hick who wouldn't know dynamite from his dick."

Gabby's brows furrowed. "I didn't mean you're an idiot either."

He crossed his arms and regarded her. "No?"

"I don't want him hurt, but I couldn't say anything. I'm his guardian, but you're his dad."

"We could remedy that, just say the word."

"Stop changing the subject."

Declan sighed. "You know what? Maybe that's the first thing we should talk about. It's hard to orchestrate the parenting thing from the cheap seats."

"Excuse me?"

He gritted his teeth, but tried his best not to snap at her, laying his hands gently on her shoulders even if all he wanted to do was throttle her. "You can't tell me what to do as his dad, if you're not going to step up as his mom."

With those words he left the room and let her stew. Declan would get pissed at Gabby, but it never lasted. Not when he remembered her heartbreak all those years ago. But she'd known Theo was her son for almost three weeks, and there was only so much he could take before he blurted out the truth. They should be talking about how to break it to him.

Not this hovering over his shoulders telling him how to be a dad.

Fuck that.

Declan wasn't an idiot. He and Levi planned a meeting with the production crew. They were filming in an indoor set that was made to look like a cave. The flooring was padded, and the fake rocks were made of foam. Concussion or not, that would have been the case anyway. Gabby should have known better.

And yet he could see where she was coming from. She'd lost someone close, and her job dealt with death, so she was jumpy.

"Roarke! Levi!" Theo's arm was around Emma, but he released his girl and pushed through the people giving him a pat on the back to get to him and Levi. They exchanged fist bumps.

But that wasn't enough. This was his son and he was a badass.

"Come here, Ace," Declan muttered. He hauled the teenager up with one arm before engulfing him in a bear hug. "So proud of you, Theo."

Son.

When they pulled away from each other, Theo's face was etched in a slew of emotions and Declan imagined his was the same. Rehearsing fight scenes involved a level of trust and it paved the way in their own personal relationship as father and son. Theo was thawing in viewing him as a mere sperm donor, but they still had a long way to go before Declan could measure up to Peter as his father. He may never measure up at all, and Declan was okay with that.

"Thanks," the teenager said sheepishly. Then he glanced away, looking for his girl, spotting her behind him and tugged her close.

Declan cleared his throat. "You guys wrapping up for the day?"

"Yeah, the crew wants to go out to Chateau Marmont, but Gabby's been harping about this Korean cafe on Beverly Boulevard and my girl here"—he gave Emma an extra squeeze—"wants to try it."

He'd heard Gabby rave about the restaurant. "Scoop by Pi?"

"That one," Emma piped in.

Levi immediately brought up his phone and searched. Glancing up, he said, "It's a family restaurant. Think you'd be okay to just walk in?"

Theo checked his own phone. "Gabby said she could do

an early dinner. It's a Wednesday. Hopefully, it won't be as crowded."

"SPAM FRIED RICE AND KIMCHI? SERIOUSLY?" Kelso eyed her plate of steaming rice, the popular canned cooked pork, and the smelly preserved cabbage. "You know we're going to Beverly Hills after this, right? We've got to interview a witness who may or not be an accessory to murder."

"She's guilty," Gabby said, ignoring her partner's first statement and digging into her plate. "How's your Kimchi pork in cold noodles?" she asked Theo.

The teen held up his hand as he slurped the end of one noodle. "Spicy, but damn, this pork belly just melts in your mouth."

"Save room for the Oreo cheesecake, baby," Emma said.

"Says the girl who ordered the kimchi carbonara," Theo teased back.

These two would give her a toothache, Gabby thought with a smile.

She glanced over to the counter where Declan and Levi were waiting for the rest of their order.

Scoop by Pi was a family-owned Korean restaurant which started as a dessert cafe. The visual displays reflected this. But there was a secret menu where the chef's creativity high-lighted savory dishes. Scrumptious Korean-culinary creations were plated with a skill one would expect from a fine dining restaurant, which clearly this place wasn't.

Case in point, it was located in a strip mall. Gabby was pleasantly surprised that Theo and Emma had no qualms meeting at this restaurant.

The interior was bright and lively, painted in pinks and greens with light maple colored tables and chairs. Orders were placed at the counter and delivered to the table, but with the waitstaff starting to get overtaxed by the influx of customers, Declan and Levi decided to wait for the rest of their meal where the kitchen expediter was grouping the orders by number.

When the men returned with a tray of food and drinks, Declan held out a tall glass of a milky white shake with a cherry on top. "Lychee shaved ice?"

Emma raised her arm and was promptly handed her order.

"Mango's yours," Declan put the yellow drink beside Gabby. He distributed a few more dishes. Their table ordered a ton of food.

Gabby thanked him through a mouthful of rice and laughed when grains nearly fell from her mouth.

"Don't you know it's not polite to talk and eat at the same time?" Declan teased, settling into the seat beside her.

"Clearly you've never been a detective," Gabby told him after she gulped down the rest in her mouth. "You take and make calls in the middle of your lunch hour which is frequently late. You never know when that one call can blow the investigation wide open." She shrugged. "I'm not usually this unrefined. Just so happens the food is too good." She took another hearty bite, just to make a point. She chewed more slowly, but her jaw hurt in an effort not to laugh.

Declan chuckled and nudged her with his shoulder. "Just teasing, Angel."

"They're so sweet!" Emma gushed as she bumped Theo with her shoulder, who promptly rolled his eyes.

Gabby's face heated to the roots of her hair, and it had nothing to do with the kimchi in her fried rice.

"Barf," Theo muttered, but the corners of his mouth lifted.

She glanced at Declan who had his chopsticks ready to lift a pork belly dumpling out of its milky broth when her own chopsticks made its way to his bowl.

"Ooh, let me try," Gabby said.

Declan's chopsticks blocked hers from impinging on his dish. "Nope."

Gabby gave a mock gasp and turned to the two teens. "Is this what you're calling sweet?"

"Aw, Dec," Emma said. "Don't burst my bubble now."

The man beside her chuckled and picked up a dumpling and held it out to Gabby. "Is this better?"

Everyone exploded in laughter, but Gabby didn't waste any time, snatching the tasty morsel with her mouth. "I should have ordered this too," she said after savoring it with purposeful bites. "Wanna swap?" She waggled her brows.

Declan lowered his chopsticks and sat back in his chair, eyeing her with a not so PG stare. "What's in it for me?"

Kelso coughed. "Minors in the house."

"Yeah," Levi muttered.

"You two are just jealous," Declan told them, then turning back to Gabby, he asked, "Sure you want this?" He motioned to his bowl.

"Nah." Gabby winked at him. "Just testing if you l—" she caught herself. She was about to say love. Her face was probably bright red by now. "L-like me more. Me or food?" she finished, giving her attention back to her fried rice.

Kelso cleared his throat again.

Suddenly, she felt a warm breath by her ear. "Well, in case you change your answer, Angel, we can talk about it later at home."

Declan kissed her temple before finally starting on his meal.

"So," Gabby said brightly in an attempt to quell the heat that rose between her and Declan. How could that man turn a conversation about dumplings into sex? It wasn't sex, it was something more. "You all said you took a video of Theo's fight scene."

Emma held up her phone and handed it to Gabby.

And with that, the subject was changed.

"I'M SUCH A DORK," Gabby announced when she climbed into the SUV beside Kelso, leaving the others in the restaurant to check out more desserts. Interestingly enough, Theo and Emma didn't get mobbed. Most of the patrons were the regular LA crowd, not the tourists who were the typical autograph seekers.

"Seems like Roarke's got your number."

"He's just …" She couldn't put it into words. "He just keeps me on my toes and throws out unexpected innuendos."

Kelso pulled into traffic and gave a brief snort. "Innuendo? I think you're past innuendos, partner. That man has branded you as his. Besides, I thought you guys picked up where you left off."

"Well, not exactly," Gabby said. "And I'm not a cow to be branded."

She never got around to having that profound conversation with Declan, partly because after the captain's funeral there was a shakeup in their Division that occupied a lot of her head space. Mostly she was sticking her head in the sand because she was overwhelmed with everything coming at her. Staying in stasis seemed like a good idea. Except Declan appeared to have reached the limit of his patience. He wasn't hiding how he felt anymore, but he wasn't voicing any feelings either, merely being demonstrative and … well, hinting.

"So, are you exes with benefits?"

"Ah … we're more than that. I think."

"Are you guys gonna try and make a go of it?"

"I don't know."

"So you're just fucking?" Kelso stated, deadpan.

"You're getting annoying."

"And you haven't told Theo that you're his mother."

"None of your business."

"I give a shit about you, Gab," her friend's voice grew rough. "I know it's eating you up inside. This is one problem that has a solution, and that solution is to stop hiding the fact from your son and come clean."

"It's not that simple."

"Oh? Explain."

"Theo is under a lot of pressure."

"Doesn't seem so to me. He seems to have it made."

"You know better than that," Gabby said. "I'm a living example of a teen-star has-been."

"That was by choice."

When their SUV stopped at a red light, Kelso turned to her. "Look at me, Woodward."

Gabby did. Her partner's eyes were serious, earnest. "Roarke seems like a great guy. That man cares for you. I hope you see that. It's not about Theo. It's about you. You should see the vibes he gives off whenever guys at Division are around you—"

"You don't have to point that out. Delgado teases me enough about it," Gabby grumbled. "And that's another reason. Theo just found out Declan is his real father. Revenant Films is coming up with a press release before the season premiere because the tabloids have just been going to town about this."

This was one thing Gabby was relieved to have Nick handle. After their Rodeo Drive field trip, the tabloids started speculating, and a picture of Gabby and Declan from when they first got married was printed. But that news was soon eclipsed by a possible bioweapon in play in LA, and the mayor was still trying to calm the public.

"Isn't the season premiere next summer? That's another eight months. The longer you sit on this, the more Theo will react badly." Kelso's face softened. "He looks up to you, Gab, and you've tried everything to find out the truth."

"I know, but he's vulnerable at this age. The point of identity and existential crisis. He's at the top of his career right now. Can you imagine what he'll feel when he finds out he's been living a lie?"

The light turned green and Kelso returned his attention to the road. "You have a point, but I still maintain Theo is as level-headed as they come—for an entitled teen actor."

Gabby laughed. "He's his father, I guess."

"No, he's you," Kelso said.

She would disagree. It was more Declan who'd had more responsibility as a teenager than he should have had until he met Gabby. She shook her head. She wasn't going to think of that past anymore, what should have been. There was only now and what needed to be done. There was still a chance for them to become a family, right?

"I'll tell him," she whispered.

As low as her voice had become, her partner heard her. "Atta, girl."

"I'll talk to Declan when I get home." It was time they defined what they meant to each other. No more skating the line of exes-with-benefits.

Their radio crackled from dispatch. "Detective Kelso, what's your twenty?"

"Heading west to Beverly Hills on Beverly Boulevard."

"You need to head to Inglewood."

"What do you have?"

"Possible homicide related to the Ortega case."

Kelso glanced at her as he clicked the mic to answer. "We're on our way."

22

TWO BLACK AND whites with lights flashing were already parked on the curb beside an alley. The ambulance was pulled in across from it.

As Gabby and Kelso stepped out of their vehicle, a uniform approached them.

"Is the scene secured?" Gabby called out, whipping out a pair of gloves from her back pocket and slipping them on.

"Of course," the officer grumbled. "We haven't touched anything."

Gabby nodded. It wouldn't have been the first time patrol officers were too eager when they were at a crime scene and contaminated the area in their haste to investigate. They frequently forgot it wasn't their job to do so. She'd been there, done that. "Were you the one who called GHD?"

"Yes." Hastings, as his nameplate stated, ran a finger across the top of his mouth. "There was a message on the body."

Passing a smattering of spectators huddled in groups, they ducked under the police tape. Residents frequently avoided the cops, the fear of getting hauled in overcame their curiosity. But sometimes, passers-by became nosy.

"Who found the body?" Kelso asked as they made their way down the narrow alley.

"A homeless person rummaging through the dumpster."

"A homeless person?" Gabby asked. "Who just happened to have a phone?"

"That's what dispatch said," Hastings replied testily. "He was gone when we arrived."

"Sounds fishy to me," Kelso drawled as they neared.

Gathered around the dumpster was a man in an apron, probably the cook from the diner that used the dumpster. Beside him stood another uniform.

"That's my partner," Hastings said. "And the owner of the deli."

The owner was Ivan Smirnov and he operated the Russian grocery/deli located in the building on the right. He looked distraught and disturbed.

Kelso crouched down near the vic, Gabby noted the face was covered in blood. The hair was close cropped, probably blond.

"Victim is Caucasian male, around six-four, two hundred and twenty pounds. Put the age around late twenties to late forties." Kelso rattled off his initial observation. "Blunt head trauma, red welts on the arms—possible defensive wounds. We need Nadia to estimate time of death."

"Did you know our victim, Mr. Smirnov?" Gabby asked.

"He frequently comes in to Mechta," the man sniffed. "Loves the stuffed cabbage. His boss loves the cakes. Pays in cash. Not unusual."

Crap, Gabby thought. No receipts to trace. "When was the last time he came in?"

"The other night."

"Was he a long-time customer?"

Smirnov shook his head and pondered the question. "Maybe two weeks ago."

Kelso and Gabby exchanged glances. "Do you have surveillance at the grocery?"

"Of course. We keep thirty days' worth."

"Gabby," Kelso called her attention to a note stapled to the dead body. "It's the number for GHD and said we shouldn't have interfered with Ortega. Does this look like a cartel hit?"

"Hard to say."

"Hastings, can you shine a light on the face?"

The patrol officer did as he was told, and Gabby crouched down to look closer. There was something oddly familiar about the man. Like she'd seen him once before, but where? Blood obscured his face, probably on purpose, but why call GHD here and be mysterious about who was killed if the perp expected a reaction?

Someone was messing with them.

Gabby turned rigid and straightened to look around, wondering if they were being watched. Some perpetuators of crimes were egomaniacs who thrilled in witnessing the aftermath of their handiwork. Who was ...*son of a bitch*. Her eyes flew back to the body on the ground as recognition sunk like an anchor in her gut.

"It's one of Claudette's bodyguards," she said.

"THERE. PLAY THAT BACK AGAIN," Gabby told Nadia and pointed to the footage of the grocery store surveillance. It was grainy and the technology was as old as Theo, but there was a frame that clearly showed Lance Logan, South African mercenary. But where was look-a-like Douglas Smith? Those were their names on their passports as security for Claudette Dumont, but she doubted they were real, given the vast resources of Antonio Andrade.

The FBI had reached out to the Brazilian billionaire. But as far as Gabby knew the man had evaded their efforts and had made no inquiries into Claudette's whereabouts. At first Gabby thought the Biotech businessman used his connections to smuggle Claudette out of the country, but now she wasn't too sure. Declan said her ex-stepmother had asked for his help in exchange for information about Ortega. There were certainly no public sightings of Claudette who was now a person of interest for carrying a biological weapon into the country.

Was she dead?

Gabby's chest tightened.

As much as she hated the woman who stole her baby and caused her endless heartache, Gabby still wouldn't wish her a brutal death. Although she'd imagined her murder a couple of times over the years and, most recently, after the captain's death, she wanted justice to prevail.

"Looks like him all right," Nadia agreed. She pulled up the photo taken by immigration when they first arrived in LA. "The CSI team is almost done cataloging the scene. I'll head back to the lab if you don't need me here."

Before Gabby could answer, her rover—remote out-of-vehicle emergency radio—crackled.

"Gab." It was Kelso. He was canvassing the neighborhood for witnesses, showing them pictures of Logan, Smith, and Claudette. They'd been at this for a few hours. Even if Nadia wasn't the medical examiner, she had enough experience to estimate time of death and Logan had not been dead very long. They had to act quickly to preserve evidence.

Fishing out her rover, she clicked. "Give me good news, Kelso."

"A townhouse."

"Fucking A. Where?"

Kelso gave her the name of the building. It was only a few blocks from the grocery. "Okay, we can consider this exigent circumstances since one of the tenants was murdered.

However, I'll get Chen to get a retroactive warrant from Judge Mackey."

It wasn't the first time they'd awakened a judge at two in the morning to approve a retroactive search warrant, so they knew which ones to approach. Mackey was one of the judges who would err on the side of public safety. After several dead ends by their Division and the Feds to locate Claudette, she didn't expect pushback. "Besides it's only ten. He shouldn't be too grumpy."

Signing off, she made the call to Chen who said he was on top of it. He didn't sound pleased, but knew it was time sensitive.

"We're done here. Just make a few copies of the videos for our file," Gabby told Nadia. She got up from her chair, but Nadia grabbed her arm.

She glanced at the other woman questioningly.

"Be careful, okay?" Nadia said. "Logan was a big guy. That was a lethal blow to the head that caved in his skull like that."

"I will. Don't worry."

Now she had to shoot off a text to Declan so he wouldn't worry too. *"Sorry. Caught up in a case. Don't wait. Long night ahead."*

EDEN PARK HOMES was a townhouse court configuration common for multifamily living. It was a series of detached buildings sharing a common courtyard. The manager, Mr. Shah, was cooperative, especially after they'd informed him that one of his tenants was dead.

"I'm so sorry to hear about Mr. Logan." The man looked genuinely troubled. "Of course, you have my full cooperation. The lease was under his name."

"Do you get a lot of tenants paying three months in advance? Cash?"

"Cash payments are not unusual." Mr. Shah looked down at his hands.

"I wasn't implying any wrong-doing. We're just trying to find a paper trail."

"I'll admit some of my tenants are less than savory characters," Mr. Shah's South Asian accent slipped out. Judging how he mostly spoke like a regular California native, he'd probably been a first-generation immigrant at a very young age. "I'm just the property manager. We do background checks, but that would only go so far if they're in town for extended business and not in the state database."

Gabby already knew from the quick hack by Nadia that the majority of tenants in Eden Park were Eastern European.

"Do you want to see the unit now?" Mr. Shah asked. The manager had tried to call the number he had for Logan on file, but it went to voicemail.

She checked her phone and saw the go-ahead from Chen.

Kelso came in from the outside. "Found it." Meaning Claudette's Porsche.

"Where?"

"She wasn't really hiding it. Basement level of the garage across the street."

"So the metallic blue Toyota Camry noted on the lease was a secondary car."

Even if Gabby's question was rhetorical, Mr. Shah nodded. "Yes. Like I said. I deal mostly with Logan. Maybe late at night I see the other guy."

"Have you ever noticed any altercations or disagreements between them?"

The manager shook his head.

"Guess we'll see what we can find out," Gabby said. She told Kelso and the other two officers accompanying them. "We'll knock first. If no response, we'll have Mr. Shah unlock the door."

23

Sorry. Caught up in a case. Don't wait. Long night ahead

Declan exhaled a frustrated breath and tossed his phone on the couch. Reading a book was useless, he couldn't concentrate, and he never watched TV unless it was with Theo or Gabby and even that was new to him. Levi had already turned in for the night since Theo had a four o' clock wake-up call, which meant Declan did, too.

It was eleven and he'd hoped to spend some time with Gabby, but that wasn't looking promising at the moment. He should get used to being with a cop and roll with it. His phone buzzed from a number he knew was a new one Garrison had used.

"Roarke."

"Is Theo home with you?" The CIA officer asked without much preamble.

"Yes." A pause. "Why?"

"Raul Ortega escaped the CDC holding facility."

"What? How?" Cold fingers of fear wrapped around his heart.

"Explain later. Pack up. Until we know what his game is, we need you mobile on short notice."

"What about Gabby?"

"We'll catch up with her."

"Not good enough."

"Goddammit, Roarke!" the man growled with an unusual lack of control. "Check KCAL9 and get your shit packed."

He needed to update Gabby. He tried to call her but immediately got her voicemail.

Fuck.

He jumped up from the couch, grabbed the remote, and switched the TV to KCAL-9.

On the screen, the footage of red and blue lights, ambulances and fire trucks seared into his vision.

He quickly scanned the caption as he turned up the volume.

"We're on the scene of what looks like another fentanyl attack. Witnesses reported an explosion and then people who were running out of the club started dropping like flies…"

"Holy fuck." He spun on his heel and stalked toward Levi's room, pounding on his friend's door.

"Jesus, Roarke, what is it?" Levi asked when he opened the door, clearly jolted from sleep.

"Pack a bag and get ready."

His partner backed away from the door to let him in and headed to the bathroom to throw water on his face and gargle mouthwash.

Declan leaned against the jamb leading to the bathroom, arms crossed, impatiently waiting for his partner to properly wakeup. "Garrison just called and we're code red. Ortega has escaped confinement."

Levi stilled, finished his gargling, and looked at him sharply in the mirror. "Just now?"

"Yes. There's also been another fentanyl attack. I don't know if it's the same case Gabby …" Declan wasn't liking these developments. Two weeks of nothing and then this? "Dammit! I don't like coincidences."

"No shit." Levi walked back into the bedroom, his body alert.

"Garrison's not sure what Ortega's end-game is, but we need to be ready to leave if Theo is still a target." And Gabby. Who would protect her when she was out there and he was here? He'd never felt more powerless in his life.

"Agreed. Our perimeter surveillance drones can only do so much if we have an all-out assault on this place."

"What's going on?" Theo's voice came from the open door.

"Pack a bag, kid. We might need to leave," Declan told him.

"Not until one of you explain what's going on!" The teenager's eyes flashed defiantly. "Does it have something to do with that nightclub attack? It's all over twitter."

Declan's jaw hardened. "Partly."

"Or did you two screw-up? Playing Russian roulette with whoever got the captain killed and now I'm the target?" Theo said. "I'm not a dumb kid. I know you're all not plain body-guards or fight instructors pandering to the whims of teen-actors or the studio."

"That's actually my job description," Levi said dryly.

"Bullshit."

"Theo!" Declan snapped. "Pack a bag. We'll explain later."

His son still wouldn't move. "Did Gabby agree to this? Why isn't she home yet? Is she at the scene? That's why she's not answering my texts, right?"

The look of worry on Theo's face escalated the anxiety he'd been trying desperately to reign in. He swiped her number again. Failing, he tried to raise Kelso. Straight to voicemail as well. Dispatch lines were clogged.

"Can't get hold of her. We'll have to go through other means." Other means meant going through the police scanner which could take a while. Declan jerked his head at Theo. "Get going."

"You can't order me around."

"Mouthing off isn't gonna help me find your sister, so knock it the fuck off."

"What about Emma? I can't just disappear and not tell her."

"You can't have any contact with her, Theo," Levi said.

"No fucking way."

"For fuck's sake!" Declan growled. "If I have to hogtie you and stuff you into the trunk of a car, I will. Your safety is our priority and the nightclub attack is only the beginning. Happy now? Will you just do as you're fucking told?!"

His son clenched his fists at his sides. Declan's cool was fast evaporating—he was about to hit his limit with the kid.

Levi turned away from their standoff and started packing his gear.

"I'm not you," Theo said finally. "I'm not going to turn my back on the girl I love when the going gets tough. That's something cowards do."

His son backed away slowly, holding Declan's eyes in defiance, and then pivoted on a foot and exited the room.

At that parting shot, Declan's anger deflated, his chin dropped, and his eyes stared blankly at the wooden floors. Those words slammed into him harder than any gunshot.

"He's never going to forgive me for divorcing Gabby." His voice was hoarse, barely above a whisper.

Levi's bare feet appeared in Declan's line of vision. "The kid didn't mean that."

"I had nothing to offer her back then except heartbreak … and my trust in her was shot."

"Your situation and Theo's are different, but maybe we should look at it from his point of view instead of dismissing how he feels," Levi said.

"Are you saying I have a stick up my ass?" Declan gave a brief smile.

Before Levi could answer, the perimeter alert sounded off. That meant the car approaching couldn't be IDed by their app from the list of permitted vehicles on premises.

Declan quickly left Levi and went for his M9 pistol under the sink of the hallway guest bathroom. It was closer than the weapons he had in his bedroom.

Flattening his body against the wall by the entrance door, he took a peek behind the shades. The newcomers weren't even pretending to hide themselves.

He recognized the driver Migs—the man Garrison had undercover with Ortega and the man who Gabby had confronted in the alley outside the clinic. Exiting behind the driver's side was Garrison helping a disgruntled woman from the vehicle.

Ariana.

Rounding from the passenger side was Bristow…the nurse who Declan now suspected was more than a nurse.

Declan opened the door. "What's going on?"

"Don't touch me!" the woman hissed.

"Just helping you down, princess," Garrison drawled.

"Come on, Ari," Migs grasped the woman's arm, but she yanked it away from him too, and hugged herself protectively.

"Stay away from me too, pendejo!"

Bristow came up to Declan. "We need to leave."

"What the hell?" Levi said, striding up beside Declan. "Is there some kind of party and we don't know about it?"

"No time to explain," Garrison said. "Something is about to go down in Inglewood."

"The club attack was in West Hollywood," Declan said.

"There are enough first responders at the scene, but that's just a diversion," Garrison said. "One of Claudette's body-guards is dead."

"What?"

"Yeah, we nearly missed it on the police scanner," Migs said. "Ortega wants us focused on that."

"So Ortega really escaped?" Declan demanded.

Garrison nodded. "And his enterprise is operational. We're thinking Ortega and the cartel have struck a deal, but this wouldn't be possible without interference from Andrade."

"Claudette's boyfriend?"

"Yes. We suspect they wanted some research we had at the CDC. We've narrowed down the inside man there," Garrison cut off, waving his hand in irritation. "I'll catch you guys up later." He turned to Declan. "You need to leave immediately with Bristow."

The red-haired man had already gotten into the driver's seat of the Escalade. Declan looked at Levi, but it was Garrison who answered the directive in his eyes. "We'll take care of Theo. Don't worry."

Declan didn't say any more and jumped into the SUV beside Bristow.

Executing an awkward three-point turn, the hefty vehicle screeched out of the driveway.

"We should be at the scene in fourteen minutes," Bristow looked at the dashboard GPS.

"Do you have an idea what Garrison is talking about?"

"About how Ortega escaped?"

"Yeah."

"One of the virologists at the CDC is working for Antonio Andrade. Guess the promise of money that's ten times more than government salary is worth betraying a vow to save lives." Bristow cast him a derisive look. "That's not including sign-on bonus."

"Jesus."

"Feds are still investigating the break-out. Ortega was always meant to survive the virus from initial reports. He'd been given the antiviral before he'd infected himself. Not even sure the chemo shit is real."

"Somebody really screwed up the intel there."

"That can only be done by someone with money. To be able to feed false intel into an agency like the CIA?"

"This Andrade guy?"

"Suspect number one."

"Counterintelligence is not new."

"Tell that to Garrison. He's pissed."

"I hadn't noticed," Declan deadpanned.

His phone buzzed with an unknown number. Thinking it was Garrison again with a new burner, he answered. "Roarke."

It was a voice he didn't recognize. "I'm sending you a link. Click on it. Don't click on it, it's up to you. It's too late anyway."

The line went dead.

A notification popped up on his screen. Declan's phone had several levels of security against malware, so he clicked on the URL without hesitation.

At first, he couldn't tell anything from the grainy video— just a group of shadows moving along a courtyard until he heard Gabby's voice and her face became clearer from the camera that appeared to be positioned at the entrance.

A text banner lowered on his screen and he quickly checked it.

"Such a waste. She's a pretty detective, isn't she?"

Dread clogged the words in his throat.

"What is it?" Bristow asked.

"Gabby," Declan choked through the paralyzing fear that froze his entire body. He couldn't take his eyes off the screen, as if he was helplessly watching an accident about to happen, a sense of imminent loss constricting his airway. Then rage exploded. "Step on the gas, Bristow. Don't fucking stop for anyone."

24

"LISTEN, people, we want to help our guys in West Holly-wood, but we stand a better chance finding answers here," Gabby said.

Their investigation of Claudette's unit was delayed when news of the Hive nightclub attack hit their rovers and phones. First bulletin was all hands-on deck, but Chen told them to wait for further instructions before abandoning their scene. They cooled their heels for twenty minutes and when Gabby tried to raise Chen again and their watch officer, all lines were clogged.

Text messages weren't being delivered and calls weren't connecting. The Hive nightclub attack must have sparked an overload of cell and data service.

There were four officers remaining at their scene; two accompanied Gabby and Kelso, while the other two continued to try and reach Chen. As they approached Claudette's town-house, Kelso signaled the rest to switch off their radios and mute their phones. Gabby held out the handheld-motion radar device used to detect movement through the door. It was another high-tech piece of equipment that was quietly being used by their division, but not advertised because it was a hot topic for civil liberties advocates. With the warrant, their team was less apprehensive about using it and the safety of everyone involved was priority. She nodded at her partner to go ahead.

Kelso gave three sharp raps on the door.

Seconds passed. No sounds from within could be heard and no movement on her radar.

"Ms. Dumont, this is Detective Kelso. We need a word with you, please."

After twenty seconds. "Ms. Dumont, we have a warrant to search your townhouse. We will be entering the premises."

Kelso signaled to Gabby to open the door. She pocketed the radar and pushed the door open. The safety wasn't engaged. They gestured at the two cops to be on alert as everyone drew their weapons.

Gabby entered first. Her partner, being taller, had the flashlight at full glare, ready to blind whomever might have a weapon pointed at them.

She had her own flashlight supported under her gun hand as they moved from room to room. There was a sink full of dirty dishes, blood on the floor, and overturned tables and chairs strewn around. A sign of a struggle.

After clearing the first floor, Gabby turned to the stairs and headed up. It had always been their play with her going first and low, because Kelso being bigger would block any shot made by Gabby. She was lucky enough that her partner was man enough to let a woman take the lead if it meant a better tactical plan. Flattening against the wall and slowly ascending the stairs, she made a forward signal with her hand, indicating for Kelso to check the other rooms as she entered the first bedroom. From the jeans and shirts strewn on the floor, she knew it wasn't Claudette's room. She aimed her flashlight at the bathroom and saw a trail of blood and a bloodied white tee. Looked like it was Logan's partner who killed him but didn't escape unscathed himself. Why leave evidence?

"Woodward!"

The urgency of Kelso's voice had her dashing out of the room and into the next one. Her partner had turned on the lights, but was nowhere in sight. She heard movements in the bathroom and headed straight there. The smell of something rank hit her nose.

In the bathtub was Claudette, deathly white, her lips bloodless, with vomit dried up on her chin and clumping chunks of her blond hair.

"Oh my God, Claudette," Gabby whispered as she crouched down beside Kelso, staring at the woman and taking an inventory of her possible injuries. There were some finger marks on her arm and visible needle bruises.

She had on a nightie, no panties. There were no bruises on her legs, thank God.

Kelso checked for a pulse.

"Except for the marks on her arms, there are no other visible injuries or trauma. They made her sit up so she wouldn't choke on her vomit," Kelso muttered.

"They forcibly drugged her?"

"Looks like it." He patted her cheek a couple of times. "Ms. Dumont, can you hear me?"

A low moan escaped Claudette's lips. It was rare that she saw her ex-stepmother without makeup. Rarer still for her hair to be tangled and filthy as it was now.

"Don't touch me," the other woman whispered.

"We're here to help you. Remember me? Gabby's partner?"

"Leave me alone."

Gabby beat back the stab of sympathy. It was there, but she had to remember that Claudette had brought this on herself and had to treat her like a job. And as much as she hated it, Claudette was innocent until proven guilty.

"Detective Woodward."

Rising from her spot beside Kelso, she turned to see one of the officers who accompanied them.

"House is empty except for our vic."

"Not sure she's the vic. Have our boys made contact?"

"No."

"Have you called the EMTs?" Kelso started running a face towel under the sink to clean Claudette without disturbing much of the evidence until the CSI team got here which could be the next morning or the next day.

Gabby let out a frustrated huff. "Dammit, Hastings—"

"I tried," the officer cut her off. "Radios are jammed. That's why I sent my partner hustling back to command post."

Frowning, she glanced back at Kelso who was quietly trying to calm the disoriented Claudette. She was weakly fighting him off—or her version of it.

"I'm going to try and raise someone." Anyone. This communication darkness was starting to nag her. Pulling out her rover, she walked out the bathroom and to the window. "Command post, this is Woodward."

Static. She turned the knob and tried another channel. "That's weird." She fished out her phone and checked that too. "No signal."

"Looks like there's a jammer," Hastings said.

The cop was right, but why?

"Get out of here," she growled at Hastings.

"Why?"

"Get out! That's an order!"

Not waiting to see whether the cop complied or not, she ran back to Kelso who was in the process of hauling Claudette out of the tub.

"Up you go, Ms. Dumont"

"Kelso, wait!" She jerked him away from Claudette and got in between them. Her partner landed on his ass behind her while her stepmother fell back into the tub.

"What the hell, Gab?" Kelso glared at her.

"It's a trap. They've jam—" Her breathing constricted, and her vision tunneled, meeting Kelso's horrified eyes and then she was falling…

"Gabby!"

THE THREE WORST moments in Declan's life revolved around Gabby. The third one was when he found her in bed with Nick. The second? When he found out she was in the hospital because she was mugged without knowing the extent of her injuries.

Watching Gabby fall to the floor unconscious via live video was the most terrifying moment of his existence. Even being surrounded by Yemeni rebels with the barrels of seven AK-47s pointed at him didn't measure up to the excruciating dread of watching the woman who was his everything, walk into a trap, and possibly her doom.

As he and Bristow raced through the courtyard of Eden Park Townhomes, following the lead of the officer who'd been with Gabby, he found himself praying.

That he wasn't too late.

That he'd get the chance to tell Gabby he loved her.

That fate wasn't so cruel this second time around.

The door was wide open, and the lights were blazing by the time they arrived. Bristow made them put on respirator masks. If Declan never saw one of these for the rest of his life again, it would be too soon.

The first floor was empty.

"Gabby!" He yelled and charged straight for the stairs. Kelso was at the top of the staircase, but he was on his ass, slouched against a wall and having a hard time breathing. Gabby was on her back unmoving.

"I tried," Kelso wheezed, getting a hand up from Bristow. "It got me too. Hastings, help him." He told the other cop.

Declan couldn't breathe as he dropped to a knee, gathered Gabby into his arms and sprang up to run down the steps and out into the open.

"Lay her down on the ground," Bristow ordered. "Help her breathe." The nurse led Kelso to sit on a nearby bench.

Ripping off his respirator, Declan lowered his mouth and breathed through Gabby's own.

"Do it a couple of times, Roarke."

The nurse drew out a packet from his saddle bag and ripped it open, expertly fixing the Narcan tube to the inhaler. "We'll do one dose and see how she reacts. She might need two depending on how much she inhaled." He held Gabby's fingers tightly as Bristow shot the anti-overdose drug into her nose. It was only then that he noticed the officer laying down another cop on the grass.

"You doing okay there, Kelso?" Bristow called out as he used his teeth to tear another packet of the drug.

"Yeah, help Hastings. I'll keep."

"I think Ms. Dumont is dead," the officer said.

"Claudette?" Declan mumbled, suddenly remembering that he'd seen her in the video too.

Kelso shook his head. "She was in a bad way. She wouldn't have survived that fentanyl aerosol."

"You sure that's what it was?" Bristow asked.

"Positive."

Claudette was dead. Decency told him to go in and get her, but Declan couldn't bear to leave Gabby's side. No one was making him budge until he was sure she was okay.

It might have been a minute, it might have been two before the officer returned with Claudette's body. Bristow gave Kelso a dose of the Narcan as well, and then he worked on trying to revive the other woman.

And yet Gabby had not opened her eyes.

"Why isn't she waking up?" Declan demanded.

Bristow glared over his shoulder. At the moment he and the other cop were giving Claudette CPR. "She's breathing, Roarke, and her heartbeat is strong. Let's worry about the waking up later. I've got bigger problems here."

Angst. He didn't do well with angst, so he directed it to the unconscious woman who was the cause of it. "Angel, you better wake up," he whispered harshly.

Nothing.

He brought both her hands to his mouth and kissed the back of her fingers. "You and I are gonna have words when you wake up. You need to be more careful. I'm this close to locking you in the house."

Not a single twitch. Then he watched her chest stop rising and falling.

He leaned in to check her breathing. Nothing.

Heart pounding, he put a finger under her nose. "Bristow!" he bellowed. "She's not breathing!"

The nurse quickly returned to their side, shoved Declan out of the way and checked. "Fuck!" he muttered. "She needs another dose."

A swarm of EMTs with gurneys arrived. "Take that blonde." Bristow instructed them. "I've given her one dose of Narcan. She may need another one. I need to stabilize Detective Woodward before you take her away." He zeroed in on Kelso. "You. Ride in the ambulance. You need to be monitored." And then turning back to the oncoming EMTs he barked, "Officer Hastings has had one dose of Narcan."

Blowing out a breath, Bristow returned his attention to Gabby and blew through her mouth as another EMT prepared another syringe. "Come on Detective Hottie, don't you quit on me."

Declan sat, ass on the ground, hands in his hair, trying to keep from losing his shit.

Bristow took the drug and administered the second dose.

"Come on. Come on," Bristow mumbled.

"How many can you give her?" Declan asked.

The nurse ignored him and spoke to the EMT.

"Shouldn't you take her to the hospital now?"

"We're doing everything we can," Bristow snapped. "She's breathing, but it's shallow. We have to wait a few minutes to administer another dose."

"Goddammit!" Declan shifted to a crouch, ignoring Bristow's warning glare and the first responder's discomfort with having a near-rabid man breathing down their necks.

"Her mouth is turning blue!" Declan roared.

"Calm your shit, Roarke, before I have you ejected from here," Bristow warned as he prepared another dose.

Not willing to risk getting separated from Gabby, he redirected all his fears to her again. "You better wake up, Angel, or I'm gonna paddle that ass red." He inhaled sharply before expelling the words he couldn't say to her. "I love you, dammit! You're not dying on me, you hear? I don't care if it's heaven or hell, I'm gonna hunt you down and drag your ass back to me. You. Are. Not allowed to fucking die!"

"Jesus," the EMT said.

The walls were closing in on his chest and he was having difficulty drawing in a breath. Maybe he needed to be dosed with the same meds. "I'm serious, Gabrielle Woodward. You wake up—"

"Asshole."

The single whispered word was music to Declan's ears.

He shoved Bristow aside and cupped Gabby's face. "Say it again." His eyes rested on her face, searching for that sign that he wasn't hallucinating, and he heard her speak.

Her eyelids fluttered, but they didn't open. Her mouth moved with no sound.

"Angel, please, talk to me."

"You talk too much."

He could barely make out her words, but he chuckled,

more from relief and maybe so he wouldn't break down and cry. "I love you, Angel." Now that he'd said the words he couldn't stop saying them.

"Hate to break this up," Bristow said behind him. "But let's save the mushy stuff for later, shall we?" The nurse motioned to the EMT to transfer Gabby to the gurney.

Declan stayed close as they strapped her in. Even as they wheeled her away, he refused to be more than a few steps behind her.

She was alive.

She was his oxygen.

He needed her to breathe.

25

EVER SINCE THE first fentanyl attack nine months prior, hospitals and first responders were better equipped to handle terrorist attacks of this nature. There were fewer fatalities this time, six as opposed to the thirty who died in the shopping center tragedy. Among the six, half had died from injuries caused by the stampede.

Declan stood inside Gabby's room as the doctor checked her vitals. Since getting her loaded into an ambulance, she hadn't regained consciousness. That was an hour ago.

"There's no reason for her not to wake up," the doctor said. "Fentanyl can cause lethargy and her body is dealing with expelling the drug. The important thing is her breathing is almost back to normal, but I'd recommend we keep her overnight."

Sounds good to me, Declan didn't say, but he nodded. The physician marked off her chart and walked up to Declan. "She's tough. I know it's hard to see her laid up this way, but the Narcan was delivered in time. I'm not seeing any long-term side effects from this. Probably a headache for a couple of days."

When the doctor left the room, Theo came charging in,

followed closely by Levi. "How is she?"

"She's okay. Just sleeping it off."

Theo's face turned troubled. "I received a call from the hospital that mother was here."

Startled, Declan glanced at Levi, but his partner gave a shake of his head. Theo meant Claudette. He didn't even wonder if that woman was alive or dead and didn't know how to talk to Theo about her.

His son looked him straight in the eye. "Can I talk to you for a minute?"

"I'll stay in the room," Levi said.

"Any change in her breathing—"

"Roarke," Levi's tone was firm. "I got this, bro. Talk to your son." A lot of meaning dripped in that last statement. Declan was reluctant to leave Gabby's side, but he had a strong compulsion to tell Theo she was his mother. Gabby could have died not once embracing Theo as her son. The lies of the past seventeen years no longer stood between them. His jaw hardened. This had gone on long enough.

When they left the room, Declan led Theo to the stairwell. It seemed like a common enough place where private conversations were held.

"You doing okay?" Declan asked.

"You look like shit," the teenager returned.

He puffed a laugh. "Thanks. How did you find out Gabby was here?"

"John? You refer to him as Garrison, I think. He told me. He also told me he didn't know Claudette's condition after we got the call from the hospital."

Declan's brows raised to his hairline. "He told you just like that."

"He said, and I quote, 'You need to learn the truth. I'm surprised those idiots haven't told you yet.'"

"Oh, that's rich, especially coming from him."

"He's CIA, isn't he?"

"No comment."

"You work for the CIA?" Theo sounded excited, then his face took on that apprehensive look again. "He told me to ask you about Claudette, but I think I already know."

"You do?" He probably didn't, otherwise he wouldn't be so calm and matter-of-fact.

"With her in the hospital at the same time as Gabby, did she have anything to do with Ortega? Or the virus that scared the shit out of everyone?"

"How did you come to this conclusion?"

"Hollywood, dude," Theo said as if Declan should already know. "I've heard things all my life. Drug-addicted has-been actors accusing Claudette of ruining their lives. Then they'd turn up dead on the wrong side of town. Sometimes I see the bimbo that married my dad. Sometimes I think it's a façade and she's conniving as hell. So," Theo blew out a breath. "Am I right?"

"Nothing is certain …" he started, eyes wary.

"Stop protecting me," Theo burst out, his maturing voice suddenly cracking a brief falsetto. He winced at the change, but shrugged it off, clearing his throat. "For once, let's not keep any secrets. Because I don't want to be that person who hates his mother for no reason."

Tell him!

"You know what's fucking me up?" he continued. "I have no desire to see her, but I would lose my mind if something happened to Gabby. My sister, who, until recently, didn't even pay me any attention, who isn't even related to me by blood. My sister who now might be warming up to me because of you."

"What? No. No, Theo, you've got that all wrong—"

"Have I? Huh?" The register of Theo's voice was now all over the place, but the teenager seemed to stop caring. "She's tolerating me because I'm your son." Hurt was written all over his face and before Declan could correct him, he added. "I'm sorry about what I said this morning, all right? Levi told me I wasn't being fair—"

"Levi's got a big mouth."

"He's a good man, just like I know you are." He bowed his head, a wry grin tilting one corner of his mouth. "So you know where all my resentment is coming from."

"Gabby bitched at me about your blind fight scene," Declan reminded him. "She was concerned for your safety, and it had nothing to do with me. That scene wasn't even my suggestion, so when I agreed to it without consulting her first, she was really pissed off."

"Why do you need to consult her? She's not my mom."

Tell him!

"That's where you're wrong," Declan said quietly.

His son's eyes narrowed before widening. "What?"

"Gabby didn't lose her baby when she was mugged that day. Someone stole you from us."

Theo stared at him blankly, growing pale before he turned away. His head dropped to his chest as his hand came up, probably hovering around his mouth. He faced Declan again. "Claudette?"

Declan nodded.

"You're sure?"

"Positive."

A mixture of anger and hurt flashed through the teenager's face. "Gabby knew all along?"

"Only for the last two weeks."

Theo looked away again as if sorting through his memories of that time frame and then started shaking his head. "I don't know. I've known her as my sister for far too long, I can't picture her as my mom. Wait! Did Dad know about this?"

"Not until after he divorced Claudette. Look, it's complicated, and we've spent way more time away from your sister's room than I'm comfortable with. We'll explain to you what we know, but not now. I need to focus on Gabby, all right?"

"Mom——"

"What?"

"You said sister." He shrugged. "She's my mom."

"Let's not shock her with this, okay?" Apprehension rose inside him as they made their way back up the steps. Gabby was gonna freak at him for breaking the news to Theo without her, but maybe not. Declan did the hard work, dammit. Besides, Theo appeared to absorb the news well.

So it was with much surprise when they got out of the stairwell that Theo made a beeline for the nurses' station.

"I need Claudette Dumont's room number," Theo said.

The nurse registered recognition and stuttered. "Mr. Cole … I, I'm afraid she's not allowed to have visitors even from family."

"Who do I need to——"

"Come on, kid, leave the nurse alone." Declan wrapped an arm around Theo's neck, pulling him close and leading him away.

His son jerked himself out of his hold and glared. "You think I'm just gonna let her get away with this?" Eyes, so like Declan's, filled with tears. "She stole my life. My life with you and Gabby."

"You didn't turn out so bad."

"Fuck you!" The boy stalked away, already attracting attention. This wasn't what he wanted to deal with. Teen drama in a hospital full of people, even if his son did have every reason to be angry.

Declan kept pace with Theo, until they were in a less busy area of the hallway. He grabbed his son's arm and immediately put his hands on his face, locking their eyes together.

"Look at me." No more kid gloves. Theo was gonna listen. "What the fuck did I say? Gabby needs to be our focus? Can you give me that, Theo?" He squeezed his jaw to make a point.

The teenager was breathing hard, face ruddy with his fury,

but Theo not struggling this time meant Declan was getting through to him.

He dropped his hands from Theo's face and the teenager's head dipped briefly.

"You're not going to throw tantrums when we get to Gabby's room," he warned.

"I don't throw tantrums."

"Could've fooled me."

The teenager's mouth tightened, before emotion made it tremble, and then his face crumpled. The heart of a parent couldn't deny that his son was in agony and tough love went out the window.

"C'mere." He clasped the back of Theo's head and drew him into a tight hug. The teenager's arms were loose at his sides and Declan held his breath, ready for rejection. Then, in slow degrees, he clasped Declan around his waist, before convulsively returning the hug.

Father and son stood in the hallway, oblivious to people surreptitiously snapping pictures of the teenage star. They would deal with the fallout later.

At that moment, all that mattered was family.

IT WAS dark and she walked on a black plane of shallow water. In the distance was a speck of white. As Gabby got closer, she realized it was a claw foot bathtub gilded in gold. Claudette sat in it, covered in bubbles, her golden curls piled up high on her head exposing her swan-like neck. And with much-affected grace, Claudette lathered her arms and legs.

"You took a while," her former stepmother told her.

"Why did you steal Theo?"

"I did it for love. Don't we all do things for love?"

"Not at the expense of others. You denied me seventeen years of Theo's life."

"What can I say? I'm selfish," Claudette's tinkling laugh grated against her skull. "And I want Declan."

"I thought you were in love with Ortega."

"You took Declan from me." Claudette glared at her, putting down a pink sponge. "He wasn't supposed to fall in love with you. He was only supposed to stay close." She snorted in disgust. "But what did he do? He married you. Then you cheated on him." She clucked. "Stupid girl."

"I didn't go through with it," Gabby whispered. Her head began to throb.

"Well, you got your family back." Claudette threw the sponge in the water. "But good god, woman, did you have to kill me?"

Gabby blinked in confusion. The scene changed. The clawfoot tub was gone, and in its stead was a filthy replacement. Mildew turned the once pristine tub green and gray. Claudette scowled at her.

"I didn't."

"What will you tell Theo now? He's gonna hate you for killing his mother."

"I'm his mother!"

The other woman smiled. It wasn't a pleasant smile. It was a smile full of conniving and malice. "I'm taking him with me."

"No!"

"You're too late."

Gabby sprung forward, jumping into a void and screamed.

Fingers gripped her shoulders and she fought.

"Gabby!"

Her eyes flew open, locking into green concerned ones—bloodshot, and creased with worry at the corners, lines that weren't there before. "Dec?"

"Oh, Jesus, Angel." His eyes were suspiciously bright. "Thank God, you're awake."

"What? I'm in the hospital?" Her tongue felt like dried cotton balls and her nose twitched at the smell of antiseptic.

Her hands were gripped tight in his as his mouth pressed on the back of her fingers. "You wouldn't wake up," he said hoarsely. "It's been sixteen hours and we were worried that Kelso missed that you hit your head again."

"He caught me. I think."

"Your CT scans are clear, but dammit, you gave me a scare."

"Us." A voice spoke behind Declan.

"Theo." A surge of fear pushed up her throat. "I'm so sorry."

The teenager's brows drew together. "For what?"

"I wasn't able to save Claudette."

"She's alive." There was a flatness in the boy's tone that vibrated with underlying anger.

Their conversation was cut short by the arrival of the doctor, who was followed by Bristow and two other nurses. "So, how's our favorite detective?"

For once in her life, Gabby wasn't annoyed by the pokes and prods of the medical staff. It gave her an opportunity to find her bearings under the scrutiny of the two men who'd become her world.

Claudette is alive.

Did that mean Gabby saved her? It was a weird feeling when she had so much hate for the woman all her life, but her heart felt less weighed down. Duty to serve and protect won over vengeance. Because vengeance wasn't hers and she would let due process take its course.

Besides it would be a form of vengeance to see her in orange. Claudette would be appalled. It would clash with her blond hair.

A chuckle escaped her.

The doctor's brow arched. He lowered the penlight he had on her eyes. "Something funny?"

"Nothing. Just remembered something."

"Are you sure she didn't hit her head?" Theo chortled.

Gabby rolled her eyes, extended her arm and gave him the middle finger.

She heard a choked laugh from Declan, and her lips curved into a smile.

Theo, the little shit, wouldn't shut up and gave a mock gasp, but the words that followed almost gave her a heart attack.

"Now is that the right way to talk to your son?" Theo said, deadpan.

She pushed the doctor's probe away and turned to face the two guys. Levi edged to the door. Bristow had his mouth covered, controlling a grin.

"Well then," the doctor said.

"Everyone out," Gabby said slowly, her eyes riveted on Declan who muttered a curse and turned to their son.

"Did you just throw me off a cliff?" He asked Theo. "What did I fuckin' say?"

"You couldn't help yourself, could you?" Gabby's question was directed at her ex-husband.

"The timing was right, so I took it." Declan shrugged. "I did tell wonder boy here to avoid giving you a shock."

"Aren't we all tired of secrets?" Theo asked.

"You're taking this well." She finally had the courage to look into his young eyes which had taken on a mature glint since the last time she saw him.

"Do you blame me?" Theo asked, his voice low. "Claudette never had the motherly gene. I didn't go looking for it. I had Dad and he was enough. I was just a statement piece to Claudette, much like one of her Chanel bags or Manolos."

"You were a beautiful kid," Gabby said. She was sitting at the edge of the bed and now took a tentative step down. Both guys rushed to help her, but she fended them off.

"Goodness, I'm not helpless. I'm fine."

"Then," Theo said, looking at her warily. "Can I hug you now—Mom?"

If there was a heart-in-her-throat moment, this was it. Her eyes grew warm as she nodded.

Theo took a tentative step toward her and Gabby closed the distance. He was a lankier version of his dad, but he was solid and warm. Their arms wove around each other tightly.

"You're my son," she said in wonder.

"Yeah," he replied. "I may slip and call you sis, or Gabby," he whispered.

She gave a watery laugh. "I don't care."

"Mind if I join in?" said a rough voice beside them.

Without looking at him, Gabby reached for Declan and drew him into their tiny family circle. His much broader frame engulfed them. His strong arms kept her standing when she was buckling with emotion. Tears tracked down her cheeks. She wasn't sobbing yet, but she felt wetness at the side of her temple and on her head.

She didn't know how long they stood there without words when Levi's voice came through them from the door.

"I can't let you in. They're having a family meeting."

"Family meeting? What the hell are you talking about."

Nick.

"We just want to see Gabby."

That came from Emma, and Theo leaned back from her. "Can I let her in?"

"It depends. Am I still your best girl?" Gabby teased.

Theo flashed her a cocky grin before pulling away from her to open the door. Declan engulfed her in an embrace, and she settled contentedly against him. There were still many things to talk about, adjusting to a new normal, but she couldn't help anticipating this second chance of happiness that was within reach.

"Hi!" Emma spied them by the bed and took a step in.

"I've got things to tell you," Theo told the girl.

"Gabby, how are you?" Nick asked, obviously unhappy at seeing Declan in the room.

"I'm fine."

"Gabby is my real mom!" her son declared to Emma. It warmed her heart to see how proud Theo seemed.

Nick's head whipped around toward Theo. "What did you say?"

"The boy has no filter on his mouth," Declan muttered.

"Tell me you didn't know this, Nick," Gabby asked.

"What are you all talking about?" the other man said, bewildered. She knew him enough to note that his shock was genuine.

"I don't think he did," Theo said.

"You sure about that?" Declan drawled. "He could be a better actor than I am."

"Anyone's a better actor than you are, Roarke," Nick shot back.

"Ouch! Is that supposed to hurt?"

"Would you two stop with the dick fight?" Gabby said in irritation.

"Hey, minor here." Theo covered Emma's ears. "Ah … I think we need to let you grown-ups talk it out. Nick's gonna handle our press anyway."

"Don't go too far!" Roarke called. "And get Levi."

"Yeah, yeah …" Theo waved.

Emma hesitated. "But my Dad wants to say hey to Gabby."

"Your dad is here?" Theo asked.

"Yes," the teenage girl replied. "Dad wants to show his support—"

"You sure he's not here as Claudette's attorney?" Gabby blurted out before she could stop herself.

Emma's face reddened. Declan squeezed her shoulders and, when Theo scowled, she knew she'd gone too far.

"Come on, baby," Theo said, ushering the girl out the door. "Let's see Mr. Haller and bring him up here. It's okay. Right, Mom?"

Gabby winced at the coldness in her son's voice. Wow, the warm and fuzzies fizzled pretty quickly as she watched Theo close the door.

"I don't think I can handle any more visitors." She massaged her right temple.

"I'll talk to Theo," Declan murmured by her ear.

"I guess I'm not his best girl after all," Gabby muttered.

Declan chuckled and turned her in his arms so he could stare into her eyes. "Does it matter if you're mine?"

She couldn't help the goofy grin that formed on her lips.

A clearing of the throat reminded them they weren't alone. They turned their heads to see Nick glowering at them, a vein throbbing at the side of his neck.

"Sorry to interrupt this lovers' reunion," he spat. "But could we talk about how we're gonna spin this to the press? And do we have—"

Declan advanced menacingly toward him, blocking Gabby's view. "You're bringing this up now?"

"It's not only Theo's career on the line here."

"Do you even hear yourself?" Declan growled. "Gabby almost died yesterday and that damn well outweighs any fucking career anyone has. Got me?"

Gabby laid a hand on Declan's back, his tense muscles bunching underneath her palm. She needed to diffuse the situation before he threw Nick out of the room.

"Dec, I got this."

"No, you're not well."

"I am well enough to talk to Nick myself," she cut in sharply. Gabby was realizing that in the face of their imminent reconciliation, she needed to set a few boundaries. Declan had always been overprotective, and she could see this becoming a nails-on-the-chalkboard habit if she didn't put her foot down.

When she turned to face her other ex-husband, his expression was contrite.

"Declan is right," Nick said, pressing his mouth together as if trying to find the words. "I'm not gonna lie. It's hard to see you two together and I just lashed out."

"I'm taking a few days off. Why don't you call me and we can set a time to hash this out, okay?"

He nodded. "I'm glad you're all right, Gabby."

"Me too."

They exchanged brief hugs, the men exchanged curt nods, and then Nick left the room.

Gabby turned to face Declan, hands on hips, about to berate him about jumping down Nick's throat, but he beat her to it.

"Don't even fucking say I overstepped," he warned. "He was out of line and you know it."

"Did you have to be that confrontational?"

"Thinking that you've been married to that son-of-a bitch? Yes, I did."

"Are you saying you're jealous of him? I thought we're past that?"

"You and me? We're past that. Me and him. Never."

"But why?"

He stared at her as if she should know. His mouth stubbornly set in a thin line.

"Oh my god. You give me a headache."

Remorsefulness marked his features. "You need something? A pill?"

"It's not too bad yet."

Declan looked like he was about to say something when the door opened, and Levi stepped in.

His partner looked around, his brows drawing together. "Where's Theo?"

26

"YOU LOST HIM?" Declan growled.

"What's going on?" Gabby gripped his arm. Fuck. This was not the way he wanted her to find out about the Ortega escape.

"No time to explain." He glared at Levi, who was returning his glare full force. "Where's Bristow?"

"Here," the ginger-haired pretending-to-be-a-nurse CIA operative appeared by the open door.

"Stay with Gabby. Explain the situation to her."

"I will if—" Bristow broke off. "Where the fuck is Theo?"

"Good question." This time it was Levi who responded.

"Come on." Declan exited the room, ignoring the outrage in Gabby's voice as she demanded to know what the hell was going on again.

"We got complacent," Declan told his partner as they both prowled the hallways, looking for the teenager. He shot a text off to Theo, praying he'd respond.

"We?" Levi barked a mocking laugh. "Need I remind you we were ordered to leave the room. He was in your care."

"Agreed. Theo left with Emma to go look for her dad. Where were you?"

"I had an update from Garrison. Had to go somewhere to take the call."

"His phone is showing up in the parking garage," Levi said, but instead of relief, his friend's face darkened with worry.

This couldn't be good. Theo wouldn't be dumb enough to go to the garage with Emma. When the elevator they took opened at the ground level, Levi checked the tracker on his phone again. It led them to a trash bin by the bank of elevators.

"Son of a bitch!" Declan spat. He raked fingers through his hair, wanting to pull it out.

Levi's shoulders slumped. "I failed Theo."

"We both did," Declan admitted. "Theo shouldn't have taken one step from that door without you. I told that damned kid to look for you, but emotions were high and he probably didn't think of it." He blew out a frustrated and pained breath. Just when their family was whole, something ripped them apart again. This was gonna kill Gabby. She didn't know about Ortega yet.

"Let's see if the hospital security can pull the surveillance tapes," Levi said.

GABBY LISTENED, as calmly as she could manage, while Bristow explained what they knew about Ortega's escape.

"Has this been relayed to GHD?"

"Garrison said the CDC just informed them."

"I'm not about to simply sit here and wait for news on my son," Gabby said. "You're going to take me to Claudette."

Bristow hitched a brow. "I don't think Roarke's gonna be pleased if you leave this room without him."

"I don't answer to Dec." And as if a thought occurred to her, she asked, "And while I get into my clothes, you mind telling me what exactly do you do? I doubt you're merely a CIA asset."

She walked to the duffel Levi brought in earlier, thankful there were jeans, sneakers, and a sweater. Gabby felt a bit woozy, but it wasn't anything she hadn't been through before, so she sat on the couch as she carefully slipped her jeans on.

"Need help?"

"No. Start talking."

"Counterterrorism task force proposed under the CIA."

"The CIA can't command anything on U.S. soil."

"Garrison's been given authority by Homeland Security and FBI since he's more knowledgeable of how all the players work together or who's fighting against whom. The U.S. healthcare system is vulnerable. Inject a super bacteria or virus into the system and tens of thousands could die. Ground Zero is Southern California whose borders are more vulnerable to the entry of terrorists in the guise of true asylum seekers."

Gabby stood up and fished a bra and shirt from the bag and turned away from Bristow. She slipped off her hospital gown. "Go on."

The door opened. "What the fuck?" Declan growled. "Cover your eyes, dammit."

"Nothing I haven't seen before," Bristow quipped.

She hooked her bra and was about to pull on the sweater when she felt the electric presence of Declan behind her.

"I know you said you're used to guys in the locker room, but would you give me a chance to get used to it?"

Rolling her eyes, she pulled the sweater gingerly over her head as Declan helped her the rest of the way. Then fingers clasped her shoulders and turned her around, her heart sinking at the turbulence in his green eyes.

"Theo?" For the few minutes Levi and Declan were gone, she'd clung to the hope that they were overreacting ... their son couldn't be taken in the blink of an eye.

He gave one shake of his head. "Found his phone in the trash."

"Oh, god." The instinct of a cop warred with the instinct of a mother and she clung to his forearms as if to steady herself.

"Gabby ..."

She focused on what she could control. "Bristow's taking me to Claudette. You do what you need to do. Surveillance tapes—"

"Got the ball rolling on that."

"If Ortega has Theo, let's hope he'll make demands." The alternative was too painful to comprehend.

"He will and you don't need to see Claudette," Declan and Bristow exchanged a look, and the nurse nodded. "We know what he wants."

27

"You've got to be fucking kidding me!"

Gabby stared, open-mouthed, at the man standing beside Ariana. She yanked her hand out of Declan's. No wonder he'd been evading her questions on the way home. What did he think she was going to do? Ask for a gun and shoot Biker Guy from the alley?

"Gabby ..." Declan started.

"Don't you dare *Gabby* me," she snarled, avoiding his attempts to grab her hand again while keeping him, Biker Guy, Ariana, and Garrison within a forty-five degree angle of her sight.

"What's going on?" Kelso asked, moving to her side.

"This man"—she stabbed a finger at Ariana's bodyguard —"was the man I followed in the alley."

"Miguel Alcantara Walker. You can call me Migs." The man introduced himself with a smirk.

"How about I call you *asshole*?" She turned and scowled at her ex. "You played me. He pointed a gun at me and you ... arrgh—I can't even." Gabby started pacing, waiting for someone to offer an explanation, but the room lapsed into silence, so she stopped wearing a hole through the floor and glared at Declan. "What? Nothing to say?"

He had his thumbs hooked in the front pockets of his jeans, his feet braced apart as he rocked back on his heels. "Nothing. Just letting you cool down and realize that what I did was the best option."

His whole posture and words incensed her further. "Oh, really? What about saying 'don't shoot him—he's on our side'?"

"My cover was important," Migs retorted.

"Your cover ceased being important the second you got your ass caught by a police officer," Kelso joined into the fray.

Gabby turned her displeasure on Garrison. She was getting more and more furious with each second that went by that these men thought what they did was okay. "Don't think because you're this hotshot CIA officer that you can run roughshod over interagency protocol. This wouldn't have happened if we'd been brought into the loop. Someone could have gotten hurt."

Garrison regarded her and her partner for one beat, two beats, and then said, "Right. That's a risk we take—"

"Don't start spouting collateral damage to me—"

"—but now that we've established that we're on the same side, can we focus on getting the teenagers back?"

Silence.

Gabby knew he was right, and she knew that the CIA operated on a different wavelength. They could break laws in other countries, but not U.S. laws. She just wanted to get the steam out of her head, otherwise she'd explode later. "Come on, Kelso, let's hear what these spooks have to say." She didn't look at Declan. Needless to say, she was fuming at every male in the house except her partner.

Gabby sat on the couch, motioning Kelso to sit beside her.

She could feel Declan's glower in her direction, but she continued to ignore him, so he moved to stand beside Garrison. Bristow, who'd been standing by the door all this time, moved to join the CIA team.

"Ortega never had cancer," Garrison said. "He spread that rumor to make him appear weak and flush out the people conniving to bring him down. This is what we've gleaned so far from his CDC tests and his actions of the past few months."

"Do we know who broke him out?" Declan asked.

"At first we thought Andrade had a plant inside the CDC but a source of mine indicated that he was completely in the dark about the Z-91," the CIA officer continued. "Heads are apparently rolling in his organization, but the damage is done. The virus is out."

"Ortega escaped with the Z-91 pearls?" Gabby demanded.

"No. Those have been safely transported to Atlanta, but Ortega himself has become the carrier. It's still too soon to say, but there are indications within the CDC audit trail that a Z-92 has been synthesized using its equipment and research files."

"We cannot discount that Andrade is still behind this," Migs said. "He has the means for misdirection."

"Agreed."

"And the cartel?" Kelso asked. "How do they fit into all this?"

"They're waiting to grab power," Ariana said. "It's gotten my brother so paranoid. I … I still can't wrap my mind around how he faked his cancer."

"I know how we can flush Ortega out," Gabby said. She stared at the other woman, trying to remain objective and hoping that in no way was Ariana complicit in her brother's actions that killed Peter. "There's one person Raul Ortega loves."

"No," Migs growled.

Gabby raised a brow. "I haven't said anything yet."

"You don't have to," he snapped. "You're going to suggest using her as bait."

"Gabby has a point," Garrison said, looking at Ariana and ignoring the fuming biker beside her. "At this point, we're banking on Ortega to be desperate to find out what happened to you. We've tracked numerous calls made to the numbers you use. We nearly captured someone who's been staking out your business in Beverly Hills.

"Unfortunately, Andrade wants Ariana, too. That's the real reason why we put Migs undercover," Garrison said, turning back to the room. "And why we needed her to stay hidden. See who makes the first move. Ortega did. We haven't picked up any movement from Andrade's end ... but like Migs said he has a vast network to cover his tracks."

Gabby's own division had been looking for Ariana but she seemed to disappear off the face of the earth, and now she knew how. This was fucked up on so many levels, Gabby couldn't even comprehend going rogue on this.

That is, if Theo and Emma's lives weren't on the line.

The surveillance footage showed the teenagers being intercepted by two men dressed in scrubs. It was at a distance from the camera and their abductors appeared to know how to avoid having their faces seen.

They needed to act quickly before the kidnapping reached the mainstream media. It would be harder to execute a rescue under the scrutiny of the public. Nick had not called her yet, but she expected a frantic call when Theo and Emma failed to show up for shooting. There was also the LAPD to consider.

"Neither of them will get to you," Migs told Ariana fiercely. "That I promise."

"Raul won't stop until he sees me. He wouldn't hurt me."

"Don't forget," Gabby seethed. "Your brother killed my father. He ordered a hit on me and Theo—a seventeen-year-old boy. He's a sociopath!"

"I know that!" Ariana cried. "No matter how much he

tries to protect me, a part of me knows what he is. That's what got our other brother killed. But he's still my brother." She ended on a whisper.

"Ari," Migs said. "If the family dog becomes rabid, it's kinder to put him down."

Ariana didn't seem to take offense to Migs comparing her brother to a dog. It appeared they'd had this conversation before. As far as Gabby was concerned, a rabid dog was better than Ortega—she wanted the whole book thrown at him, and to have him rot in jail for an eternity.

"Will you testify against him?" Gabby asked the other woman. "If we get him back?"

"It's too soon to say if this would even go through the courts," Garrison interjected.

"What the fuck?" Gabby stared at Declan who was across the room from her. "You think I'm going to stay quiet about this." She glanced at Kelso for support.

"Thinking," her partner clipped.

As it was, the coffee table seemed to be the dividing line between the law and the lawless.

Garrison, Levi, Declan, and Bristow were standing across from the long couch where she and Kelso were seated. Migs sat on the arm of the big single couch where Ariana lounged.

"We uphold the law," Gabby stressed. "Always."

"Sometimes we have to bend it a little," Declan said finally.

"You won't bring your mercenary ways onto my turf, Roarke." Gabby surged up from her seat. "Your lawlessness has no place in LA—"

"Oh, and you speak for the entire LAPD?" he cut in. "Our son's life is at stake."

"I don't appreciate you making me feel that I'm a mother who'd put her job ahead of her son—"

"I'm not—"

"People! Focus!" Garrison barked. "This is the worst time

for infighting. We need to focus on getting Theo and Emma back."

Everyone turned surprised eyes on the CIA man who'd been known to be ruthless, who had no problem with collateral damage.

"What?" he shrugged. "I watch their show. All their dossiers go through me. I've learned enough about them. Good kids. Besides, two dead teenagers won't look good on the force we're trying to establish here. This is just the tip of the iceberg, people."

"We get Ortega. Then what about Andrade?" Migs asked.

"We're in the long game. For now, Andrade is not our focus, Raul Ortega is," Garrison said. "He was an annoying splinter before, now he's literally a malignant disease we need to eliminate. My analysts are combing through his properties and finances. There's a very good chance he's keeping the kids in one of them, but we're looking at all his cronies too." John's eyes landed on her. "We'll get them back."

Gabby nodded, unable to speak as her walled-up emotions threatened to buckle under Garrison's kind words. As a cop, she was used to hardening herself when she was told to suck it up. But in the face of having Theo stolen away from her a second time, the trauma that had fallen on her eighteen-year-old self echoed emotions from long ago.

Fear.

Terror.

Agony.

An uncontrolled sob made its way up her throat. She held her breath, trying to control it, but she started shaking.

Her hand flew to her mouth as the ragged sob finally broke free and tears scalded her eyes and spilled onto her cheeks.

Kelso got up beside her and tried to fold her into his arms, but she resisted. He settled by putting a hand on her shoulder, head lowered close to hers. "You heard him, Gabs, we'll get him back."

Her ears were ringing as she continued shaking her head, continued fighting back the terror that had seeped deep into her marrow, until finally she heard him.

"I've got her."

HISTORY HAD a way of repeating itself, but Declan wasn't that insecure boy anymore. Watching Kelso get up to comfort Gabby punched him straight back to the time when he saw Nick escort her to the awards show on TV. It exhumed the pain that still had the power to stab him in the chest.

But circumstances were a helluva lot different now.

For one thing, they were different people. Shaped from the mistakes of the past, but for the better.

His strides were already taking him across the room before it registered in his mind. He saw her stricken face before she attempted to hide it, and he wanted nothing more than to wrap her in a cocoon of reassurance.

Her shoulders rose and fell in her attempt to stay strong.

"I've got her."

Kelso lifted his gaze, their eyes exchanging an understanding that it was Declan's place to comfort Gabby.

His touch was tentative on her shoulder as he gently eased her into his embrace. "Angel."

"Declan," she cried softly and buried her face on his chest, his lungs expelling a breath of relief that what she refused from Kelso, she accepted from him.

One hand cupped the back of her head and the other cleaved her body to his. "Shh … it'll be all right. We'll get him back."

"You don't know that."

"My gut does and it's rarely wrong."

She puffed a watery laugh. "Is that so?" She blinked up at him and they stared into each other's eyes as if they were the only people in the room.

The others turned away, giving them privacy, but Declan was anxious to get Gabby to their room anyway. "Come on."

With his arms around her, he supported her weight just in case her feet weren't steady. She'd just checked out of the hospital after all. The doctor wanted to keep her for another night, but Declan knew staying there would be akin to putting her in a straitjacket with Theo missing.

When they entered her room, he led her to the bed and sat her down. He knelt, removing her sneakers from one foot and then the other.

"I can do that," she said quietly.

"Yes, but I'm faster. Lie back."

She did as she was told— robotic—as if all the life had been sucked out of her and she was going through the motions.

Declan didn't say anything. Asking if she was fine was a dumb question when he himself was feeling far from fine, but this woman who'd always owned his heart needed him to stay strong.

"I'm sorry," she said.

His brows drew together. "Why?"

"Breaking down out there. I tried to hold it together—"

"Gabby," he called her name firmly. "Stop acting like a detective for once and cut yourself some slack. Our son was taken. We shouldn't even be on the case."

"You think Garrison will keep us out of any rescue?"

"Not sure."

"I'd like to see him try." She shook her head. "This is not sitting well with me. Not reporting it to the LAPD."

"But you know this is the best option."

Gabby nodded reluctantly. "I can't help but think that fate is conspiring against us being a family."

"No, Gabby." He got to his feet and started pacing. "Don't you see it? Our past is giving us another chance to make this right." He faced her squarely, his own emotions laid bare. She was looking at him in confusion. He returned to the bed and sat on its edge, gathering her hands in his. "This is our second chance," he repeated. "We didn't survive our problems before, but the biggest test of our life is now, babe. Are you with me on this?" His eyes searched hers and she still wasn't getting it. "Do you remember when I said I loved you?"

Her eyes shined, a smile tugging at her lips. "I seem to recall a dammit somewhere in there. Also something about dragging me back from heaven or hell."

Declan chuckled. "I got through to you, didn't I?"

"So bossy, even when I'm dying."

His heart clenched. "You scared the shit out of me, Angel." He leaned in and pressed a kiss to her forehead and a light one on her mouth before pulling back. "Don't do that again."

"I can't help it, Dec," she said seriously. "Are you sure you can handle being in a relationship with a cop?"

"I'm handling it, aren't I?"

She shook her head. "Are you going to inject yourself into every operation that I'm on when there's a potential for it to go bad?"

"No."

"You're two for two."

"There were extenuating circumstances."

"Dec, if anything between us has a chance of succeeding, you have to let me do my job without interfering."

"I'm trying hard, Gab." He couldn't make false promises. Never again. "I love you. My instinct is to protect you—"

"Dec," she protested.

"But you're a damned good cop. It's not you that I don't trust to do a great job but the people around you. I trust

Kelso, but you've got patrol officers having your back, and some rookies—"

"Dec—"

"But," he said firmly. "I understand it's part of the job. I'll get there, Angel." His arm reached out to tuck a lock of hair behind an ear. "I'm here to stay. You have my word. Even if you try to kick me out, I'm going to try even harder so you can't live without me."

"You make it so hard not to fall in love with you," she breathed in a resigned sigh.

Declan barked a laugh. "Don't sound so glum." Then he deadpanned. "You sure know how to stroke a guy's ego."

"I don't think I ever fell out of love with you," she whispered.

"I know." He gave her his roguish smile. The one he knew would elicit an eye roll from her, but he didn't expect that cute lip pucker reminiscent of eighteen-year-old Gabby. That was a sucker punch, transporting him back to their lost years.

"The panty-melting smile," she grumbled. "You practice that often?"

"I'm Pavlov's dog with it. It only comes out when you're around or when you pout."

"I do not pout."

He laughed again and leaned in to kiss her. It was their moment of respite from the underlying anxiety of not knowing their son's fate, but the levity didn't last long and the mood in the room turned somber again.

"When do you think Garrison will have something for us?"

"I honestly don't know," Declan said. "It could be hours or days."

"Twenty-four hours would be really, really bad."

Every hour that Theo was gone diminished the chances of finding him. Their eyes met and he knew in their unspoken words, she'd thought the same.

Fear entered her eyes. "We need to get a lead soon."

"Why don't you rest?"

"I'm afraid to close my eyes," she shuddered. "I don't want to have bad dreams about Theo. It's going to mess with my ability to think when it's time to rescue him."

"But you need your rest if you want to be effective. Go on, I'll watch over you. Would that make you feel better?"

"You don't have to be out there? Talking to the guys?"

"I don't want to see their ugly mugs. I'd rather be with you."

Gabby didn't answer. She merely smiled, and settled on her side, tucking her clasped hands underneath her cheek, and closed her eyes.

Declan kicked off his boots, dropped his jeans, and crawled over her body to settle behind her back, spooning her. She scooted her ass into his crotch, and he couldn't help the bolt of lust that shot to his groin, but Gabby needed rest.

He waited for her breathing to even out, before he gave in to his own exhaustion.

28

THEIR PHONES WENT off at two in the morning.

Gabby jerked awake, flailing, hearing a grunt followed by a curse, and remembered Declan was behind her.

"Sorry," she mumbled. He must have tried to reach over her to pick up his device as well and she elbowed him somewhere on his anatomy. "Woodward."

"Briefing in the living room," Garrison said and ended the call.

As a cop, going alert from zero to sixty seconds was a skill developed over the years, but this time the adrenaline flushing through her was different. The kick in the heart and tightening of her chest indicated that the stakes couldn't be higher.

Declan rolled to the other side of the bed, and got to his feet, briskly striding to the bathroom without saying a word.

Then they were both in the bathroom, going through the motions of washing their faces, gargling on minty mouthwash to further jolt them awake.

"You okay?" Declan spoke for the first time since they'd woken up, stepping back into his jeans. Her eyes seemed to follow the track of the zipper. He left the top button open. "Gabby?"

"As fine as I ever could be." Anxiety and adrenaline affected people differently. For Gabby, ever since Declan returned, any heightened rush translated to a sexual need only he could quench. Their eyes met and his eyes reflected a heat equal to what was thrumming through her veins.

She changed into a jogger and put on her slip-on shoes. Declan opted to stay barefoot and they exited the room together, but not touching. Stranger still, when they got to the room, they separated, Declan moved to where Levi stood, while Gabby took her place beside Bristow. Physical distance and distraction were what she needed to get through this briefing.

"Your room okay?" Gabby asked Bristow.

"Yeah," he answered. "I can sleep anywhere. You should check out the cot in the on-call room." He looked her up and down. "You? Breathing back to normal?"

"Yup."

Garrison, who was on the phone, ended the call and turned back to them.

"Where's Kelso?" Gabby asked.

"He's keeping an eye on Emma's dad."

"Has he gone to the police?"

The CIA officer snorted a derisive laugh. "He wouldn't."

"What's going on?"

"He lured Theo and Emma to a deserted area near the stairs where Ortega's men were waiting."

"What? Why put his own daughter at risk?"

"My analyst broke into his text stream. Emma was being threatened. He'd defended Ortega's associates in a couple of low-profile cases. Deal with the devil you get burned and all that. Now Ortega double-crossed the lawyer and took Emma, too, probably to keep the lawyer on the hook."

"The nerve—accusing me of his daughter's kidnapping!"

"According to Kelso, he said if it weren't for Theo, Emma wouldn't be in this deep shit."

Gabby's hackles rose. "Son of a bitch."

"Do we have a location for Raul Ortega?" Migs cut in while she was still stewing in her motherly outrage.

"A property in Baker. I'll have more information on the occupants and guards. Possible location of the kids."

"Have there been any demands at all?" Gabby asked.

"No—" Garrison started.

"Yes," Declan countered, holding up his phone, his jawline tense. "Just got this from the same number that sent me the live feed of the raid in Inglewood. He knows we have Ariana … wants to swap her for the two kids."

"No," Migs growled.

"Where is she?" Gabby asked.

"I said no," Migs repeated. "We'll find another way."

"Shouldn't that be her decision?" she challenged.

"He won't let go of Theo. Mark my words," Migs said.

"Migs is right," Declan said. "He will need Theo as insurance. The most he will do is let Emma go." He glanced at Garrison. "But I still say we use Ariana as bait."

Garrison gave Migs a look, like he was expecting the decision to come from him, which was bullshit.

Gabby fumed.

"I'm only considering this because they're kids, and Ariana wouldn't want their lives on her conscience," Migs said tersely. "I'll ask her. But if she says no, I can't force her. If she says yes, I'm with her at all times. Deal?"

"Let me talk to her," Gabby offered.

"No. She doesn't fucking know you from fucking Adam," Migs snapped.

Declan moved fast and he was in Migs's face in a split second. "Don't fucking talk to her that way again."

"Hey." Levi got between the two men. "Knock it off." He turned to Migs. "You sure you should be the one staying close to Ariana?"

"You're one to talk, Levi. You're the one who lost Theo."

It was rare for Gabby to see Levi lose his cool. In fact, she never had. But his face was mottled in fury and now she had to step in.

"Stop it!" She inserted herself between the trio. Declan and Levi appeared ready to pound Migs to a pulp, but Gabby saw a man who was afraid for the woman he cared for—deeply, apparently. "Stop behaving like an asshole," she told him. "You're afraid for Ariana, we get that. You care about her. Oh, don't bother protesting—you wouldn't be getting your testicles in a twist if that wasn't the case." Somewhere behind her, someone snorted. "But for Declan and me, Theo is our son. And I know you could argue we didn't know this until a few weeks ago, but he's always been my brother. He's also Theo Cole. He's larger than life and lovable even when he's a pain in the ass."

"Pain in the ass is right," Declan muttered.

"And technically, this is Theo's house. He's offering you and Ariana sanctuary. LAPD is looking for her, and my job is on the line keeping your whereabouts from them."

"She's innocent of her brother's crimes."

"We know that," Gabby said. "Still want her for questioning. And I'm sure you don't want her exposed until she's safe from her brother's organization."

"Sounds like a threat."

"Take it however you please." Gabby gave him an arctic smile and stepped back.

"Are you all done arguing?" Garrison asked dryly. "Has no one even thought that a swap might be the easiest for us?" He looked at Declan. "Did he say where he wants to do this?"

"Not yet."

"Tell him you're considering it."

Declan started typing into his phone.

"And if he doesn't bring the kids, we know where they are," Levi said. "We just need to make sure we have a team on the property ready to infiltrate in case Ortega double-crosses us."

Everyone waited for a response.

It was immediate.

"He'll wait an hour for our response. He's not making another deal." Declan read another text. "He said he'll disappear with the kids. We'll never see them again." His tortured gaze met Gabby's.

There was a stretch of silence as everyone considered this.

"What"—Declan gritted finally—"do I tell him?"

"Use me," a voice said from the hallway.

Ariana.

"Make the deal."

29

ROUTE 15 WAS AN ALMOST three hundred mile stretch of highway that began in San Diego and ended in Nevada. It took Gabby almost two hours from 210 to get to the junction right outside San Bernardino where the road cuts into the last big town of Victorville. After that, twenty-five miles of desert loomed before them.

Seated beside her in the Honda SUV was Ariana.

The rest of the team was tracking them at a safe distance. Kelso and Garrison choppered it to Baker, landed on an airstrip, and took a vehicle to the property where Ortega was suspected of holding Theo and Emma.

Nadia was already in the area. To Gabby's surprise, she was Garrison's analyst. Nadia confirmed Ortega's presence on the property using one of her high-tech Wasp drones.

She also confirmed that the crime lord had left in a convoy of three black Escalades. He and the kids were in the middle one.

Levi was with Declan in one vehicle while Bristow was with Migs in another. Once they had passed Victorville, their vehicles split up, taking different routes to the meeting location.

"I'm getting out of the vehicle first," Gabby reminded Ariana.

"You shouldn't have agreed to his demands," Ortega's sister said. "Theo needs his mother."

"I'm not expecting Ortega to let him go," she said as she made a turn into the dirt road that would lead to their rendezvous point. "It has always been me and Theo he wanted to destroy. I bet he was the one who ordered the hit on our car. Peter's death wasn't enough satisfaction for this perceived transgression." All because Claudette had an affair with a dangerous person.

The ride was bumpy. The sun wasn't going to rise for another few hours. Headlights shone over bushes and thirsty earth. This area between Victorville and Barstow was what Division called the desert somewhere on Route 15. The place was a keeper of secrets. The birds of prey circling above during high noon or the coyotes hunting at night bore witness to lovers burying their trinkets of true love, friends burying time capsules, or hitmen burying their victims.

"Ortega's convoy is splitting up," Nadia said. "Do you have a twenty on them, Kelso? My signal is breaking. Switching to satellite communication."

"Roger that," Gabby replied.

There was static on the line and then Declan's voice came on. "Levi and I are on high ground at the rendezvous point. Vehicles are approaching."

"Did they see you?" Garrison barked.

"Negative," Declan replied. "Went dark when we turned off the main road."

"Same. Moving into position," Migs said. "Coming in from the east. They turned off their lights too."

"Sync up SatComs," Garrison ordered.

Gabby had taken a crash course on the fancy equipment Garrison unpacked for them to use. She had to fumble with some buttons before she got the devices in sync and saw where the others were.

"Can we keep these after this gig?" Nadia piped in.

"Focus, Powell," Garrison snapped.

"Roger that, boss." There was sarcasm in the analyst's tone.

"I see headlights at five hundred yards," Gabby said, putting in the device's earpiece. "Everyone hear me?"

She heard varying affirmative answers.

"Stay frosty, Angel," Declan said gruffly. "We got you covered."

"Thanks."

"Park behind those rock outcroppings. It's the perfect spot for our plan," Nadia said. "The terrain behind it is hard to set up. Doubt that's where Ortega's men will go."

"She's right," Migs said. "They'll take the West hills that have flatter elevated surfaces."

"Amateurs," Levi muttered.

Gabby blew out a breath to steady her nerves. Her overwhelming confidence in the team kept her calm all throughout the drive, but as the headlights of the vehicle bearing Theo grew closer, her anxiety spiked.

They were a strange squad—this mishmash of CIA, disbanded mercenaries, and LAPD cops. Declan and Migs had clashed earlier, but when there was doing to get done, they set aside their egos and worked like they hadn't almost come to blows earlier.

And Nadia, how the hell did Garrison rope her into this? And why?

"Maybe I should go first," Ariana whispered. "It's me they want. You don't have to get out of the car."

"Hell, no," Gabby said. "Ortega wants me dead, so we'll make him think he's getting everything he wants."

"He won't fall for it."

"You're forgetting your brother's ego."

"You have a point."

Gabby parked the SUV right by the cluster of boulders that Nadia suggested. Close enough so when she opened the door, it would provide a shield. The way the land formation curved, it protected much of her rear. Keeping the headlights on pretty much blinded any sniper that wanted to shoot her from the front.

The other vehicle stopped, and the driver stepped out.

"Detective Woodward!"

She got out of the SUV. "I have Ariana with me. Where are my son and Emma?"

"Send Ariana over and I'll give you your son back."

"Are we honestly playing this game?" Gabby called out. "You know how this works. We trade at the same time."

The driver appeared to confer with a passenger behind the driver's seat. Gabby squinted her eyes. "Nadia, are the kids in the back seat? I think Theo is in the front passenger one. Can anyone confirm?"

"Looking through my scope," Levi said. "Looks like Theo. Not a hundred percent. The headlights are glaring."

"*El Jefe* agrees," the driver said. He leaned into the open window of the car, giving instructions to the front passenger. Doors opened and two familiar silhouettes emerged.

"It's Theo and Emma," Levi said.

Her son immediately pulled Emma protectively to his side, but the driver ordered them to break up.

"You're up Ariana," she told Ortega's sister who was already stepping out of the SUV.

Theo said something to the driver causing the man to point his gun at the boy.

Gabby's throat closed.

"Jesus Christ, Theo," Declan growled. "Stop mouthing off."

"Move." The driver waved his gun.

Ariana started walking, so did Theo and Emma.

They were slow. Cautious. Anxiety clotted the air between the vehicles and Gabby forced herself to breathe, her gun already drawn and pointed down, hidden behind the open car door.

Whoever took the first shot would dictate how this fight was going down; she had no doubt Ortega didn't expect them to be alone.

Ego.

Or maybe he had no choice and this was his last stand.

Pop!

Pop!

Emma screamed and went down. Theo tried to catch her, sinking to his knees.

"No!" Gabby cried.

Gunfire erupted all around them.

Breaking cover, her own weapon raised, she started shooting at the driver who ducked behind his vehicle door. Ariana sprinted over to help the kids.

"You're gonna be all right." Theo's panicked voice reached her. A force threw Gabby to the ground and an unholy pain seared through her chest, robbing her of her breath.

She was shot!

"Gabby!" Declan roared as anguish crackled in her ears.

Shit! Shit! She couldn't breathe. Did the vest stop the bullet? She lay paralyzed on her back.

"Theo!" Emma cried.

Gabby blinked back the black dots from her vision and saw a brute of a man—not the driver—drag Theo to his feet, putting him in a chokehold and backing away from them, using her son as a shield.

"Kill her!" someone yelled.

The rush of voices in her ears retreated as her eyes focused on the muzzle of the gun Brute Man was pointing at her head, then pointing at Theo's. Her own gun was out of reach.

Gabby's eyes locked with Theo's.

I love you. Her mind whispered.

Theo's jaw jutted out in determination. Quick as a flash, his right arm came over Brute Man's, twisting it and at the same time jerking his head forward and dislodging the arm around his neck.

Gabby fought through the pain in her body and rolled for her gun.

Bang!

Her eyes flew to Theo and his assailant, shocked to see her son had control of the weapon, Brute Man falling on his back.

"Fuck!" Gabby pushed up unsteadily to one knee. "Get over there!" She pointed to the shadow of the bushes and desert plants.

As a hail of bullets rained down on Ortega's vehicle, Theo and Ariana helped Emma towards cover. Gabby dove behind a boulder.

"We've neutralized our targets," Bristow's words joined the cacophony in her ear.

"How about Ortega? Is—" Gabby asked.

"Are you all right?" Declan's exasperated voice cut her off. She had a feeling he'd been repeating that question for a while.

"Just peachy," she retorted. "What do you expect? I got slammed by a forty-five caliber, looks like."

"She's got her bitch on," Kelso said. "She's fine."

Despite the pain in her chest that made it difficult to draw in a breath, she smiled. Then she asked the all-important question. "So, who's coming to get us?"

"Coming for you," Declan told her. "Stay where you are and don't move."

"Aye, sir."

———————

30

"WALKER, Bristow. Keep your eyes on Ortega's vehicle. Levi and I are heading in."

"Copy that," Bristow said.

"We need him alive," Garrison told them. "If possible," he added.

Declan didn't answer him but double-clicked his mic to let Levi know he was breaking cover and for him to keep a look out for stray hostiles. The plan went totally FUBAR when Migs slit the throat of one of Ortega's snipers. It alerted the others on his crew that one of them was dead. That was when all hell broke loose and Emma got shot. Garrison said something about the biometric system these death squads were using as a way to respond to stealth attacks.

High technology was no longer the realm of the military or CIA. But technology would only get someone so far.

Declan and the rest of the team relied on old-fashioned special ops training and that was where their group excelled. As he trekked down the slope, skipping over the rocky terrain, he thanked his numerous deployments to Afghanistan and the Hindu Kush mountain range that prepared him for this day— the day when he fought to get his family back.

He passed the bodies of two of Ortega's men—one of them he recognized as Claudette's missing bodyguard. He managed to instantly neutralize the man who shot Emma, but the muzzle flash of his M4 carbine revealed his position in the darkness. It took experience to shoot and dodge. But even that experience was shaken when he saw Gabby go down, when he saw a man hold a gun to Theo's head, when he didn't have a shot as the man pointed that same gun at the love of his life, getting ready to shoot her from five feet away. Then came his son's heroic display of courage that saved his mother's life and killed their attacker.

Taking a life would hit Theo hard, but Declan would be there for him and help him through it.

Ducking behind a boulder, he clicked his mic again, signaling Levi to come down, and scanned the area for lurking bad guys. Not accounted for was the driver—who was sitting inside the car—dead or alive—and Ortega.

As Levi hunkered beside him, Declan yelled, "Theo, how's Emma?"

"We stopped the bleeding, but she's passing out."

"I'm on my way," Bristow said through comms.

"Help's coming," he assured his son. He wanted to rush over and check on them, to make sure with his own eyes and hands that they were really okay, but he needed to eliminate the threat of Raul Ortega once and for all.

"Ortega! Come out of the vehicle with your hands up," Declan shouted. "Tell that man of yours to do the same."

There was no movement for long seconds.

"You're surrounded. All your men are dead. Come out now. Don't make me come and get you. That's gonna piss me off."

Finally, the rear passenger door opened. One leather shoe and then another stepped down, the man's choice of footwear so out of place on the desert dirt. Raul Ortega appeared, wearing a suit jacket over a white unbuttoned dress shirt with gold chains hanging around his neck.

He held his hands up in the air.

Declan's scope was on him. "Where's your driver?"

"Dead."

"Open the front passenger door—slowly."

He did as he was told and revealed the body of his driver slumped across the seats.

Shouldering his rifle, Declan emerged from behind concealment and approached. "Come five feet closer and get on the ground, face first, hands behind your back."

Ortega took one step and started to kneel.

Warning bells jolted through his system. "Closer, Ortega!"

He ignored Declan's order and searched the rocks, getting fully on his knees. "Ariana," he called. "I'm so sorry, *hermana de mi corazon, lo siento mucho.*"

The alarm in Declan's gut went full throttle.

From his peripheral vision, he could make out Gabby's approach. "Stay back, Gab! Something's not right."

"Raul!" Ariana emerged from the rocks, her arm outstretched. She spoke in rapid Spanish, telling her brother to surrender.

"Get up." Declan snarled at the crime lord, but at the same time took a step back, glancing briefly at Gabby, something passing briefly between them.

"Tell her to stand back!" Migs shouted into their device.

"I'm picking up a signal and it's" —Nadia's urgent voice came over the satcom—"Get out of there! Now!"

Both Declan and Gabby scrambled for cover.

It was too late.

An explosion rocked the night.

ORTEGA WAS DEAD.

A large piece of the fucking Escalade landed on him.

As for Declan, his ears were ringing. Parts of his body bitched at him, but he was otherwise unharmed. Though it had been a close call, he didn't pass out either. Gabby and Levi reached him at the same time and were speaking, but he couldn't understand a word they were saying.

He was deaf.

Which was probably a good thing because Gabby seemed angry, grabbing him by his ballistic vest and yelling into his face as she leaned over him. He grabbed her too, and kissed her hard while the rest of the team milled around them.

He and Gabby were oblivious.

Hungry for each other.

The near-death experience had reduced them to an elemental need.

Gabby pushed away from him first and said something about Theo. She helped him up and there was his son diving into him and crushing him in a hug. When he leaned back, Theo was talking rapidly, eyes brimming with unbreached tears.

"Can't understand you." Declan pointed to his ears.

Theo gestured to where Bristow was working on Emma. Then his gaze landed on Ariana kneeling in front of the wreckage and sobbing. Migs was standing behind her, a hand on her shoulder.

The three of them walked over to check on Emma. She was pale, her smile pinched, but she was putting on a brave face.

Declan looked around for Levi and saw him with Kelso securing the scene. Garrison was nowhere in sight.

The explosion could be seen from Route 15. Keeping this op under radar was wishful thinking. The highway patrol would come, and heads would roll.

He slung his arm around Gabby, and she leaned into him. Theo sat beside Emma, giving her encouraging words.

He was proud of his son and the man he was going to be.

IF GABBY never saw another hospital for the rest of her life, it would be too soon. They'd been given a special room to wait their turn to talk to Emma. The doctor had already come in to tell them she was fine, but Mr. Haller, being family, went in to see her first. He had a lot to answer for. It took all of Gabby's willpower not to punch him in the face.

There was a knock on the door and Emma's father stepped in. His eyes were bloodshot and he looked miserable.

He exhaled heavily as he closed the door. "I don't think my daughter will ever forgive me."

No one said a word, but Gabby felt the rage vibrating from both Declan and Theo.

"I'm sorry, Theo. Ms. Woodward." He flinched when he looked at Declan. "Mr. Roarke," his voice dropped to a whisper. "I panicked. I knew what this group was capable of and I thought—"

"You should have gone to the cops."

"The cops?" Mr. Haller chuckled bitterly. "You think they'd be falling over themselves to help a defense attorney? And the dirty cops? They'd snitch on me if I had. They nearly killed you and your partner. Mitchell is dead and I'm not sure about the other two."

"Chen and Delgado are good guys."

"You sure about that?" He shook his head, looking lost. "Anyway, I came here to apologize." He looked at Theo. "Go to her. She needs you."

Their son didn't need a second prompting and left the room.

"They're keeping her overnight. She wants Theo to stay with her. Her mom is flying in from Hong Kong as we speak."

"Kelso is waiting to take you to the station," Gabby said.

Mr. Haller gave a jerky nod. "I know. He's in the waiting room." Emma's father put his hand on the knob and looked back at them again. "Thank you for getting my daughter back." Then he left the room.

"Let's go see Emma," Declan told her.

"I'M STAYING WITH HER," Theo said firmly.

Gabby raised a brow. "Did we indicate otherwise?"

"I know my kidnapping spooked you guys and you're probably paranoid and can't stand to be away from me—"

Declan put a hand on his shoulder. "You did us proud back there, kid. You had your wits about you and didn't crack. You saved your mom."

Theo smiled wide. "I did, didn't I?"

"Don't let his head get too big," Emma groaned from the bed.

Gabby's eyes turned to the groggy teen. She was doped up with painkillers, and Gabby knew they shouldn't stay too long. "Yes. One save and he thinks he's Captain America."

Theo mock-scowled at his girlfriend. "Hey, I saved you, too."

"Glad you didn't leave me," she whispered.

"Never, princess."

"Oh my god, I'm going to swoon." Gabby clutched a hand to her chest as her heart expanded at the wonderful man Theo was turning out to be.

Hands curved around her hips, pulling her back into a hard, supportive warmth. "I'm supposed to be the one making you swoon," Declan murmured by her ear.

She turned her head, their faces almost touching. "You do."

Green eyes locked with gold-flecked brown ones.

"Uh, I think you guys need a room," Theo laughed.

"We better be heading home," Declan said. "Levi's staying."

"Suite's big enough."

They both turned to leave, an urgency hastening their steps as they realized at the same time that they would have the house to themselves. Migs would be taking Ariana somewhere else.

Not caring that they were behaving like teenagers themselves, Declan opened the door.

"Dad," Theo called, and she felt Declan freeze. He turned carefully, and Gabby wasn't sure if he was breathing.

Theo walked up to them. "My courage earlier? I got it from both of you." Theo's gaze landed on Gabby. "It will take me a while to think about you as my mom, to call you Mom—"

"Theo …"

He smiled. "Just know having you both as my parents? Best news in the world."

Gabby was saved from bursting into tears when he hugged them both, saying he loved them. That was everything her heart could hope for.

31

"You think they saw us?"

Declan felt a goofy grin threaten to form as the carefree Gabby beside him reminded him of the girl he first fell in love with all those years ago. Yet even as he missed that girl, the woman she was now was the one who'd captured his soul.

"I don't know," he replied. "I didn't see them before you yanked me into the stairwell."

They being Chen and Delgado. When Gabby suddenly stopped walking and dragged him into the stairwell, Declan thought she couldn't wait to get it on and jump his bones. Ever since they left Emma's room, the sexual need simmering between them since the explosion had been threatening to boil over.

He barely registered that she muttered the two detectives' names, his imagination already thinking of the ways he'd take her against the wall, but he wanted nothing more than to put his mouth on her. It had been days since he'd tasted her. That was a tragedy that needed to be rectified immediately.

"I'm glad Levi parked in the garage," she mumbled.

According to his partner, the press had caught wind of the incident on Route 15 involving the teenage stars. Any one of the first responders could have blabbed to a reporter, and the news spread like wildfire. Gabby was getting calls from Nick, but she ignored them. They were surprised he had not appeared at the hospital yet. But after seeing Theo handle himself against Ortega's man, Declan's confidence in his son was at an all-time high. He could handle his manager.

They arrived at the Escalade and exchanged a look as they were reminded of the one that blew up. It reminded Declan that life was too fragile, and it could be taken away in a blink of an eye by people like Ortega.

"Let's go," he told Gabby gruffly.

THEY BARELY MADE it out of the vehicle. Declan parked the SUV in the garage and, the moment he switched off the engine, Gabby climbed over the console and sat on his semi-erect cock.

"Jesus," he muttered before her lips crashed on his and his semi became a full-blown erection. The fabric of their clothes became a scratchy nuisance, and the confines of the vehicle severely restricted his ability to tear off her clothes.

He yanked his mouth away and framed her cheeks with his hands. "Gabby…" he muttered.

She grinned sexily and nipped his jaw. "What? I want you. I'm so wet for you."

"Dammit." He looped her hair around his fingers and tugged down, exposing her throat and bit her skin lightly. "It's cramped in here," he groaned. "I want to fuck you properly."

Gabby stopped squirming. Thank God, because he was in danger of spilling into his boxer briefs. And they were both wearing the filth and dirt of the desert.

Her eyes sparkled. "That's like an oxymoron. Fuck and proper don't go together."

"I want to fuck you blind. Is that better?"

Leaning over, she opened the door. "Fine."

She twisted to get out, and, seeing her wince, the unspeakable fear that gripped him when he saw her take the bullet returned. The nightmares would come—of that he was certain. But they had this moment. She was safe, and soon, she would be in his arms and he would kiss away every hurt if he could. He followed her swaying ass to the bedroom as she kicked off her boots and stripped off her black cargos and black long-sleeved tee. Declan wasn't a strip tease like Gabby and pulled his shirt over his head only when he got to the bedroom.

She turned to face him. A body sculpted with muscles and softness in the right places. All that was left were her panties and cropped tank that flattened her breasts. She removed the tank a bit gingerly, hissing as the fabric passed over her skin. And that was when he saw it.

The dime-sized dent just below her breasts, the forty-five caliber burn and the large bruise surrounding it where the SAPI plate distributed the energy of the round.

"Jesus," Declan said, taking several steps toward her and gently touching the area. "It wasn't this bad when Bristow took a look at it."

"It could've been worse. Tell Garrison I'm keeping that body armor," Gabby joked.

He couldn't answer, eyes transfixed on the bruise. Seeing her injury, the storm of emotions he'd pushed back came roaring back, his gaze lifted to hers and she sucked in a breath.

"Dec, I'm fine."

He exhaled through his nose. "I have to be gentle with you."

She backed away from him. "Don't you dare," she said sharply. "If you act like this every time I get hurt, I'm going to kick your ass."

"Gabby …"

"I'm taking a shower. Join me. And if you don't deliver on fucking me blind, you're not sleeping in my bed."

With that ultimatum, she pivoted on her bare foot and marched to the bathroom.

Declan stood there, trying hard to quell the raging conflict inside him. He reeked of desperation and fear. He needed to channel the emotions so they could get what they needed from each other.

The shower started running and imagining Gabby naked and wet, well …

She needed a man that wouldn't put her in a cage, and who'd let her be who she was.

He could give her that.

Fuck her blind. His cock hardened like a steel rod at the thought.

He could definitely give her that.

Declan stripped down the rest of his clothes and stalked into the bathroom.

"Shit!" She muttered, jumping back from the hot shower spray. "That burns."

Declan opened the glass door and stepped in. She had the water on boil. He adjusted the temperature.

"Hey, don't touch that."

He moved her away from the dials.

"Hey—"

"Quiet," he ordered.

She grinned. "Aye, aye, sir."

He squinted his eyes. That was the second time today she'd said that. Her playfulness was infectious. Even if that purpling bruise remained a stark reminder of her fragility, it was also a testament to her resilience. He turned her around to shampoo her hair and soap her body. When he turned her back, her hand claimed the soap from him and her fingers worked over his muscles in seductive swirls. Trailing down his abdomen, they tangled in the mat of hair right above his pelvis before tracking lower.

One soapy palm gripped his shaft.

Stroking.

Up.

Down.

"Don't." He manacled her wrist and pulled it away. "I'm too close. Just …" He embraced her, letting the water sluice down their bodies and flush the dirt and horrors of that day down the drain, letting steam wrap them in a warm cocoon that chased away the cold, stark fear that rooted deeply into their bones.

And as the chill receded, renewed primal heat exploded.

He needed her.

The increasing urgency of the way Gabby was touching his body told him she desperately needed him too.

He backed her against the tiles. "Hold on to the bar."

"What?" she asked in a daze.

He lowered his head so they were eye to eye. "Hold on to the fucking bar. I'm gonna eat you, and I'm not risking another trip to the ER or we can—"

Her left hand gripped the bar on the wall.

Declan dropped to his knees, grabbed her left leg, and draped it over his shoulder.

He glanced up. Her lips were parted in anticipation.

And he put his mouth on her, pressing his tongue as she gave him her weight. He kept her pinned to the wall as he tasted the slickness between her legs.

He was hunger; she was sustenance. He was a junkie; she was his drug. His tongue dipped into the silky folds and tasted heaven. He sucked on her clit, swollen with the rush of blood as he felt his own make him harder. And when she cried out, her fingers tangled in his hair, arching her body off the wall to feed her core further into his mouth, he felt euphoric.

He lowered her leg and jackknifed to his feet. Turning the

dials behind them to shut off the shower, Declan opened the glass door and let the steam escape into the rest of the bathroom. He wrapped Gabby in a towel, picked her up, and carried her dripping out to the bedroom.

In the back of his mind, he knew he shouldn't be getting the sheets wet, but in that moment, all he could think of was the woman in his arms, laid out, spread out, knees pushed up, opened to him, her pretty pussy served up for him to pleasure and fuck.

In a mixture of restraint and ferocity, he lowered her gently to the bed and ripped the towel from her, laying her bare, her skin glistening from the moisture of the shower.

He prowled to the top of the bed, reached forward, gripping an ankle and yanked her closer. Her arms were spread open—a willing sacrifice— and it turned him the fuck on.

Putting a knee to the bed, he pushed the ankle in, cocking one of her legs, and then taking hold of the other, he raised that too. All through this their gazes were locked and her tongue came out to swipe at her lip.

"God, you're so beautiful," he whispered before settling between her thighs. He blew teasingly on her puffed up lips before giving her a lick. Her legs squirmed, but he kept them open. "So beautiful. So fucking mine," he snarled and dove back in to feast relentlessly. Lick, suck, nip, and more suck. He brought her to the brink then backed off.

"Dec. Don't tease!"

He gripped her ankles, pushing them wider. "Keep them open, Angel."

"Just … just…" Her fingers threaded into his scalp and kept him there.

He obliged and renewed his assault. Lick, suck, and suck some more until she screamed and sobbed for him to stop.

But driving her wild only drove him more feral.

"Oh, god, I want you inside me. Inside me now."

He went back onto his knees, crawled over her body, and

kissed the area around her bruise before paying homage to her tits. One arm was braced on the side, the other holding his cock to her entrance to lubricate the tip with her natural wetness.

"Now!" She begged.

He reared back and slammed into her, hooking one of her legs, dropping to an elbow and canting his hips as he rammed into her again and again, giving new meaning to pounding her into the mattress. She clung to him, gasping encouragement.

"Harder…. harder…"

And he gave it to her. She was as ferocious as he was. Blunt nails scored his back and shoulders. They were all over each other. He rolled and had her straddle him and she rode him, scratched his chest, then she got frustrated because she couldn't get there, so Declan took over.

He had her on all fours and scooted her close to the headboard.

"Hang on to the rails," he ordered before rooting into her deeply. She cried out, but she pushed back, grinding her ass against him, her tight walls milking him with a pleasure that almost blinded him. A sensation tingled at the base of his spine, his balls became heavy. He was close. "With me," he growled. "Come with me, Angel. Come all over my cock."

She screamed as her body sagged, the tight squeeze of her pussy set off his climax. He shuddered, reeling at the explosive finish that almost stroked him out. Gabby twisted on her side at an odd angle and he collapsed beside her, the back of one hand over his eyes as he tried to catch his breath. His pulse pounded in his ears as the most incredible sex of his existence scrambled his brain.

Gabby sighed and rolled into him. "With the stamina of your cock, not to mention the several positions we went through, I think we have a future in porn."

He puffed a laugh. This woman beside him was cute as hell and a balm to his tortured soul.

"Dec?" her tentative tone made him lower his arm. He glanced over, frowning at her pensive face.

"With your expression, I'd conclude I didn't deliver on the sex."

When she didn't answer and her face still looked troubled, he propped up on an elbow and searched her face. "What is it, Angel?"

"Is it always going to be this way?" she whispered. "Using sex to work through our fears?"

"It's a natural instinct, babe. The adrenaline has to go somewhere. Don't you feel better?"

"It's weird that I do."

"Sex is a stress reliever."

"You must have been really stressed." Her mouth curved into a smile. "You were insatiable."

"Says the woman who told me to fuck her blind. I'm glad we're alone in this house. You're quite a screamer."

She smiled at his words, before a sobering thought stole it away. "I was really frightened today. First Theo and then you. I worry about the guys at work, but having it happen to both of you, messed me up on a different level."

He leaned in and pressed a kiss to her forehead which was still glistening with the sweat of their enthusiastic fucking. "Ditto. I never want to see a bruise on you again."

Her brows puckered, her mouth turning down. "I'm not sure if I'll still have a job after going rogue today. But if I'm lucky to still be a detective after this, this is life with me. There are always risks."

He bolted over her, caging her in with both elbows on either side of her head, supporting the weight of him off her, cognizant of the bruising. "You seem to have forgotten our conversation before we rescued Theo. So I'll tell you again. It was never an easy road with you, Angel. Then or now. But I'd rather fight for this than to live without you. I want nothing more than to lock you up and wrap you in a bubble, but I'm not cutting your wings. I may lose my mind when you get hurt because I love you. I'm never leaving you again. You're worth fighting for. And I hope like hell you feel the same way."

Her hand reached up to cup his jaw and he turned into it, kissing it briefly.

"I do," she said. "Who knew we'd be polar opposites now? You work at circumventing the law, and I'm all about upholding it, but as you can see I can be flexible if it's for the greater good." She gave a brief laugh. "And this is way too serious a conversation to be having naked and on a soggy bed."

"We have the whole house to ourselves." Declan waggled his brows.

"What are you suggesting?"

"STOP WORRYING ABOUT US," Theo spoke over speakerphone. "Besides, I told Levi to block all visitors. Even Nick."

"Yes, he rang our doorbell earlier," Gabby sighed. For fifteen minutes, her second ex-husband hounded their front door. "We ignored him." Just like she ignored the three voice-mails and ten text messages from Nick that got progressively angrier.

"Just want to be alone with my girl, you know," their son continued. "Her mom is getting in tomorrow morning and she'll fuss over her. Besides, Levi is here."

"I'm overqualified to be a fucking chaperone," Levi's voice rumbled somewhere in the room.

"Are you doing okay though?" Declan asked. "Remember what I said? If you and Emma need to talk to a shrink, I'm sure they have someone on staff—"

"Got it," his son cut in curtly. "It's too soon, Dad. Emma

sleeps ninety percent of the time and I really want to do this with her, make sure she's fine."

Gabby rested her head on Declan's chest. He was cradling her across his lap when they made the call to check on Theo.

"Just reminding you that it's an available option," Declan persisted.

"Gotcha."

"It's gonna hit you later."

Theo exhaled heavily. "I know."

"All your dad is saying is he and I have experience with stuff like this," Gabby said. "You can talk to us anytime too, all right?"

"Thanks, sis."

He and Gabby exchanged looks, knowing their son was tired, probably irritable, and now was not the time to push him to seek help. It was too soon. They said their goodbyes and ended the call.

They were quiet for a while, Declan was running his hand absently on her bare thighs. Their last round of monkey sex happened in the kitchen right when Nick arrived and incessantly rang on the doorbell while alternately pounding on the door. Her cheeks grew warm as she remembered the feral heat in Declan's eyes.

Gabby cursed when she saw Nick on the surveillance monitor mounted in the kitchen. She was wearing one of her sheerest nighties, she was barefoot, and was preparing peanut butter sandwiches for sustenance so she and Declan could resume their sexual activities.

"What the fuck?" Declan growled as he stalked into the kitchen, holding his phone, looking at the app for the surveillance cameras. "He has the audacity to come here?"

"His messages were frantic. Theo wouldn't see him."

"And he thinks he can just barge in here and talk to you?"

"Look, I'll talk——" She started toward the bedroom to grab a robe, but Declan grabbed her arm.

"No," he snarled.

"Dec—"

"You and him are over."

"He—" She didn't get the opportunity to say anything before Declan crushed her mouth with his, his fingers digging into her bottom and lifting her up on the countertop, and before she knew it, he'd slammed into her.

He fucked her fast and deep. His mouth moved somewhere in the vicinity of her neck, burying his face in her hair, and that was when she saw what he was doing. Declan wouldn't be as crass as fucking her in front of Nick, he was too possessive for that. But having Gabby watch the video feed of Nick frustrated, ringing the doorbell for her while Declan was fucking her senseless was him going all alpha in claiming her and making sure she knew to whom she belonged to.

That. Was. Hot.

And utterly insane.

"Hey, where'd you go?" Declan nuzzled her neck.

"You need to reign in your alpha jealousy crap."

"My what?" he chuckled. "I don't get jealous."

Gabby pulled back and arched a brow.

"No, Angel, I'd get rid of the competition if that were the case." His green eyes gleamed wickedly. "There's no reason for me to get jealous."

"You know I'm a homicide cop, right?"

If possible, his face grew more wicked—sinister.

"Oh my god, Declan, I'm not joking about this. You cannot do this jealous possessive bullshit when I'm at work. I work with men. I don't need an overprotective boyfriend riding my ass if I need to strip naked to get into my assault gear. Got me?"

His jaw hardened.

"Got me?" she repeated.

"Marry me then."

"What?"

"You heard me."

"You want to get married again?"

He nodded. He lifted her left hand, running his thumb

over her bare ring finger. "You already know I love you. You know I'm never gonna leave you. All I'm asking is that you wear my ring so every son of a bitch you interact with knows there isn't a prayer that they're getting a chance with you."

"Can I think about this?" she squeaked. Gabby vibrated with so much giddiness, her heart hurt, but she wasn't a teenager anymore. She wasn't going to make any rash decisions.

"Of course." He didn't look happy at all and she almost said yes then and there.

"Were you really thinking about asking me or did you dream up this idea when Nick showed up?"

His face softened. "Gabby," he said in a chiding tone. "A life with you has always been my dream. Haven't you figured that out yet?"

32

RIO DE JANEIRO, Brazil

ANTONIO ANDRADE SAT UNDER A CABANA, sipping a glass of caipirinha, watching two topless women frolic at the edge of the shore as the waves swept across the sand. They were his entertainment for the day. Their young nubile bodies should set his balls on fire, but he felt nothing. His blood only craved one woman.

Ariana Ortega.

He'd been patient, knowing the beauty had a lot to prove in her business, and he allowed her the growth. He understood a woman driven by her career and admired her for it, so he waited. Ortega promised Ariana to him. Turned out, it was merely a ploy so Andrade would share his connections, his business contacts, and use his influence to keep the cartel at bay. Raul Ortega was an ambitious man and he made the mistake of underestimating Andrade's ruthlessness.

It burned like acid in his gut. The idea that Ortega used his interest in Ariana as a distraction to connive with someone within Andrade's organization to weaponize the Ebola virus.

This was completely opposed to his goal of developing a vaccine.

Andrade might be one of the world's richest men. Clothed in Armani, with a fleet of expensive cars, planes, and yachts at his disposal, people seemed to forget that he was born forty-two years ago in the slums of Rio De Janeiro. He scraped his way to the top and his rise had not been easy. Nor had it been bloodless.

His phone lit up from the number he was expecting.

"Ortega is dead," the voice said.

He closed his eyes. That meant they didn't have Ariana. "Where is she now?"

"Lost track of her. She disappeared with Ortega's lieutenant."

"The biker?"

"Yes. We think he's undercover for the CIA." This was not ideal as he had enough problems of his own as he tried to find the traitor in his organization—a business empire consisting of fifty pharmaceutical companies scattered all over the globe and twice as many research labs. And when he found the person responsible, there would be retribution in the only way he knew.

"Any news on Claudette?"

"They're about to arraign her on kidnapping charges."

He waited to feel some regret, but he felt nothing. Andrade had a fondness for the blonde. She was ambitious and her ruthlessness was amusing, but he wondered if she was complicit in Ortega's betrayal.

"What do you want me to do, boss?"

"Keep looking for her."

"Yes, sir."

Andrade ended the call and stared at the sea again.

Ariana would regret not coming to him of her own free will. She would soon find out that with her brother dead, she was unprotected. And what was once off limits for the cartels would now be a free-for-all.

He always had a backup plan.

It was a sunny day in Los Angeles. The sky was surprisingly clear of smog, allowing its deep blue to serve as a magnificent backdrop to the stunning landscape of Forest Lawn Memorial Park. Overlooking the Valley and Burbank, the cemetery was far from a depressive park. No headstones stood over the graves. In their stead were flattened markers, which allowed the tall trees, rolling hills, and beautiful statuaries to memorialize a person's life. The developer of Forest Lawn wanted to dispel the somberness typical of graveyards and make it a joyous sanctuary for a loved one's final journey.

"Park under that tree," Gabby told Declan. The last time she was here was during Peter's funeral. That was a month ago. The days following Ortega's demise, more details started to trickle in regarding his beef with her father. The pictures of Theo found in Ortega's house indicated the enmity between Ortega and Peter escalated in the last year. There was also a scathing note from Ortega found in Peter's desk. It seemed Ariana lost a few key clients in her business and it was because of Peter. Gabby knew her father had influential friends among the Hollywood elite and maybe that was why Ortega didn't make his move until now. Until he snapped.

"Ready, Angel?" Declan prodded, cutting through her thoughts of the revelations that led her here.

Gabby smiled at him. "Ready."

They both exited the SUV and, hand in hand, made their way up the slope, and passed several graves neatly arranged in a row on the grass, until they stopped in front of the one they sought.

Declan took his place behind her, hugging her close,

resting his chin beside her temple and giving her strength for this moment.

"Hello, Peter," Gabby whispered. As soon as she said her father's name, her chest contracted with her repressed emotions. "I'm sorry it took me a while to get back to you." Her voice cracked. "But here I am now. I hope it's not too late.

"First of all, we got him. The bastard who murdered you," she spoke the words fiercely. "He fell on his own sword, his own machinations. He pissed off the wrong people. But I say good riddance."

"Gabby ..." Declan gave her a squeeze, reminding her what this moment was all about. Healing from their past.

"I'm sorry I didn't email you back," she continued. "Answer your calls or return your voicemails and texts. Maybe I was too busy, maybe I didn't think I could ever forgive you, and maybe, I thought ... I thought I had more time." Her voice broke as tears tracked down her cheeks in an uncontrollable rush. Needing a moment as the waves of grief crashed into her, she turned and buried her face in Declan's chest, sobbing while he just held her.

"Pete, man," Declan said as she cried silently. "Thanks for finding me. Guess Yara's popularity had its advantages after all, and you saw my ugly mug online the one time I was her bodyguard." He gave a brief chuckle. "Kade finally came clean and told me that you suspected you were in danger and if anything happened to you to make sure I was there to protect Theo and Gabby. Although, in case you hadn't noticed, your daughter is pretty badass herself." He paused for a beat to give her a kiss on the crown of her head. "We never saw eye to eye, but I finally understood that you always wanted what was best for Gabby. What you thought at least. I won't lie, it made me bitter, but after hearing what you have done to bring us back together, I wish ..." he exhaled a puff of air. "I wish we'd gotten to share a beer."

Gabby snorted through her sobbing. She glanced up and stared into his green eyes and gave him a light peck on the mouth before she turned around and faced Peter's grave again. "Dad," she said, releasing what felt like a cleansing breath. "Thank you for everything you've done for Theo." Her chest felt lighter, and yet something different weighed on it. A good feeling. Her love for her father rekindled in a big way. "Despite his spoiled upbringing, I think you'd love the man he's turning out to be. He wanted me and Declan to do this on our own." A brief smile touched her lips. "We'll come visit soon. All three of us."

"I'll take care of them, Pete," Declan added. "I swear on my life. They'll be protected."

I forgive you, Dad. Rest in peace.

33

TWO WEEKS later

"DEC, COME HERE A SEC."

Gabby's voice distracted his attention from a box of Theo's belongings. How could a teenager pack so much shit for a two-month stay at his mom's apartment?

He lowered said box to the dining table and headed her direction down the hallway into Theo's room. There was a smirk on her face and Declan couldn't help chuckling. It was hard for her to shed the older-sister inclination to pick on a younger sibling, and Theo didn't seem to need mothering. As for his relationship with his son, they'd formed a closer bond ever since the fight scene choreography session helped Theo defend himself against Ortega's goon.

"'Sup?" Declan asked.

Gabby was standing beside a full-size bed. Theo was struggling to pull the fitted sheet over.

"Take our picture," she said, plopping across its surface and posing like a pinup girl.

"No fucking way," Theo growled. "And would you please

stand up. It's hard enough yanking this fucking sheet on it as it is."

"Such language," Gabby clucked, but made no move to oblige him and continued her pose with an elbow propping her up, hand under her chin.

"Do as you're told, kid. What did I tell you? Happy mom, happy us." Declan whipped out his phone and framed the photo. "Say cheese."

Gabby smiled wildly.

Theo glowered.

Snap.

"Let me look." Gabby jumped off the bed and glanced at the screen. "Send me the rest of the photos, okay? I'll have Nadia print them."

"There are online printing services, you know." Theo tugged at a corner of the bed.

"Too risky. Before you know it, some tabloid will be running these pictures as a front-page headline," Gabby said.

Theo straightened and looked green around the gills.

"Oh, I don't know, Angel, might improve his image, gain him more fans," Declan drawled. "Girls swoon over all this domesticated male shit."

Gabby rolled her eyes. "How many boxes are still in the Honda?"

"Two," Declan answered.

"Jeez, Theo, did you haul in your entire Beverly Hills crap?"

"Told you it'd be easier if you moved into your mansion," the teenager replied. "We could fit your entire apartment four times over and then some."

"Quit grumbling and man up," Gabby retorted. "Use this as a learning experience … what's the term they use nowadays? Method acting?"

"Do you even know what that means?"

"Theo," Declan cut in. "Why don't you help me bring in

the rest of the boxes before you and your mom end up in an argument?" There were times when their bickering devolved into hurt feelings and exploded in temper. Usually the teenager's.

"Good idea, Dad," Gabby said, deadpan.

Declan pointed a stern finger at her, trying hard not to grin. "You. Stop giving Theo a hard time before he changes his mind and says fuck it with the whole thing."

"That's right," Theo muttered.

"Come on, sport." He slung an arm around his son's shoulder and together they left the room.

"You know we could've hired movers, right?" Theo said. "Normal people also do that. Movers aren't the sole domain of rich teen actors."

"What? That's the thanks I get for rescuing you from your mother?"

Theo chuckled. "You know Gab and I are just messing around right? Old habits die hard."

"Tell me that when you give her the sullen teenager treatment after one of your so-called messing around arguments."

By this time, they were walking out the door when Declan's phone buzzed.

It was Kade.

"Yo," he answered.

"Yo?" Kade chuckled. "Hanging around your son too much?"

Declan motioned for Theo to go ahead, handing him the SUV keys, to which the teenager gave an exaggerated sigh, but took them anyway.

He followed more slowly. "You could say that."

"How's fatherhood?"

"Thankful I don't have to change diapers which I hear you'll be doing soon. Congratulations, man! Heard Yara's pregnant."

"Thanks, we're ah … excited," Kade swore softly. "I hope I don't mess this up. Any advice?"

Declan barked a laugh. "Not sure I'm the one to ask. My boy came to me fully grown with an attitude to match. He may look like me, but he's got a lot of Gabby in him."

"How's she adjusting?"

"Great, given the circumstances. Less than a year and he'll be eighteen. He's level-headed most of the time. Gabby and I are just making sure this experience with Ortega won't scar him for life."

Declan paused above the parking space where Gabby's Honda was located and watched Theo approach it. The kid glared at him and threw up his hands as if saying "Are we doing this or what?"

"He and Emma are seeing a shrink. Saving his mom and Emma's lives makes shooting the man more acceptable in his mind." By this time Theo was at the Honda, leaning against it making no move to haul out the boxes by himself.

This kid.

"Listen, I gotta go help my boy move in. I guess you were returning my voicemail?"

"Yeah," Kade answered. "Garrison mentioned the counterterrorism task force, but are you sure that's what you want to do?"

"Yup. Me being able to move within the Hollywood circuit without raising questions would give me leverage. Levi was thinking the same thing since he's getting offers from several film studios for fight training and choreography."

"Does he want to go freelance?"

"Nah, we talked about it before he left to see his kids. I think since Garrison wants us on the task force it'd be a good cover to continue being employed by ESS. It'll put us in line with Gabby's suggestion of using us as consultants for the LAPD's own task force that's being formed."

"I thought she and her partner were suspended."

Declan winced at the reminder. "Yeah, for four months—no pay." Neither Garrison nor Chen could do anything because of the media circus that followed the explosion at Route 15. He blew out a breath. "It's a blessing in a way. Gives Gabby time to connect with Theo." And me.

"Gotcha."

"Are we doing this or not?" Theo hollered from the parking lot.

"Was that Theo?" Kade chuckled as Declan started walking along the open corridor of the second level and then down the steps to head into the parking lot.

"The one and only," he muttered.

"I'll let you go—"

"Kade," Declan interrupted.

"Yeah?"

"Thanks again for Peter."

"Happy it worked out for the best."

"It did."

"Call me when you're on this coast, okay?"

"Will do."

Declan purposely slowed his strides and his boy shot him a self-deprecating grin as he bleeped the locks and opened the tailgate.

"Hold on a sec," Declan said.

Theo straightened from picking up a box and arched a brow questioningly.

"I got you out here for another reason and you're probably better at this shit than I am."

"You're asking Gabby to marry you again."

"What?" Declan muttered. "You're psychic now or something?"

"You've got the look."

His brows drew together. "The look?"

"Puppy dog eyes, following Gabby around. It's sickening if it wasn't so funny."

For a second, Declan just stared at him.

Theo erupted in laughter. "Dude. That look on your face." He clapped a hand on his shoulder. "Don't worry, your badassery can take a hit."

"Not sure about that. Puppy dog eyes aren't a good look on a badass." He folded his arms over his chest and puffed up to somehow make up for that image—imagined or not. "I've already asked her—said she'd think about it."

A look of sympathy crossed the teen's face. "What do you need? Plan a public proposal? A grand gesture?"

Declan felt the blood drain from his face. "Uh, no. If you don't want Gabby to castrate us both, that's off the table." He paused briefly before continuing. "I need a name for a top jeweler in LA. Maybe Emma knows someone? I sure as hell haven't kept up with the times or what's acceptable."

"Ah, the ring." Theo's face brightened and somehow blood returned to his head and Declan's cheeks flushed. It was embarrassing to ask a teenager for his opinion, but Declan was at a loss. Nick Carter just informed them that Revenant Films' publicity machine was about to make a formal press release of Theo's parentage and Declan would be damned before he asked his son's manager on what to do. But he didn't want to fuck up that announcement. He was all in, and though he and Gabby shunned whatever the press made of their relationship all those years ago, they had Theo to consider now.

"Yep."

"You mean you proposed without a ring?" Theo teased.

He scowled at the teenager who appeared to be on the verge of laughing again. This talk wasn't helping with his dilemma of getting his stubborn woman to remarry him.

"Why are you guys taking so long?" Gabby called from above them.

"Nothin'" Theo responded and smirked, patting Declan on the back. "Don't worry—Dad. I got this."

Great, a teenager to the rescue.

Two days later

Gabby opened the door to her partner who'd come from the gym, freshly showered and wearing a fitted exercise shirt and track pants and bearing a brown envelope from Nadia.

"Christ, Kelso," she chuckled as she let him inside and accepted the packet. Having both been suspended left them with plenty of free time and he chose to spend it in the gym. "Have you doubled in size since I last saw you?"

He flexed his bicep. "You think so?"

"Ugh, you need to stop before you become a total meathead," she commented when she noted the veins on his arms popping out.

"Ouch!" he mocked. "My training partner has been slacking. I don't have a girlfriend and I have no job. What do you suggest I do?"

She winced. "Sorry. That was insensitive."

"Hey." He punched her shoulder. "Just kidding. Don't tell me motherhood has divested you of any humor. Or maybe"—he smirked—"you're having too much sex."

Gabby's cheeks grew warm. She was used to locker-room talk, but rarely was it directed at her, and having it hit so close to home? It was hard to hide her reaction.

A dark brow raised. "Something tells me Woodward is getting good and laid."

"Shut up," she grumbled, moving into the kitchen. "You want a protein shake?"

Kelso hooted. "She's blushing and changing the subject."

"Make up your mind. Do you want one or not?"

"Sure, as long as you don't poison me or dump cayenne flakes in there as payback."

Guys in Division could be brutal with their pranks—sprinkling itch powder in someone's underwear. Gabby rolled her eyes. "I'll make one for me too."

"Man, you're less fun nowadays. What gives, Woodward?"

"Less fun? Try more mature?" She winked as she turned away so she could feed Kelso. After making the shakes, she divided the mixture between two tumblers—remembering how Declan drank out of the container this morning until she reprimanded him—and handed one to Kelso.

Funny how everything reminded her of Declan and she already missed him. She just saw him this morning for Chrissakes. She was too old to feel like a giddy schoolgirl who'd finally landed her crush as a boyfriend. She disguised her smile by taking a sip from her glass.

"Damn, someone's got that mysterious smile and dreamy eyes."

"Bite me." She plopped on the barstool.

"Hey. Nothing wrong with that." He grinned and his eyes warmed. "Thrilled to see you happy, partner."

"We need to find you a woman."

"Please don't," he groaned. "Don't turn into one of those sickeningly happy people in a couple who can't wait to pair off their single friends."

"Ha!" Gabby chortled. "Never." Their eyes met and then a somberness cut through the levity. Time to address the elephant in the room. She cleared her throat. "It still hurts, you know? Surrendering the badge and service weapon." She hitched her shoulders. "Even if it's temporary ... it's like I'm missing a limb."

"Yeah, it blows." Kelso nodded his understanding. "You regret it? Going off script with the LAPD?"

"Never. You?"

"Nope," Kelso answered without hesitation. "I knew what

I was getting into when Garrison recruited us. I'm your partner through thick and thin, Gab."

"And suspension, apparently."

They both laughed and clicked their tumblers together in a toast to solidarity. In that regard, Gabby's chest loosened a bit. There was a guilt in getting Kelso suspended alongside her, but if she learned anything in the past few weeks, it was not hanging on to that guilt. It was why she asked Kelso to come over. That, and apparently Nadia was hitting the gym as well nowadays and she was their link to gossip within Division.

"Just don't forget me when the new counterterrorism task force takes off," Kelso said. "Heard Chen wants in, but everyone thinks you should be top dog, given that Ortega was responsible for the fentanyl attacks."

"You were as much a part of stopping Ortega as I was. Revenant Films is working in conjunction with the LAPD public relations to time the announcement of Theo's parentage and Claudette's nefarious role in the whole thing."

"Heard that's gonna be a three-part series in the newspaper."

"Heaven help us."

"Probably a true-to-life miniseries in the works?"

"Declan's gonna shit a brick if that happens," Gabby snorted. "Probably shouldn't overwhelm my guy so he doesn't hightail it out of LA again."

As the words left her mouth, a realization hit her. She could joke about that now without anxiety. She was truly secure in Declan's love, having experienced the depth of his commitment as they battled through the ordeal with Ortega. They came out on the other side stronger. Except …

The apartment door rattled as keys were inserted and the door opened. The man who'd occupied her thoughts walked in, his face immediately darkening at the sight of Kelso.

Yes, things were great except for Declan's possessiveness and bursts of jealousy. His scowl at Kelso surprised Gabby right now since she was sure Declan knew her partner posed no threat to their relationship.

"I thought Theo was with you," Gabby said as Declan prowled toward them like a jungle cat.

"He was, but said he'd hang out with the film crew since it was the last shooting day."

"You didn't go with them?"

"No. I thought it was an opportunity to be alone with you." He stared pointedly at the man beside her.

"Declan!" Gabby exclaimed, mortified.

Kelso drained his protein shake and got up. "Ah, I know when I'm not wanted."

"I'm sorry," Gabby sputtered. "There's no excuse for his rudeness."

Her partner raised his arms in supplication. "No arguments here, but go easy on him. No harm. No foul." Kelso gave a wry smile as he passed Declan who acknowledged him by inching up his chin.

Gabby waited until the door closed before she lit into him. "What is wrong with you?"

He pulled her off the stool into his embrace and lowered his head to kiss her. "Hello to you too, Angel."

Infuriated, she avoided his kiss and his lips landed on her cheek, then she tilted up her chin and glared at him. "Don't try to act all sweet and innocent now, Declan Roarke. You did that on purpose."

He sighed and leaned away. "Is it so wrong that I wanted to be alone with my woman?"

"By giving my friends the evil eye that more or less tells them to scram?"

"He was messing up my plan." The way Declan was looking at her, with a mixture of frustration and heat, sent her heart pounding double time. And her annoyance with him fled, replaced by tingling anticipation.

"What plan?" she managed to squeak.

Declan swore under his breath and let her go, hands landing on his hips as he glanced away briefly before returning his eyes to hers. "Asking you to dress up. Take a ride with me to Griffith Park and then to dinner at this fancy place Theo suggested."

There was a boulder in her throat but she managed to whisper. "Why Griffith Park, Dec?"

"You know, Gab," he rasped. "I wanted to do right by you, by Theo."

"And this whole dinner at a fancy place?" her brow arched. "We never cared about that."

He stared at the floor. "Yeah."

Her heart was still beating rapidly, but it was also close to bursting with the love she had for this man. She closed the distance between them and cupped his jaw, raising it a little so their gazes locked.

"Ask me again, Declan," she whispered.

"Gabby?" His eyes searched hers, and a slow grin spread through his handsome face. She did not expect him to drop to one knee, his torso flexing sideways as he reached for something in his front left pocket.

Then he looked up at her, green irises bright with all the love that radiated off him, holding up a beautiful solitaire diamond that reflected white fire. "Will you marry me, Angel?"

"Yes."

THREE HOURS later

DECLAN AWOKE with a start and flung an arm beside him, finding the bed empty. The sun was setting, casting its golden rays through the slatted wood blinds. After Gabby had said yes to his proposal, he scooped up his woman and marched her straight to the bedroom where they made love for hours in between talking about their future. Wrapped around each other, they discussed how to navigate Theo's celebrity without losing their own identity. They even discussed the possibility of another baby. Having missed the joys and trials of raising a kid, they toyed with the idea with much giddy excitement, but they also agreed it would happen when they were ready. Their focus was on each other, how they were going to live, and the compromises they needed to make given how their roles could become more challenging at work. It was when they started talking about where to find a house to live together, and suggesting different places to scout in LA that they finally fell asleep.

So proposing again in Griffith Park and following up with dinner didn't go as planned, but things rarely did when it came to Gabby.

His angel.

She wasn't one for grand gestures.

She wanted a steadfast love that would last without the glitz and glamour of Hollywood. So did Declan.

He smiled as he swung his legs from the bed and went in search of his fiancée. He found her in the living room, wearing his tee, its hem hitting sexily mid-thigh. She was staring at something on the mantelpiece.

His chest tightened and his eyes grew warm as he finally saw what it was.

Picture frames. She was putting pictures of their family on the shelf above the fireplace.

"What do you think?" she asked, not realizing the turmoil of emotions going through him. "Nadia did a good job with the prints. I told her not to mess with those fake filters but wow, what she did with our hike in Runyon Canyon was phenomenal."

Declan stepped up beside her, his eyes riveted on the row

of simple frames. One was a picture of them visiting Theo on the set. It included Emma, who was on crutches. The girl was a trooper, showing up so soon for filming, but the writers had to scramble to rewrite her part.

The next photograph was of their hike at Runyon Canyon —one of their trio, and another of just him and Gabby. The fourth photograph was of him and Theo sparring at the gym. And last was the move-in day photo Declan took of Gabby and Theo.

"Well," Gabby prodded as she cut a glance at him. "Hey, are you crying?"

"Something in my eye." Declan cleared his throat. "They look great, babe." He exhaled a shaky breath, but she didn't notice the hitch in his breathing as she continued chattering and shuffling through other pictures, holding one out and then another for his perusal. He nodded like a robot, his heart and mind completely hijacked by the single thought that he'd found her.

The girl he'd left behind had finally broken free from the chains of the past and had come home.

EPILOGUE

3 MONTHS later

HER GOWN WAS a simple ivory sheathe with elegant lines. No tiara or veil would sit on her head. Her inner girly-girl always wanted big curls and cascading tresses, but she never figured out how to do it herself or had the patience to learn. A wedding seemed to be a perfect enough reason for a hair-stylist-to-the-stars to do it.

Her wedding.

Gabby stared at her reflection in the gilded oval mirror adorning the wall of the Beverly Hills mansion she'd inherited from Peter. A couple of weeks ago, she and Theo opened the contents of the safety deposit box her father mentioned in his will. They both suspected what was in that box and had been correct.

The original copy of Theo's DNA report that Peter ran after his divorce. Along with it was a list of people he knew were involved in the baby swap. The doctor Ortega had murdered and, of course, Claudette. He also had details of his run-ins with Ortega which she already knew from going through the crime lord's properties. With Raul Ortega gone, the control of the criminal enterprise had shifted in LA, but she would worry about that after she returned to work in a few weeks.

For now, getting married to the love of her life was her priority.

The door opened again, and Nadia walked in. As maid-of-honor, she did the last-minute run-around duties for Gabby. Following her were Emma and Kelso.

Her partner was walking her down the aisle.

"They're ready for you," Nadia said.

"How do I look?" she asked.

The stunned expression on Kelso's face was certainly reassuring. Her fingers were freezing, palms clammy; she needed all the encouragement she could get. She hadn't been this nervous since her first patrol duty out of the academy.

"Excuse me while I pick my jaw up off the floor," Kelso said slowly, an appraising gaze inspecting her from head to toe. "Damn, Woodward, you clean up good."

"Thanks!" She gave a nervous smile.

"You're the most gorgeous bride I've ever seen," Nadia gushed, and Emma echoed her sentiment. The girls had seen her earlier and they'd been endlessly complimentary.

"You missed your damned calling, partner," Kelso continued. "If you weren't such a kickass detective, I'd say Hollywood is missing out."

"Don't give her ideas," Nadia admonished.

The door opened again, and the wedding planner stuck her head in. "The entourage is forming. We need to go."

"Give me a minute," Gabby replied and turned to Kelso. "Thanks for doing this."

Despite reconciling her feelings for Peter, she would never forget the man who'd stood in as her father and mentor.

Her partner knew what she meant. "The captain would have wanted to be here."

"I miss him," she whispered as a bittersweet ache settled on her chest.

"Hey! No crying or you'll ruin your make-up, delay the wedding, and Declan will kill us," Nadia warned even as her own eyes filled. "Judging from my encounter with him a few minutes ago, he's ready for this to be over."

Poor Declan. The press was camped out at the gates, and since he rode with Theo who loved grandstanding for the fans, they did a mini photo op at the entrance.

"He just wants to be married to you," Kelso said softly, offering his arm. "Ready, partner?"

She linked her arm to his. "Ready."

A CELEBRITY OUTDOOR wedding in Los Angeles was a no-no unless you wanted the whole ceremony to be drowned out by helicopter noise, or the chairs and arrangements to be tumbled by the rotor wash, not to mention guests with permanently scrunched up faces—not ideal for photographs.

Thankfully, Gabby's Beverly Hills mansion had a ballroom, albeit a tiny one. It could accommodate two-hundred fifty guests, which was tiny by Hollywood standards. But Gabby and Theo were Hollywood royalty after all. After the revelation three months ago, the public was riveted on the story of their little family—book, movie, and series proposals hounded them and showed no signs of abating just yet. The bride-to-be wanted to honor Peter by replacing the memories in this place with happier ones. The beginning of their future together.

"You okay?"

Declan turned his attention to Theo.

"Yeah. You?" They were both wearing Tom Ford suits

because, according to Theo, that
Declan couldn't give a fuck about
was more concerned about fit
damned glad the suit wasn't suffoc

"Just peachy," Theo replied.

They both shared a chuckle.
expression whenever she was ann
one way to annoy his mom—affect

"You're gonna be a celebrity s
he said. "Told you not to trim your beard. Now everyone will
be wanting us to do a father and son movie."

"Fuck that. Not a chance."

A clearing of a throat drew their attention to the minister,
and reminded them of their surroundings.

Theo jabbed him with an elbow and they both turned to
the ballroom door where the entourage was making their
procession down the aisle. On any other day, his son would
have made a smartass reply to the wedding officiant, but he
was on his best behavior except that little scene he offered at
the gates.

Nadia walked under the arched structure that marked the
beginning of the row of chairs, timing her steps to the strains
of the quartet. Two flower girls—Theo's child star buddies
from the *Hodgetown* series—scattered flower petals on the wine-
red carpet.

Declan saw a flash of white fabric before the door swung
shut again and his throat closed in anticipation.

Among the wedding guests were some big-name actors, as
well as politicians—mostly invited by Revenant Films. Gabby
had her LAPD crew. From Declan's side, he had Kade and
Yara, Levi, and Bristow as well as several Ranger buddies and
men he'd worked with at ESS, and as a private military
contractor.

The chatter of the crowd faded when the beginning keys
of the familiar Wedding March played on a grand piano.

The door sw
His brid
her befor
"ooh-
whi

ung open.

glided down the aisle in a way he'd never seen
. Declan was enthralled. All around them everyone
d" and "ah-ed." Gabrielle Woodward was a vision in
te, reminiscent of old Hollywood glamour and beauty.

His Gabby.

Simply luminous.

"Breathe, Dad," Theo whispered in his ear.

"She's so fucking beautiful," he said softly, his eyes unwavering on the woman he'd loved for so long … the woman he
never stopped loving.

She was fucking his, and this time, he was never letting
her go.

When his bride and Kelso reached them, Declan immediately stepped up to take Gabby.

"Take care of her, man," Kelso said.

"Count on it," Declan replied and then to Gabby, he
grinned. "Ready, Angel?"

She gave his arm an extra squeeze. "Always."

As THE ROCK band they hired started playing "In These
Arms" by Bon Jovi, the newlyweds were escaping their reception through the mansion's kitchen.

"I can't believe we're leaving when they're playing my
favorite song—our song!" Gabby groused as Declan led her
through the kitchen that was teeming with catering staff.
Minutes before their wedding caper, her husband maneuvered
her out of the ballroom through a side door and pushed her
straight into a gigantic cellar. At first, Gabby thought Declan
wanted a quickie, but then she was immediately ordered to
strip and put on jeans, boots, a shirt, and a leather jacket that
were packed in a duffle. He changed into similar clothes.

"Please, can we just dance. Remember, this is your song for me," she pleaded, digging in her heels and refusing to run.

Declan stopped and cast her an offended look over his shoulder. "No. That was your song that you declared was my song for you." He resumed walking, dragging Gabby through the kitchen, ignoring the curious looks of the staff, until they reached the rear door. He opened it a crack to peer outside.

"Well, it was the song you sang that made me fall in love with you."

He gave a derisive yet humorous chuckle. "You need reminding that it was your dare that coerced me to audition for the lead role in that rock musical movie?" Declan gave an exaggerated shudder. "I couldn't even sing."

"But you tried." She smiled at the memory. "And I fell in love with you."

The chorus of Bon Jovi's rock ballad reached their ears and Gabby danced a jig, clutching her heart, and belted out how the flowers wanted the rain, and how poets thrived on pain.

"Wrong lyrics, babe," Declan laughed, squeezed her to his side and kissed the top of her head. Pulling away, he pushed at the door again and this time a silhouette approached.

It was Kade. His friend tossed him what looked like keys which Declan caught with his right hand. "All yours. Garrison gives his congratulations."

"He's here?" Gabby asked.

"He was never here." Her husband and Kade declared in unison.

She rolled her eyes. "Tell him to quit being so mysterious. I'm on to him. He's a big softie."

Both men laughed.

"Angel, you could be right," Declan said, and then to Kade. "Thanks again, man."

His friend said his goodbyes to her, exchanged a man hug

with Declan, and wished them well before disappearing back inside.

"What are you up to, Roarke?" she whispered as he tugged her toward the motor court behind the mansion that led to the service gate.

"Whisking you away. Who knows? I might sing you that love song." Even if she couldn't see his face, she could feel the exhilaration emanating from him because she was bursting with the same feeling.

"I'll hold you to that and—" Her words cut off as they stopped in front of a black sporty motorcycle.

"Damn. Garrison came through," Declan said as he handed Gabby a helmet.

"Are you serious?" Gabby exclaimed, taking a step back and refusing the head gear. "Do you know how long the hair-stylist spent on my hair?"

Declan, at least, had the grace to look contrite.

"Fuck, I didn't think about that," he muttered, lowering the helmet to his side. "Sorry, Angel. I thought this was a great way to bypass the press and paparazzi what with the face shield and all, and not expecting us to leave from the service entrance."

Gabby couldn't help laughing and, after her initial horror at having her beautiful waves turned into helmet hair, she grabbed the controversial object from her husband and put it on. "It's a brilliant idea cooked up by a CIA guy. I don't know if you've recruited more people than Kade into this plan, who I believe is special ops, but none of you thought about what this would do to a woman's hair? Tsk. Tsk."

The man stood dumbstruck, just staring at her.

She shouldn't torture him. Obviously, he wanted this day to be perfect for her. Cupping his jaw between her palms she stood on tiptoes and brushed his mouth with hers. "I love you, you adorable man."

He held her close and prolonged the kiss, and before they

started a full make-out session out in the open, Declan pulled away. "Come on, hop on before I forget about the lurking paparazzi and take you right here."

His tone turned gruff and it made her squeeze her thighs together.

He swung a muscled leg over the bike, and she climbed behind him. He gunned the engine, but it had the lowest hum Gabby had ever heard from a vehicle of its kind.

"I don't think I've ever seen anything like this before." And in LA, she saw every kind of motorbike.

"You wouldn't." Declan strapped on his own helmet. "The agency has a special contract with Ducati. High performance stealth motorcycles."

"And he simply gifted one to you?"

He grabbed her hands and positioned them over his torso. "Let's say"—he disengaged the kickstand and the bike started to roll forward—"It's a sign-on bonus."

And off they went, motoring through the gates, inconspicuous as they left the Beverly Hills mansion that was a part of their past. They were riding toward their future. They made the turn on Sunset Boulevard and sped between swaying palm trees so incongruent with the billboards and concrete jungle, but this was LA, a city full of contradictions.

She expected Declan to take her to Griffith Park, but he surprised her by taking the left on Blue Heights drive which was a steep road that went up and up. The Ducati didn't even sputter. So smooth was their ride that Gabby was tempted to remove her helmet and feel the wind in her hair. She felt free. Free to love without fear, her heart open to forever with this man.

Finally, as they reached a crest on the hill, they encountered a cul-de-sac and Declan pulled beside a gate that was divided into three panels. He flipped the lid up on a control box, exposing a keypad and entered a code. The smaller of the three panels swung open and he guided the motorcycle through.

She tapped his shoulder. "Who owns this?"

"Hush, don't spoil it."

"Declan, is it yours?"

His answer was to turn off the engine and engage the kickstand. Removing his helmet, he shifted in his seat. The look on his face was part exasperation and part amusement. "Trust me."

Getting annoyed at her husband on their wedding night was not ideal, so Gabby called on every ounce of her patience as she got off the bike and followed him down a flight of steps to the entrance—not unusual for hilltop houses.

At the bottom of the stairs was a slate patio bordered by railings on two sides. The house itself had a rust-red entrance door beside a brief expanse of solid wall that transitioned to floor-to-ceiling windows. Gabby walked to the edge of the patio to see how far the wall of windows went. Part of the house was cantilevered off a cliff, but there appeared to be another level.

She glanced back at Declan. "Basement?"

He was holding the door open. "View is better in here."

The foyer provided an excellent perspective of the open floor plan. The first thing Gabby checked on during their house-hunting field trips was the kitchen, but her gaze was drawn to the glass panels that surrounded the living area.

"Three bedrooms and yes, a basement which I've converted to an armory and a bunker."

She barely heard him. And she knew she should ask him if the arms he kept there were illegal, but that was a conversation for another day. Gabby moved to the windows, a hand pressing against the cold glass. A majestic view of Los Angeles and the ribbon of light that was the strip were on full display below.

"It's breathtaking."

"To love you is to understand your love for this city." Declan's words were close to her ear and sent a shiver up her spine, a heat low in her belly. "Your need to protect it. I hope you understand my need to protect you."

Gentle hands eased her around to face him. "I'm your husband," he said. "It's my instinct to shield you from harm. You're my cop. You belong to me, too, and I protect what's mine. I love you," he rasped. "So damned much, Gabby."

Was it possible to see need, frustration, and adoration on a person's face at the same time?

Yes. Those emotions were written all over Declan's face. How could she explain to him that she felt exactly the same way about his clandestine association with Garrison?

"I hope you know what you mean to me too, outlaw," she whispered. "Every time you step in to protect me, you infuriate and make me love you even more. How is that possible?"

He grinned. "Because we're perfectly matched?" His hands started roving up and down her body, stealing inside her shirt, and caressed bare skin. Gabby leaned into his warmth, ready to climb the sexy beast that was her husband.

She hummed against his mouth. "The outlaw and the detective."

"That's right." His mouth closed on hers and they began a slow dance of feverish kisses.

They nearly tripped over something and Gabby wrenched her mouth away from him, looked down at what nearly caused them to break their necks and saw a stack of boxes. "What are these?"

"Boxes from my condo in Virginia. I had Kade ship them over."

"But you were in LA the whole time. How could you let other people pack your stuff?"

"After my time overseas, I never unpacked."

"We'll need to remedy that."

"Later," Declan murmured as he drew her back into his arms. "Much later."

*** The End ***

Thank you for reading! If you liked this book, please consider leaving a review. It's much appreciated!

Migs and Ariana's book is next in PROTECTOR of CONVENIENCE.

ACKNOWLEDGMENTS

The Ex Assignment had been in the works since late last year. I wrote the bulk of the first draft in December 2019. January 2020 brought about a rebranding of almost all my covers because I had to create paperbacks for a book signing in March. But then suddenly, the world tipped on its axis. It had been a long road to finding my reading and writing mojo again. Cooking and baking became my therapy much to the despair of my jeans. I bet most of you have made banana bread at least once, right?

Little by little, I put my writer brain back together, and with renewed determination, polished up Declan and Gabby's story. I also finished Migs and Ariana's book—Protector of Convenience, which is slated for an October release. So you all can say, I got my writing mojo back and then some.

None of these would have been possible without my favorite people in the Book World.

A big thanks to my developmental editor, Geri, with whom I've spent countless hours of brainstorming fun. We both like the same tropes. Although we don't necessarily agree on our preference for alpha males or recipients of unrequited love, we agree on the elements that make a story great. You also ground me when my plots tend to veer into the wild side. Maybe I need to write that urban fantasy series after all. I remember one of your first comments to me was: "Vee! You have enough plot here for four books!" :D

I'm so lucky to have an amazing editor in Kristan Roetker. You and I have worked together for years and I love how our relationship has evolved over several books. You continue to polish my manuscript and make it shine without changing my voice. Working with you has been effortless and I look forward to working with you for more years to come.

My special thanks to Sue—one of my very first readers. You've provided me valuable insight over the years and this book was no different if not requiring a bit more discussion. The complicated relationship between this couple was the subject of many email exchanges. Your feedback on getting clarity on the timeline regarding Gabby and Declan's past contributed to the overall cohesiveness of the story. And your eagle-eye is always appreciated!

Thank you to Victoria Colotta of VMC Art & Design and Lynn Hurley for beta reading my unedited work. Your feed-backs have been immensely helpful!

Thank you to Dana Curlett-Dunphy of A Book Nerd Edits. Not only did you provide final eyes on the manuscript, but I also enjoyed our zoom buddy reads.

To Debra Presley of Buoni Amici Press. Thank you for being a badass on all things author-related that enable me to concentrate on writing!

To readers, bloggers, and especially my group, Very Important Paige readers, thank you for your continued support!

And lastly, to the hubby and Loki. Both of you are always understanding of the times when I lock myself in my writing cave. You both make sure I have what I need to thrive in my author life whether it's sustenance, hugs, or doggy kisses. Love you both to the moon and back.

CONNECT WITH THE AUTHOR

Find me at:

Facebook: Victoria Paige Books
Website: victoriapaigebooks.com
Email: victoriapaigebooks@gmail.com
FB Reader Group: Very Important Paige readers

* Sign up for my newsletter and receive **Beneath the Fire** for free.

facebook.com/victoriapaigebooks
twitter.com/vpaigebooks
instagram.com/victoriapaigebooks

ALSO BY VICTORIA PAIGE

Deadly Obsession

Captive Lies

The Princess and the Mercenary

* All series books can be read as standalone

Printed in Great Britain
by Amazon

32572821R00200